Jacquelyn Middleton is an award-winning freelance writer. She previously worked in television broadcasting, and lives in Toronto. When she's not writing, you can find her hanging out in London, waiting in a comic con line with her husband, or chasing after her *very* bossy Schipperke. 'London Belongs to Me' is her first novel.

Follow Jacquelyn on Twitter @JaxMiddleton, Instagram @JaxMiddleton_Author, or visit her webpage at www.JacquelynMiddleton.com

A NOVEL

JACQUELYN MIDDLETON

**KIRKWALL
BOOKS**

KIRKWALL BOOKS

USA – CANADA - UK

This is a work of fiction. Names, characters, places and incidents either are the product of the author's imagination or are used fictitiously. Any resemblance to actual persons, living or dead, business establishments, events or locales is entirely coincidental.

London Belongs to Me

ISBN: 978-0-9952117-1-1
Copyright © 2016 Jacquelyn Middleton
First Paperback Edition, October 2016
Second Paperback Edition, February 2018

For Mum—my heart, my inspiration, the love of my life.

Miss you. xoxo

ONE

"Anything's possible if you've got enough nerve."
– J.K. Rowling

Alex couldn't understand the public address system's garbled instructions. The distorted voice, amidst the din of several hundred passengers in the baggage claim area of London's largest airport, sounded like Charlie Brown's teacher. Tucking her shoulder-length waves behind her ears, she slowed her pace, but the announcement didn't repeat. She held her breath, her eyes darting from passenger to passenger, searching for a reaction.

Panic? Raised voices? Tears?

Nope.

She shrugged and tossed her long bangs out of her eyes, continuing on her way. Slow walkers, and abandoned suitcases stacked high on carts like a haphazard Hadrian's Wall, threatened to impede her progress, but she dodged around the obstacles like a Super Bowl-winning running back. Her feet barely touched the floor.

A beloved line from poet Friedrich Schiller popped into her

head—*'In thy breast are the stars of thy fate.'* Inspirational quotations rocked. Alex rattled them off like Drake reeling off rhymes, her Pinterest collection tailor-made for moments like this one. Sitting back waiting for fate to come calling? Not her style. Destiny may sprinkle clues along your path, but it's up to you to act on them.

Her latest leap of faith—flying here to London, a city she loved from afar but had never visited.

'Passengers arriving on Jet America flight #429 from Miami, please report to the courtesy desk in baggage reclaim beside carousel twelve'

The announcement echoed through the hall. Alex's ears pricked up. Like a sprite on a sugar rush, she veered off-course from Heathrow's luggage carousels and bolted towards the courtesy desk, her knees buckling as her backpack—almost double her size—thumped against her back with each stride. A deke past a doddling family here, a swerve around a barrier rope there, and the jostling mob of passengers fell in line behind her. She draped her small frame over the counter, shifting her bottom-heavy *Doctor Who* laptop bag across her body onto her hip. She greeted the airport employee with a grin her freckles couldn't control.

"Hello! My name is Alexandra Sinclair. I was on the Miami flight."

A tall, middle-aged woman with straw-coloured hair twisted into a harsh bun squinted over the rims of her glasses. She referred to a computer printout in her hands.

"Good afternoon, Miss Sinclair. May I confirm that your air travel began yesterday on Thursday, May 21 at Tallahassee Regional Airport in Florida? And you made a flight connection at Miami International Airport for London Heathrow?" Her plummy accent sounded like Lady Mary from *Downton Abbey*.

"Yes, that's right." Alex couldn't take her eyes off the woman's thick dark roots.

"I'm sorry to inform you, but there was a problem at Miami Airport. The checked luggage from the Tallahassee aircraft was transferred to the wrong trans-Atlantic flight. Your two checked cases haven't arrived in London, Miss Sinclair."

Alex's smile slipped from her heart-shaped face. *No, no, no.*

The tall metal walls of the terminal leaned in, squeezing all the air out of the room. The beat of Alex's heart accelerated, as if it wanted to break free of her chest and make a run for it. Perspiration glistened on her palms, and each swallow pulled her throat into a tighter knot. She yanked at the overstretched neckline of her faded *Captain America* t-shirt, causing its damp threads to peel away from her slumped shoulders, exposing her small comedy and tragedy mask tattoo.

"What? I don't understand. Can you check again, please? This must be a mistake. Please…check again." Nauseating waves bubbled in her stomach, and a tinge of sourness assaulted her tongue. "How can my stuff be missing? Where… where *is* it?"

The woman with the inky roots curled her lip. Now she'd done it. Pissed off the clerk. The employee spoke again, but her words floated and vanished in the air like soapy bubbles blown into the wind. Alex didn't catch any of them, her mind tethered to the worst-case scenario.

Don't faint. DON'T FAINT. Not now!

Tears pooled in her eyes. "What am I supposed…to do?"

"Fill out this form with your address and phone number in the UK, and give it back to me. NEXT."

Alex grabbed the form as an arm shoved her backpack out of the way. The navy blue sleeve belonged to a squawking New

York accent, having a go at Ms. Dark Roots. Alex's load teetered, jerking her sideways, her leg kicking into the air. A swarm of rampaging travellers elbowed her back onto both feet and devoured the small pocket she had just occupied against the desk. She rebounded through the herd, clutching the crumpled paper like a Get Out of Jail Free card.

She dumped her backpack on the floor, giving her rubbery legs a reprieve. A nearby wall offered welcome support. Her damp back bounced against its surface as she slid down to the floor, her eyes overcome with stingy tears. She whispered a mantra she relied upon to combat her panic attacks: "You can do this. You can do this."

Her trembling hands juggled her cell phone. Hugging her knees to her chest, she pressed a saved number. A familiar voice with a British accent drifted through the speaker.

"Alex, honey! You've arrived. You're finally on our side of the pond." It was her dad, Michael.

His daughter failed to respond, shifting his jubilant tone to worry, her gasped half-breaths a concern. "Alex, what's wrong?"

"Dad, my luggage ... they lost it. Something happened in Miami. I...had two checked bags...all my clothes, books... gone..." Her voice trailed off, replaced by a wheezing rattle.

"Alex, listen. Everything's going to be okay. Breathe with me; take slow...breaths. You're going to be all right."

She didn't answer.

Michael swallowed, stifling his worry. He chose his words cautiously, careful not to send Alex into a deeper anxiety spiral. "We'll get through this, love—together...one breath at a time. We've dealt with a distance larger than 200 miles, haven't we? I'm here for you. Now, what belongings *do* you have?"

She blew her nose three times into a tissue, flinging the

room into a jerky spin reminiscent of an out-of-control amusement park ride. "I have my laptop, one of my plays… but my playwriting books, my notes for my latest projects… are lost. I need them for what I'm writing now…"

Alex stalled for air, dropping her head on her knees.

"Aw, sweetheart. You've got your laptop and your play—that's what you need most, isn't it? Do you want us to come down there? We can catch the train and be in London in a few hours."

Tears played follow the leader down Alex's cheeks. She craved a hug from her dad and step-mum Helen, but having them travel down from northern England on a rescue mission? No way. That would prove she couldn't look after herself. Besides, she hated asking for help. Ever.

"No, Dad, really…it's okay. Hearing your voice makes me feel better. I pictured my arrival differently, you know? I hope this screw-up isn't a sign that moving here's…a mistake. I…can't go back…"

"I know, love, I know. It's easy to feel like everything's against you when something unexpected happens, but things will be okay. You're doing great; I'm so proud of you…did you speak to an airline rep?"

"They gave me a form…"

"Honey, fill out the form, hand it in, and then go to the flat. Your luggage will turn up. The airline will be tracking it, but you need to be at your flat to receive it. Is Harry meeting you?"

Harry Manville was a twenty-three-year-old British exchange student Alex met last September during her senior year at Atlanta's Emory University. She had spotted the tall fellow standing alone, his shoulders rounded and his eyebrows scrunched over a map. When she asked if he needed assistance, his gloomy frown melted away into an eager smile. Lost on campus, he couldn't locate his business lecture hall. His posh London accent captured Alex's heart. How could she not help this charming British stranger?

That moment sparked a deep friendship. Harry offered Alex brotherly advice and in exchange she teased him like the cheeky little sister he never had. They even looked alike: their blond hair and blue eyes often misled people into thinking they were siblings, an untruth they playfully adopted with over-the-top Cockney accents on more than one occasion.

Harry's arrival in her life felt like serendipity, a happy accident. His companionship came when she needed it most. Just before Halloween, Alex suffered a betrayal by the person she trusted most, the one person she believed would never hurt her. The discovery ate away at her; the 'Freshman Fifteen' she had carried for two years whittled away, and she considered dropping out of college. Harry lent a sympathetic ear at all hours of the day and night, held her hand through panic attacks, and pulled her back from the brink. He also suggested that she follow her passions for writing, theatre, and London, and move abroad after May graduation. She could stay in a spare room in his flat, a temporary home until she could find something permanent. With barely a year's rent money saved in her pocket, his hospitality would grant her twelve months to make her mark. Harry offered an escape from her problems, and a glimmer of hope for the future.

Now aged twenty-one, the ink on her Bachelor of Arts degree still wet, Alex had taken that leap, turning her back on the only life she had ever known, looking for a new start. Arriving in London was the first piece of the puzzle and each decision, each chance taken, would snap into place, unlocking her picture perfect future.

Talking about Harry, Alex's gasps for air lessened, and the room no longer resembled a Tilt-a-Whirl, but the receding attack left her with the usual souvenirs—self-consciousness, exhaustion, embarrassment.

"Yeah, he's meeting me. I can't wait to see him. I wish I had a change of clothes though. I'm stuck with yoga pants, a baggy tee, and my denim jacket. Talk about making a terrible first impression. I'm meeting his girlfriend for the first time today. She'll think I'm a total loser."

"Don't be silly. She's lucky to be meeting *you*. Now…are you feeling better?"

"I am. Thanks, Dad."

"Fill out that form and go see Harry. Call me tonight once you're settled?"

"I will. Love you."

Alex tapped the screen's red button and blew her nose one more time. She peered into her compact's mirror and cursed the pimple sprouting above her right eyebrow, as well as yesterday's decision to wear mascara. Raccoon eyes stared back at her. She dampened a tissue with bottled water and dabbed her eyes, the melted black makeup staining her hands. Several tries later, she almost looked human again.

The lost baggage form proved tedious, but Miami's airport code had a sense of humour—MIA. *MIA luggage*? A tired giggle escaped from Alex's throat. Oh, the irony. She rose to her feet, shaking the pins and needles from her legs. She pushed through the restless throng suffocating the courtesy desk and handed her completed form to the now frenzied airport worker.

"Miss Sinclair, your bags will arrive at the address provided within seventy-two hours. Unfortunately, I cannot give you a more precise ETA. Your patience is appreciated." Ms. Dark Roots pulled her thin red lips into a taut pout and with a single finger jab sent her sliding eyeglasses back to the summit of her ski sloped nose. Fancy an argument? Like a Rottweiler guarding a juicy bone, her expression snarled 'approach at your own risk.'

Alex raised her right hand in surrender and backed away, her nerves still on high alert. She scraped her hair into a lopsided ponytail, then dragged her backpack and laptop bag towards the elevators leading to the high-speed train into Paddington Station. Hunger growled in her stomach, leaving it hollow and tight—a wobbly combination. So much for her breezy trans-Atlantic re-invention.

She sagged into her seat on the train, hauling her bags to safety under her feet. She opened Facebook on her phone. Wonder Woman smiled back at her—Alex's profile photo, complete with black wig and corset, taken during cosplay at last year's Florida comic con. Her alter ego, the woman she wanted to be: in control, powerful, confident with nary a worry. If only life could imitate art. Her thumbs flew over her phone's keyboard, drafting a status update when an unexpected text burst onto the screen.

"Alex. Welcome to London. So sorry. Last minute change of plans…"

TWO

It was Harry.

'I have an emergency at the club. I'll be stuck in Mayfair today. Don't worry. Tom's home. He'll give you the grand tour! See you later. H x'

Alex gulped. Shoot. A stranger—instead of Harry? Who's Tom? Harry had never mentioned a Tom. She played with the silver A charm on her necklace. Is Tom the landlord? A room-mate? Harry and his girlfriend lived there, but did others as well? Alex rubbed her throbbing temples. She'd only been in London for a few hours, and old demons were yanking her backwards. *Get a grip, girl.*

She turned to a favourite companion—the London Underground app on her phone. She greeted the yellow, blue, red, green, black, and pink Tube lines that zipped and twisted across the map like old friends. Back in college, she had studied the map dozens, probably hundreds of times. She could pinpoint specific Tube stations in her sleep. If that made her a London transport geek, so be it.

One by one, the charming station names—Oxford Circus,

Pimlico, Chancery Lane—danced across her phone's screen, but Alex meant business. She selected a saved journey within the app, reminding her that once she arrived at Paddington Station, it would take roughly forty minutes to travel eastward across the city to her final destination where Harry resided—London Fields, in the borough of Hackney. A few train and platform changes were on the cards, but several transfers meant more time exploring the Underground. Day made.

The express ride into Paddington took less time than a pizza delivery back home in Florida. She followed the other passengers off the train and into the concourse. Such a circus! London's commuters stamped, shoved, and sneered through the station's roving obstacle course of lost tourists, weaving suitcases, and skittish pigeons. No wonder Paddington Bear had such an unsettling introduction to London at this station.

Aw, Paddington. Alex needed her luggage to arrive if only to rescue her own Paddington Bear, a stowaway in one of her missing cases. Even an aspiring playwright about town needs her scruffy childhood pal on an overseas adventure. He would've made a rather fitting selfie accomplice right now, too.

Alex dodged many of the rampaging Londoners, but her swaying backpack had a mind of its own, body-checking commuter after commuter.

"Sorry! I'm so sorry. Whoops," she said, cringing at the "Tsks!" "Watch its!" and "Heys!" of its victims.

She spotted the iconic London Underground sign and zigzagged towards it. Standing in front of the ticket wicket, she plunged her hand deep into her laptop bag to grab cash for an Oyster travel card, but her British bank notes played hide-and-seek.

Her chest tightened as she scrambled to free up space in her crammed bag. She fumbled and dropped her laptop charger, a loud plastic clack rising from the station's floor. *Klutz*. She snatched it up by its cord and fished further into the bag, yanking out her headphones, chewing gum, and a small bottle of hand sanitizer, but still no wallet.

"Just a sec, my money's right…here."

A heavy exhale landed on the back of her neck.

"Excuse me, love. Do you mind stepping aside? I'm really late."

Alex looked over her shoulder. A well-groomed man sporting a bowtie, a three-piece suit, and a leather briefcase fussed behind her, shifting his weight back and forth from one leg to the other. He bobbed his neck, checking his watch like the agitated white rabbit from *Alice in Wonderland*.

A woman in a baggy tracksuit twitched behind him, a snotty-nosed baby screaming in a sling tied to her chest. The infant heaved its pacifier and rattle to the floor, his watery eyes cursing Alex's existence. He resembled a mini-version of the Bond villain Blofeld minus the fuzzy white feline. The young mom huffed and puffed, sticking out a defiant hip.

"Hurry up, will ya? Bloody tourists." Her surliness bounced off the kiosk wall.

Alex wanted the floor to swallow her up. Weren't British people supposed to be polite?

She peeked at her watch. 3:10 p.m. "Sorry. One more look, and I'll get out of your way."

Shoving both hands into her bag, she lifted the laptop. Underneath, she spied a purple leather corner. *Phew!* No need for an international incident.

"Got it! Can I please get an Oyster card with fifteen pounds on it?" Alex threaded a twenty-pound note through the small opening at the bottom of the glass wicket.

The Tube employee rolled his eyes and shoved a blue Oyster card back—Alex's first piece of London identification.

"Yes! It's all happening!" She spun on her heels, avoiding the glares thrown by the queue swelling behind her and headed towards the Hammersmith and City line.

She waved the Oyster card against the round yellow reader on the ticket barrier. It squealed an electronic beep and released its rubber panels with a clumsy shudder. Alex slipped through; successfully maneuvering her two bags clear of the gate's grip. The mechanical clunk...clunk...clunk rhythm of rising and falling escalator steps filled her ears, a metal-on-metal invitation to the Tube's dizzying precipice. The escalators plunged sharply into the subterranean depths of the city, but the locals breezed down the steel steps as if on rails, completely unfazed by the steep drop.

Alex stood on the right side of the escalator, mesmerized by the succession of theatre posters passing by on the walls: *Kinky Boots, Billy Elliot, The Curious Incident of the Dog in the Night-Time*. Every advertisement celebrated a different production. She salivated.

If one of those posters were advertising MY play, I would DIE!

The path to the Hammersmith and City line sent commuters along cartoonishly bendy hallways, and up and down several heart-pounding flights of stairs, like an underground fitness test. Alex arrived just in time. The first carriage screeched into the station, the train's whoosh morphing the platform into a temporary wind tunnel and blowing her ponytail over her head.

Her first impression upon climbing aboard—the train looked like a toy. Round in shape, its carriages mimicked the tunnel, and wacky patterned material from a bygone era covered the cushions. The train rocked out of the station as Alex's Tube companions hid behind newspapers or closed their eyes, some lost in private headphone symphonies—all immune to the Underground's charms—but not Alex. Giggling to herself, she wriggled in her seat like a sleep-deprived kid on Christmas morning. At each stop her wide eyes danced, capturing snapshots of the ads stretching the entire height and length of the curved platform walls, promoting films, cheap airfares, and cheesy tourist attractions. King's Cross, Euston Square, Barbican—all the station names passing by the window captivated the Anglophile, but Baker Street, home to Sherlock Holmes (the Benedict Cumberbatch version), delighted her the most.

With one line change and eight Tube stations under her belt, Alex checked her app. Liverpool Street station beckoned, her second and final transfer…

Five minutes later, rising to street level on the escalator, sunshine greeted her eyes. She raced across the light-filled concourse and boarded the Overground line; three more stops—all above ground. Bring on the sights! She cozied up against the window as the train rattled away from the station, each minute unveiling a fleeting blur of London's East End.

What the—?

Alex wilted. Instead of black taxis and quaint shops flying by, glimpses of obnoxious graffiti tags, rear entrances of squat apartment blocks, and the circular metal gasholders of Bethnal Green whizzed into frame. Not a picture postcard scene in the bunch. She collapsed into her seat, pulling her denim jacket tightly around her. What happened to the pretty London she adored in books and movies?

Ten minutes into the journey, the breezy blue sky darkened

with a menacing scowl. An unrelenting deluge, the kind of gusty cloudburst that drowns sewers, disembowels umbrellas, and drenches pedestrians. The train pulled into Alex's destination, London Fields station. She swallowed hard. *Damn.* Her raincoat and umbrella safely stowed in her luggage—her MIA luggage— no use to her now.

The doors slid open. She ducked her head and lunged for cover under the outdoor station's metal shelter, its roof popping non-stop as wave after wave of fat raindrops met their maker. She exhaled and stood back, allowing the other passengers to exit down the steps. First challenge completed.

Alex 1, Rain 0.

A blinding flash illuminated the sky. She gasped and snapped her eyes shut, bracing against her laptop bag.

Wait for it…

An earsplitting clap of thunder shook the elevated train platform. Alex shuddered, the zipper pulls on her backpack and laptop bag jangling with uneasy solidarity. Some people fear spiders, others heights. Alex's phobia? Thunder and lightning. Mother Nature really knew how to twist the knife. She walked gingerly down the enclosed staircase to ground level. Was it too much to ask for nature's car wash to complete its cycle by the time she reached the exit?

Flickering flashes and snarly rumbling threatened through the downpour. Alex hugged her laptop tightly against her chest like a life preserver and ran for it. She splashed along Mentmore Terrace, coming face to face with a red phone box. Perfect timing. What newcomer to the United Kingdom didn't love this famous icon? And right now, Alex loved it even more. She heaved on the door and squeezed inside.

But her love proved fickle. She could barely move. Her

Converse All-Stars battled for space with crushed beer cans, and her eyes watered, tormented by months—or years, maybe?—of drunk men using the enclosed refuge as a urinal. This was *not* an Instagram-worthy moment. She held her nose, stifling her gag reflex. Her dripping clothes and bags created a design resembling a Rorschach test on the floor while the breath from her mouth fogged up the greasy windows, lending a fuzzy Daliesque appearance to the people and vehicles rushing past outside.

A spike of nausea gurgled in her throat. *Urgh.* That stench! She stumbled outdoors and bent over, her lungs pleading for fresh air.

Another searing flash lit up the street. Alex's heart jolted, an out-of-control jackhammer pounding her chest. Her only choice—run. She sloshed through puddle after puddle, each step splattering filth up to her knees. Pummeling raindrops stung her face, while her jacket offered no defence, its denim sucked onto her bare arms like a second skin. A patch of goosebumps rose underneath her sopping t-shirt, now a useless sponge.

She gave up the race. Alex 1, Rain 1.

"London, I love you, but you're treating me like an ex, not your new crush!" she hollered to the whipping rain while turning onto Martello Street. With each step, the loose shoelace of her left Converse slapped through the overflowing puddles like a bloated noodle.

London Fields, a large green park dotted with old trees, stretched beyond the street's right side. The wet grass gave off a fresh springtime scent. Three and four-storey buildings stood shoulder-to-shoulder along Alex's left. She trudged along the sidewalk, avoiding the park's canopy of trees and its waving invitation to the lightning gods. In between booms of thunder, an eerie quiet amplified the emptiness of the street, a dead end. It terminated in an old red and white brick building, retrofitted with modern apartments and blue balconies. A tall metal fence embraced its forecourt; a few cars and wheelie trash bins occupied the limited parking spaces. Alex straightened her shoulders and lifted her chin. No more running from the storm. *This is it.* Harry's flat.

She sped up her pace, the intercom affixed to the fence just an arm's length away, but an exiting car sprung the gate open. She slipped onto the property unannounced and headed towards the front door. A glass awning, peaked like a raised eyebrow, offered a dry welcome.

A year ago, Alex would've scoffed at the suggestion of packing twenty-one years of belongings and memories to live in a city she loved but had never visited. A lot can change in a year, and heartbreak can spur you on to do the previously unthinkable. Buoyed by each deep breath, Alex's heart danced a little faster. Why not attempt the outrageous, the unexpected? If you don't try, you'll never know. She adjusted her wet jacket and smoothed down her bangs.

She pressed the buzzer for apartment 2B.

Nothing happened.

THREE

"Seriously? 2B or...not 2B? Did I press the wrong one?" Alex retrieved a soggy email printout from her jacket pocket. Blurry and beginning to shred, the page offered little assistance.

She leaned on the circular button. BUZZZZZZ!

Ten seconds passed. Is anyone home? Where's the mysterious Tom?

Alex stepped backwards and tilted her head to peer through the glass awning, the windows above it staring blankly into the park.

The squeal of a hinge pierced her eardrums. The front door swung open, its metal frame missing her chin by an inch.

"Hey!"

Her backpack's swaying momentum tipped her back onto her heels. Her arms flailed around and around like the sails of a Dutch windmill until she regained a shaky balance.

"Oh, *sorry*. Didn't see you." The half-hearted apology slipped from the lips of a pretty thirty-something redhead toting a briefcase. She struggled with her trench coat, fumbling its belt with one hand, her half-unbuttoned dress—no longer a secret—

lurking underneath. A severe case of bed head and a faint smear of pink lipstick below her mouth betrayed her; someone had an energetic session between the sheets this morning.

Thunder rumbled overhead. "That's not the smartest place to stand." The woman sneered, eyeballing Alex from head to toe.

The Floridian's knees wobbled, and yet the urge to put this pushy chick in her place pestered her brain. Who shoves open a door without checking first to ensure the coast is clear? What a bitch.

But could this girl be one of her flatmates? How would that look?

Alex bit her tongue. She'd have to get used to dealing with difficult people; egos and tempers ruled the theatre world.

"I'm looking for Tom. Does he live here?"

"He's in 2B," said Sex Hair, taming her unruly bob. She released the door and opened her umbrella with one hand. Alex lunged, catching the door with both hands. A huge sigh escaped from her mouth, along with a 'thank you' that hung in the air, unclaimed. The woman, now a blur, skirted around puddles at the forecourt gate.

Squish...splotch...squeak. Alex's saturated shoes protested up the stairs to the second floor, where four apartment doorways punctuated a narrow hallway. 2B stood to her immediate right. A park view from Harry's flat? Score!

She knocked three times, her knuckles leaving behind a wet splotch on the white paint.

The door flew open. A good-looking guy, lanky with messy brown hair stood shirtless, clad only in tight Calvin Klein boxer briefs. His pores emitted a vile cocktail of sweat, cheap beer, and cigarettes. A crooked grin inched across his face while his half-

24

mast eyes swept upwards from the floor.

"Darling, am I *that* irresistible?"

"Um…" Alex blinked.

His leering smile evaporated. "Shit!"

The door slammed shut.

Warmth flooded Alex's cheeks. *Now what? Knock again? … Text Harry?*

The door opened again, and the disheveled fellow reappeared, pulling a badly creased 2013 Glastonbury Festival t-shirt over his six foot two inch frame, his long arms struggling for freedom through the holes. Black, skinny jeans with a torn knee covered his bottom half.

"Sorry, love. Can I help?" Dark, puffy circles propped up his piercing blue-green eyes.

"Hi. I'm Alex. Are you…Tom? Harry arranged for me to have the spare room?"

"Right, right. Sorry. When I heard the knocks I thought you were…oh, never mind, come in." He waved Alex into the apartment and yawned so widely, she counted all of his fillings.

A new tightness pinched her chest as she looked down at her dripping clothes. What a nightmare of a first impression. During her flight, she played her arrival over and over again in her head. She'd show up at the flat all carefree and charming, greet Harry with a big hug and win over her his girlfriend instantly. If only. And this Tom fellow…he didn't exist in her dream at all.

"Are you a friend of Harry's?" Her eyes wandered, snooping down the long hallway to her left. She counted four doors, two tennis rackets, and a bicycle.

"Yes, I'm Tom Chadwick-Smythe. Nice to meet you." He pulled Alex close and stooped down, delivering a kiss on each cheek. His patchy stubble scratched her skin. "I completely forgot you were arriving today. My mind's a sieve! Thank goodness I was home."

Such a hands-on introduction…with a smelly stranger. *Ew.* Wide-eyed, she squirmed out of Tom's intimate greeting.

"Thanks…so…how many people live here?"

"Well, you already know Harry, nightclub owner extraordinaire. My younger sister Olivia lives here too. She's Harry's girlfriend. And me. I moved in a month ago, actually."

Tom kneaded his bloodshot eyes. "Acting jobs have been few and far between lately. My landlord chucked me out, the rotten swine, so Olivia took pity on me."

Alex raised her eyebrows. Living with an actor—that's new.

"Speaking of which, my sister will kill me if she comes home to a dirty flat." Tom shrugged. "Our cleaning lady was here yesterday but isn't due back 'til Monday. I was supposed to tidy up last night's mess when I woke, but…got distracted."

Alex's cheeks warmed again. She placed her soaking bags against the closet door in the entryway and folded her jacket on top. The dirty All-Stars—off they went, too; wearing germy outside shoes indoors gave her the willies.

"*Doctor Who* fan, I see," said Tom, pointing at the computer bag. "I always preferred David Tennant to Matt Smith. Tennant's arched eyebrow was a stroke of acting genius."

"It was, but Matt Smith had a charming, boyish quality. He was totally endearing," said Alex. Hurray, another *Doctor Who* fan. Fangirling about *Doctor Who*, a favourite pastime.

"True. True. We'll have to debate their qualities later. But first, riddle me this. How did you get so drenched? The nearest exit from our Overground station is only thirty seconds from our gate."

Alex rubbed the back of her damp neck. "Seriously? I exited onto Mentmore Terrace. I guess I took the scenic route?"

"Ha, that you did." He cracked his knuckles. One. Finger. At. A. Time. And then the popping extravaganza moved along to his other hand. *Snap. Snap.* Alex's face blanched. So fidgety. *Snap.* And annoying. *Snap.* Like an over-wound toy, the guy flittered on the spot. He played with his unkempt hair and leaned to his right, raising an eyebrow at the floor behind her. "You must have more bags than this? Where's the rest of your gear?"

"Misplaced. They're en route somewhere over the Atlantic."

"Oh shit, that sucks. I'd be lost without my stuff." His hand climbed underneath his t-shirt and scratched his chest. "Anyway, before I tidy up, I'll show you around. Then you can make yourself at home." Tom pointed in front of them. "This room's the lounge."

The large, rectangular-shaped space looked like the lair of a bohemian traveller just back from Marrakesh. To the left, a purple velvet sofa rested on an angle, overwhelmed by brightly patterned Moroccan throw pillows and a blue ikat print blanket. A white dress shirt and grey trousers lay discarded on one of the sofa's armrests.

A pair of distressed wooden crates stood guard on either side of the sofa, covered in gypsy-inspired lanterns and a jungle of dangling houseplants that spilled precarious green tendrils. Atop a square wood coffee table, fashion magazines on the verge of toppling over fought with crumpled newspapers, overflowing ashtrays, and tea-stained mugs.

Alex spotted a grease-smudged delivery box nestled into a white, fuzzy area rug beneath the coffee table. Its torn lid and strong smell hinted at a half-eaten pepperoni pizza lurking inside. She cringed, itching to save the furry textile from the oily cardboard. Not only would the box's contents attract flies, but it could also leave an irreversible stain, if left there too long.

"Want me to grab that box?" Alex pointed at the leftovers as she hopped around a minefield of beer and wine bottles, and two garish Suzani pouffes.

Tom laughed over his shoulder. "You haven't even moved in, and you're already taking Olivia's side. Nah, leave it."

To her right, a low, dark wood cabinet stretched diagonally in the corner, displaying a techie nerd's dream set-up: a large, fifty inch flat-screen television as well as a DVD player, a cable box and a gaming console. Built-in shelves, surrounding an antique fireplace, climbed up the wall behind her. They displayed a mahogany carriage clock, two rows of hastily piled DVDs, a stack of books—titles by Richard Branson and Malcolm Gladwell…probably Harry's—and silver-framed photos of smiley, well-dressed people. Discarded beer bottles intermingled with pieces of driftwood and a collection of conch seashells.

A bright flash of lightning pulled her eyes back to her right, and three large windows peeking out behind patchwork silk scarf curtains. On a sunny day, natural light would probably spill across the honey-hued hardwood, but today the greyness from the incessant deluge lent a chilly, lonely vibe. More thunder rattled the flat, keeping Alex on her toes.

Tom grabbed an armful of dirty mugs. "Follow me around the corner, and check out our kitchen." He waved her forward towards a small teak dining table with four mismatched chairs. "It's a tight squeeze in here—especially on curry take-away night when we're elbowing each other for the chicken tikka masala."

Curry. Alex didn't care for curry, but her stomach growled

28

at the mere mention of anything edible.

With Tom out of sight around the kitchen corner, she doubled back to the coffee table and liberated the disgusting box from the white rug. She bounced into the galley kitchen, placing the cardboard on the edge of the slate grey kitchen counter, careful not to shove it into a crusty stack of white plates, a lipstick-stained wine glass, or an opened tin of baked beans that balanced on the metal rim of the sink. Two slices of whole wheat bread peeked out from the toaster. Buttery toast would be lovely right now…baked beans, not so much.

"Don't worry about that." Tom gestured at the smelly can. "I was making breakfast when you arrived. Just call me Jamie Oliver."

Alex eyed the microwave's digital clock, its bright blue light blared 4:43 p.m. Tom clearly operated on an unconventional schedule.

"Harry said you're from Florida. Why would you trade all that glorious bloody sunshine for rainy London?" He hid the mugs in the dishwasher.

Alex's eyes lit up. "London is theatre geek heaven. You're an actor. You know!"

He leaned against the opposite counter and held his stomach.

"I'm a total fangirl of the London theatre scene." She waved her hands, excited to spill. "There's a perfect mix of plays and musical theatre here. It's such a thriving community. I desperately want to be a playwright. I graduated two weeks ago with a joint major in playwriting and theatre studies, and couldn't get on a plane fast enough…"

A hint of green tinged Tom's face, and sweat stains began to sprout across his Glastonbury tee. His attention… drifting.

"Are you okay?"

He belched. His watery eyes settled on the stale pizza.

"I just need something to soak up the booze." He fought with the box until a piece pulled free, knocking the wine glass into the dirty plates; Tom made no attempt to save it.

Alex's stomach gurgled, loud enough to elicit a frown across Tom's face. He slouched, pointing the cheesy triangle towards her. Pepperoni, especially on a cold, congealed pizza? Disgusting. How do guys eat this stuff? She squinted and shook her head, launching back into her answer.

"...the playwrights and actors I admire call London home. I'd be crazy not to live where my playwriting idol Isabella Archer lives. Where else would I want to be?"

She shrugged with a smile. "Besides, look at me. Florida's heat and sun are my enemies. Fair hair and pale skin don't exactly make me beach body ready. I think I'm more likely to fit in here. I love London. I watch British movies just to see London streets. Isn't it weird how you can fall in love with a place you've never even visited?"

He gave Alex an appreciative once over and sniggered between bites. The salty greasiness of the pepperoni hit the spot. "Well, I don't want to burst your balloon, but it's a tricky field, playwriting. Not everyone can make a go of it. The competition's fierce."

Tom's words kicked a deep pit into Alex's stomach. Geez, did he steal ice cream cones from excited little kids, too? Why is he such a downer? She swallowed hard.

"...Well, hopefully I'll beat the odds."

She turned her head away and fiddled with a soft tea towel tossed on the stovetop, her eyes following the continuous downward trickle of raindrops on the kitchen window sandwiched between the two counters.

"I'm chasing a deadline, too. I've saved enough to cover the rent Harry's charging me for maybe twelve months. My plan is to concentrate on writing and get a play accepted into a development program —"

Tom interrupted. "You'll have tons in common with my sister. She's got a Bachelor's in playwriting and works in theatre fundraising on the South Bank." He tossed the last scraps of the pizza crust into its box, licked tomato sauce from his fingers and headed around the corner into the lounge. "Mind you, she seems to spend more time schmoozing with a glass in her hand than at her laptop."

Alex cleared her throat and blinked several times before following him. Tom's negative comments still echoed in her ears. She didn't travel this far to be a failure. Giving up and going back to Tallahassee weren't options.

"Harry said his girlfriend was in the arts, but I didn't realize we're on the same path."

"She'll be home soon, actually. You'll *love* her." Tom laughed, weaving through the beer bottles on the floor. "Everyone adores *darling* Olivia."

Something in the way Tom delivered that last statement made Alex pause. Did everyone adore Olivia? Was she the doting sister, perfect friend, irresistible lover? Or was Tom being sarcastic in that charming yet confusing way Brits can be?

FOUR

Alex appreciated Tom's 'tour', but it kept her from her most urgent desire—her room. Once introduced to her own private space, a little freshening up—perhaps a relaxing bath or warm shower—she'd feel more at home. With Olivia expected to walk through the door at any moment, she couldn't think of anything else.

"What's with the face?" said Tom.

Alex scrunched up her eyebrows. "My face? Nothing. That's just the way it is. I look pouty if I'm not smiling."

"Some girls I know pay a small fortune to get luscious lips like yours." Tom threw a heavy arm over Alex's shoulder and pulled her into his chest. "Come along, Miss America, the next stop is the sleeping quarters."

She let out a nervous giggle and shifted slightly away from him. Tom was attractive and charming in an odd, still drunk way, but she didn't like strangers invading her personal space, especially if they needed a shower. And was he *flirting* with her? All that touching, hugging—she didn't want to flatter herself, but...seriously? Compared to the pretty girl on the doorstep,

Alex shouldn't register on Tom's hook-up list *at all*: short, A-cup breasts, freckles, and a slight gap between her front teeth. Picking up her backpack and laptop bag by the door provided the excuse to slip out of his touchy-feely grasp.

"The redhead I ran into downstairs…is she your girl-friend?"

"Who? Oh…nah. She just popped 'round for a cup of sugar," Tom winked. "Actually, I met her last night in the pub by the park. I doubt I'll see her again." His response surprised her, but then Alex wasn't a one-night-stand kind of girl.

"So what about you? Did you leave a boyfriend behind in Florida?" They swerved around an expensive looking road bike propped up against the wall. Shiny without a blemish, it still dreamt of its first outing.

Alex bit her nails. "How much time do you have?" she said, intentionally being evasive.

"Ooh, a lady with a past. Love it. You'll have to tell me everything."

Alex's long bangs concealed her eye roll. Tom seemed even more interested now. *Great.*

The first two doors along the hallway were closed, the bathroom, and the bedroom belonging to Harry and Olivia. The third door was open—Tom's room—and much like the man himself, a mess. Cluttered with empty take-out cartons, crumpled magazines, and clothing, both designer and casual, haphazardly strewn over every surface, it looked like a hurricane had hit recently.

Her eyes widened at the chaos. She struggled to find something nice to say. "Looks…cozy."

"It is," said Tom, not picking up on Alex's neat freak-inspired disgust. "I haven't been here long, but I've certainly made it my own."

Alex smirked. "Yes, you have." Stifling a giggle, she turned away from him and set her sights on the final door. Her room. A smile slowly crept across her face.

"And here we are, my dear." The door stuck, so Tom gave it a hearty push. It swung open and clobbered something in its path. He swept his left arm out in front of his body like a game show model revealing a breathtaking prize. "Ta-da!"

Alex gasped.

And shook her head.

The 'prize' hidden behind door number four could hardly be classified as a winner or even a bedroom. A storage closet, maybe, but only at a stretch. A narrow wardrobe leaned crookedly against the wall, its wire hangers dangling precariously over a twin-size futon that hogged most of the floor. An ugly ceramic table lamp lay sideways on the hardwood, its green shade bashed in—the casualty of Tom's door shove, perhaps?

If Alex wanted a dresser, desk or chair—forget it. Even her backpack and laptop bag faced a struggle for real estate. High-end shopping bags from Harvey Nichols, Burberry, and Matthew Williamson appeared to be multiplying like rabbits in the remaining floor space and on top of the futon. Clothes, purses, and who knows what else overflowed from their cardboard and paper constraints. Suitcases, old Christmas decorations, out-of-season clothes belonged here, not humans.

No window. Only one visible power outlet. Her crappy dorm room back in Atlanta was easily three times larger.

Tom looked at Alex open mouthed, staring silently at the floor. "Shit. Harry told Olivia to shift these bags, but she must've had a breakfast meeting and forgot." He grabbed an armful, tossing them into the hallway. "It's a shame this room is so titchy, but at least you're travelling light, Alex."

Her chin trembled. It took every scrap of self-control not to burst into tears at Tom's joke. For months she had been picturing this moment, how she'd skip into her own room, jump on the fluffy bed and instantly make herself at home with her books, clothes, and cherished mementos. Her London bedroom was supposed to have been a comfortable haven from which she'd launch her career and in the process, figure out who she was destined to become. She should've known better. In Alex's experience, real life and dreams never synced; this room, her latest proof.

Slumped soaking wet against the doorway of the 'titchy' broom cupboard, her confidence and excitement had pooled on the floor along with excess water from her clothes. She didn't feel how she was *supposed* to feel at all. She shivered, hiding her face behind her hands. *I'm an idiot.* Kiss goodbye to any semblance of cool in front of the new flatmate.

Tom tugged at his t-shirt. "Was it something I said? Oh…" He legged it.

Alex rubbed her eyes until they watered. Tom popped back in the room, holding a grey cotton sweatshirt adorned with red fabric hearts.

"A peace offering?" His previously relaxed posture, now rigid. Tom and upset women—not a good mix. "You'll feel better in something dry and warm. Put this on. Olivia won't mind. She's always sharing clothes with her girlfriends."

A stranger's clothes? Alex scrunched up her nose and shook her head. She spotted the label inside the collar—Stella McCartney. Oh, God. Designer clothing. This top wasn't like the college sweats from home, the shirts you'd wear at all-you-can-eat wings night at the sports bar. It probably cost more than her entire wardrobe.

She pressed her lips together, and shifted her weight from one foot to another. At this point, she'd eat a slice from that gross day-old pizza or even snog Tom...*anything* to quash the damp goosebumps riddling her skin. And Tom presented a pretty good argument, so...

She nipped into the bathroom and slipped it over her head. Unfurled, it became a mini-dress on her small frame. Its soft sleeves reached well beyond her hands, and her breasts disappeared altogether. Is this Olivia girl some kind of giant? Alex stepped out of the bathroom, rolling the excess material above her slim wrists.

Tom chuckled. "Yeah, Olivia's got at least six inches on you. She's very leggy, so I can't kit you out with her jeans. But your top half's dry. I know it doesn't make up for the wee room, but at least you won't catch your death."

"Thanks. At least I won't stretch it or anything. You're sure she won't mind?"

"She won't even know it's missing, trust me," said Tom.

Alex pulled her hair out of the ponytail. "Is there a shop nearby? My toothbrush and shampoo are in my checked bags. I want to look presentable for your sister."

Alex gave a squinty grin towards the sun. Its warmth, paired with the post-shower scent of drying pavement along Broadway Market, added a spring to her step, last seen at Paddington Tube station. The two-storey shops hugging the street made her feel like she was strolling through one of her favourite British movies like *Love Actually*, or *Pride*.

Her stomach cooed blissfully as she wolfed down a Time Out chocolate bar and a small packet of Cadbury chocolate buttons. The candy bars from the States couldn't compete with the creamy silkiness of British chocolate. One of the best parts of moving to the UK—indulging her chocoholic tendencies whenever a craving hit, instead of relying on sporadic care packages mailed by her dad.

Birds chattered their bliss from lampposts while a grey squirrel frolicked across the pavement, happy for the sun's return. Locals popping out of shop doorways looked up at the blue sky and its cotton ball clouds, and grinned. Alex swung her bags of toiletries and groceries, absorbed in her new neighbourhood.

Along the curb, a black cab swerved, its front wheel plunging into a pothole brimming with grimy water. A surge of dirty muck rained over the sidewalk—and Alex, baptizing her with sludge.

"Eeeeewwww!"

Her eyes stung. The cold gasoline and mud mixture oozed through the fibres of the sweatshirt's right side, its chill spreading downward in a gunky smear.

"Fuck!" Alex stomped the ground as her gaze followed the taxi. It merrily chugged around the corner onto Westgate Street. Her throat constricted. Olivia can't see this.

Alex's shoes slapped along the sidewalk, the bulging plastic bags of cereal boxes, English muffins, and bottles attacking her legs with each stride. She leaped up the stairs two at a time, cursing her decision to accept Tom's help. If only she'd followed her gut…

She stuck her key into 2B's lock, but the door drifted open. Raised voices roared from the kitchen. One voice belonged to Tom, the other an unseen female. Alex tiptoed inside.

"You're twenty-four-years-old and still can't follow the simplest of instructions." The woman's accent sounded like actress Elizabeth Hurley's—sultry and posh. Alex bit her lip and nudged the door closed.

"You've done a piss-poor job. This place is exactly the same as when I left at seven: a pigsty. I'm sick of your excuses."

The voice barely paused for air.

"So tell me. Who was it this time? That jogging nutritionist from the Isle of Wight? Not the barista around the corner, *again*? It's busier than Piccadilly Circus in there. The revolving door to your bedroom has got to stop—"

Tom snapped back. "Why do you care? I don't pry into your sex life. Maybe I should. Is Harry working too much at Bespoke, sister dear? Too many hours in the company of hot cocktail girls?"

Alex stared down at the caked mud and gulped, her temples damp and tingly. *Damn. Olivia.*

"Shut up, Tom. You're *such* an arse."

The click-clack of high heels grew louder and closer. Alex's blood chilled. She turned to her left, slipping down the hall, but her sensitive nose tickled with a waft of sweet raspberry and peonies.

Tom's twenty-two-year-old sister stopped mid-stride on the edge of the lounge, immaculate in a stunning emerald green knee-length dress that highlighted her coltish legs and slim waist, her dark hair, corralled in a sleek, low ponytail. A square amethyst, large enough to feed a family of five for half a decade, glittered on her right hand, its brilliance dancing in the light when she stabbed the air in Alex's direction.

"And who the hell are *you*?" Her green eyes narrowed. Tom crept up behind her, his hand stroking his chin stubble.

Alex gasped, knocked senseless by a strange combo of fright and Olivia's beauty—the kind of beauty that always gets its way. She wasn't sure whether to flee or stand her ground.

Olivia curled her lip and stormed at Alex. "Tom, it's bad enough that you bring your conquests back here, but to then dress them in *my clothes...*"

She snatched the shirt's right sleeve. "Look at the state of my Stella top." Alex flinched. Olivia's nails grabbed more than just a fistful of material. "It's filthy! I've had the day from hell and now I have to deal—"

"Olivia." Tom wrapped his arm around the diminutive blonde's quaking shoulder. "Meet Alex, Harry's friend. Remember she's staying with us for a while?"

The brunette blinked her long eyelashes several times, her fingers releasing the Floridian's arm. "You're...Alex?" Her voice softened. "I'm so sorry for this misunderstanding. You know how siblings are." Olivia shot a frustrated sneer at Tom.

Alex bit the inside of her cheek, unsure if the fireworks were truly over. She eased out of Tom's embrace and rummaged with jittery hands through her plastic bags. "It's okay. I fight with my older sister all the time. What family doesn't have drama?" She tossed her bangs over her right eye. Is the zit still hidden?

Olivia's eyes travelled along the mud splatter on the top.

Alex shuddered. "I'm so sorry about your shirt. I arrived drenched and without luggage, so Tom loaned me your top. On the way back from the shops, a taxi splashed me. I'll pay for the dry-cleaning—"

"No need." Jaw clenched, Olivia snapped up several wet plastic shopping bags off the floor. She delivered one last glare at Tom and clomped down the hall.

Alex set her grocery bags on the floor, then yanked off her running shoes. So much for winning over Harry's girlfriend.

"Well done! That went well," Tom whispered, breaking into an apologetic smirk. "I'm sorry. It's not you. My laziness put her in this foul mood. She's cross at me. Our friends are arriving in an hour and a half, and this place is a tip."

Alex's eyes bulged. "People are coming over *tonight*?"

Tom peered past Alex, distracted by a clattering racket coming from the bathroom. "Yeah, Friday night…time to let loose after a busy week." He picked up several magazines and loped towards his bedroom.

The unemployed actor needs to let his hair down.

"Can I have a quick shower first?" asked Alex.

"Sure." Tom wandered down the hall ahead of her.

The bathroom door remained closed; Olivia must be inside. Alex entered her tiny room to squirrel away her purchases. True to his word, Tom had moved his sister's hoard of shopping, so the floor gained maybe ten square feet of space.

He stuck his head back around the doorway. "Towels for the pretty lady and a top to put on afterwards. Sorry it's a football shirt. I haven't got round to doing my laundry, so clean clothes are scarce."

The back of the shirt read *Terry* with a number twenty-six— a Chelsea Football Club shirt. She couldn't walk around in just her bra. "Thanks. My dad would freak if he saw this. He's a life-long Manchester United fan. The Mancs despise Chelsea."

"Tell me about it. And for the record, the feeling's mutual." Tom winked.

Alex hugged the towels and popped open her shampoo. A familiar whiff of citrus filled her nose. Home in a bottle. In a few minutes, the shower's warm water would wash away all the day's dirt and, she hoped, all of its drama.

"I've made the worst first impression. I wouldn't blame your sister if she hated me."

Tom scrunched up his nose, dismissively.

"No, Tom think about it. Some random girl you don't know invades your home, and wrecks your clothing? I'd hate me, too."

He patted her back. "Get cleaned up and then we'll get pissed. Let's forget today."

She scooped up her toothpaste and hair care products, and shuffled into the now vacant bathroom, but the claw-foot tub was already occupied—with a jagged mountain of ice cubes. Alex frowned and sank down on the tub's edge.

"Oh, sorry. I didn't know you wanted a bath," said Olivia, strutting into the bathroom with her arms filled with bottles and cans. "Curse of the small fridge. We're chilling the beer and wine in here, but you can still freshen up. I'll get you a flannel for a quick wash at the sink. People will be here in just over an hour, so best be quick."

41

FIVE

English muffins popped out of the toaster, their edges scorched. Alex's hunger didn't care. She spread a thick layer of butter into their crevices and then cracked open her jar of Nutella. The nutty chocolate flavour would overpower any burnt bits.

She checked her phone. 11:15 a.m. May 23. A Saturday. How did she fall asleep and miss the entire party last night? It must've been a rager. Discarded lemon wedges, wine glasses, and bottle caps lay strewn across both counters, and the smell of stale smoke and weed hung in the air. Two trays of half-eaten crackers, rubbery veggies, and goopy dips junked up the top of the stove. Empty bottles of wine and Jack Daniels hid behind the trash can in the corner. A cricket bat rested on the lounge floor beside the shiny bike, both surrounded by toppled beer bottles. Clearly, she was dead to the world last night.

So dead, she also broke her promise to phone her dad. One moment, she was checking Facebook at 6:30 p.m. while testing out her lumpy futon. The next, jolting awake this morning in a strange room. Blame drama and jet lag. She dashed off a text to her father:

'Dad, fell asleep and didn't wake up until this morning. Hope you didn't worry. No luggage yet. Haven't seen Harry, but am ok and getting settled. Speak soon. Alex xo'

She owed her mom, Geraldine, a message too. Letting her know that she had arrived safely in London—the mature thing to do. She'd rather skip it. The clashes between Alex and her mom were legendary in the Sinclair family. They fought over everything: clothes, Alex's picky eating, panic attacks—but her playwriting aspirations ranked as her mother's favourite target.

Geraldine always championed her older children, Kathryn and Robbie, who were twelve and ten years older than their youngest sibling. Alex never quite measured up to them despite her solid grades and talent for storytelling. Her mom didn't value Alex's artistic flair. To Geraldine, a career with prospects, status and a big pay cheque—impressing friends, family, and business associates—was the only path to take. It's all about the bragging rights.

Michael insisted that Alex follow her passion at college. Forcing her into law or medicine to become a corporate attorney or emergency room doctor like her sister and brother, would be a cruel waste of her creative gifts. He didn't have the heart to impose such an agenda on his baby girl, and as a result, Geraldine viewed Alex as her ex-husband's problem. He could worry about her, pay the tuition, and support her when her writing dreams amounted to nothing.

Her mom's harshest words were burnt into Alex's memory: *"A job in the arts isn't respectable. You'll struggle for years with nothing to show for it. You'll embarrass yourself, Alex—and worse, you'll embarrass me."* She desperately wanted to prove her mother wrong, and was determined not to return to Florida until she had made her mark.

Geraldine didn't deserve a blow-by-blow account of her new life abroad, but if Alex shirked this one small responsibility, she'd never hear the end of it from her dad. Old habits ran deep. She'd walk barefoot over shards of glass to avoid upsetting him. His voice rang in her ears: *"It wouldn't kill you to send one text, or leave a quick voicemail message."*

The five-hour time difference meant that a text or call would wake up her mom or interfere with her early morning gym session. Alex chose the least invasive option—a Facebook update. Her mom could read it at her leisure, and Alex could avoid speaking to her. Besides, most Saturdays her mom had back-to-back real estate viewings with her clients. Alex would be lucky to hear from her hours from now, if at all.

She typed a quick status update and set her phone down on the small kitchen table, its surface littered with lipstick-ringed cigarette butts, corks, and a woman's telephone number jotted down on an ATM slip. She tugged open the under-the-counter fridge. How do Brits make do with such teeny refrigerators? It looked like a mini-bar. She bent over to get a better look.

Two hands, cloaked in fuzzy black sleeves, tickled her waist from behind.

"Arrrrgh!" She flicked her hair out of her eyes...

"It's *you*." Alex's grin could've powered half of London's East End.

"Ha ha. I didn't mean to startle you. I can't believe you're actually here...in my flat making breakfast." Harry let her go and tightened his plush black robe, his dark blonde hair pointing in all directions. He smelt like freshly laundered towels.

Alex bounced on the spot, her eyes taking in all five foot ten inches of him. Even though they had last been together two weeks ago, their separation felt like an eternity.

"I'm sorry I wasn't here when you arrived. The beer supplier for the club fouled up our order and with it being the start of the weekend, I had to fix it in person. Then we had a leak in the ladies' room, and the hostess quit without notice. One disaster after another."

He pulled open a canister holding tea bags. "I didn't get home until gone three. Fancy a cuppa?"

Alex nodded and sat down at the table with her chocolate-coated English muffins. Harry's sugary tea was legendary. In college, they shared many an evening ranting about their course work over a comfy mug of tea and a plate of cookies—or biscuits, as Harry called them.

"The party was on its last legs when I got in, so I only saw Tom and Livvy briefly. He mentioned your luggage was missing. And I can see he tried to help you out. Nice Chelsea kit, Manc girl!"

Alex stuck her tongue out at him just as Olivia sauntered in to the room. His girlfriend made a point of hugging Harry tightly from behind, giving him a lingering kiss on the temple. Her long dark hair tumbled onto his shoulder as she nuzzled his neck. "Morning, darling. We missed you last night. You owe me."

Harry turned to face Olivia and kissed her lips. "I do, do I? Well, before my princess calls in her debts, I have a favour to ask you."

He fetched a third mug from the cupboard and elbowed several prosecco bottles to make space on the counter. "Alex is still waiting for her suitcases to arrive, so why don't you take her shopping for clothes this afternoon, get a few essentials to tide her over? Shopping is your cardio. Go on, you know you want to."

Alex's eyes shifted from Harry to Olivia.

Olivia jerked her head back, avoiding Harry's gaze. "I was planning on revising the seating plan for the young playwrights fundraiser, but…I *suppose* it can wait." She tightened the belt of her pink silk robe with a sharp tug.

Harry beamed. "Of course it can wait. It doesn't happen for another two weeks."

He poured hot water into two of the three mugs and chuckled at Alex's plate of chocolate drenched muffins. "Alex, sweetheart, I see fruit's still banned from your breakfasts. Is it safe to assume you still like three spoonfuls of sugar in your tea, too?"

Olivia crossed her arms and squinted, first at Alex, then at Harry. Her mouth fell open, but no words came out.

Alex shifted in her chair, one foot jittering underneath the table. "Yep, guilty as charged. My dentist was in tears when I left Florida."

She smiled at Harry, and chewed a mouthful of English muffin, but the butterflies whirling in her stomach and the chill creeping up her spine hinted that Olivia's eyes remained locked on her.

Harry handed Alex her steaming mug, then turned to his girlfriend. "I've switched on the coffee maker so it should be ready shortly, babe. Right, I'm jumping in the shower. Must get back to Bespoke. I'll see my two favourite girls later."

He kissed Olivia on the lips and squeezed Alex's shoulder. "Olivia will show you the ropes. Have fun today."

Mug in hand, he headed off to the bathroom leaving the two women submerged in a suffocating silence. Only the ticking carriage clock and the hissing shower head pierced the quiet. Olivia kept her head down, leaning against the counter, scrolling manically through Twitter on her Swarovski-jewelled iPhone. Alex counted the seconds it took for the Nutella and melting butter to drown the nooks and crannies of her muffin.

Several minutes later, Tom's shuffled into sight, naked except for a pair of low-slung baggy shorts that matched the Chelsea top Alex wore. He scratched at a sparse patch of dark hair on his chest.

"Morning, ladies. Ooh, that was a heavy night."

He spotted Alex's half-eaten breakfast and rubbed his temples. "I don't think I can tolerate brekkie. When did your friends become so boring, Olivia? I had to get totally polluted to have any semblance of a good time."

Olivia rolled her eyes and shoved Alex's unopened Frosties out of her way, plucking a box of fair trade muesli from the top of the microwave. She poured a stingy amount into a bowl.

"You seemed to have no complaints last I saw you. Who was that awful girl you were snogging? You barely came up for air." A splash of soy milk topped her breakfast.

Tom ignored his sister and flopped down onto the chair beside Alex, picking up the ATM receipt. His bleary eyes focused on the handwritten phone number. He pulled a cigarette from a packet on the table.

Olivia shot him a withering dose of side-eye. "Obviously you liked what you sampled, if the moans coming from your bedroom at 4 a.m. were anything to go by."

Ick. Alex's room shared a wall with Tom's. Thank goodness for her comatose slumber. A play-by-play of Tom bumping uglies?

She also didn't want to be caught in the middle of another sister-brother squabble. She silently gathered her dishes and bundled them into the dishwasher. The siblings continued bickering, so she left them to it. She ran into a squeaky clean Harry wrapped in white towels on the way to his bedroom.

"Are they kicking off again? Take no notice. They do love each other, but you wouldn't know it."

"They're pretty hardcore," said Alex.

"Look, I feel awful about your room. You were supposed to have Tom's. I warned Livvy it was a bad idea, having him move in. He's a good laugh and means well, but once here, he'll never budge. He's not exactly a self-starter."

Alex giggled. "Yeah, he gave me that impression. He's an actor? When was his last audition?"

"A few months ago. And at this rate, he'll never be treading the boards at the National or guest starring on *EastEnders*. He got kicked out of RADA, and since then he's been faffing about. Their parents got fed up with his mooching and cut off his cash, hoping it would push him into action. No such luck."

"I wish I had a trust fund," Alex fluttered her eyelashes at Harry. "What's that like?"

Harry laughed. "Cheeky monkey." He playfully shoved her and slipped into his room.

Tom and Olivia's conversation grew louder in the kitchen, so Alex claimed the elusive bathroom. It had been thirty-six hours since her last shower back in Florida. She gathered towels, her toiletries, and clothes, and shut the bathroom door on the warring siblings.

She twisted the shower's handle and waited for a steamy surge of water. A lukewarm, half-hearted sprinkle dripped onto her head. It barely saturated her hair. *Is that IT?!* Haven't the Brits discovered *water pressure* yet? She shivered and lathered up quickly.

☂ ☂ ☂ ☂ ☂

By one o'clock that afternoon, the two women were on their way. Alex couldn't wait to kiss goodbye to her day-old flight attire, but she dreaded having Olivia as a shopping companion. Her tepid welcome was unsettling and standing next to the statuesque brunette in her fashionable red, black, and orange DVF shirtdress, and espadrille wedges, Alex—back in her baggy *Captain America* tee and yoga pants—resembled a shrimpy teenager on take-your-kids-to-work day. The pimple definitely didn't help her look older or sophisticated, either.

Alex never chased the latest trends or drained her savings on designer labels. Her go-to outfits consisted of dark jeans, t-shirts, and Converse All-Stars. When she was feeling particularly girly, she'd channel Jess Day, Zooey Deschanel's character on the TV show *New Girl,* in cute retro-influenced skirts or dresses with a cardigan and flats—comfy but presentable.

The women popped into an independent coffee shop tucked underneath the arches of London Fields Overground station. Olivia desperately craved a cappuccino to fuel the afternoon shopping excursion.

Harry had warned Alex that their Hackney 'hood was hipster central, and he wasn't kidding. Guys with big beards, skinny jeans, and hats left their bicycles outdoors and queued for coffee with women dressed in crop tops and high-waisted jeans. Alex tugged at her creased outfit. Their trendy vibe made her feel even more out of sorts. She stepped outdoors to pet two bulldogs that were whining, missing their owners. "On the outside looking in, guys. I know how you feel," whispered Alex, scratching their chubby shoulder rolls.

Drink in hand, striding through the door, Olivia took charge, proclaiming her distaste for London's most popular shopping destination. "Forget Oxford Street. I despise it." She adjusted her

Dior Sauvage sunglasses while balancing her white leather Burberry hobo bag on the crook of her arm. "One day you'll see what I mean. It's overflowing with slow walking tourists and bratty teenagers. I'm taking you to my favourite shopping area in Chelsea. It has designer shops, plus the more popular chains, something for both our tastes."

She carefully sipped her steaming cup. "And let's skip the Tube. It'll be hot and sweaty, and there are too many changes between here and Sloane Square. The drive will take about thirty-five minutes, so we'll have plenty of time to chat." She waved at a taxi. The first one in sight swerved to her command.

Alex sat down in awe, taking in her first ride in an authentic London black cab. Clean, tons of legroom—so different from the rank, dirty crampfests back home in the States. She buckled the seatbelt with no fear of finding a questionable sticky substance lurking on its strap. Her legs happily stretched out as far as they could reach; her Converse still couldn't touch the other side of the seating compartment. She felt like the Queen.

Olivia seemed softer, chattier. Maybe Tom was right and her dark moods were his fault? The questions began to flow.

"How did you move over here? I thought it was impossible for Americans to live here unless they had a firm job offer."

Alex pushed a random button, sliding the window open. A welcoming cool breeze soothed her clammy skin. "I was born here—well, not *here*, but in Manchester. I have dual citizenship."

"Really?"

"My family flew over from Florida in July '93 for my grandfather's funeral, my dad's dad..." Alex trailed off, distracted by the old pubs and quirky Bethnal Green shops whizzing past.

"Mom was seven months pregnant and went into labour the day after the funeral. I was born two months premature. Dad says Mom was furious we couldn't go straight home afterwards. She doesn't like England at all—hates the weather, hates the food, and hates my dad's relatives. I was in the hospital for just shy of two months. We went back to Florida in early September, so Kathryn and Robbie—that's my older sister and brother— didn't miss much of the new school year."

Olivia pulled out her phone to check for messages. "I had no idea you were half English."

"Yeah, I guess that explains why I adore all things British. It's in my blood. My dad was born in Manchester but moved to Florida in the late seventies. That's when he met Mom. He got hired by Walmart and worked his way up into management. When Walmart bought Asda supermarkets here in '99, he was asked to manage the transition in Manchester, but he never came home."

"That must have been tough."

"I cried myself to sleep every night for a year. I was only six. I felt completely abandoned and didn't understand why he didn't take me with him. Before he left, we were inseparable. We used to watch old *Doctor Who* episodes on VHS for hours on end; it drove my mother bonkers."

Alex calmed her flyaway tresses and closed the window, silencing the wheezing breaths of the passing Routemaster buses. "We flew over with Mom for a visit when I was seven. I guess it was a last ditch effort to salvage something, but it didn't work. Their divorce was finalized a year later in 2001. When I was old enough to understand, Robbie told me that they were having issues for a long time. Apparently, they almost split in '92, but then Mom got pregnant with me. I was an accident, so they stayed together..."

The taxi zipped around St. Paul's Cathedral, its majestic 300-year-old dome piercing the blue sky. Alex fell silent, contemplating how something so robust and massive could be so beautiful.

"Impressive, isn't it?" Olivia looked up mid-text. "I take many things for granted here, but St. Paul's always makes me smile."

"I bet. It's like that Samuel Johnson quotation: *'When a man is tired of London, he is tired of life.'* There's so much to love here. I could never be bored of all *this*." Alex steadied herself as the cab swung around a sharp corner.

Olivia smirked at Alex's grand statement, smothering a titter behind her hair. Alex didn't notice her seatmate's reaction and continued with her starry-eyed commentary. "I didn't expect it to be that magnificent; photos don't do it justice."

With the cathedral receding into the distance, Alex turned back to Olivia. "Anyway, Dad flew to Florida most years to see us, but I haven't been back to England since I was seven. I haven't visited my grandmother since then. It's weird being separated from family, especially when it's not your choice."

The Victoria Embankment, the northern side of the River Thames, blurred as the taxi picked up speed, passing signs announcing the approach of Waterloo Bridge. Alex leaned against the window, tapping her fingers, her eyes searching across the water. There! The National Theatre, rising above the river on the South Bank. She took a deep breath and didn't dare blink, absorbing the view before her eyes. "I've waited so long to see that building in all its cement ugliness, and I mean that in the most loving way possible."

Olivia took a quick sip of her cappuccino. "Yeah, I know

what you mean. It's not the daintiest or prettiest of London architecture, but there's something about it. If you love theatre, you're drawn to it."

For the first time, Alex felt a kinship with Harry's girlfriend. She wanted Olivia to like her. They had playwriting and theatre in common, as well as a fondness for Harry. At the kitchen table during breakfast, her familiarity with Harry had concerned the brunette. Lots of girlfriends are possessive, but Olivia seemed agitated by the littlest things. Alex shrugged off her gnawing discomfort, determined to become better acquainted with her new friend and enjoy the day.

Both women slipped into silence as the taxi swept by the Houses of Parliament, Big Ben, and St. James's Park, all sights that Alex couldn't wait to explore up close. She smiled, catching a fleeting glimpse of Buckingham Palace and the scarlet-coated Queen's Guard, standing tall under their black fuzzy hats. All those hours poring over magazine and online photos of Will and Kate, and the Queen's home—right here! Alex leaned closer to the window just as the cab bounced over a bump in the road. She smacked her head on the taxi's curved frame, a sharp ouch escaping from her lips.

"Sightseeing with you should come with a health warning," said Olivia, her eyes glued to her phone.

Alex giggled, but offered no apologies for her geekiness. Maybe these London landmarks were as common to Olivia as the corner diner back home was to Alex, but seeing these long-loved places was like stepping into an enchanted storybook. She didn't want to sully this first impression with distracted chitchat.

The lack of conversation didn't faze Olivia one bit. Immersed in reading texts, she only looked up after a short drive through Belgravia. "We'll be arriving in Sloane Square soon."

Six

Alex climbed out of the taxi, squinting into the eye-watering sunlight. The Royal Court Theatre stood across the square to her left. She raised her hand to eyebrow level, blocking the sun and gasped at the regal building. "Oh, wow…"

"So you've spotted it," Olivia tossed her empty cup into a bin. "I must admit coming here was somewhat selfish. I have theatre tickets waiting at the box office."

Alex didn't expect to visit the beautiful old theatre's lobby so soon. Forget curbing her enthusiasm—she swooned—wobbling up the theatre's steps.

"You're shaking!" Olivia chuckled. "I hope you don't pass out from joy."

Alex knew this theatre's history by heart. Her dog-eared copy of *The Royal Court Theatre Inside Out* was a gift from her dad when she was accepted into Emory's playwriting program. Known in the industry as one of the most supportive institutions for new and young playwrights, the Royal Court exemplified what Alex held dear in writing for the stage: innovation, creativity, and an eclectic voice. She dreamt about having her work accepted, developed, and performed within its esteemed walls. It shared top spot on her list of must-see London venues along with the National Theatre.

Olivia chatted and charmed the front desk staff. Alex didn't hover. The modern lobby invited her to peek up its stairwells and run her fingers along its walls, happy to share its secrets with someone so keen. It seemed much smaller in real life, but its intimacy made it even more captivating.

Alex hoped that someday soon she'd have the spare cash to see a play here. That was her top task for the coming week— finding a part-time job to cover such expenses. The money she saved over the past two years would cover Harry's generously low rent for a year, but it wouldn't stretch towards food, or fun like comic cons and plays. She couldn't live in this theatre-rich city and not catch a production or two. If forced with the choice, she'd go hungry before she'd skip theatre; it nourished her soul more than any meal.

A guy about Alex's age carrying a motorcycle helmet and wearing a black t-shirt, jeans, and a distressed leather jacket, strolled through the glass doors and waited behind Olivia. He unzipped the jacket, and a subtle waft of deliciousness settled in his wake. Ooh. Spicy cardamom, juniper berries, and leather; Alex guessed he was wearing Burberry Brit Rhythm. A brief spell last Christmas working in the fragrance department at Saks Fifth Avenue in Atlanta meant she could identify cologne within seconds. He raked a hand through his thick jet-black hair and caught her gaze. He smiled, his brown eyes large and dark, full of mischief and warmth.

Alex grinned back, savouring the moment.

A staff member waved the smiley stranger towards the desk. He raised an eyebrow at Alex and began speaking to the clerk. Alex wasn't an expert at accents, but she could tell a soft Irish lilt when she heard one. Good looking, friendly, and a fan of theatre—what more could a girl want?

"Got them," Olivia waved a pair of tickets in front of Alex and ushered her through the doors, down the steps past a red vintage Vespa and into the sun-soaked square.

"Let me see?" Alex squinted at the tickets Olivia placed in her hand. "May 25—this Monday. Lucky." Envy ate her up from inside.

Olivia pointed to the Club Monaco on the edge of Sloane Square. "Let's head there and get you some jeans, maybe a dress." She lowered her sunglasses over her eyes as they walked across the road. "You might want to tuck those tickets away somewhere safe."

Alex scratched her temple, confused.

"In the cab, I got a text about my fundraising meeting on Monday. It will probably run late, so I won't make it in time," said Olivia. "Go in my place and take Tom with you. He could use a night at the theatre. Maybe it will remind him that his talent's growing stale."

Alex stopped in her tracks, her eyes growing misty. She grasped the tickets to her chest and crumpled Olivia in an impromptu hug. "You're *sure*? You really can't use them?"

Olivia raised her eyebrows at Alex's embrace and pulled away, smoothing her dress. "Nope. Mustn't let them go to waste."

"Thank you, thank you, thank you!" Alex couldn't stop beaming. She grinned all the way into Club Monaco, past the racks of khakis, jeans, and dresses. A play in forty-eight hours? Nothing else mattered. How bad can the world be when you have Royal Court tickets in your wallet?

The clerk at Club Monaco snipped off the tags from the jeans and the flowery blue blouse Alex purchased, so the yoga pants and *Captain America* t-shirt were dumped into one of her bulging carrier bags. In her new attire, she seemed to sprout up three inches—shoulders back, chin up—and she zipped about like Tinker Bell, interested in everything.

She followed Olivia into Hugo Boss and Whistles. One glance at a price tag hanging from a pretty beaded skirt in All Saints, and Alex swore her wallet flinched. Olivia, however, managed to buy several tops, two dresses, and a soft motorcycle jacket in white leather.

While ambling through the racks of bras and underwear in the Peter Jones department store, Alex decided to broach the subject of her friendship with Harry. Olivia seemed jovial and on the heels of her spur-of-the-moment generosity with the theatre tickets, the timing couldn't be better.

"So tell me about uni in Atlanta." Olivia beat her to it. She tilted her head to the side. "Harry said the two of you were inseparable."

Alex let out a half-laugh, shaking her head. "I wouldn't say we were inseparable. Our programs were in different parts of campus for the most part. I'd only see him if we planned to meet up." Alex replayed her words in her head. Oops. That didn't sound reassuring to a possessive girlfriend.

Olivia shoved the bra hangers along the rack two at a time, their plastic edges squealing in protest with each push. "Did you meet up *a lot*?" She wouldn't look Alex in the eye.

"Once or twice a week. We both had heavy course loads, and I was doing a double major," Alex's hands grew clammy. "We studied together sometimes. That's where my fondness for his sugary tea comes from. It kept me going into the night when I started to fade. You know what it's like when you have a lot of ground to cover and only a few hours to do it? Studying and assignments owned me twenty-four-seven. A social life? What's *that* like?"

Her breeziness didn't crack Olivia's intense facade. She pursed her perfect red lips and glared at the sexy push-up bras. Alex half-expected the lingerie and its promotional photo of model Cara Delevingne to spontaneously combust.

"Harry helped me through a heartbreaking time." Alex rifled through a table of cotton bikini briefs.

She looked up through her bangs to gauge Olivia's reaction. There wasn't one.

She slipped behind the table's chest-high sign proclaiming *Buy Two, Get the Third Free.* "I missed my brother Robbie. He's always been in my corner, a great listener. Harry filled that void. He kept my spirits up and told me not to drop out of college." She picked at her cuticles. "If it wasn't for him, I doubt I'd be here. I'm so grateful to Harry—to *both* of you—for letting me stay in the flat until I find something permanent."

Olivia bit the inside of her cheek and looked away towards the hosiery. Alex's stomach cramped, waiting for a response. Say something, anything.

The brunette remained silent. A toxic cloud of speechlessness filled the room. Suffocating, Alex burst out in a ramble. "Harry's such a sweet, wonderful guy, and he loves you so much. He always talked about how he couldn't wait to get back to London."

Still nothing.

"He's been a great friend...nothing more." Why did *she* sound so defensive?

Olivia swallowed hard and took a step back. Alex's worry-meter shot into the red.

"You're right. He's wonderful," said Olivia. "Lots of women would love to have what I have with him. We've been together for four years, so I've seen plenty of girls try to steal him away, but that will *never* happen."

She snatched two lace bras off their hangers and marched towards the customer service desk. She didn't look back to see if Alex followed.

The girls stepped outside into the late afternoon warmth, but the air between Olivia and Alex held a chill. Alex didn't know what more to say without shouting '*I only slept with one guy in college and it wasn't Harry!*' If Olivia's freeze continued, those words might be her only ticket towards forgiveness—forgiveness for a fling that never happened.

Alex offered an olive branch as they walked away from Sloane Square. "Are you hungry? My treat as a thank you for today."

Maybe the friendly Olivia last seen thirty-five minutes ago could be coaxed back with food. Some skinny girls get angry and weird when they're famished. Alex tore the three-pound price tag off her new black sunglasses, waiting for an answer.

Olivia lit a cigarette, her shades coolly masking her emotions. "There's a Pret south of here on the King's Road."

Economical and somewhat brisk, but a response nonetheless.

Olivia didn't utter another word. She stuck her nose into her phone, scrolling through texts. Alex turned away, absorbing her surroundings: so many small dogs being carried by so many well-dressed women; no homeless people; leathery-skinned men leaning against foreign cars; very little trash—definitely a wealthy area.

A few blocks down the King's Road, Olivia erupted in a laugh. Alex snuck a sideways glance. Had the spell been broken? A vague grin trespassed across Olivia's face while reading something on her phone. Her moods seemed to change with the shifting breeze.

"Everything all right?" Alex bit her tongue and waited.

Olivia slipped her phone into her purse. "Just Harry. Being Harry. Bless."

Whatever that meant.

"What are you working on play-wise right now? Anything promising?" said Olivia.

Alex exhaled. "I'm fine-tuning the play that was my final college assignment. I think it could work quite well here. It's based in the UK and delves into the British suffrage movement. It's an empowering women's story with an all-female cast. Even the male characters will be portrayed by women."

"Sounds ambitious. Do you think you can pull it off?" Olivia took a final drag on her cigarette and flicked its glowing embers to the curb.

"I hope so. I keep fiddling with it, editing, adding scenes. That's my problem. I'm always tinkering, trying to make it perfect. Sometimes I don't know when enough is enough. What about you?"

"I have a few ideas on the go," said Olivia as they entered the King's Road branch of the Pret a Manger sandwich chain. "I tend to juggle several and dip in and out. There are a few new writers' workshops and development programs coming up, so I need to figure out which play to submit."

A question about these upcoming programs hesitated on Alex's lips, but Olivia changed the subject.

"I drank far too many calories last night, so I need something light. What's got a low calorie count?"

Alex didn't care about calories or fat grams, but she did care about her picky tastes. On her right, chilled stainless steel racks displayed tidy rows of fresh sandwiches enclosed in triangular-shaped cardboard boxes. Alex had never seen anything like it. Pre-packaged sandwiches weren't a take-out option in Florida or Georgia.

She stood wide-eyed, blocking one of the shelves, many of the sandwich filling combinations beyond her comfort zone. Avocado and Toasted Pine Nut wrap? *Pass!* Most of the customers knew exactly what they craved and didn't hesitate to reach around her, snatching their prizes.

A meaty bicep flew out of nowhere, its owner reaching for a veggie wrap from the highest shelf. Alex ducked backwards. She stumbled, crashing into an employee balancing a pyramid of sandwiches. Chicken Avocado, Classic Super Clubs, and Pret Pickle triangles sailed through the air, landing with a succession of muffled cardboard *thwumphs*. The grand finale—the jarring clang of the round silver tray on the cement floor. A few patrons sarcastically cheered, "Wahey!"

Alex didn't know whether to hide or take a bow. Olivia rolled her eyes, distancing herself from the spectacle by zeroing in on her phone. She pretended to have no association with the American klutz.

Sweat broke out on Alex's brow. Most customers stared, others tutted, looking inconvenienced. Being the centre of attention killed her appetite in one fell swoop. She dropped to her knees, her shaky hands corralling the wayward sandwiches, plucking each triangle one by one out of harm's way. She looked over at the Pret employee she had accidentally tackled. "I'm so sorry. I didn't hurt you, did I?"

The employee, a twenty-something black woman wearing a Pret server's cap, slowly knelt down and barely batted an eye at the smorgasbord of sandwiches strewn across the floor. She didn't even glance at Alex. She just calmly piled the sandwiches on her tray. "No worries. Most of the boxes stayed sealed…"

It couldn't be…

Alex paused her frantic sandwich recovery. The tattoo on this girl's toned bicep, an elaborate Cyberman, a robotic villain famous for threatening Doctor Who and his companions, was instantly familiar. She stared at the employee's face, partially hidden by her curly hair. She had to make sure.

"Wait. I *know* you…I would recognize that tattoo any-where."

The woman lifted her left eyebrow but kept stacking sand-wich boxes.

"Lucy? Lucy Hardy? It's me, Alex…Alex Sinclair from Florida?"

The Pret employee looked up, puzzled. She did a double take. "Oh my God! It's not. It's not!"

Their shrieks in unison alerted Olivia, who peered over her sunglasses from the safety of the beverage fridge. Alex and the employee were on their knees, embracing in the middle of the store. Olivia turned her back, letting out a bored sigh.

Shop patrons gingerly stepped around the reunited friends and the triangle-shaped collateral damage scattered in their wake. Breathless, Alex didn't clue in to the scuttling feet nearby, her perma-grin, aching. "Of all the people to run into, I can't be-lieve it's you. This can't be a coincidence. I just know bumping into you was meant to be!"

She pulled Lucy up off the floor, her five foot six frame dwarfing the blonde by three valuable inches. Alex reminded herself to call her friend by her full name—Lucy hated it when people called her Lu or Luce.

"You still believe in signs and destiny and all that crazy shit." Lucy laughed, her brown eyes taking in her old friend. "Look at your hair. It's shorter, but other than that you're the same. I'm so happy to see you!"

She hugged Alex tightly. "What are you doing here? I thought you'd be writing up a storm in New York City by now."

"It's a long story. I have so much to tell you! It's been what? Two years since we were in touch?"

"I know. We have to do a proper catch up. I'll be finished here in about forty minutes if you want to hang around?"

Alex nodded. "Sure. I'll eat and wait for you to finish."

Lucy gave Alex a thumbs-up and disappeared into the back room with the damaged sandwiches. Alex bundled an egg mayo sandwich, a Coke, and a bag of sea salt crisps into her arms and skipped over to Olivia standing beside the baskets of fresh apples and bananas.

"That's my friend, Lucy. She works here. Can you *believe* it?"

The two of them placed their food choices on the shiny metal counter in front of the cash register. "She was one of my best online friends. We lost touch about two years ago. I can't believe she's here...and *I'm* here. It's crazy." She pointed at the hodge-podge of healthy and unhealthy choices. "Let me get this."

Olivia slid her salmon, prawn, and crab sushi, and a bottle of coconut water in front of Alex. "It's crazy all right." She

63

looked at her watch and crossed her arms. "This place is filling up. I'll grab a table over there."

Alex pulled a twenty-pound note from her wallet. "Okay, cool." Once her body-conscious flatmate turned her back, Alex waved a chocolate brownie bar at the employee and then tossed it into her bag.

Olivia wrinkled her nose. "This Lucy person. She's someone you found online? But you've never actually *met* in person before today?"

Alex knocked back a swig of her cola. "Yep. We met on Twitter about four years ago. We'd chat about *Doctor Who, Sherlock,* comic cons, books…all sorts of fandom stuff. We moved over to Facebook and email. We Skyped a lot, too. The more we chatted, the more we realized we had in common. I probably shared more with Lucy than anyone else." She peered inside her egg mayo sandwich, curling her lip. That crinkly leaf of arugula had to go.

"Isn't that a bit weird, though?" Olivia narrowed her eyes and sipped her coconut water. "How can you really know someone online?"

Alex nibbled her sandwich. "I think online friends often know you best."

She offered her crisps to Olivia, who instinctively shook her head no. "I've spent so much time online discussing things that matter to me, what touches my heart. Sometimes the people dearest to you aren't the ones you see every day. Sometimes your besties are at the end of an Internet connection, smiling in solidarity over a new film trailer or geeky t-shirt design."

Alex glanced over Olivia's shoulder and grinned, spotting her old friend laughing with a customer near the apples. "I've never had to explain myself to Lucy. She just *gets* it. She gets how you can love something or someone so much it physically hurts. We have fangirl shorthand."

"Fangirl? Like One Direction fans…aren't you a bit *old* for that?"

Alex stifled a laugh. "Fangirls span all ages. Sure, there's the boy band type—all teenage hormones and squeeing—I've been there, but the older you get, it changes. We don't scream or stalk, but we still have a blast as fans. A new film clip, meme or collectable can make my day. I think people who aren't fans don't get that. But the coolest thing about fandom is the friendships made along the way with people who share your passions."

Olivia swallowed a bite of sushi. "I've always had plenty of real friends, so I've never had to search for kindred spirits elsewhere. I suppose if you're feeling like an outsider or have unique interests, the Internet can help you connect with like-minded individuals."

"Exactly. We've always wanted to meet. We just didn't have the means."

Alex loved talking about Lucy but could sense she was losing her audience. "Those playwriting programs you mentioned before, how do they work? I need to hit the ground running. A year will fly by quickly, so every day needs to count."

The brunette nodded. "I'll email you the details. There's a website that lists a lot of the programs and workshops available. And if you ever want another pair of eyes to look over your work in progress, just let me know."

Alex's jaw dropped. "Would you? Olivia, that would be *fantastic*. If you could give my suffragette play a read through,

I'd really value your opinion."

"Happy to." Olivia crumpled up her napkin and stuffed it inside her empty sushi container. "I might have some time later before Harry and I go out—"

"That would be fab." Alex added her empty sandwich box to the pile of trash on their silver tray. "There's a hard copy sitting on top of my laptop bag. The cover is marked with date stamps and professor's comments. You can't miss it. I'll be busy with Lucy for a few hours, so you won't have me snooping over your shoulder."

"And on that note, I'll leave you to it." Olivia held the hem of her dress and pivoted gracefully off her chair. "Check Facebook. I sent you a friend request." She gathered her shopping bags. "Your Wonder Woman profile photo threw me; I had to stare at it to make sure it was really you. I'll see you back at the flat tonight."

"Absolutely. And…thanks for today, Olivia."

Without a second thought, Alex opened her Facebook app and accepted the request.

SEVEN

At six o'clock, the Pret staff began to pack away the day's remaining sandwiches, cookies, and salads, destined for their charitable program that feeds London's hungry and homeless. Lucy sauntered out from behind the counter, stuffing her hat, and white and burgundy Pret shirt into her beat-up satchel. Her wild curls skimmed her shoulders, and her eyes—always smiling, even when her mouth wasn't—danced when she said goodbye to her coworkers. Alex wasn't surprised that Lucy's off-duty wardrobe consisted of faded jeans and an *Iron Man* t-shirt. Some things never change.

"Hiya!" She hugged Alex. "I never thought I'd be leaving tonight with you by my side."

"Tell me about it. Do you work here every weekend?"

Lucy held the door open for Alex and her abundance of shopping bags. "It's a total fluke you found me here. I started at Pret's head office in Victoria as the Operations Manager's PA two weeks ago. Part of the training includes in-store shifts, so you learn how the products are made, how customers are given the 'Pret experience', and all that jazz. Today's my last in-shop session."

"See?" Alex laughed and playfully smacked Lucy's legs with her bags. "That makes our meeting even more incredible. Someone wanted us to meet. I just *knew* the sun shining this morning was a sign that something good was gonna happen today."

"Something good? More like something fucking awesome." Lucy stuck her arm into one of Alex's bags, partially pulling out a navy blue dress with a scalloped neckline from Club Monaco. "Look at all this stuff. Win the lottery?"

"I wish. The airline lost my luggage."

"Fuck, no. I would freak if that happened to me..." Lucy stopped, her eyes scanning the King's Road. "Wait, do you fancy a drink? I'm dying for one, and I bet you've worked up a thirst exercising your credit card."

"Bring it," said Alex.

🌂 🌂 🌂 🌂 🌂

"Stake a claim on the couch. I'll get the drinks in." Lucy helped Alex tuck her bags under the wood table and skipped back towards the bar.

She whooped it up with the Fox and Hounds bartender like he was an old friend. Lucy was always extroverted and bubbly over email and Skype. Thank goodness her online and real life personalities mirrored one another. Sometimes meeting online friends in the flesh is like encountering a stranger. The most outgoing, hilarious person online ends up being a shy shell of a soul who squeaks out four-word sentences, or the sweet, caring person on Twitter transforms into a rude, know-it-all—or worse. But being with Lucy felt easy and familiar. No stranger danger here.

Lucy returned with a pint for herself, a vodka and orange for Alex, and packets of pork scratchings, and cheese and onion crisps.

"This place is perfect for my first drink in London. It's so cozy." Alex's eyes skimmed the red walls, paintings of hunting scenes, and chocolate brown floorboards. "Exactly what I imagined a London pub would look like."

Lucy whipped out her phone. "We have to document our first drink together. Ready? Say 'I Am Sher-locked'." Alex held her drink aloft and grinned widely beside her long-lost friend.

She tore open a crisp packet. "These chip bags are so small compared to ours in the States. Where are the rest of them? Seriously, you'd have to scarf down six British chip packages to equal one American bag."

Lucy raised her glass for a 'cheers' with Alex. "Listen to you. Chips...that's a different thing over here."

"I've been juggling all the different names. I'll never blend in if I keep calling crisps, 'chips', and flats, 'apartments'. Once an outsider, always an outsider. You'd never know my dad's British."

"And so are you. Accent aside, you're one of us." Lucy popped the pork scratchings open. Her eyes widened at the crisp bag in Alex's hand. "Oh shit. Sorry. Creature of habit. Freddie's a cheese and onion addict. I buy that flavour automatically. Hope I didn't poison you."

Crumbs coated Alex's fingers. "Nope. I inhaled them." She showed Lucy the bag's shiny interior.

"You have to meet Freddie. You'll love him."

"He's got great taste in crisps—and friends—I'm sure I will," said Alex.

"He's my gay bezzie mate. We get into all sorts of geeky trouble together. That's how we met. In 2011, waiting for the *X-Men: First Class* red carpet arrivals...James McAvoy, Michael Fassbender. God, Fassbender's so freaking hot. They were both great about us taking lots of selfies. That was a night I'll never forget."

"I remember seeing photos on your Facebook page two years back...didn't you meet Daniel Radcliffe at a film premiere or something?" asked Alex.

"That was the 2012 BAFTAs red carpet at the Royal Opera House. Our film awards, yeah, we camped out for hours. So worth it."

"I'd love to do that."

"Stick with us, kid. You'll see all your favourites," said Lucy. "We've got a brilliant track record. My most recent selfie's with your favourite, at least I *think* he's still your favourite...Ben Whishaw? A bird pooped on my jeans about thirty minutes before I ran into him on the street. Talk about a superstition paying off."

"Really? Ben! So lucky. I hope you cleaned yourself up before you met him."

Lucy laughed. "What do you take me for?" She quickly scrolled through the photos on her phone, searching for him. "There he is."

Alex smiled at the image of Lucy and the actor snapped on an East London street. "Aw, Whishy. I adore Ben so much."

"I practically wet myself. It was sweet of him to stop like that," said Lucy.

"If I could cast actors in a play, he'd top my list," said Alex. "It's a shame some people only know him from the Bond films... and look at his hair. It's always epic."

"Isn't it? He's surprisingly shy in real life, though." Lucy swigged her pint. "This makes me happy. Two years on, you're still crushing hard on the same actors. So loyal, not switching to the flavour of the month...I really should reactivate my Facebook and Instagram accounts, get myself back online."

"Do it. I've missed your pop culture posts. If I didn't love you so much, I'd be disgustingly envious. I remember you posting photos of your old ticket stubs from concerts too. So how many times did you see the Arctic Monkeys in the end?"

"Nine times," said Lucy. "Yeah, I went a bit mad there for a while. Dancing my face off, letting the music sweep away my worries...I also got into Years & Years, big time."

"Whishy's in their *Real* video. I don't know much else about them, though," said Alex.

"They're brilliant. I'll make sure you're properly schooled in the best Brit bands...but before I forget, I've been dying to ask...who was that girl with you in Pret? I don't mean to sound nasty, but what are you doing with Little Miss Snooty?"

Same old Lucy, never mincing words. Alex smirked. "Olivia? I met her yesterday. She's the girlfriend of my friend Harry from Emory. I'm staying in his flat in Hackney for a few months."

Alex sipped her drink. "But never mind her, what's new with you? Last we were in touch...well, I can't imagine what that must've been like for you..."

Lucy stared straight ahead and picked at a damp beer mat. "My world collapsed. Nothing else mattered except Gran's cancer diagnosis. I stopped drawing, dropped out of my animation course at uni—Gran was so upset about that, but I wanted to look after her. I went into full-on caregiver mode."

"I don't know how you coped," said Alex. "It was always

you and her against the world, right?"

"Yeah, more so than ever. My shitty excuse for a boyfriend dumped me because I wasn't there for him all the time." She tossed torn shreds of the beer mat onto the table. "Such a selfish fucker."

"He didn't!" Alex spluttered on her drink. "Well, you're better off without him." She laid a hand on Lucy's back. "I'm so sorry. I should've tried harder to stay in touch. I just didn't know what to say."

Lucy shook her head. "*I'm* sorry. I vanished. One day I had Facebook and Twitter accounts. The next, they were gone. I just couldn't deal with anything but Gran at the time. I felt so bad, disappearing without telling you how bad things were. I've never forgiven myself. I wasn't *avoiding* you."

Gentle tears swelled in her brown eyes. "Things went from bad to worse. They said she'd have a year, but she only made it to six months."

Alex pulled her friend into an embrace. "Oh Lucy, I prayed for her to get better. I wanted to see how you were doing, but I was afraid to intrude. It was a stupid, naive decision on my part. I should have been there for you." She dug some tissues out of her bag for Lucy and tightened her hug.

Lucy dabbed her eyes. "I was a mess. And then there's all this stuff you have to take care of when someone dies. I wasn't prepared for any of it. I was only twenty. What did I know about dealing with wills, making funeral arrangements? And relatives you haven't seen for years, claiming what they believe is theirs. It was bad enough losing Gran's flat in Upton Park and being forced to find a new place to liv—"

Alex jumped in, loosening her hug. "Did your mom show up?"

"Thankfully, no. I wouldn't recognize her if she did, it's been so long. But my aunt showed, sniffing around like a rat for any tasty crumbs left behind by the mother she couldn't bother to visit. So pathetic." She blew her nose. "Freddie was a lifesaver. He stayed with me afterwards…until I got turfed from the flat."

"Thank God he was there, Lucy. It's about time someone looked after you for a change."

"He's the best. I don't know what I did to deserve him. Now I can't get rid!" Lucy laughed and wiped her eyes. "Now I just want to enjoy my friends and my new job. I'm done with drama for a while, you know? Bring on normal life for a change."

"Are you drawing again?" Alex pulled the straw from her lips. "Your hands! They were always covered with ink when we'd chat on Skype."

Lucy shook her head. "I haven't even looked at a sketchbook for at least a year. With everything that's gone on, I've kinda lost my passion for it." She shrugged. "And it's hard getting back into the starving student routine when you're used to a regular pay packet. Never say never, though…"

She sipped her pint. "So that's me all caught up. Please tell me that I'm the only sad sack around here? I hope the last two years have been kinder to you." She touched Alex's hair. "I love the shorter 'do."

"Thanks. New hair, new start."

"So who's this Harry? Have you snogged?" Lucy winked. "And what happened to that bloke from your theatre class… Damon, Davin…what was his name?"

"Devin Lockhart. Yeah, I met him at the start of my freshman year."

"Go on. Spill."

Alex's voice went quiet with a slight smile. "He was lovely.

Six foot tall, a year older than me, deep blue eyes. He wasn't the cutest guy in my theatre studies class, but he had this gentle, centred way about him. He wasn't arrogant or showy like some acting students, and he always knew how to make me laugh."

She slowly spun her glass around with her fingers. "Living away from home for the first time, we leaned on each other for support and friendship. He was there for me during some tough moments. His parents were dead set against him being an actor, just like my mom hated my playwriting aspirations. For the first time, I was in sync with someone and didn't have to explain why I was so keen on this unstable career. He did a lot of community theatre in his spare time, and I wrote a play for his acting group. We clicked on so many levels."

"Did you fall hard?"

Alex nodded. "Completely. My schoolwork began to suffer. I was totally infatuated with him. I couldn't stop thinking about what it would be like to kiss him, not to mention sleep with him. So I decided not to torture myself any longer, dove into the pool feet first. I made the first move."

"You? Seriously?"

"I did! There was no way I was letting another theatre student snap him up. That first kiss, though ... it seared through me. It took every ounce of my strength not to tear his clothes off on the spot. Thank goodness we were in a crowded bar."

Lucy laughed. "The perils of being a virgin. All that sexual energy aching to be released."

"I know, right? He was my first proper boyfriend, my first *everything*. And I was totally blind to any consequences, if he thought I was sleazy for making the first move or if he'd bolt once he learned all my secrets, but he didn't."

"He sounds wonderful."

"He was. It was so new, being that vulnerable with a guy. I felt good around him, safe. We fooled around, but he didn't rush me. Two weeks in, my vow to take it slow fell to his dorm room floor along with my clothes."

Lucy raised her hand for a high-five. "Put it there, girl. Someone was getting shagged senseless. Sexy Lexy!"

Alex's cheeks grew warm, and she met Lucy's hand with a giggle.

She cleared her throat and retreated back into a soft grin. "Funny. That's the nickname Devin gave me…Things moved pretty quickly from there. I barely slept in my own bed. It was like this new secret world was unlocked and I couldn't get enough. We even skipped lectures to stay in bed, but he was a real gentleman. He's from Louisville, Kentucky and had this warm, respectful southern charm about him."

Lucy smiled above the edge of her glass. "Lucky duck, Lex…an amazing boyfriend, your dream course, talk about the picture perfect uni experience. You weren't in a sorority too, were you? Please say no." She laughed.

Alex shook her head. "Me…in a sorority? Only if their Greek traditions were swapped for Geek…but I did become best friends with a girl in my Reading for Performance course. Taylor McCoy. I had plastered my dorm room's walls with tourism photos of London. She came over to study one night, but we ended up talking about how badly we both wanted to come here."

Alex opened the second packet of cheese and onion crisps. "We bonded over the silliest things like our love of Mindy Kaling. We joked about our fondness for Will and Kate, and shared an addiction to Twizzlers."

Lucy looked confused.

"Twizzlers?" said Alex. "They're strawberry licorice twists.

We'd eat package after package while binge-watching *Gossip Girl* episodes. She could also match me song for song at Friday night karaoke."

"Belting out the tunes on the piss. Love it," said Lucy.

"Yeah. I'm a sucker for musical cheese from the sixties and seventies. No era does schmaltz better." Alex crunched a handful of crisps.

"During our sophomore year, Taylor and I decided to plan a post-grad trip to England, taking a few months to live it up before work commitments owned us. I even convinced Devin to come along too."

"Nice one. Being an adult can wait." Lucy downed the dregs of her pint.

"But when we started our senior year at university, something seemed off...Devin—"

Lucy interrupted. "You wouldn't be here on your own if you were choosing a china pattern together. I'll kill him if he broke your heart..."

Alex plucked the cutlery from the table. "I better hide the knives, then."

"No. Really? *Wanker.*" Lucy banged her pint glass down on a beer mat.

With a final sip through her straw, Alex finished her drink. "I couldn't put a finger on what it was, but around Halloween, I spotted a Snapchat video Devin received from Taylor. Their secret was out."

"Ew. A video? It wasn't dirty, was it?"

Alex stabbed at the ice in her glass. "Put it this way, if she uploaded screencapped images to Tinder, she'd set a record for right swipes."

Lucy scrunched up her face.

"I still don't know when it started, what happened exactly."

Lucy shook her head. "That's horrible—to cheat on your best friend, to cheat on your girlfriend!"

"I couldn't sleep or eat. I felt sick, so I confronted them. I used my phone to record her Snapchat video so they had no choice but to admit it." Alex crinkled up the crisp bag. "I was done. They were dead to me, but I couldn't avoid their smug faces for seven more months. If I skipped the courses we had together, my degree would've been in jeopardy."

"God, talk about rubbing your nose in it," said Lucy.

"I spent most of my senior year replaying everything in my head, trying to figure out what I did or maybe *didn't* do that caused this to happen. I'm still at a loss. Coming to London is my chance to move on, leave them behind and start over. This time the happy ending I write will be my own."

Alex stared down at the table. "Still, there are times when I can't help looking back, rehashing events, what I did wrong—"

"I'm sure you didn't do anything wrong."

Tears blurred Alex's vision. "I wish I knew...but I keep coming back to a pattern. I can't depend on people. Every time I do, disaster strikes. They leave me."

A cascade of tears spilled down her cheeks.

"Dad left when I was little. Mom and Kathryn never had time for me, and Robbie moved to Orlando for work. And then this mess with Devin and Taylor. People don't stick around. I always care more about everyone else than they do for me. Time and time again, I take a chance, rely on them, and they let me down. I always end up alone. I'm easy to walk away from." Alex felt the pangs again...she was dispensable, broken.

Lucy yanked her friend into a side-by-side clinch. "Don't be daft, you silly cow. You're spewing complete bull. No wonder your self-confidence is in tatters. Look, I'm gonna be selfish. I'm glad these other people buggered off because it means there's more of you for *me*. I don't have to fuckin' share."

Alex snorted, snot unexpectedly bubbling from her nose. A half-laugh escaped amidst the tears.

Lucy howled and thrust a clean tissue under Alex's nose. "What are we like? Both blubbing in the pub. They'll lock the doors the next time they see us coming."

"I wouldn't blame them." Alex scanned the small room to make sure no one was witnessing her nasal explosion. "So much drama. I need another drink."

"Definitely." Lucy scooted off the couch. "Stay here and clean yourself up, you cry-baby, you. When I'm back, you can tell me about Harry. I bet he's lush."

Alex shrugged. "There's nothing to tell. He's blond. Not really my type."

"Ah, I love a blond, me. Well, that's settled, then. We need to find you a fit boyfriend. I'm on it. And don't worry, whoever I find, I won't snog him."

While she waited for Harry to come home, Olivia indulged in some quiet time, reading through Alex's suffragette play. The strong characters and detailed writing surprised her, and the story arc held all the hallmarks of an engaging and popular play. It needed some work, some fine-tuning, but it had good bones. Little Alex had talent. Who knew?

Olivia logged onto her computer to read through her own script. Scenes weren't exactly flowing, and a few of the characters lacked substance. Her attempts to flesh out the story about the colourful Hackney neighbourhood on her doorstep left her less than satisfied. It would require a lot of massaging, but eventually she'd get there.

At twenty after nine, an apologetic text from Harry interrupted her editing session.

'Babe, so sorry! Kitchen's sprinkler system's on the fritz. Chef freaking out. Must cancel tonight. Be home after closing. Love you. H xo'

Olivia scowled at the last splash of prosecco in her glass. Another cancellation. The fourth date this month—all at the last minute.

She lit a cigarette and leaned on Facebook for company. Scrolling through her newsfeed, Alex's accepted friend request popped up.

The Floridian's Facebook page screamed 'geeks gone wild'. Olivia's stern frown softened with each photo click. Such a weirdo. Alex was dressed as Wonder Woman, Supergirl, some Doctor Who person Olivia couldn't care less about, and a character called Captain Marvel; none of Alex's profile photos were without a silly costume. Even her cover photo was totally dorky. It featured a long rambling quotation by actor Simon Pegg about how 'cool' it was to be a geek. *Yeah, sure it is.*

Olivia sank back into her chair. She now cringed at her pangs of jealousy in the kitchen over breakfast and her treatment towards Alex on their shopping trip. This silly, odd little American girl, she's really quite sweet. And certainly no serious competitor for her Harry's affection. How strange to react so…defensively? She put it down to a reflex reaction. Harry was one of the most eligible bachelors in London. She'd grown accustomed to warning off so many Pretty Young Things during their blossoming relationship four years earlier. Old habits die hard, it seemed.

She finished her prosecco and raised her eyebrows at the overabundance of pictures. Ms. Alex Sinclair certainly liked to overshare her meals, family get-togethers, and American holidays like the Fourth of July and Thanksgiving. Olivia smiled. She remembered sexting Harry on the Thursday morning of that long weekend to offer a scantily clad '*Happy Thanksgiving, Pilgrim*'. He responded, saying he would be spending the four-day weekend stuck alone in the library, plowing through a mountain of course work.

She clicked through Alex's album for Tallahassee Thanksgiving 2014, and snickered at the photos of her mother putting on airs. Nice try, lady! But in the jumble of faces, someone familiar caught her eye.

…Harry. Her Harry—without textbooks or laptop—in Tallahassee, not Atlanta.

She clicked from photo to photo, her pupils constricting into defiant dots, shocked by the images flaunted one by one across the screen.

Harry lied. Why the HELL did he lie?

Her abdomen constricted, cramping into a knot, its heavy weight tying her to the chair. A sourness rose in her throat. No amount of swallowing could make the distaste, the anguish wash away. She slammed her laptop closed and with a sweep of her hand, sent her wine glass flying towards the floor.

EIGHT

Alex stumbled into the lounge, wiping sleep from her eyes. She sideswiped a pouffe, her feet just missing a stray cricket bat.

"Hey, Sleeping Beauty." Tom threw cushions off the couch and shoved his hands forcefully into its deepest recesses. "You were late last night. You dirty stop out."

The brightness leaping through the large windows taunted Alex's pounding head. Her mouth tasted sticky and metallic, like it was coated with wallpaper paste. She hugged her stomach, clad in newly purchased blue plaid cotton pajamas.

"Where is everyone? What are you doing?" Aspirin. She needed Aspirin. She rummaged in the kitchen cupboards. Her head spun like a wound-up ballerina inside a jewellery box.

Tom nudged her out of the way and liberated a bottle of Paracetamol from a high shelf. "Harry's taken Olivia out for the day. She made him feel guilty about missing Friday's party and cancelling their date last night."

He shook two tablets into Alex's hand and handed her a bottle of water. "God, she was in an epic mood last night. I don't know what's eating her. She was fine when I left for the pub.

81

Olivia and her moods, eh? They change like the English weather."

They both smirked. Alex may have only met her forty-eight hours ago, but Hurricane Olivia was already an erratic force to be reckoned with. She swallowed the two tablets and plunked herself face down onto the kitchen table, just missing a bundle of flowers suffocating in layers of orange tinted cellophane. A slight head shift alleviated the pressure on her now mountainous zit.

"Have you seen my wallet? This place is such a tip." Tom snapped his knuckles. "If I show up at the match without cash again, the lads will skin me. I'm already half-hour late."

He knocked over Olivia's muesli box from the top of the microwave, showering oat flakes and dried fruit onto the floor. Alex lifted her head. The swaying microwave's clock glared 12:36 p.m. at her.

"Oh, two things...a delivery came for you yesterday afternoon." Tom ignored the spill and wrestled a card from the flowers.

"Can you read it to me? Everything's...fuzzy and... moving," said Alex. The muesli mess scattered on the hardwood didn't help, lying there begging to be swept up.

"It says '*Beautiful flowers for a beautiful daughter. Just a little something to make you feel at home. Love and kisses, Dad, Helen, and Joan xo*'. Aw, that's sweet. They're not roses. What are they?" Tom pressed on the plastic wrap.

"Probably snapdragons. If they look like funny little jaws, they're snapdragons. My favourite," said Alex, her head still in a face plant.

Tom shrugged. "Weird choice."

He moved back towards the unruly counter congested with

dirty plates, overflowing ashtrays, and several empty wine bottles. "And your suitcases showed up last night around seven…bloody hell, *there* it is." He plucked his missing wallet from behind the Styrofoam clutter of last night's kebab take-away. "Man, your cases are big. They wouldn't fit in your room, so I tucked them in mine. Feel free to unpack in there and then leave the empty cases in the lounge. One of us will stow them later…somewhere."

A flush of relief interrupted the nauseating ripples in Alex's stomach. She raised her head, taming the errant strands of hair that stuck to her oily face. "Oh thank God. My entire life is in those bags. That's my day figured out, then."

She let out a big sigh and dumped her forehead on the table. "Baggage. Everyone's got some. Sometimes it just takes a while to catch up to you."

Tom adjusted the collar of his Chelsea shirt and snorted. "That we do, oh Wise One. Well, I'm off. Can't keep the Blues waiting! Good luck with the hangover—and the unpacking."

One steamy bath followed by a buttery English muffin and an overflowing bowl of sugary cereal, returned Alex to the land of the living. Just in time, too.

Her mission: to unpack…so daunting, like a life-size game of Tetris, but instead of puzzle pieces, her clothes, books, and personal items had to find their most space efficient positions.

Alex hung each item of clothing individually in the wonky wardrobe, testing its stability. Would the weight send the cupboard crashing down on top of her? She grounded its base with her heaviest books including her chunky volume of *Bartlett's*

Quotations, a prize for earning the highest grade in English during her senior year of high school. Pairs of motorcycle and ankle boots, and Chuck Taylors also lent their heft.

Books sorted by size—paperbacks on top expanding downward to coffee table tomes on the bottom along with two large spiral-bound photo albums from her childhood—scaled the walls of the room in three Jenga-worthy towers. Without shelves or a desk to display her framed pictures, she placed them atop the book stacks. Photos with her brother Robbie and of the family cat shared pride of place alongside comic con shots hamming it up with Elijah Wood, Hayley Atwell, and Matt Smith.

She tucked away her final necessities—several bashed in boxes of Lucky Charms cereal, Pop-Tarts, and packages of Twizzlers. If she smartly rationed her stash, it could last until September. Home *sweet* home.

She stood back to admire her work. No limbs were crushed underneath falling furniture; no books were sacrificed. Mission accomplished.

With the unpacking behind her, Alex relaxed, her mind reacquainting itself with all the things she deemed important enough to cart across the ocean: her mementos, clothing, food. But her packing list—a strict roll call of what to bring, what to leave behind—wasn't infallible. What you leave behind says as much about you as what you bring along.

Her shoulders sagged under the weight of her memories. The seldom mentioned, the unseen—the people left behind—haunted her heart. She hated herself for feeling a shred of sadness over leaving her mom. She shouldn't let it bother her. Usually it didn't. From an early age, Alex knew her mom didn't love her like she did Kathryn and Robbie. It was as if Geraldine blamed Alex for delaying the inevitable—the divorce from Michael. If Alex hadn't come along, she wouldn't have wasted seven years tied to a dead marriage. But when their union crumbled for good and they stormed towards a permanent split, Geraldine wouldn't let Michael take Alex to England, denying him what he wanted most. She'd rather hold on to the daughter she didn't want than allow her ex to 'win'. But at the airport four days ago, it was as if Michael had finally triumphed. Dropping Alex at the curb, Geraldine didn't cry, her face hard and defiant. Alex hoped for a last minute emotional reprieve, a hug, some sniffles even, but got nothing—her mom didn't crack.

Alone with her thoughts, Alex knew she shouldn't be disappointed by that reaction, but it did bother her, more than she had expected. You can be belittled, ignored, and rejected, and eventually fly the nest, hoping never to return, but those familial bonds still pull and twist, making you yearn for what you don't have and probably never will. Sure, her mother was more invested in the older kids, her smarmy politician boyfriend, and her precious job, and she seemed to dole out affection to Alex in meager amounts, bit by bit—none of that behaviour was new—but she was still her mother. Your mother is supposed to love you unconditionally.

And so are your boyfriends. Well, one boyfriend. There was only one. Devin. All the other flirtations didn't count—stolen kisses in clubs, clumsy fumbles at house parties…little crushes, little infatuations, but nothing that prepared her for the full-on tidal wave of all-consuming love and devastating heartbreak that Devin brought to her life. It was easy to purport to Lucy that he was out of her life—gone, banished, never to be thought of again—but the reality wasn't that simple or painless.

The last two-and-a-half years were all Devin. Calendars and dates didn't matter; life events were bookmarked according to what she and Devin were doing at the time: her first A on a play came just after they slept together for the first time; her stint in the university's brief production of *The Unravelling*—on the heels of their first fight. Everything linked back to him. Her life tied to his and vice versa. He may have moved on back home with Taylor, and Alex may be a world away on another continent, but she still struggled with letting him go. It was during quiet moments that she felt the strings painfully tugging all the more.

She brushed away a few hot tears and breathed deeply. Old hurts weren't so easy to leave behind. In the excitement and desperation to get away, perhaps it was naive to believe that only the items jotted down on her packing list would accompany her on this journey. Four days ago when she was packing in her Tallahassee bedroom, it seemed much more black and white.

One loyal companion from her old zip code was settling in just fine: Paddington Bear. As a child, Alex loved away Paddington's fur and eyes, leaving him threadbare, so every birthday her dad gave her a new bear—until she turned six and he moved overseas. Invested with fifteen years of unconditional love, this cherished toy had comforted Alex through her parents' traumatic split and beyond. He chilled comfortably on the futon, a paw's reach from her bouquet of pink and yellow snapdragons, smiling their lopsided grins and lending much needed joy to the bland space.

The Sunday stillness of the abandoned flat beckoned Alex to tell a story. She hugged Paddington, burying her nose in his matted fluff. Returning the bear to her pillow, she curled up with her laptop, its keyboard letters scuffed from years of typing and its scratched case decorated with half-peeled superhero stickers. She eyed the hardcopy of her suffragette play, lying on top of her laptop bag with its cover page bent backwards. Olivia must've read it last night. She placed it on top of her thesaurus, opened the saved version on her laptop, and started typing.

NINE

The shower's taps squealed, waking Alex on her first Monday morning in the flat. She turned over, dozing until a new sound assaulted her ears—the urgent stutter of Olivia's high heels. Their sharp *clickclickclick* meshed with Harry's stern voice instructing someone over his phone. He paced in the hall and then wandered out of earshot. Alex tossed the covers over her head and closed her eyes, hoping to squeeze out another twenty minutes of sleep.

The front door slammed shut. Silence. Alex waited fifteen minutes in case Tom stirred, but the flat remained still. Perhaps he never came home last night.

She wandered through the lounge and into the kitchen where Harry's cup and tea bag, and Olivia's lipstick-kissed mug sat abandoned near the sink. A plate of half-eaten toast smeared with strawberry jam grew cold, a lone fly plodding across its stickiness. Thai food cartons, new additions to the lingering mess from Friday, lay jumbled in the sink. How do they live like this? Alex dumped the trash into the smelly bin and loaded the dishwasher.

LONDON BELONGS TO ME

Still no sign of Tom. Alex grabbed a pen and scrap of paper from the counter, and scribbled a note, displaying it prominently on the kitchen table:

'Morning, Tom! I hear you're coming with me to the Royal Court this evening. Curtain rises at seven thirty, so I'll meet you back here at five. Alex'

The bathroom was finally hers, the shower dousing her skin warmly this time. Bliss. Thank goodness for a late start and a replenished water heater. She missed the wake-up call of American-level water pressure, but at least her teeth didn't chatter while lathering up today.

The cleaning lady arrived at ten o'clock in the midst of Alex's last milky spoonful of Lucky Charms. She spoke to the middle-aged Polish woman, but the lady just smiled and nodded. Alex grinned politely, loaded her bowl and cutlery into the dishwasher, and flew out the door to tackle her to-do list. The most pressing tasks: sorting out her health care number with the National Health Service and the purchase of a new SIM card for her phone.

On route to her first errand, Alex spotted bright red letters screaming 'Help Wanted!' from the window of a small café on nearby Mare Street. The part-time job sounded ideal—a few hours mid-morning until after the lunch rush, leaving most of the afternoon free to write. She completed her application for the crinkly-eyed owner and flashed her brightest American customer service smile.

🌂 🌂 🌂 🌂 🌂

Alex and Tom rushed into the Royal Court Theatre just ten minutes before the play's start. Tom couldn't be trusted to show

89

up on time. Next time—if there *was* a next time—she'd meet him at the venue and spare herself his contagious lateness. She rubbed her jaw. It still ached from clenching it tightly on the packed Tube journey.

Excited theatre patrons swarmed the lobby and streamed up the stairs from the downstairs bar. Alex envied them, soaking up the pre-theatre atmosphere, sipping drinks, and browsing the theatre's bookstore. She purchased a program at the door and followed Tom straight to their seats, her blue flowery blouse, black knee-length skirt, and crisp beige trench coat fitting in with the dressy-casual vibe.

She gave tardy Tom the benefit of the doubt. Perhaps an audition or meeting with his agent ran long. "Hectic day racing between auditions?"

"Auditions? You're kidding, right?" He shoved the arms of his black blazer up to his elbows and shifted his denim-clad butt back into his seat. "I was lending Harry a hand at Bespoke."

Tom gave off a pungent whiff of alcohol as he spoke. If lending a hand meant tasting the libations on offer, then his tale was true.

Seated seven rows from the stage in the stalls, Alex's head scanned up and down, back and forth, like a curious owl surveying new territory. Tom looked up from his phone. "You'll give yourself whiplash craning your neck like that."

"I can't believe I'm here!" She clasped his forearm, giving it a shake. "*The Royal Court*, Tom. I've waited years for this moment."

He rolled his eyes. "You're a freak. It's just an old building."

Alex took a break memorizing every corner, every row of the theatre and flipped through the program.

"This is crazy." Alex pointed at a page. "This thing has every single line from the play. It's not a program at all. It's a proper book. They should do this on Broadway. So much better than a Playbill."

Tom shook his head, his finger swiping up a storm on his Tinder app. "It's a play text, Alex. It's hardly the second coming."

The theme to BBC's *Sherlock* blared from somewhere. Alex didn't notice, engrossed in the book's cast bios. When the music didn't stop, Tom elbowed her in the ribs. *Whoops.* She fumbled in her bag and muted the ringer, sending the call to voicemail. She didn't want to be *that* person.

🌂 🌂 🌂 🌂 🌂

Alex ambled outdoors into the brisk May air, play text hugged to her chest and Sharpie in hand—tools of the fangirl trade—hoping to meet the play's star, Amanda Abbington. She adored Amanda's portrayals of Mary Watson in *Sherlock*, and Miss Mardle in *Mr. Selfridge* but TV roles didn't match the magic of watching her on stage. Amanda's live performance imbued the playwright's words with an icy passive-aggressiveness that made the audience despise her character. The play was satirical and thought provoking, the kind of story that tumbles around in your mind for days afterwards.

Several other enthusiastic theatregoers gathered in the stage door alleyway, as did four paunchy 'professional' autograph hunters, equipped with binders of eight by ten publicity photos. These slimy guys—all beer guts and baseball caps—gave theatre geeks a bad name. Once signed, they'd hawk the promotional photos on eBay at exorbitant prices. Not cool. Neither was it cool to show up at the stage door when you hadn't even seen the play. A cluster of 'fans' ran out of the Sloane Square Tube station and joined the queue. The theatregoers in front of Alex shook their heads and grumbled into their chests.

"Tom, when Amanda, oh…where are you?" Also not cool—Tom's disappearing act.

Alex peered around the dark alley and couldn't see him. A clique of pretty girls, underfed and willowy like a gang of runway models, swarmed the side entrance of the Royal Court, smoking, posing, and tossing their glossy manes. When three of the tallest members shifted, she spotted Tom ensconced in the middle of the group, bumming a cigarette and flirting. Typical.

She stepped out of line. "Tom, when Amanda comes out, I'll need your help. Make sure you're beside me, okay? I'd love a photo with her, a proper one on my camera, not my phone. Its flash isn't bright enough."

He nodded and waved his hand in dismissal. His fan club of seven rolled their eyes and chuckled behind their hair at Alex, and then continued with their discussion about Mayfair's trendiest clubs.

Alex shivered intermittently, the spring chill amplifying her nervousness. She smoothed her bangs. Thank goodness that pimple on her forehead was no longer mountainous, but now just a mere pink dot, easily covered with foundation. No filters would be needed to make her look half-decent in the photo with Amanda. To pass the time, she checked the voice message left before the curtain went up. A jocular Cockney voice burst through the phone. The part-time café job—hers, starting Wednesday—two days from now. Alex smiled. Things were looking up!

She leaned towards a short woman with curly blonde hair wearing a black beret. "Excuse me, I've never done a stage door in London before. How long's the wait usually?"

"My friends were here last week. Amanda came out quickly, within twenty minutes. Shouldn't be—" Squeals erupted a few feet ahead, cutting off the girl's answer.

Alex's eyes flew towards the red stage door. Amanda! In the flesh. Goosebumps tickled her neck while her mind danced with questions: Did Amanda spend time with the playwright during rehearsals? Did they collaborate? How does she feel about working with new writers?

Alex's two passions, playwriting and fangirling, were colliding so spectacularly this evening. How often do you get to bend the ear of a favourite actress?

Fans took turns receiving autographs and photos. Amanda chatted with each person and doled out hugs. Alex held back, tapping her foot and looking back towards the theatre. Where's Tom? He and his girl gang must have snuck away to the Royal Court's downstairs bar. She yanked open the lobby door and galloped down the steps.

Her heart plummeted. No sign of him.

Screw it! A badly-lit selfie would have to do.

She raced up the stairs and tripped on the top step, crumpling in a painful heap against the glass door. Did anyone notice? A rip in the knee of her tights mocked her attempt at a graceful recovery. She smoothed down her skirt and dashed outside.

Laughter hung in the cool spring air as fans happy with their autographs and photos headed towards the Tube entrance next door. Her chest heaving, Alex bobbed through the dwindling crowd. Her reward—a glimpse of the theatre's security guard closing the stage door firmly behind him.

She threw her arms up in the air. "Great. Thanks *a lot,* Tom."

"No worries! Thanks for what?"

Tom strolled out of the shadows behind Alex, casually rolling a cigarette between his fingers. He struck a match, its sharp glow briefly illuminating the abandoned alley. He inhaled deeply on his cigarette and broke out into a carefree grin. "Those girls are *hilarious*, trying to drag me to a new dance club."

He tilted his head, blowing smoke at the stars. "I was halfway down the road and thought, *Bugger*—I'd better check with you first in case you want to tag along—"

She pushed her bangs out of her eyes. He didn't even offer a whiff of an apology. Enough of this tomfoolery. "No, I don't. Just go. I'm going home."

Tom stared at her with squished eyebrows. "Suit yourself, Miss America. Laters!" He turned on his heels and loped off into the darkness.

Alex stomped towards the Sloane Square Tube entrance, muttering a vow under her breath. The next time she tried a stage door, she wouldn't place her trust in someone else. It was *always* the same old story.

You can only rely on yourself.

TEN

Texts, Twitter retweets, and Instagram images flew back and forth in the week since Alex and Lucy crashed back into each other's lives. Old inside jokes were resurrected and debates on who was the hottest actor picked up where they left off two years before. But best of all, this relationship originally cultivated online was blossoming into a tangible friendship, and Lucy brought with her a ready-made posse; today on the final Saturday in May, Alex would meet Freddie Ryan.

To Alex, meeting new friends was almost as thrilling as meeting a potential boyfriend. While growing up, Alex didn't have the largest pool of friends to rely on, just a casual group of kids she hung around with on the soccer field or at swimming lessons. She'd have a best friend here and there, someone to share secrets, crushes on boys, and dreams for the future, but too often the best friend moved away or eventually dumped her for someone cooler. Unfortunately, a love of reading, writing, and theatre didn't top the popularity charts with the in-crowd at her sports-loving American high school. And during her senior year at Emory, many of her classmates fell by the wayside, too, casualties of their mutual friendships with Devin and Taylor. Alex was used to making friends and then losing them. She had joked to her dad that she had a degree in solitude, having spent so much time alone over the years.

She hoped life in London would put an end to all that, and this Freddie fellow's advance billing was stellar. By day, he toiled as a TV program scheduler for the BBC. By night, the twenty-three-year-old morphed back into his devoted fanboy persona, hanging out in theatres and cinemas. Lucy said he loved James Bond films, romantic comedies, pub quizzes, and dancing. Alex was already enamoured.

"I wouldn't share Freddie with just anyone." Lucy scratched at the shoulder of her blue 'Impossible Girl' tee and plonked down on Alex's futon, picking up her friend's suffragette play.

Alex was half-dressed in cotton bikini briefs and a thin, long-sleeved striped sweater, its blue hue making her eyes pop. She straightened her hair frantically while Lucy kept the conversation flowing. "He means the world to me. I know he'll fall head over heels for you. How could he not?"

"Aw, thanks."

With straighteners in one hand, Alex reached towards her tea on the floor with the other. She reached around the dwindling burst of snapdragons, careful not to bump into the book towers teetering close by, but her awkward stretch creased a big L-bend into her locks. "Damn it." She clamped the flat iron's plates back into position along the kinked section of hair, but it just made the curve worse.

"Sorry, Lucy. We should've been on our way by now. Can't believe I slept through my alarm."

"No rush. Take your time. You're probably still getting over jet lag."

Alex shook her head. "No, it's all Tom's fault. He's such a shag monster. He's had noisy sex four out of the eight nights I've been here. I feel dirty hearing everything through the wall, but it's impossible to block it out, even wearing earbuds. I finally fell asleep around three fifteen this morning. One thing's for sure, the guy's got stamina."

Lucy laughed. "Lucky girlfriend."

"Girlfriend? I don't think he knows the meaning of the word. A different chick stumbles out of his room each morning. He's such a man-whore!"

Lucy flopped over onto her stomach, her denim-covered legs just missing the leaning wardrobe. "Geez. You weren't kidding. Even a Hobbit would feel claustrophobic in here."

"I know, right? I feel like I'm in solitary confinement. No daylight. No space. I keep bumping into my stuff, but the rent's practically non-existent, and London Fields is to die for. I'm trying to focus on the positives."

Lucy flipped to the first page of Alex's play. "Good idea. Just don't let that bohemian rhapsody in the lounge give you a headache. So many patterns…"

"Blame Olivia," said Alex. "Tom said she fashions herself as some sort of bohemian culture vulture. She used to be obsessed with Kate Moss and Sienna Miller, making inspiration boards out of *British Vogue* clippings. Now ten years later, that boho vibe's overtaken her home décor. She hasn't even *been* to Marrakesh."

Lucy sneered. "Typical."

"I don't care how the flat's decorated. I'm just happy I found a job close by. That's a big worry off my shoulders."

"Now we can have proper fun—nights out, theatre, films," said Lucy. "Watch out, London!"

"My pay cheque's not much, but it's something." Alex slipped the flat iron along the last section of hair, resisting the urge to rush. "The worst part's coming home smelling like egg salad sandwiches. I swear I made 100 of them on my first day."

She unplugged the straighteners from the wall and began a struggle with her skinny jeans, jumping up and down on the spot. A final tug brought them up over her hips. "I want to impress Freddie. Is that weird? And he works at the BBC. How cool is *that*?"

Lucy's stomach cried out as she glanced up from the page she was reading. "Freddie's the last person to call himself cool. He's a total geek. There's no need to avoid pervy discussions about Hiddleston or Cumberbatch either; he's all in. Chill, girl. You're being too hard on yourself."

Alex kept fussing. "I hate this top. I think I left some clothes in the dryer. I'll be right back."

"Take your time. Your suffragettes are keeping me company."

Late morning crowds had already sprung up around the piazza of Covent Garden. Alex rubber-necked under her burgundy-hued umbrella at the rows of shops and a pair of street performers wearing suits and top hats, covered in silver paint.

Both girls upped their speed. The persistent mist teamed with unseasonable gusts made their walk a chilly, windswept chore. Alex kept tabs on her black Converse, splashing along the slippery cobblestones, hoping to clear the square without a twisted ankle.

She pouted. "I shouldn't have bothered straightening my hair. I've gone all frizzy."

She held Lucy's umbrella while her friend gathered her wet flyaway curls into a low ponytail. "Tell me about it. Story of my life. I'm glad you did it, though. It gave me time to read your suffragette play…it's riveting."

A drenched, overly theatrical magician hollered at a swarm of passing tourists. Alex was unsure what Lucy said. "You *liked* it?"

"*Loved* it, so far. I felt like I learned something, too."

"Really? Thanks." Alex always felt relieved when people complimented her writing—receiving criticism left her cold. Her back usually went up with suggestions for improvement. "I did a ton of historical research for authenticity."

"Do you submit your work to anyone, to theatres?"

"Not yet. I keep finding things to change. Once I start revising, I can't quit. I'll submit it once it's ready. It's got to be perfect, though."

Lucy narrowed her eyes. "Are you sure you're not just delaying a decision? At some point you should see if your ideas fly. Maybe you're not finishing your work so you don't have to face rejection? Or you're worried that it's not good enough? Just a thought…"

Alex's eyes widened. She admired Lucy's blatant honesty, but when it came to her playwriting, she was protective and stubborn like a momma bear hovering over her cub. Lucy's words stung somewhat, but she knew her uncensored remarks rang true. She always worried if she was up to the task—in relationships, in writing, and everything else.

"No, it's not that…it just needs a few final tweaks. And I have to find the right place to send it."

The girls weaved through the throng in Covent Garden and into a Boots drugstore. Lucy cooed at a big nosed monster smiling manically from a colourful bag of crisps. "C'mere, big boy."

Alex's eyebrows tightened into a knot. "What the hell is *that*?"

Lucy did a little dance, waving the bag under Alex's nose. "It's *Monster Munch*. Otherwise known as today's breakfast. These corny hands will do nicely."

She wasn't kidding. The yellow snacks were shaped like four-fingered hands.

"Brits eat *strange* things." Alex purchased a packet of Cadbury chocolate buttons and tore it open as they stepped back onto bustling James Street.

Lucy juggled her umbrella, chomping through her breakfast. "So how's the glamorous flatmate? Is she helping your writing quest?"

"Not really. I mean, she told me about playwriting workshops, and I think she had a quick read of my play, but I haven't seen her much this week."

Alex reloaded on chocolate buttons. "And when I have, she's been a total grump, so there's been no chance to ask her opinion. We haven't had a proper conversation since last Saturday in Pret. Tom says she can be moody. So far, he's right. She's up and down like a yo-yo."

"She sounds high maintenance," said Lucy, crossing Long Acre to reach Neal Street. "Maybe it's a good thing, not getting too close? I don't know if she'd be supportive. Just a feeling I get."

"I think it's too early to tell." Alex crumpled up the deflated purple Cadbury's wrapper, stuffing it in the pocket of her red raincoat. "I've seen both warm and cold Olivia. And not just with me—with Tom and Harry, too. If she hated me, why give me theatre tickets? Maybe she's having a tough time at work or her writing isn't going well. You never know. I get grumpy when my characters aren't cooperating."

"Thanks for the warning." Lucy balled up her empty bag. "But speaking of cooperating, I think you should send some of your work in for critique or to those workshop sessions. You never know. Something might stick."

Lucy flung her arm around Alex's shoulders like a geeky Willy Wonka, ushering her theatrically inside Forbidden Planet on Shaftsbury Avenue. "Welcome to Fandom Heaven! All your obsessive desires—graphic novels, anime t-shirts, posters—await inside these doors. And like the TARDIS, it's much bigger on the inside..."

London geeks were out in full force. Alex had never seen a comic book and collectables store so rammed. They squeezed past shoppers standing four deep just inside the front doors, all gawking at a wall of glass cases displaying intricately designed statues and busts of all the major fandom players: Batman, Loki, and Frodo—to name just a few. Most were limited edition and all boasted jaw-dropping price tags.

"My God, Lucy. The prices! Please tell me this isn't a window shopping expedition?"

Lucy squeezed Alex's upper arm. "Not to worry, my fangirl friend. There's plenty we can afford, and when we're done, we'll do Show-and-Tell in the pub."

Around the corner to the left, *Doctor Who* memorabilia owned several shelves and crept up the wall to the ceiling. Action figures, t-shirts, mugs, even stuffed toys—the shop had all Whovian merchandise covered. A tall wisp of a guy wearing a black suit jacket, grey t-shirt, and black skinny jeans stood in the middle of the display, carefully stacking a series of small boxes into a pile purposely placed out of reach from two boisterous ten-year-old boys. Lucy rushed forward.

"Freddie!"

His head jerked to attention, sending his floppy fringe of dark brown hair cascading into his green eyes. His face lit up with a broad grin. "Lucy Hardy, if my eyes aren't deceiving me. Late as always, darling. I was about to audition a new best friend, but the potentials were devastatingly *boring*."

He drew his pal into a tight hug, but released his grip to focus on Alex, fidgeting with her dripping umbrella. "Alex, I've heard so much about you. Don't be shy. Give me some lovin'."

She willingly tucked beside Lucy into Freddie's group hug. All week Lucy had rambled on about him, so Freddie felt more like an old friend than a stranger.

In the midst of the embrace, Freddie crooked his head over his left shoulder to check that his stash hadn't been pilfered. "You've caught me in my natural habitat, ladies. Hunting for blind box *Doctor Who* Titan variants. I'm shameless in my pursuit."

Lucy grabbed his stubbly chin. "Yeah, shameless and a little bit stupid. You know you'll end up with the figures no one wants. It's a total gamble, and you *always* lose. That's the problem with blind boxed collectibles; you never know what's inside when you buy them. Don't throw your money down the drain."

"Yes, it's a gamble, but one I enter willingly. I've got to get my kicks somehow. Care to place your bets?" He picked up one of the boxes and held it up to his ear as if it might whisper its secret, held within. "Will this box contain the elusive green-windowed TARDIS or the ultra-rare eleventh Doctor with blue shirt?"

Freddie shook and listened to each small box. Lucy guffawed. "Stop it. That looks weird."

She nudged Alex. "Last time he did this blind box thing he got three blobby Adipose figures—all identical—and a clockwork robot. Hardly worth shouting from the rooftops. He frequently hits his overdraft limit buying these things. Freddie, you're such a shopaholic."

"Ye of little faith. You'll see when it's Show-and-Tell time. I'll amaze you with my uncanny ability to uncover the best collectables in the store." He spun around, and embraced his stockpile of small boxes. He strolled towards the *Star Wars* figures, muttering, "Please be a green-windowed TARDIS, please be a green-windowed TARDIS..."

"You're a nutter," laughed Lucy as she dodged out of the way, escaping the lunging advances of a sticky three-year-old dressed as Spiderman. "I'm going to show Alex the *Sherlock* and *Walking Dead* stuff. Meet you downstairs by the graphic novels?"

☂ ☂ ☂ ☂ ☂

After Forbidden Planet, Freddie made them all grab lunch at the baked potato van in Covent Garden's piazza. Such odd fast food choices. First, triangle-boxed sandwiches, and now hot baked potatoes, slit open from end to end and heaped with cheese, chili, baked beans or chicken curry. While Alex stuffed her face with melting strings of cheddar cheese and starchy spud, Lucy pointed to the sign above the counter—*jacket* potatoes. If only Brits and Americans spoke the same language.

In the three hours that followed, no corner of Covent Garden remained unexplored. The shopping trio scoured the Apple Market, Paperchase, Benjamin Pollock's Toyshop (Alex especially loved their toy theatres), the Moomin store, the London Transport Museum, and the seven streets of Seven Dials that stretched outward from the junction into the West End like spokes on a bicycle wheel. Worn out from battling the Saturday afternoon hordes, they decamped northwards atop an iconic double-decker bus. Destination—Freddie's one-bedroom flat on Holloway Road in Archway. He had plans to see a play with his friend Mark later and welcomed the opportunity to drop off his purchases before setting out again.

"How British is *this*? You live above a fish and chip shop!" The comforting smell of crispy beer-battered cod hung in the air of the narrow stairwell to Freddie's flat. Alex's mouth watered as they trudged up the stairs, past the pockmarked and scuffed walls; scars from moving nightmares of the past.

"Yep. It's like having room service downstairs," said Freddie. "Greasy carby goodness."

"Mmmm, carbs. You know what a load of carbs is? A food hug," said Lucy.

Alex laughed. "It is. My happy place. I could get used to fish and chips twenty-four-seven though."

"I swear one of my recent flings only stuck around for those delectable fish and chips," said Freddie. "I yearn for him whenever I catch a whiff of mushy peas."

"Freddie, do you need a flatmate? I'm ever so tidy and don't mind sharing household chores." Half joking, anything would be an improvement over the windowless prison cell Alex currently slept in.

"Sorry, hon, but I've got the perfect set-up." Freddie shook his umbrella one last time, splattering raindrops on the dingy dirt-encrusted linoleum. "My flatmate's rarely here. He's a medical resident at University College Hospital. He kips on the sofa-bed when he can't get home to Reading. I only see him once or twice a week."

Lucy tugged on the back of Alex's raincoat. "And before you change your address, dear Lex, I've first dibs on this place. I've bored Freddie into submission complaining about my annoying flatmates and their grating band."

"You live with a band? How cool!" said Alex.

"Oh, it's *so* not." Lucy crowded Alex on the top step. "They're a couple, a folk duo called Cider with Rosie. Their hippy-dippy cooking and vomit-inducing pixie music is doing my head in. I'd leave today if the rent wasn't so affordable."

"You mean downright cheap, Lucy." Freddie winked at her and unlocked the door. "Make yourself comfy, girls...but not *too* comfy. I just need to feed Jim Moriarty, and then we're off."

Freddie's flat was little more than a small box with a row of shoulder height windows along the back wall. The sparse lounge, painted lavender, contained a grey sofa that might uncomfortably seat three people, and a secondhand oak coffee table. White floating shelves hovered along the far wall, showcasing his Titan collection, carefully curated novels, and his favourite DVDs. A large framed photo with Lucy smiled brightly on the middle shelf, hugged by selfies with Kit Harrington and David Tennant. A small flat screen television clung to the wall facing the sofa along with a framed Madonna poster from her *Sticky and Sweet* world tour. Underneath, a low wooden rectangle supporting a turntable and speakers housed a sampling of vinyl—albums by the Stone Roses, the Charlatans, and the Happy Mondays lay scattered on the beat-up hardwood floor.

To the right, his kitchen was an afterthought. A row of three

Tiffany-blue painted cupboards hung above a short, white counter with a single sink, a tiny fridge, and a two-burner cook top. It faced a breakfast bar, crowded with a crumb-covered toaster, kettle, a pyramid of Pantone mugs, and a plastic mountain of stuffed shopping bags from Topman, Beyond Retro, and Forbidden Planet. His tiny bedroom and a bathroom—with just a shower, no tub—were just to the right of the front door.

Lucy stomped into the flat like she was trying to scare away evil spirits. "Keep that thing away from me." She planted herself at the far end of the sofa. "I *hate* black cats. They're creepy soul stealers."

"Your cat's named after *Sherlock's* Moriarty?" asked Alex.

The suspicious feline darted underneath the single side table. Alex stooped down, her hands trailing through his velvety hair. "*Awwww*, I miss our cat so much."

Moriarty purred and slinked up against her bent knees. "It's the perfect name, too. You're a man after my own heart." Alex laughed. "*Marry me*, Freddie!"

"Aw, if only, my love, if only."

"Cats, Moriarty, *Doctor Who*, you're my perfect match. Damn it. Why are all the good ones gay?"

"Bless," said Freddie. "If only you were muscular and male." He sighed. "One day my dream fella will commit, and I'll be blissfully ensconced in my little love nest."

Lucy snorted. "Freddie, you are such an incurable romantic … and a drama queen, but a pretty one at that."

Alex pivoted to face Lucy. "And you're a superstitious spaz. What's next, avoiding ladders, stepping over cracks in the pavement?"

"Always. I have a thing about spilt salt, too." Lucy created a battle scene with a cluster of Titans on Freddie's narrow coffee table. "I really hate that black cat. I'm glad you're on the scene now, Lex. *You* can be his friend."

Freddie bent down to set Moriarty's bowl on the floor. "He needs all the friends he can get. You hate him. Mark's allergic. My poor fur baby. Okay, let's go!"

"Not so fast, Titan terror. Did you forget Show-and-Tell?" Lucy sprung from the sofa. "If you're not bringing your toys, you have to open them here. Now. I'm not letting you sneak away from this embarrassing moment."

"I suppose I have to give in otherwise I'll never hear the end of it. Must be quick, though. Can't keep our Mark waiting." Waving his arms with a flourish, like a cheesy magician, Freddie snatched Titan box number one from the breakfast bar, singing an old show tune about luck being a lady tonight...

ELEVEN

A rowdy but jovial crowd basked in the late afternoon sunbeams stretching through the large windows of the Castle pub in Islington. Freddie planned to meet Mark around six at the Pentonville Road hangout for a relaxing pint, before heading to the Old Red Lion Theatre down the street.

Lucy's hunger pangs proved impatient and wouldn't wait for their final guest to arrive, so she ordered barbecue chicken wings and fries to share with Alex. Freddie opted for the massive Angus beef cheeseburger. He purchased the first round of drinks at the yellow-painted bar and ambled behind the two girls towards the last available table, tucked into a discreet nook between a wall and the pub's side door entrance.

"All right, bitches, it's selfie time." Freddie scooted the tray of drinks across the distressed wooden table and plonked down on the banquette. He pulled out his phone, snapping a burst of photos cuddled together with the girls—drinks aloft, silly faces, and falling off Lucy's lap.

He shifted to a vinyl-padded chair on the vacant side of the table. Lucy pushed the banquette's yellow, purple, and green throw pillows out of the way and pointed at the price of the cheeseburger on the menu, giving Freddie an incredulous stare across the table.

"What?" Freddie shook his head. "I'm starving, and there's nothing worse than a grumbling stomach during a quiet spell in a play." He grabbed the menu from her hand. "And I know how expensive it is. I'll curtail my alcohol consumption accordingly, so I won't overspend, but thanks for the warning, Miss Moneypenny."

A budgeting lecture from Lucy was coming, so Freddie changed the subject. "So, Alex, I hear you have a Manchester connection? I love the place! Went to uni there."

"His ex lives there, too," said Lucy.

"He did. Not sure he still does." Freddie looked back at Alex. "When are you visiting your dad?"

"Don't know. I want to be settled first. If I don't have things clicking along, he'll nag me about staying in London when I could live up there rent-free." She fiddled with her necklace's clasp, returning the A to its spot above the rounded neck of her blue and white-striped Breton top. "I don't think he's realized that I'm twenty-one, not twelve. And he worries about me. *A lot.* It's actually quite sweet because Mom never does."

"I know what that feels like. My mum only worried about her empty rum bottle—the lush." Lucy handed napkin-wrapped bundles of forks and knives to her friends. "So that's where your worry wart genes come from."

"Yep. Blame Dad. I'd be lost without something to fret over."

A rushed server ducked through the crowd to place two hot plates on the table.

"Feeding the greater London area tonight, Freddie? That

thing's massive." Lucy chuckled at the mountainous burger.

"Sod off! At least I can eat all of this and not put on a pound." Freddie spun the plate around, finding the burger's best side. He captured its magnificence on his phone.

Lucy pouted and dipped her fries into a metal pot of ketchup. "You and your bloody metabolism. I'm so jealous. That said, if we're still hungry after all this, let's share the warm chocolate brownie with ice cream. I don't care if I can't button up my jeans tomorrow."

"Sometimes I order dessert as my *meal* if I don't like anything on the menu," said Alex. "And it has to be sinful and chocolatey. No fruit allowed—ever."

"But you're downing vodka—and orange. You must like *some* fruit, then?" asked Freddie.

"I like strawberries, bananas, orange juice. Love citrus scent. Can't get enough. But eating the actual orange segments? That gross stringy white skin? Hurls-ville."

"Says the chick from bloody *Florida*." Lucy elbowed her friend. "You freak!"

Freddie clasped Alex's hand across the table, prompting a smile to creep across her cheeks. "*Pleeease,* Lucy? Can we keep her? We can be freaks together."

When their laughter abated, Alex caught the last strains of *Habits* by Tove Lo over the pub's sound system. A chill embraced her heart. She was back in Devin's car—feeling loved, feeling content, holding his hand, singing along at the top of their lungs. She stared at her hands, empty in her lap. She had to let go—she knew that—but her heart still needed to catch up to her head. Devin played that damn song all the time, and even here, over 4,000 miles away, she couldn't escape it or how it made her miss him.

"…See, Lucy? You're wrong. I don't have a big gob."

A welcome distraction came with Freddie's comical attempts to eat his monster burger. He raised the stack of beef, cheese, and tomato to his lips but couldn't stretch his mouth wide enough. He fumbled with the cutlery cocooned within a tightly wrapped napkin and scowled. The pub's playlist shuffled onto Lady Gaga's *Bad Romance*. His scowl grew into a snarl. "Nooo. I despise Gaga. Bring back what you were playing earlier …the Monkees, Taylor Swift…I've lost my appetite now."

"You don't like Lady Gaga? But she's so creative, so theatrical." Alex laid a napkin on her lap. "I thought you would like her…because…"

"What? Because I'm gay? That's…homophobic."

Alex's face dropped.

"I'm kidding." Freddie squealed. "No, I don't like her because she feuds with my beloved Madonna. Mess with Madge, you land on my 'Don't Play' list. Simples."

He removed the bun from his burger, slicing the oversize patty with his knife and fork.

"But didn't Lady Gaga and Madonna kiss and make up?" asked Lucy.

"Doesn't matter. The damage has been done." Freddie looked at Alex. "So…about Manchester…let me know when you plan to visit. I'd love to tag along."

"Promise, I will." Alex raised her voice in order to be heard over the increasing din in the lively pub. "But I must warn you that Joan—*I mean*, my grandma. I'm so used to calling her Joan—will want to meet you both."

"You call your gran by her first name?" Freddie blotted excess relish from his upper lip. "Do all Americans do that?"

Alex licked barbecue sauce from her fingers. "No, she always told us to call her Joan instead of Granny or Nanny because she felt too youthful to carry around those so-called ageist 'labels'. She's feisty. Dad says some people find her quite intimidating. I've only met her in person once. She's this unfiltered force. Lucy, you'll love her."

"I love her already. My kind of woman." Lucy tossed a chicken wing bone onto the pile on her plate.

"What play are you seeing tonight, Freddie?" Envy lingered in Alex's question. She desperately wanted to devour as many productions as possible, not only for pleasure but also for any lessons they might hold for her. Watching professionals in action—the best way to learn.

Freddie rummaged in the inside pocket of his jacket. "I wish we had extra tickets so you two could come along. It was at the Fringe Festival in Edinburgh last year. Some two-hander starring Mark's friend and some old guy, I'm not sure of the title. Mark's bringing the tickets. At least I *hope* he is. He'd forget his head sometimes if it wasn't attached."

He put on a pair of black-framed eyeglasses and checked his phone. "Speaking of Mark, I hope he arrives soon. I haven't heard from him all day. He's rubbish at keeping in touch."

"You wear glasses? They suit you," said Alex.

"Cheers. Yeah, I don't wear them all the time. I'm a bit far-sighted…unlike *some* people I won't mention who aren't visually compromised and only wear glasses to make themselves look more intelligent at work."

Lucy smirked and gave him a cool dose of side-eye. "I don't know *what* you're talking about."

"But anyway…we'll see something together," said Freddie. "Isabella Archer's new play opens this autumn at the Almeida. It's supposed to be really innovative and weird from what

Mark's told me."

Alex sputtered on her drink, unsure if she heard him correctly. "Isabella Archer? THE *Isabella Archer*? The one who won her third Olivier Award last month?"

"That's the one."

She smacked the table. The shock rippled through the drinks causing them to shimmy on the spot. "Oh my God. She's my favourite writer, Freddie. I own all her plays. She's been the darling of London's theatre scene for, what, the past ten years? I mean, who wins an Olivier with their first play at twenty-three?"

She stopped to catch her breath. "Go see her play? I'd *die*. I would. I hope you're not pulling my leg—"

"I'm not. I wouldn't. Look, if you don't believe me, ask Mark…"

Freddie stood up to hug a guy with jet-black hair who had wandered up to the edge of their table. Alex did a double take. It was the handsome Irish stranger from the Royal Court lobby. Freddie delivered a roguish smooch to Mark's forehead. The guys laughed, but she couldn't make out what the two friends said to one another. Raised voices and the venue's blaring music made for a deafening mix.

He was a few inches shorter than Freddie and a few pounds heavier, but then everyone weighed more than Freddie. The scruff of whiskers above his lip and along his jaw line matched his friend. He playfully slicked his hair back away from his forehead and leaned across the table to embrace Lucy, giving her a peck on each cheek.

Sitting down across from Alex, he looked at her with his soulful brown eyes. They lingered a little too long as if they were memorizing every freckle. He shrugged off his beat-up leather jacket to expose a loosely knotted purple tie and a fitted, white dress shirt that hugged his chest when he moved. He leaned over the table full of drinks and plates, extending his hand to her. His handshake was warm and firm. She hoped he couldn't detect her racing pulse.

"Hello, I'm Mark Keegan. You must be Alex."

Laugh lines gathered around his eyes, and his smile was easy and genuine, just as she remembered from the theatre.

"Have we met before? You look familiar."

Alex's stomach did a back flip. "Were you at the Royal Court box office last weekend?"

He blinked rapidly and then his eyes widened in recognition. "That's it. Wow, small world."

Lucy laughed. "What a crazy coincidence."

Mark's kind welcome and charming Dublin accent captivated Alex, but before she could say much more to the soft-spoken Irishman, Freddie broke the spell.

"And here I thought I was introducing two strangers. Fancy a pint, Mark?"

"Hell yeah. My shout. Same again, ladies?" Mark leapt off his chair and disappeared into the swarm of Saturday night revelers.

"Mark's an actor," Freddie blurted out to Alex as soon as his friend was out of earshot. "You two should have plenty to chat about. He's done everything: radio dramas, voiceovers, theatre. I met him in the Beeb's canteen two years back. He was taking a break from a radio play, and he scooped the last cheese and onion pasty. I could've *throttled* him, but he was too bloody adorable. And did you check out that arse? He looks so fit in those black trousers."

Alex smirked, unsure of Freddie's relationship with Mark. Was he Freddie's partner? No mention had been made about a current boyfriend, so she didn't know what to assume. She wasn't great at reading new people.

When Mark returned with a tray of drinks, Freddie commandeered the conversation. Alex noticed that Mark didn't mind. He seemed perfectly at ease letting Freddie take the lead. He interjected his thoughts a few times, but he wasn't boisterous or an attention-hog like some actors tend to be. And when he laughed, his entire body became committed to the cause. He threw his head back with abandon and chuckled explosively, a contagious giggle that enticed everyone to join in the hilarity.

Alex yearned to share a few words with him. Why did she feel so needy for someone she'd just met? Sure, he was attractive, but lots of people ticked that box. But she didn't hang on their every word as she did with him. She studied every smile, nod, and laugh. His presence, intoxicating. If only Freddie would take a breath or a bite of his burger and give her a chance...

"Alex, are you enjoying London so far?" Mark grabbed a moment to jump in while Freddie chewed a large mouthful.

"I love it." She sat up straight. "I can't believe I'm actually here. It doesn't seem real."

"I was the same when I first arrived five years back. Everything is brighter, more vibrant than you expect. I'm still discovering areas of the city I never knew existed."

Lucy jumped in. "That's because you're a workaholic." She turned to Alex. "We rarely see him."

The Irishman raised his eyebrows. "Oh, come on now. I'm not that bad. Can't a guy love his job?"

Alex smiled. "Did you see the play at the Royal Court?"

"I was supposed to. I got called into work, and had to return the tickets."

"See?" said Lucy. "Workaholic."

Mark swatted across the table at Lucy, liberating a chip in the process.

"Did you see it?" he asked Alex.

"I did!" Alex's eyes danced at the memory. "It was terrific, and the Royal Court…" She placed her hand over her heart. "…blew me away. Freddie says you're an actor."

Mark nodded. "I am. Graduated two years ago from the Guildhall School of Music and Drama. I've done some theatre and plenty of voiceovers for adverts back in Ireland. A few radio plays for the BBC. Auditions keep me busy. What about you?"

Freddie adjusted his glasses and volleyed back into action. "Alex is a playwright and a geek. Today, we baptized her at Forbidden Planet, and in turn she dragged us around…*wait for it*…the London bloody Transport Museum!"

Alex sank into the banquette. Nerd alert.

"Really?" Mark winked reassuringly at her.

Freddie went to take another bite of his half-eaten burger but thought better of it, so he could continue talking. "I *particularly* enjoyed fighting through screaming rug rats to climb on the double-decker buses on display. And those wax mannequins in period costumes on the Tube carriages really freaked me out."

"God, they were awful. I swear the shaggy-haired one looked like a cross-eyed Boris Johnson. This Covent Garden talk reminds me, it's Show-and-Tell time…" Lucy reached towards her feet and dropped a plastic bag on her lap. "Go on, Lex, show us what you bought."

Alex opened her handbag, looking for her purchase, but Lucy's eye caught a glimpse of something red and plastic.

"What's this?" Lucy snatched the rectangular packet and held it aloft. "Twizzlers? Are you always packing sweets?"

Alex grabbed it out of Lucy's hand and chucked it into her

bag. "It's a comfort thing, and they're hard to find here." She shot an anxious look through her bangs at Mark, who smiled kindly.

She flashed a small transit pass holder. "All I could afford was this *Sherlock* Oyster card cover. Maybe Benedict's lovely face earns me a few points for trying?" Her eyes wandered back to Mark.

He held her gaze. "I'd say it does." Alex bowed her head with a slight grin.

"Never feel bad, never. It was your first go." Lucy stole some fries off Freddie's plate. "At least you didn't buy an *Elementary* cover. Then I would've been concerned. You can't compare the two shows. It's like *Empire Strikes Back* versus *The Phantom Menace*. Just wait until you get your first pay packet. You'll be loading up on *Doctor Who* Titans just like Freddie."

"I refuse to accept that comment as an insult." Freddie raked his hand dramatically through his hair and swigged his pint.

"Mark, he did the bloody blind box thing again," said Lucy. "Came away with three Oods and a Cyberman. I think the collectible gods threw in the Cyberman to prevent Freddie from doing something desperate. I laughed so hard I nearly gave birth to my kidneys."

"Oods...remind me?" Mark scratched his head. "I'm not into *Doctor Who* like you lot."

Lucy wiped her mouth with a napkin and launched wide-eyed into her explanation. "They're the aliens that have human bodies, squinty reptilian eyes, and squid-like tentacles that hang down where their mouths should be. They carry these glowing orbs that are attached to their bodies by an umbilical cord."

"Ah, right. *Those* guys." Mark shook his head at his friend. "Yeah, that's not a score, Freddie."

Freddie couldn't defend himself. His cheeks bulged with hamburger like a squirrel hoarding peanuts.

"Never mind the fandom failure over there." Lucy dove into her plastic bag. "Correct me if I'm wrong, and I'm sure I'm not: I win the prize for best find today." She held a Marvel comic a loft called *A-Force #1*, a cluster of colourful female Avengers vaulting from its cover, faces unflinching, and arms thrust defiantly towards the heavens. A powerful golden glow radiated their unspoken confidence. "It got a great review online. Alex, you can borrow it after me if you'd like."

The blonde nodded enthusiastically. Any book or comic celebrating strong female characters immediately claimed the top spot on her must-read list.

"While we're on the topic of writing…Alex, it's brilliant you're a playwright." Mark's tone was soft and indulgent.

"Well, I hope to be if all goes to plan."

Mark leaned closer, so he'd be heard above the booming pub soundtrack. That scent again…the same one from the Royal Court lobby. He smelled yummy.

"I'm in awe of people like you, bringing an idea to life on the page. If you ever want your work-in-progress performed, let me know. My actor mates and I love workshopping new plays and helping up-and-coming writers."

His dark eyebrows rose to punctuate his point. "We're all in this performing lark together. Theatre's a team sport. Us creative types need to support each other, you know?"

Alex blushed at his unexpected offer. "Thanks so much. I'd like that."

His kindness sounded genuine, and in Freddie's words, he was *adorable*, but what if he wasn't everything that he seemed? She'd trusted an actor before and look how that turned out.

☂ ☂ ☂ ☂ ☂

By 7 o'clock, Freddie and Mark were on their way to the theatre, leaving Alex and Lucy to juggle a pressing decision—whether to pool their resources to purchase two more drinks or to call it a night and disperse into the brisk London air. In lieu of a decision, Lucy bit her lip and stared at Alex.

"What? Do I have ketchup on my face or something?"

Lucy cocked her head to the side, eyebrows raised as if to say "you know what I mean."

"Mark?"

"Pretty *fit*, right?" said Lucy, toying with her petite ruby and gold ring, a cherished heirloom from her gran.

Alex stalled cautiously, not knowing if Lucy had her eye on Mark or if they had history. And she still wasn't sure if he was seeing Freddie. So confusing...

She went the non-committal route. "He's lovely, yeah."

"I knew it. You drooled over him like he was a cartoon steak!"

"I did *not*." Alex carefully chose a different line of questioning. "Are he and Freddie...together?"

Lucy burst out laughing, knocking over her pint glass. "Freddie *wishes*!"

She snatched the remaining napkins strewn in front of her, blotting up the fast moving trickle of beer. "No, they're just mates. Mark's as straight as they come. Freddie flirts with him in fun, and Mark thinks it's endearing. He's a cool guy, very protective of Freddie. I have to admit, I fancy him. I mean, how could anyone *not*? And as far as I know, he doesn't have a girlfriend..."

TWELVE

Alex swore she had spring fever. Excited and optimistic, she had kicked the sleepy haze that had troubled her during her first week. Now with two weeks at the Tasty Munch café under her belt, she slapped together bacon 'sarnies', chip 'butties', and all-day breakfasts with aplomb. Regular customers raved about Alex's scrambled eggs and milky coffees, and began asking the owner for her by name. She even scored a few healthy tips. Best of all, she finished her shift at one and had plenty of energy left to tackle several hours of writing at home.

It didn't feel like the first Friday of June. It felt more like July in Tallahassee based on the short-sleeved tops and light fabrics Londoners were sporting. An unexpected heat wave hugged the southeast of England, and London basked in its humid embrace. Jolly Brits skipped out of work early, spilling onto pub sidewalks across the city, toasting the beautiful weather with their well-earned pints and glasses of wine. Sunbathers, rambunctious toddlers, and excitable canines dotted every grassy square and park. Even Londoners temporarily stuck commuting underground seemed softer, more open and friendly. The dank days of May were truly over, and London couldn't wait to chuck its brolly and wiggle its toes in the lush green grass.

Alex popped on her sunglasses and practically danced out of Tasty Munch. The weekend starts now! At seven, Freddie and Lucy were meeting her at St. George's Tavern on Belgrave Road. A short walk from Lucy's office, it made for the perfect venue for a departing coworker's leaving do. Payday was still another week away, and cheap entertainment options were currently few and far between. The promise of free booze and sausage rolls—too tempting to ignore.

And then tomorrow, Bespoke's official opening bash, but first, a date with a coffee shop and her writing. A quick pit stop at home for her laptop, and she'd be all set.

She glanced at a guy wearing a helmet, straddling a red Vespa parked by the curb.

"Alex?"

She slowed her pace, lifting her sunnies from her eyes and following the voice, escaping on the breeze.

"It *is* you!" The mystery man lifted the visor and pulled off the helmet, revealing a beaming, tousled Mark. His black hair pointed up and sideways while his brown eyes sparkled in the sunlight. "Hello, stranger!"

"Mark! You live around here?" Alex's eyes darted between his smile and the scooter.

"Not even close. My flat's in East Acton…west *west* London." He smoothed down his hair, the grin taking up permanent residence. "I had an audition at the Hackney Empire this morning. Crazy running into you here."

"I live beside London Fields, and I work *there*." She pointed to the tiny Mare Street café.

"You landed on your feet. Hackney's cool."

"It's only temporary. I'm staying with a friend."

"Well, that's the best way to feel at home in a new city, living with friends. When I moved here, an actor mate set me up with his spare room. I think he wanted me there as a buffer from his other flatmate. He's a dentist, so he drones on about bicuspids and root canals. Wanna trade?"

Alex tugged on the hem of her *Batman* tee, pulling it towards the pockets of her skinny jeans. "Ooh, that's tempting, but he'll probably confiscate my licorice. Can't have that."

"That's true." He leaned forward. "What are you doing now?"

"Just off to do some writing. Why?"

"Fancy a little London adventure? Ever ridden a Vespa?"

Alex bounced up on her toes. "Really? I'd love to!"

"It's your lucky day then." Mark handed the helmet to her. "Put this on. I've only the one, but I'd feel better if you wore it. Hop on and hold tight."

Alex eased a leg over the seat, her chest brushing against Mark's back. Her open knees grazed the outside of his upper thighs. She inhaled, seduced by the light Burberry scent lingering on his neck. She held her breath and wrapped her arms around his waist. The muggy weather meant he wasn't wearing a jacket, just a black button-down shirt paired with dark jeans. Her hands felt the outline of toned abs underneath the fabric—not too bulky or six-pack perfect—Mark was just right. She felt self-conscious, hugging him so closely...so intimately.

"Don't be shy," said Mark, reading her mind. "Hold tighter. I can't risk losing you, can I?"

☂ ☂ ☂ ☂ ☂

Mark took advantage of the chance to give his new Anglophile friend a proper taste of London. He zoomed through Hackney and Cambridge Heath towards Whitechapel. He pointed out the pubs where Jack the Ripper was rumoured to have stalked his victims and then sped off towards central London.

Pressed against Mark's back, Alex was deliriously giddy. She couldn't blame the sights whizzing past her. Mark's intoxicating scent, and the heat of his body underneath her arms, her chest, her cheek...such a heady cocktail. She worried about hyperventilating—so unattractive!—but Mark's gentle words, wafting over his shoulder at every red light, checking to see if she was okay, calmed her runaway imagination. He was so much more than just a pretty face.

They stopped for an ice cream outside the Tower of London, stumbled across St. Bart's Hospital—scene of Cumberbatch's famous 'Reichenbach fall' in *Sherlock*—and got sore necks gazing up at the heavens inside St. Paul's Cathedral.

"You've got to see the old narrow streets across from St. Paul's." Mark hopped back on the Vespa. "Bow Lane, just off Watling Street...you'll feel like you're in a Dickens novel...well, apart from the hairdressers and take-aways."

"How do you know all these cool hidden streets?"

"Perks of being an actor, I guess. My cast mates dragged me to the Ye Olde Watling pub after our one-off performance at the Bridewell Theatre."

"A closing night party...for a *one-off*? That's hardcore." Alex stretched a leg over the Vespa's seat and lifted the helmet above her head.

"Welcome to London, kid. Any excuse to end up in a pub," said Mark with a laugh.

The Vespa dodged double-decker buses, honking taxis, and tourists stepping blindly into traffic. Trafalgar Square, guarded by its pride of four bronze lions, begged for a photo op. Who was Mark to decline? He snapped several selfies with Alex, the two of them huddled between a lion's mammoth paws.

They zipped through the majestic Admiralty Arch, down The Mall with its Union Jack flags waving in the breeze, and around the sweeping roundabout in front of Buckingham Palace. At Alex's insistence, Mark parked and let her treat him to a thank you lunch from a refreshment kiosk in St. James's Park. They lazed in two of the park's famous green and white striped deck chairs, soaking up the unrelenting sunshine while ducks bobbed and swans honked in the nearby pond.

"You're a bad influence, Mark Keegan. I should be hunched over my laptop, surrounded by coffee-sipping hipsters, not eating cheese sandwiches in the park."

"You were surprisingly easy to corrupt. I *like* that in a woman," said Mark, raising a cheeky eyebrow and stealing her sunglasses to try on.

Warmth flooded Alex's cheeks. She refreshed her parched mouth with a sip of cola. "Don't let this innocent face fool you. Maybe it's the other way around...I'm corrupting *you*."

"Really now?" His brown eyes popped over the rims of her sunglasses. "Hmm. Well, I did have a monologue to learn this afternoon, but I couldn't disappoint you. Your eyes! When you sussed my Vespa, they lit up brighter than Blackpool Illuminations. I had to snatch you away."

"Perceptive! Yep, you got me—guilty as charged. I'm using you for your wheels. I love scooters. Can't get enough of

Quadrophenia."

Mark gasped with a smirk. "You only want me for my Vespa? Shame, that." He took a swig of his lemonade. "But if we're being honest, full disclosure...I only like you for your American accent..."

"I thought Europeans hated Americans?"

"Not this one." He shook his head and handed back her shades. "I'd love to visit one day. What's Florida like?"

"Warm, sunny, and crammed with tourists."

"Kinda like London is now." Mark squinted into the cloudless blue sky. "Do you miss it?"

"I don't, well, at least not yet. Still feels like a holiday." She raked her hand through the thick grass. "Do you miss Ireland?"

"I do, yeah, sometimes. Late at night when I'm alone, or when it rains. I miss the *smell* of rainy days in Dublin. And I miss my family. When my older sister got married last year, she moved to Wales, so our mum's on her own. I get back as often as I can."

Alex smiled softly. "I bet Dublin's beautiful."

"It's lovely, yeah. St. Stephen's Green—the park in the city centre—that's my favourite. I could people watch there all day, great for an actor...well, for anyone, really. Maybe one day I'll show you around."

She leaned forward, nodding like one of those bobbing dogs in the back of a car. "And I'll take you to Disney World in Orlando..."

A few steps away, a toddler dropped his ice cream in the grass. He slipped, landing with a thud...a face-plant in the gooey pink mess. He wailed on contact, all distraught milky strawberry tears. His impatient parents snatched his sticky hand, dragging him away. A rambling Jack Russell caught wind of the sweet scent and followed in hot pursuit.

Mark and Alex looked at each other and burst out laughing.

"...Just don't make me go on the rollercoasters," said Alex. "I hate them."

"How can you hate rollercoasters?" said Mark. "They're thrilling, fast, a great excuse to scream like a girl..."

"Like a *girl*?"

"Shit. Now you know my secret."

Alex giggled. "Well, if that's the case, I'd be a terrible host if I didn't offer to ride *with* you...and maybe—*maybe*—I'll let you hold my hand for safety."

"Deal," said Mark with a wide grin.

Bruno Mars began to warble from Mark's deck chair. Alex put on her sunglasses while Mark stretched, fishing his hand into his front jeans pocket. A scowl greeted the phone screen. He jabbed the glass, sending the call to voicemail. "I lost all track of time. It's just gone four, so I really should head back. Sorry to break up our adventure. It's been ace."

Alex's heart dipped. If only they could steal another hour or two. She twisted strands of hair around her finger. "You're a wicked tour guide, Mark. Thank you. I've loved every minute."

"Oh, before I forget...our photos are on here. How 'bout you type in your number so I can text them to you?" He slid his phone into her palm.

It was still warm from his thigh. Alex bit her lip.

And the screensaver? A photo of a muddy soccer team. "I didn't know you were a soccer—sorry, *football* fan. What team's this?"

"Mine. Well, my old one back in Ireland. I lived on the pitch. But as a jobbing actor, I can't show up at auditions on crutches, or with a concussion. Sometimes you have to move on, you know?"

Alex sighed. "So true."

She saved her digits as Bruno sang again, an incoming call from a 'Julia'. Alex handed his phone back, but Mark ignored the caller.

"My family, the Manchester side, is football mad. My dad even named me after Sir Alex Ferguson, much to my mom's annoyance."

Mark threw his head back, laughing. "That's fucking brilliant! Your dad's a legend. I'm a lifelong Red, too."

They both stood up, shaking off sandwich crumbs and the laziness of the afternoon.

"Can I give you a lift home?"

Alex swallowed the 'yes' that threatened to escape from her lips. She couldn't take advantage of his kindness. "It's kinda far, isn't it? I don't want to make you late." She threw their trash into a bin. "I can find my way back. Part two of my adventure."

"At least let me drop you somewhere. St. James's Park station is close by." He checked an app on his phone. "The Circle line will take you to Liverpool Road and the Overground to London Fields. Can't have you wandering about…God knows who else you'll corrupt."

Forty minutes later, Alex floated through the door of her flat. Fueled by Mark's impromptu London tour and with two hours remaining before meeting Lucy and Freddie, she felt inspired to write, her latest brainwave based on a conversation she overheard in the café two days earlier. Three hard-hat toting workers, ploughing through their Full English Breakfasts, were discussing Waterloo Bridge and how *women* were largely responsible for its construction. The topic sounded too good to ignore and possibly too good to be true, but a quick Google search on her phone while frying eggs came up trumps—it was true!

Since her discovery on Wednesday, her fingers had flown over her keyboard, doing research and outlining the facts for a potential play. And the timing couldn't have been better. Earlier in the week, she smacked into a brick wall with suffragette edits. Alex always found that the best way to climb out of writer's block was to put the troublesome piece aside and start something fresh. The Waterloo Bridge idea—so cool, so London—was the perfect diversion.

But first, she had to contend with a jagged stack of books threatening to keel over. Some of the largest books in the tower, originally at its base, now leaned precariously from the summit. Every time the cleaner visited, she knocked something over. Bless her. The fact that she even *tried* to clean Alex's box room was a huge ask. There was barely any floor space to vacuum and yet she made the effort. The kind lady had tried to rebuild the stack, but it was one nudge away from bludgeoning Paddington. Alex had ignored it yesterday when she got home, in such a hurry to write, but the breeziness of today made her take the time to fix it, and return her con photo with Matt Smith to the top.

A few minutes later, Olivia and Tom burst into the flat, fracturing Alex's quiet refuge. Olivia's young playwrights fundraiser was tonight, and she barked commands at her older brother. Alex couldn't tell through her closed bedroom door if Tom had screwed up or whether Olivia was just super-stressed about the weighty responsibility. They thumped and squabbled around the flat and…vanished. Welcome silence settled in their wake.

Alex ventured into the stuffy kitchen and filled the kettle. Discarded clipboards, revised guest lists, and torn up name cards were left behind by the Chadwick-Smythe whirlwind. Did they ever pick up after themselves?

A few minutes later, a key clicked in the lock.

"Honey, I'm home," joked Harry, as he strode through the door.

"Your honey's gone out with Tom," Alex hollered from the kitchen, unplugging the kettle.

"Ahh, I thought I might miss her." He walked in and rested four large bouquets of white and pink lilies on the counter. Alex's jaw dropped. Did he knock over a florist?

"The Piccadilly line was murder. There was a power outage for a while, and it backed up all the trains."

He reached into a cupboard above the stove and removed two large vases. Alex whirled a spoon round and round in her tea, the three lumpy teaspoons of sugar hesitant to dissolve. She watched Harry fight with the crinkly cellophane wrap cradling the blooms.

"Olivia will be pleased with these when she comes home tonight," he smiled. A final pull released the elegant flowers from their plastic prison. The burst of fragrance prickled Alex's nose.

"Ah—choo!...ah-choo!...ah-choo!"

"You done yet?" Harry laughed, filling the vases with cool water and then dunking the stems. Eyes watering, Alex pushed open the kitchen window; the influx of fresh air calming her sneezing fit. Several houseflies took advantage of the open window and sailed inside on the June breeze.

"What's wrong with you Brits? Haven't you heard of window screens?" Alex swatted the air, urging the bugs to leave while submerging her nose in a tissue. "Those flowers are epic. What's the occasion, or are you in the doghouse?"

"Nope. These are 'congratulations on a brilliant event' flowers. You see, I'm officially a great boyfriend. Now, time to clean myself up and get going."

Looking at Alex, he did a double take. "Why are you dressed like *that*?"

Alex glanced down at her comfy combo of jeans and *Batman* t-shirt, and scrunched up her face. "Like this? Why? What's wrong with it?" She slouched against the counter.

Harry shot her an expectant look. "Aren't you going to the fundraiser tonight? You're young. You're a new playwright. This party's made for you."

"Well you see, Harry, there's this thing called an invite— and I don't have one. It's no big deal; I'm not bothered. Besides, I have plans with Lucy and Freddie."

"No, you don't. Call your friends and tell them you'll meet them later tonight." He plucked the mug out of her hand and chucked its contents into the sink.

"Harry, wait—" Alex hated surprises, especially surprises involving dressing up at the last minute, big crowds, and—worst of all—schmoozing with strangers.

He gently pushed her towards her room, continuing his hard sell. "Olivia's had a lot on her plate; your invite must've slipped her mind, but we'll fix that."

"Maybe I don't *want* you to fix it…"

Harry wasn't taking no for an answer. He kept nudging her until they reached her wardrobe.

"This event's a huge deal. Trust me, you need to be there. All the movers and shakers will be in attendance, and it'll give you the perfect opportunity to toss your name into the playwriting ring. You want these people to remember you."

"But...I've never been to a fundraiser...*thing*," said Alex with a pinched expression. "What would I even wear?" She rubbed her eyebrow, searching for a pressure point. "God, I hate wearing heels..."

"A dress would be perfect." He browsed through the clothes hanging up in her wardrobe. "It doesn't have to be expensive, but choose something summery. This weather's glorious, and let's face it, you should be spending tonight outdoors with us, not shut away in a pub."

THIRTEEN

"Thanks, darling." Harry winked at the hostess with the guest list as he and Alex sailed through the front door of Bridgewater House. Alex craned her neck, gawking at the ornate glass domed ceiling of the Great Saloon and the huge murals adorning a far wall. This place was no ordinary London address. The Victorian mansion overlooked Green Park and shared its posh neighbourhood with several royal residences, including St. James's Palace and Clarence House.

"I knew you were good at this stuff, but I didn't realize *how* good," said Alex in a hushed tone, her eyes washing over his Richard James pale blue linen suit. "Should I call you *Prince Harry* from now on?"

Harry chuckled and got down to business. "Look, here's the one rule you need to know for tonight. Have your elevator pitch ready. There are all sorts of producers, directors, and theatre money here."

Alex gulped and wrapped the delicate chain of her clutch around her finger.

"Don't worry, Alex. Just be your charming American self.

They'll love you."

The wide cement patio and lush green garden of the impos-
ing building reverberated with laughter, conversation, and plenty
of clinking glasses. Harry whisked two champagne flutes off a
passing silver tray and handed one to Alex. She took a large sip,
keen to quench her thirst while gaining some much needed courage. The bubbles tickled her nose and throat. A Coke or mixed
drink was more her style, but she didn't want to leave Harry's
side to search for the bar.

She stuffed her clutch under her arm and adjusted the gap-
ing v-neck of her light blue and purple dress. At least if she fell
out of it, no one would notice—the only advantage of small
boobs. Harry picked up on her fidgeting. "Don't fret. You look
lovely."

His kind words coaxed Alex's pale pink lips into a smile,
but her outfit was in a lower league than everyone else's. The
other women in attendance looked immaculate. Not all wore designer threads—far from it—but the many who did lived on another planet as far as Alex was concerned. Stilettos were a popular choice, despite the garden party theme.

She glanced down at her own feet clad in simple black flats.
"Don't these women realize they're going to sink into the grass
wearing heels?"

"I think that's the least of their worries. They're here to be
seen. Fashionable, rich, and a supporter of the arts—that's their
M.O."

Harry squinted through the crowd, somewhat agitated, as if
late for a meeting. "Most won't leave the safety of the patio.
That way they're closer to the booze and their Jimmy Choos can
live to see another party."

"I'm surprised you know what Jimmy Choos are," said

Alex.

"You can't date a woman like Olivia and be in the dark about such things."

A muffled ping escaped from Alex's clutch, then another …and another.

"Is that yours?" asked Harry, watching the door.

She snapped open her bag. Like an attack of hiccups, her phone interrupted every few seconds.

"Sorry. Can you…" She handed her champagne to Harry. "Thanks. Must be spam. I'll mute it."

She caught a photo of Mark dodging fountains at Somerset House. Then one of herself hugging the ice cream van outside The Tower—each text message, a different shot taken by Mark: Alex pointing at The Monument, Mark lying on the ground where Sherlock fell at St. Bart's, Alex in front of the gates of Buckingham Palace…The final text included a message:

'Alex, a few mementos from our London adventure. Shame I didn't capture that toddler face-planting into his ice cream! I hope you had as much fun as I did. London is definitely better with you in it! See you soon, Mark'

She re-read his last sentence— *'London is definitely better with you in it!'* She blushed and relaxed into a smile that was more genuine than all the other grins circulating around her, but Harry stepped away, tapping his foot, his eyes scanning the garden. Now wasn't the time to share her snapshots. She dashed off a brief reply:

'Mark, love the photos! Thank you for being so kind and making a lost American feel at home. Strawberry Tears Forever! Alex'

She slid the phone into her clutch and retrieved her glass from Harry.

A waitress paraded past, handing out pamphlets listing the items up for auction. Alex accepted one, and began fanning herself with it. The late day sun sizzled and showed no signs of leaving the party.

"Ah, *there* she is."

Harry rushed to the far end of the patio where Olivia, perfectly presented in a Christopher Kane lilac lace dress, held court surrounded by a gaggle of women. Alex followed a few steps behind, keeping his blue elbow within reach. He greeted his girlfriend with a discreet kiss on each cheek, conscious of her current company. In turn, she inserted herself under his right arm, claiming ownership. The ladies swooned over the glamorous pairing.

Noticing Alex, Olivia stiffened, throwing her an incredulous stare. Her mauve lips pinched briefly, before releasing into a plastic smile worthy of a beauty pageant contestant.

Alex blinked several times, confused by Ms. Chadwick-Smythe's disdainful welcome.

Olivia tilted her flushed cheeks back towards her boyfriend, fluttering her false eyelashes and stroking his face. "I'm so glad you made it, darling. It means a lot, taking the night off from Bespoke to be here for me."

Harry pressed his lips tenderly against his girlfriend's forehead. "I wouldn't have missed it for the world."

Olivia beamed at her faithful female audience and absorbed their rapt appreciation. Her confidence seemed effortless, like she was born with it, another win in the genetics lottery along with long legs and blemish-free skin.

Alex broke her stare. She'd been gawking at their public display of affection for too long. Nausea toyed with her stomach. That's what you get for guzzling champagne under the influence of the sweltering sun. She surrendered her empty glass to a passing waiter.

She glanced in the opposite direction. Geez, was that *Kevin Spacey*? He used to have something to do with the Old Vic Theatre, so maybe?

Several feet away from Maybe-Spacey, she spied Tom, tie askew in a summery white suit, leaning against a large cement plant container. Glass in hand, he whispered in the ear of a pretty Asian girl. She was wearing an expensive silk mini dress that floated around her hips like a cloud. Great. Another person that made Alex feel under dressed. The silk cloud didn't care for what Tom was proposing because she shot him a disdainful look and glommed onto the first person passing by. Poor Tom. Such a trier. If he put as much energy into his acting career as he did shagging around, he might be winning BAFTAs by now.

Since Harry found Olivia, Alex hadn't spoken a word. The clique surrounding the brunette felt incestuous like they all knew each other and weren't open to outsiders. To be fair, Alex knew she wasn't the best at initiating conversation with strangers. The thought of it made her even more feverish and dizzy. She pondered an escape. A bench beckoned under a shady tree, but Harry stepped in to the rescue.

"Ladies, before we get too carried away discussing the pros and cons of ten quid theatre tickets, let me introduce you to a new voice on London's theatre scene. Meet my good friend Alexandra Sinclair. She's a recent playwriting graduate from the States."

"Welcome to London, Alexandra," said one theatre supporter, extending her hand. "How long will you be staying?"

Alex grinned, shaking her hand. "Forever, I hope."

"Such a pleasure to meet you, Alexandra," said another.

Alex didn't dare glance up at Olivia. She didn't have to—her silent contempt pricked Alex's skin like a pesky heat rash.

"Yes, Alex is here to test the waters, and we're doing everything we can to help," said Olivia. "It's hard coming from so far away with no contacts or support. An artist can't flourish in isolation."

The group agreed with a chorus of approval, and continued to ask Alex about Florida. One of them enquired whether she had attended the polo season there. Oh, how her mom would've *loved* this. She stifled a giggle. "No, I haven't, but—"

Olivia jumped in before she could finish. "The auction will begin in an hour's time, so be sure to look over the list and see what grabs your fancy. There's an afternoon tea at The Ritz with Sir Ian McKellen that's certain to be hugely popular."

Her words worked their magic, sending her affluent associates scurrying off to the Great Saloon to take a gander. While one group of arts patrons departed, another arrived, doling out handshakes to both Harry and Olivia. One member of this three-person team Alex recognized instantly.

Isabella Archer.

Alex gawked. Isabella was only in her mid-thirties but in the flesh could've easily passed for mid-twenties. In a venue populated by designer dresses and trendy fashion statements, her quirky style made her all the more charismatic. She defied tonight's fashion rules in black jeans, a white t-shirt, and beat-up cherry red Doc Martins. A glittery black and silver scarf snaked through her belt loops. Alex had read that Isabella *never* wore dresses or skirts. A haphazard bun spilled curly dark blonde tendrils down her long neck. She stood out like an Oreo cookie amidst a jarful of Jammie Dodgers. Isabella didn't follow the crowd and didn't care. Alex adored her for it.

Isabella had created a buzz on the UK theatre landscape as a twenty-three-year-old wunderkind from the small town of South Elmsall, up north in Yorkshire. Her edgy debut play was picked up unsolicited by the Soho Theatre and went on to earn her an Olivier Award. The Royal Court snapped up her second work a few months later, and in the ten years that followed, Isabella's plays captured awards and entertained packed theatres across the country. Alex couldn't have chosen a worthier idol; a young woman forging her way in a tough business, ripe with rejection and shattered dreams. Her hard work, talent, and drive were legendary, plus she had a reputation for mentoring young writers.

"Olivia, it's nice to see you again; thanks for inviting me. Congratulations on tonight's festivities. Impressive. You should be proud. Nights like this one can really make a difference for young playwrights...such as yourself."

Isabella introduced Olivia and Harry to the two people by her side. Their names flew over Alex's head. Only Isabella remained in focus. Her role model stood just a *handshake* away. She dried her clammy palms on her dress in case salutations extended in her direction.

The celebrated playwright shifted her attention towards the short blonde. "Hello. I'm Isabella."

Alex met her hand halfway. "Hi. Alex Sinclair. It's a thrill to meet you, Ms. Archer."

"Lovely! You're American. Call me Isabella, please."

Alex dissolved into a tongue-tied stupor. She had so many things she'd love to ask, but her mind collapsed into her bubbling stomach.

Harry smirked and sipped his glass. He'd known Alex long enough to recognize an internal freak out. She needed a parachute. "Isabella, Alex graduated top of her playwriting class at

Emory University this spring. She's really talented. I think she'd make a great candidate for your upcoming writing workshop."

Olivia looked away, rolling her eyes. Her sour reaction flew under everyone's radar.

Alex's cheeks grew warm.

"It's wonderful to meet a new face." Isabella's smile didn't hold back. "The London theatre world can be quite cliquey and insular. New ideas, new voices are always welcome. It's the only way our community will thrive."

The Floridian nodded, fazed to be in the presence of her idol.

"Funny that you mention my workshop, Harry." Isabella turned to Olivia. "Are you submitting a play again this year? Rejection is never fun, but I'm sure you learned from some of the constructive criticism last year." She handed her empty glass to a passing waiter. "And will our new American friend be submitting as well? The final deadline is only two weeks away, though. Think you'll be ready?"

Olivia pushed her shoulders back. "I will." Her words stepped all over Isabella's. "I'm working on something special that celebrates British women."

Harry pulled her close. "Leave it to my girl to come up with something riveting *and* socially responsible." He released Olivia from his clinch, letting her take centre stage.

Alex tossed her bangs out of her eyes, looking wide-eyed at Olivia. Her idea must be impressive. She's in such a hurry to share. Hopefully her own idea wouldn't pale in comparison.

Isabella folded her arms in expectation. "Okay, Olivia. Elevator pitch—go."

The brunette ran her hand through her sleek blowout, her amethyst rock glinting in the sunny haze. "It's a British story of strong, courageous women and their devotion to a cause that was viewed as illegal and threatening by their men and society at large—the suffragette movement…"

What? Did she hear that right? Alex's jaw dropped. A rush of adrenaline pulsated through her body, jolting the peach fuzz on her arms to attention. Her hand clamoured for the charm on her necklace.

"…Today we take our equality for granted, but back in the early 1900s, the idea of women voting, of having a say in governmental affairs was verboten. My play, featuring an all-female cast, even the male roles will be portrayed by women—"

Isabella interrupted. "I love it! A twist on gender and traditional acting roles. Go on."

Alex glared at Harry's girlfriend, but her stare wasn't met. Olivia's eyes stayed glued to Isabella the entire time. Nothing could come between Olivia and her pitch.

"It will expose the trials, tribulations, and violence that brought radical change to British society and show people whom to thank for the advancements women enjoy today." She held her chin high and swung her arms loosely behind her back. Job done.

Harry couldn't praise his girlfriend enough. "Babe, that's incredible. I thought you were set on that Hackney hipster idea, but this one's even better." He wrapped his arms around her waist, emanoured. "Love the feminist angle. I couldn't be more proud."

Harry couldn't be more proud.

Alex couldn't be more horrified.

Beads of perspiration formed on the back of her neck, threatening to soak through the fine weave of her jersey dress. She needed to simmer down—stat. Her furious waving of the auction pamphlet, in time with her rapid-fire heart, flapped an unreliable breeze that did little to curb her sweating. She shivered while her face grew hotter and hotter.

Olivia continued to elaborate on the amount of research she had apparently completed and why this story had to be told now. Isabella ate it up. The two older arts patrons, planted like bookends on either side of the award-winning playwright, nodded their approval as well. Harry beamed so hard, Alex worried his face might crack.

Short, shallow breaths slipped from Alex's mouth. She pieced together a few scattered thoughts. Olivia had stolen not just the idea; she had stolen her *entire* play. *Why?* Why would she do such a thing? And right in front of her…and Harry.

Her stomach lurched as if she had just missed a step walking down a flight of stairs; funny how you can plummet into the dark pit of anxiety when your feet are still planted on solid ground. The looming circle of Olivia, Isabella, the two theatre bigwigs, and Harry began to stretch and twist over her head, the sky's flossy pinky clouds stuck in their hair like cotton candy.

A jubilant Isabella turned to Alex. The American's pounding heart filled her ears, leaving all sounds muffled, as if underwater.

"What will you be submitting, Alex?"

It felt like all eyes in the garden were locked on her. She struggled to focus, to find the words. Her Waterloo Bridge idea…way too early to share.

"Go on, Alex. You must have some great ideas brewing…" Harry's voice and raised eyebrows urged her to announce a passion project.

With her body acting out, losing control, her frayed mind couldn't process what to say. The creased pamphlet slipped from her hand.

A half-smile raised the corners of Olivia's lips, its silent threat forcing Alex's stomach into a sickening death spiral.

She swallowed but couldn't wash away the excess saliva flooding her tongue. Choking back tears, she dug her fingernails into her palm. The desire to simply melt like butter through the patio stones, overpowering.

"I was working on something, but…" Her sideways look at Olivia captured the brunette's smile reaching further across her rosy cheeks with each passing second. Alex's breathing disintegrated into jerky, garden-swaying bursts, this rollercoaster ride showing no signs of stopping. "But I…I'm sorry…please excuse me…"

A surge of nausea stung her throat. She scurried away towards the washroom without uttering another word.

Alex's whole body shuddered with each violent spell of vomiting, her throat raw, her face slick with sweat and unrelenting tears. Her left foot lay bare, its corresponding shoe missing in action. Dizzy and scared that she'd pass out on the cold floor, she gripped the toilet bowl to retain some control.

If her career suicide on the patio didn't rank high enough in the humiliation stakes, a jagged shred of light blue and purple material dangled from the metal toilet paper dispenser above her head. She patted a hand over her chest and along her waist. The tear sliced near the hip. Her dress must have snagged during her desperate plunge to the cubicle floor. Forget escaping from this nightmare with her dignity intact. How could she cover up? The warm weather had dictated no need for a coat.

The restroom's wooden door swung open, and a sole female

entered. Alex braced herself in the hopes that she wouldn't vomit while she had company.

Harry was right. These people *would* remember her, but for all the wrong reasons. Her body lurched forward once more, but her stomach had nothing left to expel.

A sterile click of stilettos on the tile bathroom floor halted outside of Alex's stall. She didn't think anything of it until one of the heels kicked her missing shoe underneath the opening of her cubicle's door.

A familiar voice echoed against the walls of the vacant loo. "It must be you. You're the only person who would wear cheap ballet pumps to a society event. Don't bother getting up."

The heels turned towards the wall of mirrors facing the row of stalls. Alex heard a clutch snap open and assumed Olivia was reapplying her lipstick. "Well, that didn't go to script. You weren't meant to be here tonight, but what's a theatrical presentation without a little improv, eh?" Another snap stabbed the quiet.

Alex shook intermittently, waiting for Olivia to speak again, but no further words floated over the stall door.

Olivia strode purposely towards the exit. The washroom's air filled with loud music and enthusiastic voices. A slight breeze wafted in from the open doorway.

The door slammed shut, leaving Alex alone once again.

FOURTEEN

"All the art of living lies in a fine mingling of letting go and
holding on." – Havelock Ellis

Alex climbed into the black cab and fell into the warm embrace
from Lucy and Freddie. Her fingers clung desperately to the rip
in her dress, maintaining what little modesty she had left. Lucy
unfurled a cardigan across the jagged tear, prompting Alex to
release her iron grip. The sickly white hue occupying her blood-
deprived knuckles began its slow retreat. A blush of sunburn
brightened her nose, in contrast with the tear-soaked smudges of
mascara and eyeliner that gave her pale skin a spooky Goth-like
aura.

"Thanks for rescuing me, guys. I didn't know what to do."

"I'm glad you called me. We're here for you no matter
what." Lucy held onto Alex's clutch. "I cannot believe the nerve
of that poisonous bitch. God help her if we're ever face-to-face."

"Actually, you did us a favour," said Freddie, attempting to
make Alex smile. "Lucy's co-workers are *tragic*. If I had to hear
one more word about the 'optimum crunch of a baguette', I was

going to throw myself from the bloody Shard."

"Freds, shush." Lucy turned back to her distressed friend. "What do you want to do? You don't want to sleep there tonight, do you? Should we swing by yours, grab some clothes, then head to mine?"

She shook her head. "No, can we go straight to yours?"

"Sure. I'll loan you some comfies to put on." Lucy leaned towards the cab's plastic partition. "Excuse me, mate. We're headed to Henshaw Street in Southwark. Cheers."

She rubbed Alex's back. "Once we're settled, do you want to go out? It's only eight o'clock. We could go to the pub, whatever you want..."

"No, but I could murder something to eat." Alex wiped her red nose with a shaky hand. "God, I haven't been that sick for ages. I only drank a little champagne."

"I blame that snobby bitch," said Freddie. "Betrayal will turn your stomach every time."

🌂 🌂 🌂 🌂 🌂

Alex stepped out of the teeny upstairs bathroom clad in a pair of Lucy's tracksuit bottoms, an oversized blue Ravenclaw t-shirt, and a dark grey hoodie. She looked like any other recent college grad, except for her puffy eyes, swollen nose, and hunched shoulders.

She wandered downstairs to the living room and flopped on the flowery love seat, tucking her legs underneath her and laying her head on the overstuffed cushions. Freddie claimed the spot to her left, wrapping her in a sympathetic squeeze. Alex sighed, thankful for his gesture.

Lucy's rental was a typical London terrace house. Two

rooms on the ground floor, a small bedroom upstairs along with the bathroom and some storage, and Lucy's bedroom on the third floor—cramped but cozy. The front room of the main floor was the place to hang out, with a small TV and a hodgepodge of DVDs. Lucy's tastes fought for space with her flatmates' favourites. Thankfully, Lucy's were winning. There were far more DVDs dedicated to superheroes, antisocial detectives, and aliens than there were earnest folk rock documentaries. The bongos, spiky plants, and Jethro Tull vinyl clearly didn't belong to Lucy.

A small round table with two chairs gave way to a kitchenette tucked in the back of the house. Lucy popped out, looking pleased. "Good news. Cider with Rosie are boozing it up at a craft beer festival in Camden, so the place is ours. What do you fancy: pizza, fish and chips, kebab?"

"Can I have a grilled cheese sandwich? I'm craving old school American comfort."

"Got it." Lucy disappeared behind the kitchenette's wall.

Freddie pushed the TV remote and a few magazines to the corner of the tiny coffee table so he could stretch out his legs on its surface. "Make me one, too, please?"

Lucy poked her head around the corner, saluting with a spatula in her hand. "Cheese toasties coming up."

Alex rested her head on Freddie's right shoulder, scratching at her swollen eyelids. "I didn't think for a second she'd steal my play. She even pitched Isabella the bit about the male roles being portrayed by women. She didn't leave *anything* behind."

Freddie wanted to say something nasty about Olivia, but held back, sensing Alex's need to vent. He got up to grab the box of tissues near the TV.

"I feel so stupid. I've no one to blame but myself. I handed it to her on a silver platter."

Freddie gave Alex a dismissive scowl.

"I did. I let her read the entire thing. I should never have accepted her offer to 'read it' over." A warm trickle fled from her right eye down her cheek.

Lucy thumped into the room and handed Alex and Freddie each a plate with a grilled cheese sandwich. "Bollocks! You didn't *ask* her to nick it. What did she graduate in? Advanced Bitchery?"

She rushed back into the kitchenette and returned with a tray crammed with her sandwich, ketchup, and several cans of beer and cola.

The cheesy warmth of the toasted sandwich melting on Alex's tongue felt like a little slice of home. She closed her eyes, sending stray tears towards the corners of her mouth. "I've been working on this play for a year, fine-tuning every bit of dialogue, every character, doing research for hours on end, and then in a split second—it's gone. I'll have to start from scratch with another idea." She inhaled sharply. "I have to tell Harry. Let him know what his cow of a girlfriend's done."

Freddie nodded between bites and nudged his glasses up his nose with the back of his hand. "I bet Harry would be livid if he knew that idea was yours. Girls like Olivia need to be brought down a peg or two. Entitled bitch." He cracked open a can of lager. "She shouldn't get away with it just because of who her daddy is or how much bloody money she has. Yeah, you have to tell him."

Lucy furrowed her brow. "Freddie, c'mon. Do you really think that's a smart move?" She violently shook the ketchup bottle and popped the cap. A large red puddle engulfed her sandwich. "I'm not sure telling Harry's such a good idea..."

Alex frowned. "Why?"

"I'm the first person who runs *into* a fight, you know that, but in this situation you're taking on more than Harry and Olivia. I hate to say it—I'd just let it go if I were you."

"Let it go? Harry needs to know what Olivia's really like before it's too late! He doesn't know her." Alex's nails tore desperately at the box of tissues as a collection of new tears conspired in her eyes. "And if I do it soon, maybe I can get my play back."

"Lex, listen, babe. If you tell Harry, he'll take his girlfriend's side." Lucy sat on the loveseat's armrest. "He's known you for what...eight, nine months? How long has he been with Olivia?"

Alex sniffed. "Three, four years? I'm not sure..."

"*Exactly.* They've got history. They have a bond that goes far beyond your uni friendship. You may think he's your friend, but when the chips are down, he'll side with Olivia every time." Lucy dunked her sandwich in the ketchup. "Harry won't want his precious girlfriend upset by some chick he barely knows."

Freddie frowned. "She might have a point."

"Great." Alex abandoned a crust on her plate.

"Telling Harry might make you feel better, but you'll be setting yourself up for a massive shit storm," said Lucy. "I wouldn't want to be there when that comes rolling into town. That girl's a nutter."

Freddie narrowed his eyes. "But don't you have a hard copy of the play?"

Alex nodded.

"So Harry can see that Olivia stole the whole thing. There's tangible proof!"

"Freddie, you know that doesn't matter." Lucy lowered her brows. "So Lex has a hard copy...big fucking deal. Are you forgetting that Harry and Olivia are both stupidly wealthy? They're a different breed from us. He won't be fazed by her theft. Rich people lie, steal, and build their wealth on the backs of little people like us, and if they're threatened—they close ranks. They always look after their own and to hell with everyone else. People like *us* don't matter."

"Down with the bourgeoisie! Up with the proletariat!" Freddie pumped his fist in the air.

Lucy scowled. "Freds."

He shrugged. "Actually, I don't think I'd make a good communist...their fashions are *dreadful*. Carry on."

Lucy sipped her cola and reloaded.

"Olivia and Harry are on track to get engaged—apparently it's only a matter of time. I Googled them both a week back. Harry's family owns one of London's largest and wealthiest property development companies. Olivia's dad is head of the second oldest law firm in England. They're an up-and-coming power couple, Lex—just a few rungs on the social ladder from *royalty*. You really think they'll let all that be derailed by some Yank with a sob story about a stolen play?"

"Fuck me..." Freddie put his head in his hands.

"Harry won't *care* if I have proof?" Alex blew her nose so forcefully it honked. "So, basically, I'm screwed, and no one will believe me? It's such a big fat mess...and on top of that, I've blown it with Isabella."

Freddie interrupted. "I'm sure you didn't."

She shook her head. "You weren't there. Isabella must think I'm a joke. One moment I'm shaking her hand. The next, I'm struck dumb like I'm having a stroke, and for an encore, I run away hyperventilating with my hand covering my mouth, trying not to barf."

Her shoulders twitched at the memory, the embarrassment seeping further into her bones. The remaining half of her sandwich lay on her plate untouched, her hands choosing instead to clutch a wad of disintegrating tissues.

"My idol thinks I'm a blithering idiot."

"Maybe it wasn't as bad as you think?" Lucy shrugged.

Alex pressed her palms against her warm cheeks. "I didn't want to say anything, but…you've both been so great. You should know the whole story about me."

Lucy and Freddie looked at each other.

"I get panic attacks, bad ones." Alex avoided the gaze of her friends. "When they hit, I can't breathe, can't swallow. I get nausea, sweats, dizziness—the works. They started when I was a kid just after Dad left. Stressful or unexpected situations can set them off, but sometimes they arrive out of the blue. It's like a black cloud of dread is suffocating me. My heart pounds out of control. I just…fall apart."

"I used to have a coworker who had them," said Freddie. "She'd be in tears in the loo, and I'd try to talk her through it." He rubbed Alex's left arm. "I had no clue, honey. It must be so difficult."

Alex nodded. "I had one at Heathrow when my bags went missing. It was bad, but at least I didn't faint; I did that once in a store back home. Talk about mortifying. I hate losing control."

"Aw, Lex, please don't feel embarrassed. It's okay." Lucy hugged her. "I'm a terrible friend, so self-absorbed. I should've known."

"You, self-absorbed? As if. How were you to know? I never mentioned them. It's not something I talk about. I've learned that people look at you differently when they know, so I hide them—deal with them on my own."

Alex dropped her chin to her chest. "I thought I had left them behind. After Devin and I broke up, I had a bunch, but then they petered out. Since February, I'd only had one. But I've already had two here—in two weeks. First Heathrow, then again tonight. I can't believe I'm back in the anxiety pit. It scares me. I never know when I'll have another one."

"I'm glad you told us," said Lucy. "It's nothing to be ashamed of. The next time you feel one's coming on, call me, okay? I'm here for you."

Freddie nodded in agreement.

"Thanks…but please don't tell Mark."

"Our lips are sealed," said Lucy.

Alex tugged her hair, somewhat relieved to have spilled her secret. Her mind wouldn't rest though, switching gears. "You know, I think Olivia hates my guts because of my closeness to Harry."

Freddie's eyes lit up. "Really? Do you *fancy* him?"

"No! Harry's just a friend…but it's like she's threatened by the attention he gives me, how well we get along. I wish I could give her head a shake, make her listen."

Freddie grabbed the teetering plate from Alex's lap, placing it on the table. "Well, if you do confront her, tread carefully. God knows what else that toffee-nosed cow has up her sleeve."

A yawn escaped Alex's lips. "It probably won't ever come to that. Right now, the only thing I plan to tackle is sleep…if my mind would just chill out."

"That's my girl," said Lucy. "Things always seem better in the morning."

🌂 🌂 🌂 🌂 🌂

Lucy shuffled down the staircase, bundled in the fuzzy blue co-coon of her *Doctor Who* TARDIS bathrobe. Still groggy, she stopped at the bottom, catching Alex at the front door. "Where are you going? It's only just gone seven."

"To the flat. I need to do this. I need to tell Harry the truth, then have it out with Olivia."

Alex zipped up Lucy's hoodie, her eyes puffy and red. She didn't get much sleep last night. Cider with Rosie tromped in at three in the morning with four slurring pals in tow. The front room became an impromptu sleepover. Crunched for space on the loveseat, Alex tossed and turned, tormented by her thoughts and the rattling snores rising from the floor. It didn't help that she woke up with a painful kink in her neck, either.

Lucy scratched her head. "I thought you *weren't* going to tell him?"

"I know, but I have to. And if there are consequences, so be it." Alex adjusted the waistband of Lucy's borrowed sweatpants.

"Well, I'll come with you. I don't agree with it, but I can't let you face them alone." Lucy turned to climb up the stairs. "Give me a sec to throw on some clothes."

"No, enjoy your Saturday lie-in, what's left of it. If I get there before eight, Harry should still be around."

"Are you sure? I don't mind tagging along with—"

"I'm sure." Alex peeked at her phone. She wanted to get going, now. "I need to do this on my own."

"Well, call me if it goes tits up, okay? I can swing by in a cab; get you and your stuff? Don't worry about my weird flat-mates. I'll smooth it over with them."

Alex turned the door's lock. "Will do."

Lucy grimaced and hugged her friend. "God, the breakfast from hell. I'm glad it's you and not me. Go get 'em, tiger."

Fifteen

Alex took a deep breath in the hopes of reigning in her galloping heart. Her right hand trembled, so she propped it up with her left, turning the key in the lock. The aroma of fresh brewed coffee drifted past the open door. Harry didn't drink coffee; neither did Tom.

Silence hung over the flat apart from the stern tick-tick-tick of the carriage clock. Alex stepped out of her shoes and approached Harry's two towering vases of lilies standing regally on the coffee table. She pinched her nose walking past, the lilies' scent waging war on her nasal passages. A single figure sat further on at the dining table, backlit by the early morning sun spilling from the kitchen's east-facing window.

"I wondered when I'd see you today." Wrapped in her silk robe, Olivia lifted her cup and took a dainty sip. "Have a seat. Care for coffee?"

A simple black hair band held the brunette's tresses off her face, and a slight flush of pink brightened her cheeks. The hue looked effortless and fresh, like the complexion of a china doll.

The blonde shook her head. "No, thanks." She sat down tentatively as if her pockets held a hoard of raw eggs.

No ranting or raving, Olivia seemed calm and friendly, like she was meeting an old friend for breakfast. She placed her coffee gently back on the table, barely making a sound.

Alex looked around the room. "Where's Harry…and Tom?"

"Still asleep. Last night went late."

Olivia stroked her cup with her fingertips, her scarlet manicure shone in the encroaching sunlight. "We had a lot to celebrate. My soirée raised a record amount for charity. All the auction prizes were a hit. We even had a bidding war on the tea with Sir Ian McKellen. I couldn't cross the ballroom without someone hailing my efforts. Even Kevin Spacey congratulated me. It's just a shame that not everyone left the party with a smile." She cocked her sights on Alex.

"It wasn't a night I'll forget." Alex spoke in a hushed tone. She needed to choose her words with care to keep her emotions in check.

Olivia nodded. "Me neither."

Enough with the niceties. This *friend* ship had sailed…and was lost at sea. "Why did you take my idea? Why would you do that to me?"

"I didn't take anything, Alex." Olivia parroted the Floridian's low volume and pushed her shoulders back. "Ideas are commonplace. You can't copyright an *idea*. It's one of the first things we're taught in writing class at university. Don't you remember? Maybe you were sick that day or they skipped that chapter at your *American* school…" Olivia shook her head gently. "…You're so naive. It's quite endearing, actually—but it won't help you in London's theatre world. You need to develop a thicker skin and realize that a good idea is often held by many. Coincidences happen."

Alex crossed her arms. "A coincidence? Really?"

"Quite. Like I said, ideas are *ten a penny*. It's rare to find a good idea that no one else has pondered. You're getting your knickers in a twist over something that's unavoidable in this business." She shrugged and picked up her cup. "Best you learn now, I suppose."

Alex leaned across the table. "But you didn't just hear about an idea. You read the *entire* hardcopy of my play. You took everything—my plans for casting, the relevance to today—all of it. Maybe we should wake Harry so *he* can decide whether what you did was theft or not?"

Olivia stifled a laugh and took a slow sip. "Oh, Alex. You have no idea how bad things can get for you." She raised her eyebrows, returning her coffee to the table. "If you share your stories with Harry, your life here will be over before it even began."

The sharp tick-tick-tick of the carriage clock filled Alex's ears, each strike of its hands chipping away at her confidence.

"One—you'll lose Harry's friendship. Don't think for one *second* he'll believe your schoolyard tales of theft. Do you honestly think he'll believe you over me? He'll take one look at your body language, your shaking hands, trembling lips, and *frankly* unattractive perspiration, and conclude that you're hiding something...just like you are now. Good God, you're actually making the table shake." She snickered softly. "Harry was right. You do have a *little anxiety problem*, don't you?"

Alex jerked away from the table, the jolt sending a flurry of dust particles dancing through a warm sunbeam. Oh God, Harry told her? She wrapped her arms around her waist.

"Two—you'll be homeless. Harry's very protective of me. I'll see to it that he has no choice but to throw you out. Kiss goodbye to the cheapest room rental in London. You won't be able to survive on your earnings from that pathetic café job."

She folded her hands on the table, the amethyst a sparkly reminder of the chasm between her background and Alex's. "And three—you'll be ruined professionally. Did you see the people at my event last night? I'm very well connected. My professional contacts are the crème de la crème of London's theatre world. I'll do everything I can to make sure that no doors are left open to you."

Olivia licked her lips. "And then there's Isabella. Your idol will never forget the American girl who imploded."

An urgent need to pee flooded Alex's bladder. She crossed her legs and scrunched further back into her chair.

"I was mortified on your behalf, truly." Olivia plucked a cigarette from a silver case with OCS engraved in a swirly script on its front. "You should've seen yourself, quaking in front of her, spluttering. That's no way for an aspiring playwright to behave in front of a potential mentor, is it? And when you froze and then scuttled off, sobbing…that must have sealed it for Isabella. You weren't up to the task, and, frankly, would you ever be?"

She lit the cigarette and took a long drag. "If you tell Isabella your little story about this supposed theft, she'll think you're mad. If it was your original idea, why on Earth didn't you say something there and then? A good playwright stands up for what she believes in, and you didn't. You missed your chance. Oh, and FYI, here in England everyone *hates* a tattletale."

Alex's eyes followed the twirling ribbon of cigarette smoke as it floated above Olivia's hand.

Olivia leaned forward, her shadow engulfing Alex. "Now, *hypothetically*—if one *were* to hijack someone else's play—what would spur one on to do such a thing? Envy? Hmm…no. Laziness? Far from it. Perhaps it's payback for a different *kind* of theft?"

She stared at Alex. "I feel it in my bones…you and Harry. I know something went on."

Alex itched her puffy eyes and reminded herself not to shout. "I've already *told* you. He's a friend—nothing more. We never kissed. We never slept together. Why are you fixated on Harry and me?"

"Of course you'd deny it. That's human nature," said Olivia. "Give the girl a gold star for predictability."

Unsure of how to reply, Alex rested her forehead in her clammy hands—anything to avoid Olivia's shark-like eyes. She just wasn't getting it. What's wrong with her?

"I don't blame you." Olivia shook her head. "Every girl wants Harry. He's gorgeous, kindhearted, sees the best in everyone—usually to his own detriment."

She tapped her cigarette, nudging a long ash from its tip into a small glass plate. "He works too hard at Bespoke, and he doesn't need to. The Manville family is old money, and they're successful at keeping it. They're also quite adept at weeding out people who don't belong in their circle. You may see Harry as a friend, but to him you're nothing more than a charity case; a girl who needed temporary shelter, that's all. Funnily enough, his family does have a charitable fund for the homeless…"

Olivia's lips continued to sneer and flap, her words fading in importance as jagged breaths escaped from Alex's mouth. The room began to swing slightly in time with the maddening tick-tick-tick…

No! Not in front of her—not again. Alex concentrated on her breathing, clawing her way back.

"...and let's face it. He's a typical bloke. You may have had your fun, but it didn't mean anything to him. He and I are in it for the long run. He knows what side his bread is buttered. He'd be a fool to let me slip away."

"If you're so convinced Harry and I slept together, why don't you just *ask* him?" Alex struck back like a cornered animal.

"You really don't know how it works in our world, do you? The secret is to keep the upper hand, not to let your man discover *what* you know. Cracks appear in a relationship when you start asking questions. My goal, next to becoming a successful playwright, is to protect what's rightfully *mine* at all costs. I'm going to marry Harry, and no one—certainly not some piece of trash from the Florida swamps—will stop *that* from happening."

Olivia crossed her long legs and reclined comfortably in her chair. "I'm prepared to make a deal with you...It's Harry's big night. We've got dinner and Bespoke's official launch in a few hours. You keep your mouth shut about this silly play, and I'll let you stay here until you find somewhere else to live. But you have to find something soon. I think that's fair, especially when you ponder the alternative—tell Harry, and you'll be tossed to the curb this afternoon. It's that simple."

She inhaled on her cigarette slowly, then allowed an elegant swirl of smoke to escape from her tight lips.

Alex stared at the ceiling. Her toes tapped against the chair leg like a determined woodpecker. Last night, Lucy had called it. Harry would take his girlfriend's side, and there was no way she could triumph over Olivia's reputation or wealth.

Giving in, surrendering...she had no choice. "Fine."

Olivia squinted. "I'm sorry?"

"FINE," Alex repeated, a little too loudly. "I won't say anything, and I'll look for somewhere else to live. I've never felt welcome here anyway."

"Good girl," said Olivia. "If you move soon, you'll be doing Harry a favour. You were only staying here as a token of his good will. It wasn't meant to be permanent. And that room— well, it's hardly even a room, it's a scandal."

The floorboards behind Alex creaked. Her eyes darted over her left shoulder. "I thought I heard voices," said Tom, scratching the sprouting whiskers on his chin. "What are you two whispering about? Girls and their gossip."

Alex let out a deep breath while Olivia's face brightened with a fake smile. "We were just talking about dinner tonight and Harry's official unveiling of Bespoke."

"Argh, the *dinner*. Can I skip it?" He rolled a prescription bottle around in his hands. "Mummy and Daddy dearest are gonna give me an earache."

Olivia scowled. "No! You can't. If you stopped your Tinder shagging spree and went to an audition or two, you'd earn a reprieve."

He rolled his eyes. "And if you got a play commissioned, maybe I'd finally understand why you're the Chadwick-Smythe golden child..."

When Olivia didn't bite, he carried on. "I'm going to hit Bespoke *hard*. Can't wait to get totally trolleyed. Drinks always taste better when they're on someone else's tab." He rifled through the kitchen cupboards, clinking mugs and glassware.

"Well, that someone else will be up soon." Olivia stubbed out her cigarette. "Sooner if you keep banging about."

Tom blanked his sister, pulled an Evian from the fridge, and swallowed a tablet. He tossed the small prescription bottle on the table; the pills rattled as the container rolled across the wood.

"What happened to you, Alex?" He snatched a packet of cigarettes off the counter. "I didn't see you last night."

"I was there but had to rush home. Upset tummy."

Tom's pill bottle stopped, label up in front of her—Azithromycin.

"Gross." His hand scratched his crotch. "Listen, I'm headed to Broadway Market to wander the stalls, maybe grab a bacon butty. Care to join me?"

Olivia hopped to her feet. "I will. I'd like to get something yummy for Harry's lunch, and I fancy a walk through the park. Let me get dressed." She tiptoed towards her bedroom.

"Ooh, lucky me. Spending the morning with Jekyll and Hyde." Tom straightened his jacket over his t-shirt. "Coming, Alex?"

She scrunched up her eyes, desperate for a pee. "No, I seem to have lost my appetite."

☂ ☂ ☂ ☂ ☂

After a quick loo break, Alex retreated to the safety of her room. After jousting with Olivia, she needed some alone time to smooth her feathers. She didn't know what to say to Harry when she saw him anyway. If she kept to herself, perhaps she could avoid him until dinner and have time to figure out what lie to spin about last night's disastrous exit. She collapsed on her futon and dashed off a text to Lucy:

'I'm fine. No getaway car required. Spoke to Olivia. You're right. She's certifiable. Won't speak to Harry. Don't worry. I'll fill in the deets later. Have fun with Freddie today. A x'

She hit send and stared at her laptop…but wait a minute…where *was* the play? Did Olivia take the actual hardcopy?

Alex dived to the floor, checking the small stack that held her thesaurus, dictionary and a few other reference books. The last time she referred to the hardcopy and the professor's notes handwritten in its margins was Wednesday before she switched to the bridge play. She swore that she had left it on top of the thesaurus but in all the craziness of the week, maybe her memory was playing tricks?

She shuffled through the pile of books, then another. Nothing.

Maybe it got shoved in her laptop bag? She tore it open, tossing notebooks on her futon. She fluttered through their pages—just in case. Nope.

Her heart upped its pace, tripping in her chest. She looked around her room, her legs like jelly. Her trembling hands rummaged through her wardrobe, under her futon...

The water pipes in the shower groaned; Harry's up.

She dabbed the sweat on her forehead. Even if she could summon the nerve to ignore Olivia's threats and tell Harry—the rich bitch had left no trace of her heist.

SIXTEEN

In the limo ride from Hackney, no one spoke about last night's fundraiser. Nothing about Alex's hasty escape, Isabella's reaction or how much cash Olivia raised. Harry didn't even ask her how she felt today. Just call her The Invisible Girl.

Instead, the conversation swirled around Olivia's organization of tonight's celebratory feast. She chose the restaurant—Winston's in Mayfair, just a few blocks from Bespoke—the guest list and menu. She even dictated the flowers and the exact brand of candles decorating the tables.

"If the playwriting game doesn't work out, sis, you could reinvent yourself as an upscale party planner." Tom adjusted his red paisley tie in the window's reflection, a cigarette dangling from his lips. Olivia's cheeks warmed, the colour matching her boho-style dress. She motioned 'just stop it' while Harry enveloped her into his black Louis Vuitton suit for a smooch-filled clinch.

Never mind playwriting or party planning, thought Alex—Olivia would make a brilliant actress—cold and biting one moment, loving and charitable the next. Spin the roulette wheel; get a different emotion every time.

She stared at the cutout hem of her navy blue sheath dress. The sting of the last twenty-four hours gnawed at her. Her worry over the missing copy of her play intensified the unshakable ache.

The restaurant staff whisked them through their VIP entrance, checked their coats, and led the way into the private dining room at the back of the venue. Alex lagged behind, her feet already throbbing from her heels. Luxurious carved wood fittings, gleaming antique Art Deco mirrors, pristine white tablecloths, and buttery leather chairs competed for her awe. She had never seen such an opulent restaurant or been treated like a VIP. How long would it take for someone to twig that she didn't belong here?

Harry and Olivia greeted each arriving guest with laughter, air kisses, and handshakes. Close friends, family members, and business partners made the list. The older women in attendance looked waxy—too many cosmetic procedures, perhaps? —the younger women like they'd stepped out of *British Vogue*, and the men, regardless of age, oozed wealth and power in their made-to-measure three-piece suits.

Drink in hand, Tom flicked the collar of his navy blue Ted Baker suit and snuck away, presumably outside to torture his lungs with more cigarette smoke. His parents were busy fawning over Olivia, seemingly unaware of his escape.

Alex stood to the side, alone. She accepted a glass of water from a waitress, hoping that the cool liquid would ease the thickness plaguing her throat. Chattering people passed by her without offering a word. Invisible, again.

The wait staff ran ragged during the cocktail hour, refilling champagne glasses, ensuring that every guest stayed lubricated.

The private room could easily accommodate about sixty people, but tonight's exclusive bash held half that number. Three oblong tables of ten provided plenty of elbow room and comfort.

"Hello. Who are you?" A greying blond gentleman wearing a plaid three-piece suit stared down at her. He was the spitting image of Harry albeit thirty years older.

"I'm Alex. I live with Harry, Olivia, and Tom."

Olivia hovered nearby, monitoring their conversation.

"Nice to meet you, Alex. I'm Harry Sr. I've heard wonderful things about you. My son raved about your kindness while he was in the States. I'm pleased you made it over to England."

Alex's smile didn't linger. She spotted Olivia on the prowl and squeezed her glass.

Harry's dad pointed over his shoulder. "Are you sitting at our table?"

"No, Budgie, darling. Our table's for *family*." Olivia patted his arm. "Alex is seated...elsewhere." She waved her hand towards the third table far from Harry's spot. Banished to social Siberia. No need to guess who created this seating plan.

While Harry Sr. gazed towards Alex's table, Olivia seized the opportunity to shoot the blonde a smirk. "Come along, Budgie. Mustn't waste time. I'd like you to meet our *dearest* friends." She steered him away without pause.

Alex walked around the room, snooping at the names on the table place cards. She found hers and frowned—her chair sat the furthest from Harry. Any further, she'd be in another room.

A hostess announced dinner would be served shortly. Alex claimed her seat, thankful to kick off her shoes. With luck her tablemates wouldn't be stuck-up label slaves, looking down their cosmetically sculpted noses at her non-designer dress.

Tom, Olivia, Harry, and their parents were at the far table

along with three stern-looking businessmen. A few couples filled out Alex's table. Two young women sat down on either side of her.

"Hi, I'm Caprice." A buxom blonde in a plunging orange knee-length dress extended her right hand.

Alex gawped at Caprice's Rubenesque breasts. She didn't mean to stare, but her dress barely contained its voluptuous cargo. Alex shook her hand and gulped, her eyes skimming over her own meagre chest. "Alex. Nice to meet you."

She felt like a thirteen-year-old next to chesty Caprice.

A brunette with a pixie cut sat to Alex's immediate right. She smiled. "Hello. I'm Rosamund. Quite the night, isn't it? How do you know Harry?"

"We met in Atlanta when he was on exchange at Emory. Now I'm his flatmate, well…just temporarily…"

Rosamund's eyes widened. She ran her fingertips over the neckline of her black asymmetrical dress. "Oh, you're the American. Right. Olivia had mentioned you."

Alex shifted in her chair, fussing with the A on her necklace. "I'm here to start my career in the theatre, in writing. How do you guys know them?"

"We go way back," said Caprice. "How long have we been friends with Harry and Olivia, Rosamund?"

"With Olivia, at least ten years, I think. Christ, that makes us sound old, doesn't it?" Rosamund grinned into her glass of champagne. "We went to school with Olivia at Cheltenham. Harry was a champion tennis player at Eton. In the holidays we shared the same large group of friends. All the girls had crushes on Harry. He was quite the ladies' man, but once he set eyes on Olivia, all bets were off. No one else mattered."

Rosamund smiled in Harry's direction. "He was infatuated,

and Olivia was, too; she just didn't let him know it. My God, the hoops she made him jump through! It took him the best part of a year before she agreed to go on a date. That girl played a blinder."

"Love-Forty, then game, set and match. Bitch!" Caprice laughed, finding herself hilarious.

"Olivia could write the book on playing hard-to-get. She's brilliant," said Rosamund.

Caprice looked wistfully at Harry and Olivia's table. "I wish they'd hurry up and get hitched. Now *that* will be wedding of the year. I'm already eyeing up a Dior gown for my bridesmaid's dress."

Alex didn't know what else to talk about. Since Caprice mentioned dresses, it seemed like a safe bet.

"I love the colour of your dress. It's so vibrant. Perfect for spring."

"Thanks. It's Roland Mouret. I saw Reese Witherspoon wearing it in *Hello!*, and *had* to buy it." Caprice's eyes swept down Alex's dress with nary a compliment. "I would've loved to wear the Victoria Beckham, but Rosamund called dibs."

Rosamund shrugged. "It's Olivia's, actually. She lent it to me last year." She played with a weighty chandelier of diamonds dangling from her left ear. Just one of her earrings would likely have paid for Alex's entire college education. "When I walked in tonight, she told me to keep it. Love that girl."

A waiter interrupted the banter, handing elegant menus to Caprice, Rosamund, and Alex. She looked up to thank him and gasped.

"Oh my God, Mark! You work here?"

"Alex. Hi!" He glanced at the other guests. "What are you doing *here*?" Mark seemed just as surprised as Alex to see a

166

friendly face. The black trousers, white shirt, and purple tie looked familiar; he'd worn the same thing at the Castle pub last weekend. A lock of black hair fell mischievously over his forehead. She desperately wanted to sweep it back in place.

So giddy, seeing him unexpectedly, Alex's cheekiness ran away with her tongue. "Pleased to see me then?"

He stifled a laugh, and leaned in, his tone conspiratorial. "More than you'll *ever* know."

Alex couldn't stop smiling. "Actually, my flatmate Harry, his club's officially opening tonight, so we're celebrating."

Caprice and Rosamund stared silently at their menus, obviously eavesdropping on the conversation.

"He picked quite the place. The food's extravagant and beautifully presented." Mark ignored her tablemates, hesitant to take his eyes off her. He leaned in and whispered. "You look amazing, by the way."

Alex's toes curled. She pinched her hand under the tablecloth as a reminder to breathe. "How long have you worked here?"

"A year. A struggling actor has to pay the bills somehow." He continued down the table and beamed back at her while discretely handing menus to the guests. Alex gave his butt a good stare, but she wasn't the only one.

"Ooh, he's yummy. I know what I want for my main course." Caprice couldn't peel her eyes away. "He'd make a nice change from my monthly pity bonk with Tom." She redistributed her chesty arsenal, like a courtesan preparing to seduce a reluctant prince.

"Stop flashing your assets, Caprice. Can't take you anywhere." Rosamund glared at her friend, then looked back at Alex. "How do you know the Irish hottie?"

She winced at their interest. "He's a friend."

"Just a friend? That sparkle in your eye tells me you fancy him," said Rosamund.

Alex fiddled with the cutout hem of her dress. Shoot, too obvious.

Rosamund licked her lips and excused herself from the table. "I need to reapply my lipstick. I'll be…right back."

She pranced away in her Louboutin heels, stopping briefly at the far table to whisper in Olivia's ear. They both laughed, and she toddled off. Olivia glanced over, smiled, and raised her glass to Alex.

"I'd like to propose a toast." Harry's voice commanded his guests' attention in the private dining room. "As you know, Bespoke has been a passion of mine for some time. Creating a refined, upscale private members club for my friends, family, and business associates is a dream come true. A place to unwind, enjoy fine beverages and food, and network without the intrusion of the general public—Bespoke is for all of you."

All of us? Alex squinted at her water glass.

"It's taken plenty of blood, sweat, and tears to reach this point. Bespoke is officially open tonight. And I'm thrilled to be able to share this moment with you."

Harry smiled and looked at his dad sat two seats away on his right. "I would be amiss if I didn't thank two people. First, my father. He could've easily dissuaded me from taking on this challenge and ushered me into commercial property development like his dad did with him. But he took a gamble, put his trust and a few quid behind me, and well…here we are."

The three tables erupted in applause and cheers. His dad

raised his hand to acknowledge their kudos.

"The second person needs no introduction." Harry took a deep breath, inching closer to Olivia on his left. "You all know how important she is to me. Everything I do is for her..."

"Aw, so sweet." Caprice couldn't help herself.

"...I'm a better person because of her."

Olivia stared up at him and placed her hand over her heart. Alex swore a single tear rolled down his girlfriend's cheek. She's good; right on cue.

Tom yawned and jumped the gun on Harry's toast, swigging his champagne.

Harry lifted his glass into the air and surveyed the room. "So please raise a glass to Dad, to Olivia, and finally to Bespoke—entertainment tailor-made for a different class."

The chosen few toasted Harry's speech, sipped their champagne and then returned to their conversations. Alex didn't join in. A more pressing concern held her hostage—hunger. It somersaulted in her belly. She glanced over the set menu. Options included shellfish cocktail, Dorset crab, and Orkney scallops as starters. The mains boasted Grilled Wester Ross salmon, a shrimp burger, or dressed Portland crab.

Unlike most natives of the Florida coast, Alex suffered from a serious seafood allergy. Oysters, lobster, shrimp—she couldn't eat any of it unless she fancied a date with the nearest emergency room. The only fish she seemed able to eat without problems were haddock or cod. Shame traditional beer battered fish and chips didn't make this menu's cut. Not posh enough for Olivia's palate, obviously.

A waitress placed an artistically arranged salad in front of her. Sprigs of mesclun greens stood piled high like a grassy teepee, garnished with walnuts, chunks of beets, and goat's cheese.

Alex watched Rosamund for guidance on which fork to select and began picking apart the salad's red oak leaf lettuce, baby spinach, and curly endive layers. Did any shrimp or lobster pieces lurk underneath? All clear.

The server returned, cradling a basket of thickly sliced artisan bread. Alex loaded up her side plate. Caprice and Rosamund each tossed the blonde a dismissive glance.

"Steady on, Alex. That's a lot of carbs," said Rosamund. She smirked and resumed her banal conversation with Caprice about handbags, blowouts in Kensington, and how to land a role on a reality TV show called *Made in Chelsea*.

Alex slumped in her chair, alone but for the slices of bread and a blob of butter on her side plate. Mark hadn't returned to her end of the room. Harry's table had the pleasure of his service. She watched his every move, hoping he would break away and speak to her again.

The wait staff hovered, hastily collecting empty dishes before the arrival of the dessert, or pudding course as it was labeled on the menus. Alex's plates were spirited away virtually untouched, her involvement in the meal stretching to a few seasoned spring potatoes. She thought about sneaking off to the loo to gobble her last package of Twizzlers stashed in her clutch, but spotted Harry strolling around her table, asking his guests how they enjoyed the meal.

"Olivia outdid herself again." Rosamund's diamond earrings glittered and swung with each compliment. "Such succulent scallops. Just excellent."

"Alex, did you enjoy it?" Harry smiled.

Caprice jumped in before Alex could speak. "She ate bread and potatoes. Someone's carb loading. What's next, Alex? A pre-Bespoke pit stop at the golden arches." She slurped her fourth champagne and giggled.

Alex scowled at her. "It was either that or go hungry. Or to the ER." She turned to Harry. "My seafood allergy... remember?"

"Oh bugger, right. Sorry, I completely forgot. The menu was Olivia's baby; I had no control over it. By all means, fill up on pudding. Don't leave here hungry."

"You can have mine," Caprice butted in. "It's not a good look, eating pudding."

Harry ignored her and kneeled down. "Are you feeling okay? I was worried about you last night. You weren't yourself." He leaned in, speaking behind his hand. "Panic attack?"

Why was Harry showing discretion *now*? He had already blabbed her anxiety secret to Olivia...why not the rest of the world? His disloyalty stung.

"It was all a bit much." She nodded. "The curse of the unexpected."

"I should've told you Isabella was invited, given you time to get used to the idea, so you weren't overwhelmed. I'm *really* sorry." Harry stood up, putting a comforting hand on her shoulder.

Alex wanted to tell him the truth—that Isabella's appearance wasn't to blame—but one glance in Olivia's direction put paid to that fleeting notion. Harry's girlfriend stared at her, like she could read lips from across the room.

"Look, don't worry about it." Alex's eyes dove to her lap so they didn't betray what she really wanted to say.

"I should head back. Olivia's in a foul mood."

Alex squinted. "Oh yeah?"

"One of the waiters, the Irish bloke. He's wound her up something awful. First of all, her wine was warm. Then her meal was cold, so she sent it back. She says he's getting *everything* arse-backwards. I hate seeing her irritated. She's worked hard putting all of this together. If he thinks he's getting a tip, he's got another bloody thing coming."

Alex's mouth fell open. The only jobs she'd ever held were service positions—in bookshops, theatres, department stores, and now in the café. Not easy work by any means. She guessed Harry had never served a demanding customer in his life.

He looked back at his table. "But enough about some silly waiter. Enjoy your pudding. And save me a dance at Bespoke, okay?"

A false grin flashed across her face. It didn't register with Harry. He hurried back to his seat, squeezing Olivia's right shoulder before sitting down. She cuddled into the crook of his neck.

Alex rubbed her brow. Harry's comments reminded her of that old saying—something about gauging people's character by the way they treated waiters. *Wow*. Was Harry always condescending to people serving him? How did she miss it before? She slouched in her chair as the waitress wheeled out the pudding trolley with a choice of Kir Royale sorbet, William Pear Tarte or a chocolate and clementine bomb. Alex half-heartedly chose chocolate. She'd eat around the hideous orange wedges.

Harry's words clouded her thoughts—'*He's wound her up something awful.*' She hadn't known Mark long—but he was warm and friendly, if nothing else. Surely the problem lay with Olivia and not Mark's serving skills...

She sipped her water, her eyes glued to the far side of the

room. Mark reappeared through a doorway, expertly presenting pudding with a smile for each guest. He didn't give off any vibes of impertinence or incompetence.

Next, Olivia's turn. Mark approached her left side, his arm steady and the plate's delivery smooth. But as his hand withdrew, a splash of wine flew into the air, sloshing Olivia's chest. She shrieked and jolted out of her chair like she had been zapped with a taser.

"You IDIOT!" Olivia raised her arms to shoulder height and shook them with a dramatic flourish like an injured bird trying to take flight. "You did that on *purpose*. You've ruined my Matthew Williamson!"

The empty crystal glass shimmered in the light as it rolled across the sopping tablecloth before it disappeared towards the floor, shattering into countless slivers.

Alex gagged on her water. *What the…*

An uneasy buzz swept across the room like storm clouds rolling in over a once tranquil lake. Harry shot up, shoving his chair backwards, the surge hurling it onto its side where it landed with a wooden crack.

"I'm sorry, Miss." Mark's eyes widened. "I thought I stayed clear of your glass…let me get you some towels…"

"Okay, fella. That's enough." Harry threw his napkin onto the table and clasped Mark at the shoulder, guiding him forcefully through the private dining room's door and into the public section of the restaurant. The heavy wood door slammed, concealing any further interaction between the two.

Guests exchanged accusatory whispers and indignant looks. Alex sprang up onto her toes for a better vantage point. Olivia's mother rushed to her daughter's aid.

"Oh, Mummy." Olivia wobbled on the cusp of collapse and

sank into her mother's arms.

"Just awful." Rosamund leapt out of her chair to support her friend. Caprice, on the other hand, remained planted in her seat, tossing back her fifth glass of champagne.

Grabbing every clean linen napkin handed to her, Olivia's mother blotted the chest and hip area of Olivia's pale pink dress. "Thank God you weren't drinking red," said Rosamund, snatching extra napkins from the table.

Olivia tore her hands away from her eyes, throwing her friend a dirty look. Rosamund gulped. "Granted, Livvy, it won't be fun wearing a wine-soaked dress to the club…"

Tom, with his front row seat to the pantomime, cocked an eyebrow, and stuffed an unlit cigarette between his lips. He plucked a fellow diner's full wine glass from the table. "Well, that's me done. Hope you enjoyed the show, folks. *We're here all week. Try the veal.*" He loosened his tie and strolled off laughing towards the exit. His father bristled with disapproval.

Olivia's dramatic wails continued. Alex shook her head. If a stranger had walked into the room, you couldn't blame them for thinking Olivia had been the victim of a serious assault, not a spilled glass of wine. *So* over the top.

"I had every detail organized…" Olivia laid it on thick. "…and then this *lowlife* ruins it in a single second."

Her gathering sycophants agreed and continued to tend to her ego and damp dress.

It didn't look *that* bad. A wet splotch the size of two small hands, maybe? Alex scrunched up her nose. And seriously…*lowlife*? Mark was a waiter, not a petty criminal.

Two servers dashed into the room overburdened with white cotton towels to mop up the spill. A third brought a dustpan and brush to sweep up the glass shards.

Harry slipped through the door, red in the face. He dragged his hand through his blond hair. "Sorry, everyone, can't get the staff these days!"

The room laughed at Harry's inside joke—everyone except Alex. She drooped into her chair.

As the guests returned to their seats, the owner of Winston's stepped into Harry's shadow. "I'm terribly sorry for this unfortunate accident, Mr. Manville. You can rest assured; we'll make this right." He signaled to the staff to top up everyone's glasses.

Olivia's mother piped up, a little too loudly. "Let this be a lesson, Harry. When it comes to cleaning or gardening staff, one simply doesn't have a choice. But if I were you, I'd avoid hiring immigrants as staff who deal directly with your customers."

Harry snickered. "Oh, Penelope. You know very well you can't say that sort of thing in public these days. It's not politically correct."

"After my *fifth* martini, darling, I say whatever I *please.*"

Friends and family guffawed. Alex cringed. God—Lucy's right. These people were *awful*.

The hovering owner snatched Olivia's wine-soaked leather chair and replaced it with a dry one. She gingerly sat back as he nudged it underneath her. He whispered something in Harry's ear and retreated back into the public section of the restaurant.

Harry addressed his guests. "Sorry for the unexpected drama. Enjoy your pudding and flag a server if you'd like more wine or champagne. Tea and specialty coffees are also available for those pacing themselves for the night ahead." He placed a reassuring hand on Olivia's neck and gently kissed her lips.

Alex's chocolate dessert teased and tempted, but she pushed it away without even a taste.

SEVENTEEN

Four shiny limousines whisked Harry's younger guests to Bespoke. The parade of cars didn't have far to go, only five blocks. Blisters ringed her heels, but Alex wanted to walk. The stuffy, narrow-minded snobs surrounding Harry made her want to throw up. Worse still, he acted like a completely different person. Sure, side with your girlfriend, but don't manhandle a waiter out of the room, belittling him in front of everyone.

Her eyes searched Winston's main dining area on the way out. No sign of Mark—anywhere. Wait staff buzzed around the tables, balancing large platters piled high with crab's legs and lobster. Still no Mark. She wrapped her trench coat around her slight frame and teetered outside onto the wet pavement.

"Alex. Where you going? Get in the car." Tom lingered outside Winston's with a smoke, his habit holding up the last limo from departing on its ridiculously brief journey.

"Go without me. I've got a headache. The fresh air will do me good." She also needed time to think without banal mentions of polo parties or expensive skiing holidays in France.

Tom stubbed out his cigarette on the sidewalk with his shoe.

"No, you don't. Come on. Besides, you won't get in the club if you walk up to the bouncers on your own." He slinked over to her and slipped his arm around her waist.

She shot one more look towards the restaurant's entrance and climbed into the empty car. Tom pounced in behind her, prattling on about the DJ at Bespoke and what great mates they were—like she cared. She ached to talk with Mark and make sure he was okay.

The silky voice of Beyoncé floated out the front door of Bespoke. Red velvet ropes and two burly bouncers with Bluetooth earpieces guarded the entrance like tuxedoed trolls. Tom wrapped his arm around Alex's shoulders and slid them both through the crush of models and trustfunders. He winked at Harry's PR girl. She blew him a kiss and checked off his name.

She yelled in his ear. "Who's your plus one, Tom?"

"Alex." He looked over the PR woman's shoulder, scanning the room while removing his tie.

She flipped the page on her clipboard, her eyes searching back and forth. "Alice? Your name's Alice *what*?"

Alex helped her out. "No, my name is Alex. Alex Sinclair."

"Alice Sinclair...I can't find you."

Alex rolled her eyes. "No. It's Alex... A...L...E...X.."

"Right...Found you." Her pen ticked the page. "Go in."

Tom dropped his arm from Alex's back, tuning his radar to a nearby trio of overly tanned women wearing skirts so short that they'd make a gynecologist nervous. He leaned down, shouting in Alex's ear. "*You good?*"

She winced. "I'm fine. Go. Have fun."

He scampered off, grabbing a glass of champagne from a passing tray. He disappeared under six enthusiastic orange arms.

Alex squeezed past a group of boisterous men and removed

her trench. The coat check girl gladly accepted it, handing Alex a small silver button in return. Cute. It matched the Bespoke tailoring theme.

Harry's club gleamed in polished chrome, glass, and mirrors. Modern and sleek in design, the vibe leaned more towards cool and stark than welcoming and relaxing. A narrow hall gave way to a large room, its outer reaches accessorized with onyx leather banquettes and booths. Servers of both sexes dressed in tailored black shirts and trousers doled out champagne and specialty cocktails. Another wave of staff offered fancy finger foods—mini burgers, crispy squid skewers, and black paper cones filled with fries drizzled with truffle oil. A long bar decorated in gold and black ran the length of the right side of the venue, and the DJ—Tom's new best friend—rallied the elite crowd of celeb A-listers, models, and hedge funders from a perch high in the far left corner. London's beautiful people spilled out onto the dance floor; designer mini dresses, and sharp cut suits ruled the night.

Alex limped to the bar and kicked off her right heel, bending down to inspect her foot. An orange blur bounced behind her, hollering in her ear.

"Alllll-ex. You'll never guess who's here...*Pippa Middleton*." Caprice weaved. "I wonder if her sister's hot brother-in-law came with. I would've asked her, but she's surrounded by a swarm of Russian money." She gulped her glass; a cascade of champagne slopped on her heaving breasts.

Alex backed away from the spluttering socialite, but someone blocked her escape.

"There you are." Olivia smiled down at both Caprice and Alex. "Caprice, darling, Rosamund's looking for you. Head towards the VIP area; you'll find her there. Last I saw, she was

178

chatting with Emma Watson."

Alex's pulse raced. What did Olivia want *now*? Her eyes narrowed as she stuffed her foot back into the torture device disguised as her shoe.

"Emma Wa—? I'm so there. Maybe I can bag a Russian billionaire while I'm at it. Thanks, babe." Caprice toddled off precariously, turning an ankle in the process. Her boozy haze probably numbed any pain.

"Isn't this a fantastic evening?" Olivia's eyes danced across the room. "It's turned out even better than I imagined."

Alex bit her tongue.

Olivia leaned in and stretched her right arm and fingers across the bar, like a feline unfurling its claws. Alex couldn't budge. "Rosamund told me something fascinating at dinner."

"So?"

"The Irish waiter? He was quite the dish." The brunette chuckled, her breath champagne-soaked. "When I found out you two were friends, I decided to have some fun with him."

Alex's eyebrows scrunched.

"I complained about the wine, sent my meal back." She snickered. "But actually, nothing was wrong. Everything was perfect. And he handled my outrageous requests professionally and patiently. So *boring*. So I upped the stakes."

"What?" Alex scowled.

"He didn't knock over my glass. I did!" She smoothed down her dress. Damage from wine-aggedon? Not a trace.

"I suppose most waiters would just receive a reprimand for being clumsy, but I *told* you, didn't I? Our families are well connected. We're some of Mr. Winston's most valued customers— and he was *mortified* to see how upset I was."

A tightness squeezed Alex's throat. "What did you *do*?" Her vision blurred.

"Duuurgh! *Do* keep up, Alex!" She glanced at her glittery watch. "He's probably cleaned out his locker by now…"

Alex shoved past Olivia and through the thick throng of partygoers. At the coat check counter, the numbered silver button slipped from her shaking hand, clinking and rolling amidst the Jimmy Choos and Louboutins. She knelt down, her palms padding the floor under the disdainful stares and unpredictable feet of arriving guests.

"Looking for this?" A male voice floated over her shoulder.

She swiveled to her right. Ohmagod! She blinked several times. *Rupert Grint.* Crouching down beside her, holding her coat check button. First Emma Watson and now…this…a verifiable *Harry Potter*-palooza.

"Yes, thank you." Alex accepted the silver disc from Rupert's hand. She stared at the ginger-haired actor as he lifted her up.

"Happy to help." He smiled and rejoined his friends, who were discarding their jackets.

She caught her breath and slid the button towards the woman behind the counter. At any other time, she'd be buzzing like a fangirl over Rupert, but Mark mattered more.

Coat in hand, she hobbled through the scrum at the front door, desperate to get back to Winston's to catch Mark.

"No, no, no. Please be there."

In her haste, several fleshy blisters pinched their dissatisfaction, each step like a sharp pencil piercing her toes and heels. She took a peek. Great. Splotches of blood had soaked into the lining. Screw elegance. She ripped off her heels and ran barefoot along the damp sidewalk, juggling both shoes and her clutch. The doorman at Winston's glowered at her dirty bare feet. He made no attempt to open the door for her.

"H-h-hello. I was part of the Manville private party earlier. I forgot something inside. Could I please see the hostess?"

He pursed his lips and yanked open the heavy door just as raindrops began to speckle her coat. Alex stumbled towards the hostess desk and a blonde woman wearing a striking form-fitting grey dress.

"Good evening. I was here with Harry Manville's party an hour ago. I need to speak to one of the servers who waited on our group, Mark Keegan. Is he here?" She held her breath, her heart pounding. One of her heels slipped from her hands and bounced on the floor.

The hostess blinked her smoky eyes a few times and shot a look over her shoulder. "Mark? He's…left for the evening. I'm afraid you've missed him."

Alex exhaled and tapped her fingers on the edge of the desk. "Shoot, okay…okay…right. Is he working tomorrow?"

The employee swallowed and fussed with papers on the desk. "Actually…as of tonight he's no longer employed by Winston's."

The pinball machine in Alex's stomach crashed into a game-changing tilt.

Alex's other shoe dropped, landing on her blistered bare toes. The sharp pain in her feet tingled, dissolving into a creeping numbness that swallowed her quivering legs like quicksand. "What?! Shit, Olivi—"

She caught herself. "Sorry…okay, thanks for letting me know."

Stepping carefully into her shoes, she pulled her coat closed. Out in the street, the doorman held a large golf umbrella over her head. "Taxi, miss?"

She shook her head, ducking away from its refuge. Rain beat down without mercy, her trench coat unable to keep up with the wet onslaught. Alex didn't feel a drop as she limped into the road.

He'd been fired. It was all her fault.

A honking taxi burst her foggy bubble. She staggered back onto the curb towards an antiques store, its wide green awning offering a dry sanctuary to text. Her shaky fingers fought with the autocorrect:

'Mark, are you okay?'

She shivered in the chilly rain, waiting for an answer.

Five minutes passed…nothing. Time for another text:

'Freddie, have you heard from Mark? x'

Several cars splashed by, fogged up with Saturday night pleasure seekers. Drunken patrons from a nearby bar staggered past. Alex opened Facebook on her phone, and with a few swipes and taps, unfriended Olivia. She blocked her from both Twitter and Instagram, too. The rain eased into a sporadic trickle, so she slouched off towards the nearest Tube station. Her phone finally pinged.

'Mark's here. Meet us at The Cut, the bar in the Young Vic Theatre. Southwark Tube. F xo'

Alex pulled open the door to The Cut, unleashing a lively roar that spilled onto the wet South Bank street. She ignored the busy stairway leading to the upper level and scanned the packed ground floor. Thirsty patrons three deep jostled by the bar. The rest of the space boasted scattered tables and chairs—every seat taken.

Lucy spotted her from a table tucked beside the window in the far left corner. She waved her hand, catching Alex's attention.

"Party over already?" Freddie smirked as he stood up to squeeze Alex. "What are you drinking?"

"Jack Daniels and Coke, please."

"Since *when*?" said Lucy.

"Since *now*. Shit night deserves a hard drink."

"On it." Freddie deked to the side so Alex could slip through to the vacant chair across from Mark and against the window. "Another round?" Mark and Lucy nodded, and he disappeared towards the bar.

Lucy reached diagonally across the table to hug her friend, just clearing the crowd of beer cans.

Mark waited for them to finish and stood up to hug Alex, too. His stubble tickled her cheek. Alex pressed in even closer, a dream come true. She had fantasized about his face against hers, breathing in his sexy, clean scent. But his arms held her only fleetingly like an embrace from a stranger. She stepped back with a quivery smile, her heart sinking along with her hopes for a warm reunion.

"I didn't think we'd see you so soon," said Lucy. "Then again, I didn't think we'd see Mark at all this evening."

He ran a hand through his dark hair and leaned back in his chair, angled away from Alex. "Who says there's no drama in waiting tables, eh?"

Alex sat down, hugging her clutch, her rain dappled coat still buttoned up to the neck. "Are you okay, Mark?" She swallowed, trying to soothe her dry mouth. "I know what Olivia did. She couldn't wait to tell me at Bespoke."

"Yeah, she had it in for me. Plain and simple." He tugged

at the shoulder of his white shirt, popping a button open below his collarbone. A flash of his chest teased her from across the table. "She complained through the entire meal, but I sucked it up, polite as you please. I've seen her kind before, but then she pulled a bloody kamikaze move on her own wine glass."

Alex blinked down at the table and bit her lip. "I think it's *my* fault. Those friends of hers at dinner...I told Olivia's flying monkeys that I knew you." Her voice cracked. "I think Olivia got you fired...just to prove her power to me."

Mark shrugged and crossed his arms, his lean biceps bulging under the pressure. He seemed...standoffish.

"Don't worry about it. You might want to consider finding new friends, though."

Alex jumped in, shaking her head. "Oh God, no. Olivia's not my friend. Her boyfriend Harry's my friend, although I'm starting to re-think that after tonight."

"Really?" said Lucy. "He went along with her bullshit, then?"

"All of it." Alex kicked off her heels. "He said some disappointing things, too."

"That guy seems like an arse—plus he's got shite taste in women," said Mark.

"Maybe I could say something to Harry. Get your job back? If he would just listen, I'm sure I could convince him that—"

Mark shook his head. "Alex, leave it. Seriously. Don't waste your breath."

Lucy nodded. "Didn't I tell you? Harry and Olivia are one and the same, cut from the same cloth."

"Lucy, you don't know him like I do—"

"But do you *really* know him?"

Alex sank back into her chair.

Freddie parked a round tray of drinks and crisp bags on the table. He placed a Jack and Coke in front of Alex, gave Mark and Lucy each a can of Amber Ale, and kept an Aspalls cider for himself. "What did I miss?"

"They're powerful, rich, concerned only with themselves." Mark sipped his beer, his eyes narrow. "God knows what else they're capable of. I'd drop it if I were you."

"But you lost your job..."

He let out a half laugh. "I appreciate your concern, Alex, really I do, but I'm not half as upset as you are. I hated wearing a tie for work. Glad to be rid."

"Silver lining," said Lucy, ripping open a crisp packet.

"Waiter and bartending jobs...they're easy enough to land here. I'll get another. Actually, a friend mentioned that the National Theatre was hiring bar staff. I'll head over there Monday morning and apply."

Freddie fist pumped the air. "Yes. *Free booze* when we go to the theatre!"

Mark smiled and cocked his right eyebrow. "I've just lost one waiting job, Freds. I don't plan on losing another."

Alex rested her clutch on the table and slowly unbuttoned her damp trench, leaving it to pool on the chair behind her.

"Pretty dress, Lex," said Lucy. "Shame it was wasted on *them*."

Mark nodded, his expression softening. "Before you walked in, Lucy had started to tell me about last night. Something about Olivia and a fundraiser?"

Alex frowned. "Yeah, she stole my play idea. Pitched it to Isabella Archer, right in front of me. This morning when I confronted her, she said she didn't steal anything—'*you can't copyright an idea, Alex*'. And to keep me in my place, she threatened my friendship with Harry and said she'd ruin me in the theatre community if I blabbed to anyone."

"Told you so!" said Freddie.

Mark shook his head. "Jesus, what a bitch." He leaned in. "Why are you hanging around with these people?"

Alex rubbed her furrowed brow. "They're the first people I met here. I didn't know anyone else until I ran into Lucy." A small sip of JD and Coke passed her lips.

"I've seen them before at Winston's. They're a rich bunch—fair dues, I have no problem with that—but they're elitist and full of themselves. Always looking down their noses, you know? To be honest, it really threw me seeing you there. It made me second guess what I knew about you."

His comment stung. Alex's eyes widened. "I'm hardly *rich*. Definitely not *elitist*. I work in a greasy spoon, I shop at H&M… hell, give me a few more weeks, I'll probably be addicted to that Primark chain, too."

Lucy rested her head on Mark's left shoulder. "Bet you wondered where we picked up this wealthy snob, eh, Keegs?"

He stole a few of Lucy's crisps and unleashed his devastating smile. "I did wonder…"

His grin melted away any lingering iciness. Alex caught his eye and held her breath, waiting for what he'd say next.

"But in all seriousness, Alex—*be careful*. I don't think you can't trust any of them, even Harry."

She swallowed a gulp of her drink, sending a burning torrent down her throat, but once the warmth dissipated, the heaviness in her heart hijacked her attention. Everything that Lucy had warned her about had come to pass. She'd seen how spiteful Olivia could be and how blind Harry was to his girlfriend's faults. Had she been wrong about Harry all along?

EIGHTEEN

June evaporated into July—a blur of café shifts and marathon
writing sessions at various coffee shops. Evenings and week-
ends, Alex reserved for Lucy and Freddie. The more time spent
away from her flatmates, the better, but it didn't calm the root-
less feeling that bore into Alex's restless heart. If anything, all
this shuffling about made her turbulence worse.

At some point, Olivia must have submitted the stolen suffragette play to Isabella's mentorship program. Alex didn't know
for sure. Only a few terse words had been exchanged between
the two since the night Olivia had Mark fired. Bespoke owned
Harry, so Alex never saw him. Occasionally her ears were tormented by Tom's hook-ups or she'd catch his conquests tiptoe-
ing from his room, but apart from that, she felt like a ghost rattling around the Martello Street flat on her own.

The theft of her play and the toxic flat environment extin-
guished her spark. London hadn't been kind so far.

It didn't help that homesickness soured her stomach. She
didn't pine for her mom or Tallahassee, but she longed for familiar comforts: her spacious room, her go-to diner with its mouth-

watering hush puppy recipe, and cheesy American daytime TV. She missed the family cat. She missed constant sunshine. She missed Twizzlers.

Adrift between her old life and her new one.

Freddie and Lucy tried to distract Alex by showing off her new hometown on the cheap. City-wide rides atop double-decker buses, strolls along the Thames, and excursions to Tower Bridge, the Changing of the Guard, and Camden Market put a slight dent in her wallowing, but nostalgia still threatened to yank her backwards. Despite protestations to the contrary, Alex was crap at letting go. Detaching from her old life was proving more difficult than she ever expected.

The arrival of July 6—her birthday—required extra care. Lucy and Freddie chose the Pizza Express across from the Royal Festival Hall for dinner celebrations. Thank goodness Alex wore a floaty blue and white striped slip dress. A waistband would have meant bellyache central. Garlic butter-drenched dough balls, thin pizzas, and gooey chocolate cake slices left all three diners begging for gastronomical mercy.

The birthday girl beamed. "You're too good to me. It's been a great twenty-second birthday. Thank you." They stepped outside, embraced immediately by the unseasonably humid July air.

"I've missed that smiley face," said Freddie. "Keep those cheeks warmed up; the surprises aren't over yet."

"I hate surprises," said Alex.

"Ah, shut up. C'mon!" Freddie motioned for her and Lucy to cross Belvedere Road.

Lucy hopped over each crack in the pavement, her canary yellow shirtdress billowing with each leap. Alex smiled at her friend's quirkiness, but pulled her attention away to check out the bridge stretching over their heads. Waterloo Bridge—the very bridge in her new play.

If this overpass was Waterloo Bridge, then right next door stood...

She halted in her tracks, her eyes wild in the dwindling light. "It's *not*?!" Her voice echoed against its cement arch. She sprinted past the rack of 'Boris bikes' lining the bridge's under-belly.

...The National Theatre.

"We know you're a walking Wikipedia page about this place, and you've been dying to visit, so we figured, why wait until we score tickets?" said Lucy, increasing her speed to match Alex's sprint along Theatre Avenue.

Alex gazed at the massive concrete building on her right, biting down on her smile. "Someone pinch me." Her eyes lit up when the statue of Sir Laurence Olivier popped into view near the front entrance. "All the acting legends that have tread the boards here."

"The building's a bit...ugly though, isn't it?" said Freddie.

"I think she's beautiful," said Alex.

The early evening breeze from the Thames whispered across the forecourt, tickling the leaves in the trees and propel-ling soapy bubbles from a street performer high into the pink and orange sky. Blissful pedestrians strolled in bunches, their laugh-ter lending a sweet, magical soundtrack to this birthday surprise.

Alex bounced on her tiptoes, toying with the strap of her bag. "Can we go in?"

Freddie waved her forward. "Of course."

The sliding glass doors whisked open, welcoming them into the stark yet expansive lobby of monolithic cement pillars, and soft circular benches. They passed the busy box office counter on the right and stopped just short of the bookshop, its shelves happily offering play texts and souvenirs to the bustling pre-theatre crowd.

"We wanted to give you a taste of the place," said Lucy. "We'll definitely come back and see a play here. Fancy a drink on the balcony overlooking the Thames?"

Alex laughed. "What kind of a question is that?"

They rushed up the stairs, dodging theatregoers up one level, then another. Lucy queued at the bar while Freddie and Alex went outside onto a wide cement balcony, its railing ill-equipped to contain the birthday girl's overflowing enthusiasm.

She leaned forward, her eyes spoilt for choice. The sleepy sun glinted on the dome of St. Paul's, creating a hazy fireball across the river. On the ground below, a guitar-toting duo rocked a makeshift stage surrounded by red National Theatre deck chairs, a scattering of round tables, and red, yellow, and blue throw cushions. Revellers gleefully sipped wine or nibbled on appetizers from the National's Understudy pub in between bursts of applause and animated conversation.

Alex turned to smile at Freddie, but caught a glimpse of a double-decker bus zooming across Waterloo Bridge under the watchful gaze of the London Eye.

"Thanks for bringing me here. I so needed this."

Freddie hugged her as Lucy reappeared, a tray aloft with three glasses of white wine. A wooden bench provided the perfect platform for a birthday toast.

"Me first." Lucy raised her glass.

"Lex, running into you was the best thing that's happened to me in a long time. I know I may snap at you sometimes when your perfectionist tendencies go off the charts, and I'll *never* understand how you can pack away so much sugar without bursting out of your jeans. But your friendship means everything—and I love you. And now that I've found you again, well—I'm never letting you go, and that's all there is to it! Happy Birthday, babe."

A burning tickle teased Alex's nose. She set her wine down on the bench and fanned at her eyes, fluttering her eyelashes. Do *not* blub on your birthday…

Freddie raised his glass. "Happy Birthday, sweetie. You're brave, kind hearted, and despite your affection for Lady Gaga, a top friend. Oh—and don't forget—when you turn our story into a glittering West End production, I *insist* that you have gorgeous Eddie Redmayne play me."

The girls laughed.

"Only if Chloe Grace Moretz portrays me. And Lucy gets Freema Agyeman."

"Martha, playing me? She'd be great," said Lucy.

"Perfect casting!" Alex clasped their hands. "Thanks for the fun birthday. It's the best one I've had *since*…well, I can't remember!"

"Think we're done? Nope." Freddie dug around in the left pocket of his blazer. "Just a little something I thought you'd like…" He handed Alex a tissue wrapped bundle about the size of a ten pence coin. She chipped at it with her short fingernails.

"Freddie's bad gift wrapping strikes again. Too much tape. Let me have a go." Lucy pulled it out of Alex's hand and snagged a corner.

Alex tore at the hole in the tissue. A small round brown button with 'Stage Door' in white lettering emerged.

It found a new home on her bag. "It's super cute. Thanks, Freddie." She kissed him on the cheek. "I'm now officially part of your stage door/red carpet/comic con squad."

"Wait. There's more." He pulled out a blind boxed *Doctor*

Who Titan from his other pocket. "I didn't wrap it in case the tape stuck to the box's artwork."

"Did you pick this one out *specially*, Freddie?" A crooked smile lit up Lucy's face. "Prepare yourself, Alex. I fear you're about to be plagued with..."

"...an Ood!" they announced simultaneously. They crumpled into each other, chuckling.

Freddie scoffed and pushed up his glasses with mock indignation.

Alex popped open the box and pulled apart the seal on its blue and silver foil packet.

"Freddie, I think you did good...yes, REALLY good." She waved the three-inch plastic figure in the air. "It's a fez-wearing Matt Smith."

"Of *course* it is," said Freddie, pouting.

Lucy doubled over with laughter, sloshing wine on the cement.

"Want to keep him? I didn't spot this one at your flat."

Freddie bit his lip. "Tempting, but...he's all yours. Maybe this means our luck has changed. You'll be the toast of the West End, Lucy wins a contract with Marvel, and I meet the man of my dreams."

"Blind date go badly the other night?" asked Lucy.

"The less said about *that*, the better."

Lucy rolled her eyes. "Not fair, Freds. You're always nosey about my love life. Or lack thereof."

"What's wrong with *everyone*? You're both great catches in my eyes," said Alex. Talking about dates and partners, her mind swung around to a certain someone.

"Isn't Mark working here now? Maybe we could go say hi?"

LONDON BELONGS TO ME

"He is, but we can't," said Freddie. "The workaholic's shooting a TV advert in Wales."

Lucy noticed Alex's sigh, and pulled a flat square from a plastic bag. Wrapped in colourful London scenes, it looked like it might be a vinyl record. "And here's my gift."

The wrap clung together with only two small strips of tape. Alex opened it effortlessly.

Ben Whishaw's eyes peeked out between shreds of paper. "It's genius! Is it a colouring book?"

"I made it." Lucy beamed. "The National's bookshop sells colouring books for Hiddleston, Redmayne, and Cumberbatch, but not Whishy, so I made one."

Freddie raised his glass to Lucy. "Putting those artistic skills to good use! Nice work, Hardy."

"It looks so professional. Thanks so much!" Alex flipped through the pages. "Lucy, you should go back to art college. You could create your own graphic novels."

"Maybe. One day. But for now, my creativity's *for your eyes only*."

"Before I forget...there's one more card." Freddie handed Alex a magenta envelope.

"More? You spoil me."

Freddie rested his hand against his heart. "It's not from me."

"Moriarty gives birthday cards, too?" Alex chuckled. Her eyes swept over the celebratory sentiment, pausing to smile at the cute cat juggling cupcakes on the cover. She flipped the card open...

'I was all set to jump out of your cake, but my agent (party pooper) called with a job. So I'm stuck in Wales with sheep by my side instead of you, and I'm cursing my dumb luck. How

'bout a rain check? Another Vespa adventure? London is yours—if you want it! Happy Birthday, Lex. Mark x'

Her lighthearted appreciation floated away on the warm breeze, lost along with her breath. She blinked several times. Yep, that 'x' wasn't a mirage. She stroked her neck absent-mindedly as she poured over the handwritten message again…and again.

Mark's words, committed in ink to paper, like a promise—unlike a text dashed off on a whim, only to be sent and instantly forgotten. Every looping vowel and crossed T offered a glimpse of his personality and sincerity.

Despite teasing from Lucy, Alex regularly sent handwritten cards for birthdays, Christmas, or just *because*. Having the tables turned—by Mark of all people—was a delicious surprise.

Life in London had been isolating and grim as of late, but this card and the efforts of her friends temporarily lifted the double-decker bus flattening her heart.

Leaning behind Alex, Freddie edged closer to Lucy and shielded his mouth with his hand. "Just look at her. I think our gifts have been overshadowed."

Lucy elbowed him. "Can you blame her?"

Nineteen

That birthday glow began to fade, and within a month, Alex was in the shadows again. When an unexpected bus of famished tourists unloaded at Tasty Munch, bringing rushed orders for eight all-day breakfasts and six cheese omelets, a sneaky panic attack began to rise. If everyday stressors were triggering her attacks, how would she survive writing rejections or demanding theatre producers?

Negative fixations on unimportant things, such as the schizophrenic English weather and the mess left behind by her estranged flatmates, tested Lucy and Freddie's patience. At least Alex still had her crush, but Mark's birthday offer of another Vespa adventure had yet to materialize. They'd exchanged the odd text, but she never saw him. Alex didn't dare ask Freddie about his whereabouts—girls probably bugged him all the time about his Irish mate with the killer smile—but one evening when Mark blew out plans to catch a film, Freddie joked that the only mistress in Mark's life was his work. Well, since Freddie *went* there…Alex dived in, tossing Julia the Voicemail Girl back at him over her popcorn. Freddie's floppy fringe shook defiantly;

he denied that Julia was to blame—they only went out twice. He was adamant; it was Mark's hectic whirlwind of auditions and bar shifts keeping him at arm's length. It all conspired to quash Alex's creativity. Her writing inspiration…gone on summer vacation with no forwarding address.

On the second Saturday in August, Lucy and Freddie dragged her to a London comic con in the hope that cosplayers, comics, and autograph sessions would revive her drowning spirit.

"Isn't this brilliant? Your first British con. Look, it's our tribe," said Lucy, dressed in head-to-toe PVC as Storm from *X-Men*.

A child hidden in a Dalek costume wheeled by, accompanied by a tanned Buffy the Vampire Slayer, and a pair of tall Hobbits. "If this doesn't put a smile on your face, I'm not sure what will."

Alex frowned at the *Sailor Moon* cosplayers clustered nearby. "It's kinda crap. This con can't compete with the events back home. It doesn't even have any major actors for autographs or photo shoots. The guy who played Ewok number six in *Return of the Jedi*? Hardly a must-see, is it?"

"Do you *enjoy* being a buzz kill? Seriously, Alex. You'd be more into it if you were cosplaying. Why didn't you wear your Wonder Woman gear?"

Alex shrugged, her eyes flitting over her *Batman* tee and jeans.

"Not feeling any chirpier, then?" asked Lucy.

Alex flipped through a bunch of graphic novels on a vendor's table. "I've been thinking about things a lot lately…it feels like the universe is telling me I'm not supposed to be here…in London."

Lucy slammed a *Watchmen* graphic novel down on the table, the force of its reunion with the other volumes causing the whole display to shake and a skittish Pikachu cosplayer to scurry. "Oh, come on. I know you've been out of sorts since the fundraiser, but that's no reason to second guess *everything*."

"But if it was meant to be, wouldn't it *be* easier?" Alex caught the crossed arms and cocked head of the vendor—dressed as Rorschach—and slinked away towards the Tower of T-shirts display. She tripped over the foot of a burly Angel wannabe and scowled at him.

"On my first day here, Tom mentioned how hard it is to break in. Take it from the failed actor. He knows how the industry chews people up and spits them out."

"It's not the industry at the heart of your current troubles, though, is it? It's your psycho flatmate with a jealous streak. Don't let that bitch piss on your bonfire," said Freddie, dressed as a dapper eleventh Doctor with a red fez atop his rebellious hair.

"You've only been here for a couple of weeks. Nothing worth achieving is easy or quick," said Lucy. "I think *you* told me that, smart arse. Yeah, wasn't it some quote you wouldn't shut up about online?"

"Probably, but…nothing's worked out as I hoped. London's been a clusterfuck from day one." She pulled a half-eaten Dairy Milk bar from her bag. "Lost luggage, the box room, a deranged flatmate, writer's block. And Harry. He's a bit different on his own turf. I think he really believes all that class garbage. If I knew from the outset I was just his latest charity case, I wouldn't have moved in."

She snapped a piece off her chocolate bar. "Everything sucks."

197

"Gee, thanks." Lucy threw her hands up in the air. "What about us—me and Freddie? Are we Scotch mist?"

"I didn't mean you guys."

"I should hope not." Lucy crammed a *Supernatural* top back into the t-shirt display.

Freddie draped his arm over Alex's shoulder as they squeezed through the feeding frenzy at a popular collectables table. "I get it. You're missing home. But I think that's partly because you're not feeling welcome in Hackney. It must be exhausting to work so hard to avoid spending time there—you're practically part of the furniture at mine and Lucy's after work. Not that you're not welcome…"

Alex nodded. "But it's not just that. If the theatre community here is as cliquey as it seems, I don't think I'll *ever* establish the right connections to be a success. Being American, the odds are even more stacked against me. I was supposed to fit in here, but I'm even more of an outsider than I was at home."

She flicked a stray shard of chocolate from her tee and crumpled up the wrapper, shoving it into her back pocket.

Freddie squeezed her shoulder. "Maybe, but you're not alone. We're outsiders, too, in our own way."

"Sounds like you've forgotten all the reasons why you left the U.S. in the first place." Lucy raised her eyebrows and adjusted her white wig, peeling its damp strands from her forehead. "I thought you hated Tallahassee."

"I do, but there's always New York City or somewhere like that. At least I wouldn't be circling the drain like I am here."

"Circling? Well, at least you haven't been sucked down," said Lucy. "Stop being so negative. Bring back the balls-out Alex who knocked me flying at Pret. Where'd that girl go? The one determined to write her own happy ending. The one who made things happen instead of sitting around waiting for fate to do the hard work."

"Yeah, where *did* she go? If you see her again, let me know." Alex half-joked, picking up a Jon Snow figure.

"You've got to move out of that hell hole of a flat. I thought you guys were viewing some places this week?" Freddie lifted his arm away from Alex so he could study a *Sherlock* Pop! Vinyl figure up close.

"We did, the past two evenings after work. Put it this way, if that's all I can afford, I'm moving under London Bridge. I'll probably become known as the Shopping Trolley Lady—barking at tourists, feeding invisible pigeons…"

Lucy wiped perspiration off her forehead and upper lip; wearing PVC in August wasn't her smartest idea. "I can put up with noisy neighbours or drafty windows—not a lot bothers me but the three flats we visited were a horror film come to life."

Freddie's eyes widened.

"One flat had black mould growing on all the walls. The carpet actually *squished* when you stepped on it," said Lucy.

Alex interjected. "And the drains *reeked*."

"Another had cockroaches and no hot water after 6 p.m. In the third place, the landlord had fifteen women living in a basement flat. They shared one bath and the kitchen was just a mini bar fridge, and a hot plate." Lucy crossed her arms. "It gave me the willies."

Alex leaned into Freddie to allow a girl dressed as Harley Quinn to push through to the front of the table. The cosplayer's oversized inflatable mallet skimmed Lucy's head. "I tried, but anything better is too expensive," Alex shrugged. "Even with flatmates, I can't afford a half decent place on what I've saved, not to mention what I earn."

"London *sucks* for affordable flats," said Lucy.

"I'd suggest staying with me, but the doctor had a huge domestic with his girlfriend. He's been sleeping on the sofa-bed most nights. He's totally cramping my style. Moriarty hates him," said Freddie.

"I *know* what you're going to say, but...there's always my loveseat," said Lucy.

Alex frowned. "And a cramped neck...and a folkie sing-a-long at two in the morning..."

A swarm of Trekkies clad in red command uniforms over-whelmed the *Star Trek* Titans to Freddie's left. He spun around to let a determined Worf join his Starfleet crew.

"What about asking your dad for financial help?" said Freddie. "Take a weekend trip to Manchester? If you need moral support, we can come along."

She shook her head. "I can't. He's already on the hook for my student loans. And besides, asking him for help makes me feel like a failure."

"Does he even know what you're going through?" asked Lucy.

Alex shook her head again.

"What about a better paying gig?" Lucy pursed her lips at Harley Quinn's poor mallet control. "Making egg and chips isn't going to cover first and last month's rent. Have you looked for something better paid?"

"No." Alex ran the zipper up and down on her bag. "Outside of making chip butties and writing, avoiding Harry and Olivia has been my main job lately."

A TARDIS sound reverberated within Freddie's pocket. He looked at his phone and then tucked it away again. "Sorry. Just

Mark. He says hi, by the way."

Alex's face lit up. "How's he doing? How's the job?"

"Four weeks in, so far so good. He says the people are fantastic; they're cool with him getting time off for auditions—and he's had plenty lately." Freddie settled on a Moriarty figure, handing the vendor twenty pounds. "If you're escaping the flat to write, why don't you head to the National? You can type away to your heart's content and talk to Mark about any jobs going there."

Lucy scratched her wig. "Why didn't I think of that?"

"Because I've got the looks *and* the brains, darling," said Freddie.

"Whatever." She rolled her eyes and squeezed her way out of the crowd.

Alex followed Lucy out of the throng, losing her smile along the way. "But it's so far to go each day..." Each syllable, each word, pushed her friends further away. Her heart hated that she was doing it, but her head screamed self-preservation.

Lucy yanked at the neckline of her PVC costume, desperate to cool down. "Well, if you keep nit-picking and making excuses, *nothing* will change, will it?"

Alex pouted and shuffled to the next table, alone.

☂ ☂ ☂ ☂ ☂

After elbowing crowds all day at the con, Alex craved a quiet night with Paddington, a cup of tea, and a stockpile of *Cabin Pressure* BBC radio episodes. Benedict Cumberbatch's hilarious Captain Martin Crieff always boosted her spirits. She dove her hand into a box of Lucky Charms, her dinner of choice when laziness took hold.

She finished listening to the final episode in series three and took a washroom break. The flat stood empty. Only the ticking of the carriage clock and the white noise from the fan in Tom's room, slicing through the humid August air, kept her company.

When she stepped back into the hall, a tall, shady figure approached from the lounge. Alex's heart leapt into her throat; the distinct scent of sweet raspberry and peonies...

"I've been meaning to talk to you."

Olivia strode into the hall, and stood arms crossed and legs splayed wide, blocking Alex's path to her room. The brunette's gauzy sundress sprinkled with daises contradicted her 'I mean business' demeanour.

Alex leaned against the wall, mirroring Olivia's crossed arms. "I have nothing to say..."

"Well, that's convenient because I have *plenty* to say. Guess who I bumped into at work yesterday?"

Alex shrugged.

"Isabella. We caught up over coffee, and as luck would have it, our conversation turned to you. She remembered you. Unfortunately, it's for all the wrong reasons...no tangible ideas, crumbling under pressure..."

Alex released her arms and tugged at the bottom of her t-shirt. "Would you *move*, please? You're in my way."

Olivia chuckled, her bare feet remained planted. "Reputations are *everything* in the theatre community. They're built on how you deliver—when you're granted a golden opportunity to impress. We both know your reputation crashed and burned on the runway. It didn't even make it into the air. That's one of the many differences between you and me. I don't let those chances to impress go to *waste*..."

Exhaling heavily, Alex shifted her weight from one foot to

the other.

"Your little suffragette idea's taking me to Isabella's exclusive Mentorship Program this winter. Granted, the writing's quite good, but do you want to know the main reason it got selected?" She placed a hand over her heart. "It made an impression because of the reputation of its author—Olivia Chadwick-Smythe. People know me. *Everyone* likes me—"

Alex spit back. "And most people don't see through you like I do. You may have fooled everyone else with your perfectly manicured life, but I know what you're *really* like."

Olivia smiled, ignoring Alex's interruption. "Just watch. I'll make that idea sing, better than you ever could. You didn't deserve to have it in the first place. You'll be on the outside looking in, the Girl Who Melted when it mattered most. Face it. You don't belong here. You're an embarrassment, a mistake—you said it yourself, *you're an accident.*"

Alex couldn't catch her breath, Olivia's hateful remark felt like a sucker punch to her gut, the words cutting deeper than any knife. "…Are you finished?"

"Actually, no—there's one more thing. Why on Earth are you still *here*?" said Olivia. "A deal's a deal. You agreed to move out within a week or two, and here we are…weeks later and your child-like food choices are still in my kitchen, and your ratty hair is clogging the tub's drain. You've more than overstayed your welcome."

"Don't worry. I don't want to live here, either."

Olivia laughed. "Oh, I'm not worried. In fact, I've taken matters into my own hands. I texted Harry tonight and told him how you gave me your two weeks' notice. So, I guess you're homeless in…" She checked her watch. "…T minus fourteen days…"

"You can't do that." Alex's hands tightened into fists. "This isn't your flat."

"Harry's heads down with business meetings in Ireland for the next few days, so I'm taking care of everything. Time's up, Alex. Time to crawl back to America and become a has-been. Oh...wait. You have to *be* something first *before* you can be a has-been."

Alex leaned against the wall, her balance unhinged.

"You were finished before you even began." Olivia smirked and brushed past towards the lounge.

Alex stomped into her room, grabbing her breath and her phone. She punched a saved number.

"Freddie? Fancy that trip to Manchester? How soon can we go?"

TWENTY

Alex fussed with her overstuffed backpack and stared at the departure board at Victoria coach station—National Express London to Manchester, Friday, August 21 at 17:30 p.m.

"C'mon, Lucy. Hurry up." Alex muttered under her breath, fanning her face. A dull headache squeezed her temples, the stuffy coach station air not helping. Perspiration dotted her upper lip and trickled down the back of her black tank top towards the bum of her jeans. She dumped her backpack on the floor and nudged it against her waiting laptop bag. Fingers crossed, the coach had air conditioning, but this being Britain? Probably not.

Her friends had scampered off to buy snacks for the four hour and forty-five-minute trip, and boarding had already begun. A train would've arrived in half the time but its fare exceeded their budgets. Even at seventy-two pounds return, these bus tickets were steep. Alex couldn't scrape together enough funds with her café hours, so she supplemented her earnings with a temporary evening job the past three weeks, answering focus study questions for various marketing research companies. She had roped in Lucy for comic relief. Both women hated the questions ranging from their opinions on alcohol brands to what kinds of feminine hygiene products they used. Now all those hours stuck in a small stale room felt worth it.

She stood guard over Lucy's green duffle bag with the broken strap and Freddie's shiny silver carry-on case with wheels. It didn't take a travel expert to figure out who would arrive crease-free.

"Alex!"

She jerked her head back, catching Mark sprinting towards her with his Vespa helmet under his arm. Her eyebrows lifted, releasing her first smile of the day. It had been two months since she'd last seen him.

"Good! You haven't left yet. Bloody traffic." He swooped in with a hug. "Where's the gang?"

Alex lingered against his white t-shirt, the fabric warm and glued to his chest. The rapid beat of his heart filled her ear. "Getting magazines and snacks."

Mark's hand swept along her dewy back. If she knew an embrace from him was on the cards, she would've worn a bra.

"At least I hope they are." She crossed her arms over her breasts. "Maybe they've changed their minds and done a runner."

His eyes floated around the concourse for their friends. "I'd gladly take their place. Manchester's a cool city. I did a play there last year."

"You sure get around."

Mark laughed. "Damn. Another one of my secrets, exposed."

A troop of head-bobbing pigeons noisily scattered, stealing Alex's attention away from Mark. Their dusty wings flapped into a perilous lift off, clearing a path for Lucy's galloping sandals.

She ran ahead of Freddie, her dark curls bouncing above the shoulders of her sleeveless blue blouse.

"Hiya, Mark!" Panting for breath, she pulled at the waist of her denim miniskirt. "Got 'em. Pies and pasties for everyone. Got chocolate, crisps, water." She handed Alex a paper bag containing a cheese and onion pasty. It promptly got shoved into her computer bag.

"Shame you can't come, Keegs." Freddie hugged his magazine against his black 221B t-shirt. "We could've relived that epic pub crawl. Remember when I fell into the canal, and you lost your trousers..."

Alex's eyes grew twice their size. Lost his *trousers...*?

Mark's impish gaze darted from Freddie to Alex and back. "Yeah, yeah...well, two other staff are on hols right now, so I'm working most of their shifts. Not complaining, mind."

"They're boarding now." Lucy fumbled with the broken strap of her duffle. "We should get a move on."

"Have fun." Mark helped Lucy reign in her bag. He nudged his hair off his forehead and looked at Alex, a slow smile inching through his stubble. "Don't miss your ride."

Alex blushed. She knew what *ride* meant in Irish slang— God, her mind was in the gutter.

Why did every encounter with Mark feel so *fleeting*? She loved nothing more than sharing these stolen moments with him, but they never lasted long enough. Not long enough to figure out if she meant as much to him as he did to her. He could flirt for Ireland, but did it mean anything? If it did, surely he would've made a move by now...

"Text ya later, Keegs." Freddie waved, chasing after Lucy.

Mark lifted Alex's backpack off the floor, his eyes spotting the small tattoo beside her tank's strap. "Comedy and tragedy masks? Glad to see I'm not the only one who's passionate...about theatre, I mean." He raised an eyebrow and tossed the heavy load over his shoulder, walking her to the gate. "I'm sorry I haven't been around lately..."

Lucy jumped out of the way of Freddie's wheelie case and looked back. "Lex! What are you like? Come on!"

Alex flung the strap of her laptop bag across her body. She dragged her feet and briefly closed her eyes, torn between staying and leaving. "I should go..."

"Enjoy the time with your family. I'm envious." Mark's eyes swept downwards, settling on her lips. "Give the Mancs a smooch from me."

The other side of the double bed lay rumpled but empty.

Where's Lucy? Alex kicked off the duvet, threw on her white bathrobe, and padded down the plush carpeted stairs to the main floor of her dad's semi-detached house just outside of Manchester. Muffled voices and the smell of fresh coffee signaled she was the last one up.

An assembly line of white bread, butter, and uncooked bacon crossed the kitchen counter. The kettle jittered and whistled on top of the stove.

"Morning, love."

Michael set his coffee down, ready for a hug. He was dressed in jeans and his red Manchester United shirt, which stretched uncomfortably over his slight potbelly. A few threads of silver weaved through the dark hair at his temples, defying his fifty-six years.

"I've waited *months* to hug you." His tight embrace was

warm and loving.

"Me too." Alex held on for dear life.

"You lot were knackered last night. I didn't know if I was picking up my daughter and her friends, or the cast of *The Walking Dead*."

Alex scratched her head as she pulled away. "What was it? Gone midnight or something? We couldn't get here any earlier. Blame work."

"Oh, I'm not complaining." He nudged his wire-rimmed glasses back up his long nose. "I'm just happy you're here. I was beginning to think we wouldn't see you until Christmas. You kids are so busy."

He grabbed several mugs from the cupboard. "Helen popped down to the shop to get more milk. She'll be back any minute."

"Dad, after breakfast, can I speak to you about something privately...just you and me?" Alex squeezed her robe's belt.

"Yeah, of course, love. Let's catch up before United's match comes on. If you're still thinking of going into town, Helen could drive your friends to the station, and you can meet up with them after." He placed a final mug on the counter and then counted out tea bags for each one.

"That works. Thanks. Are Lucy and Freddie watching TV?"

"They're chatting with Joan..."

"Oh no..." God knows what embarrassing tales Joan had shared with her two friends. Alex rushed through the doorway into the lounge. Joan sat wedged between Freddie and Lucy on the overstuffed blue couch, wearing jeans and her poppy red 1998 Manchester United shirt with Beckham and seven on the back. Photo albums and boxes of loose pictures covered the coffee table and their laps.

"Morning, Lex," said Lucy, clad in her fleecy Hogwarts pajamas. "Why didn't you tell us your grandmother —oh, I'm sorry—*Joan*...was so cool? I just followed her on Instagram."

"Joan, you still ride a motorbike?" Freddie peered at the picture in his hand. "Alex, you've gotta see these old photos. They're fabulous." He sipped his orange juice.

Despite being seventy-six, Joan had more crazy hobbies and pursuits than the rest of her family combined. Perhaps speaking her mind and stepping outside her comfort zone kept her young and feeling more fifty-six than seventy-six—that and not allowing anyone to call her Granny. Her tiny frame, fair hair, and pale skin hinted as to where Alex's looks came from.

"You have an Instagram account?" Alex raised her eyebrows.

"There she is." Joan shifted the heaviest photo album off her lap and into Freddie's waiting grasp. "Alex, come here and give Joan some love." She stood up with arms out, willing a hug to happen.

Alex pressed her lips together and crept forward. Joan was having none of it. She tugged her granddaughter close, kissed her on the mouth, and hugged her into submission. Her slight build and advanced age belied the fact that her suffocating squeeze would make a boa constrictor envious. Squinting over Joan's shoulder, Alex's eyes pleaded forgiveness from her friends seated below.

"FaceTime has a lot to answer for. You're taller in person. Have you grown since our last video chat on your birthday?" Joan planted a hand on each of Alex's shoulders and stepped backwards, her eyes spanning from her granddaughter's toes to her chest. "Ah, look at ya—you're a *woman* now."

Heat rose in Alex's cheeks. Lucy smirked and bit her lip.

Freddie looked down, hiding a giggle against his hand while toying with the buttons on his Henley tee. Why had she thought it was a good idea to bring her friends along? At least Mark wouldn't witness this embarrassment.

"Um, thanks?" Alex didn't know how to respond. The conversation couldn't move on fast enough. "What are you guys doing? I've never seen these photos before."

Joan kept hold of Alex's right hand, pulling her onto the couch. Lucy scooted over to the left, making space for her friend to sit down beside her gran. The ocean of soft blue cushions swallowed Alex, her bare feet dangled above the floor.

"Photos of me when I was your age. You were so *wee* the last time you were here. What seven-year-old sits still to flip through black and white photographs? You were more interested in playing with our old tabby cat. Him and that Furbie your dad bought you, remember? Oh, and you used to *love* watching Tinky-Winky—we've still got that Teletubbies DVD somewhere."

Freddie snorted, shooting orange juice out his nose.

"Argh. Sorry!" he laughed.

Alex scrunched up her eyebrows. Great. More ammunition for her friends to tease her with later. Joan plunked another large dusty album onto her lap; its cover pressed forcefully onto Alex's thighs.

"No wonder you love the theatre so much, Lex," said Lucy.

She tilted her head. "Why?"

"Joan's chorus girl past. She had a mean dance kick." Lucy held a loose photo from a box of old pictures and keepsakes, and read a faint note written on the back. "Palace Theatre, 1955." She stretched over Joan, handing it to Alex.

She stared at the grainy black and white photo of a young

blonde dancing on stage in a sparkly dress. "You performed *on stage?*" She turned back to Joan. "I never knew that. You never told me."

"It was a lifetime ago, love. It didn't help that I only spoke to you here and there by phone when you were little. And only when your mum allowed it. Thank God, we've had Skype and FaceTime to stay in touch the last couple of years, eh? Your mother thought I was a bad influence. She never liked me. Granted, that feeling was mutual."

"That I did know."

"Michael told me about how you were doing in school though—what theatre courses you were taking in university. I read all your old essays and plays."

Alex turned another page of the album. Several of the photos stuck together. She ran her fingers over the yellowing images, separating them.

"I was going to post you some photos a few years back, but your dad asked me to send nowt," said Joan. "He worried if I told you about my years treading the boards, your mum would've had a right old strop, especially with your love of theatre. I didn't care about upsetting her ladyship, but the last thing I wanted was to make things harder for you, so I kept my trap shut."

"It couldn't have gotten much worse. She practically disowned me when I accepted the spot at Emory. Refused to help with tuition, constantly belittled my choice."

Joan rubbed Alex's back.

"This one is from another production at the Palace." Joan pointed at an image where she stood in the middle of a long line of chorus girls. "The director wanted to pay us a quarter of what the men were earning. We didn't have a contract, so five of us girls threatened to walk out an hour before opening night unless he gave us a third. He caved, of course. We didn't take any guff."

"Why did you stop performing?" asked Freddie.

"I married Alex's granddad before my nineteenth birthday. Had Michael nine months after. It's what all of us did in those days, Freddie."

Alex slipped a photo from the album sat on her lap. "Oldham Repertory Theatre, 1957" was handwritten in faded pencil on the back.

"Oh, that was Noel Coward, *Design for Living*. I had a dozen lines or so, but I made the most of them," said Joan.

She continued to answer Freddie. "But you see, love...with a baby, it just wasn't possible to carry on. You were done. The day after I found out I was pregnant, I was offered a lead role—it would've been my thirteenth play. It broke my heart to turn it down. I often wonder where it might have led if I'd stuck with it. I had some grand old times on stage."

"I had no idea." Alex's eyes widened.

"Thirteen? So unlucky," said Lucy.

The kitchen rattled with clinking mugs and the metal-on-metal clatter of cutlery. The smoky, salty call of bacon wafted around the corner.

Michael stepped into the lounge, holding a knife smothered with butter. "Helen's back, and breakfast's almost ready. Let's get you all fed and watered so you can head into town. Who fancies a brew?"

"I do," said Freddie. He set his glass on the coffee table and bounded into the kitchen with Lucy in hot pursuit, snatching the back pocket of his jeans.

Joan squeezed her granddaughter's arm. "It's so good to

have you here. It means the world to us."

"Me too," said Alex with a smile as they walked into the lively kitchen. Lucy and Freddie were laughing at Michael. Helen had just told him off for pinching a slice of bacon.

"Alex, gimme a kiss, love." Helen set a greasy pair of tongs on the counter, wiped her hands on a flowery Cath Kidston apron and wrapped her chubby arms around her stepdaughter. "I tried to stay up last night for your arrival, but fell asleep."

Alex closed her eyes, resting her chin on Helen's shoulder, the squishy hug both welcoming and overdue. Helen never had kids of her own, but when she married Michael in 2005, she treated all three of his children like they were hers—albeit from an ocean away. Helen had been her dad's first love as a teen, and she boasted many qualities that Alex knew her mother lacked: she was utterly selfless, always put her family first, and appreciated each of the kids in their own right. With only a few years left until retirement, Helen had recently marked thirty-five years working as a critical care nurse. Alex adored her.

Helen eased her clinch, her round brown eyes aglow. She placed her hands on Alex's waist. "So skinny! Have they been starving you down there? You need some good northern cooking to put some meat on those bones. Bacon barms coming up, my sweet." She lifted several thick rashers of sizzling bacon onto a large plate.

"Usually it's me making breakfast for people. Can I help?" Alex leaned in between Helen and her dad who buttered several pieces of toast. She plucked a fresh cup of tea from the counter and handed it to Joan.

"Nope. Grab a mug for yourself and head to the table. I'll bring the barms as soon as your dad's finished with the toast," said Helen. "I'm making two for all three of you. These London kids, so *skinny.*"

Lucy pulled Alex aside and whispered. "All systems go for talking to your dad about a hand with rent money?"

Alex watched the bacon sandwiches being assembled, avoiding Lucy's gaze. "After breakfast when you're on the way to the train station."

Twenty-One

Alex paced around the lounge, waiting to hear the door slam to Helen's SUV. Freddie and Lucy were buckled in for a lift to the Heaton Norris train station. Within twenty minutes, they would be at Manchester Piccadilly in the city centre where Alex would join them later. Joan had returned to her granny flat at the back of the house to finish a piece of pottery, so Alex had her dad all to herself.

"You're going to wear a hole in that carpet. What's so worrisome that you shuttled your friends off, and want to speak with me on your own? Not boy trouble? Devin hasn't been calling, has he?" Michael settled into his leather recliner and slapped his Saturday morning newspaper on the small side table. "I know how hard it's been for you to let him go."

Alex crumpled into the couch, pulling her knees into her chest. She picked at a stray thread sticking out from the toe of her sock. "It's not that, Dad." She dropped her chin. "It's something else."

"I'm all ears, love."

Her nostrils prickled. "It's…not working, being in London,

writing...I feel sick admitting it, but...I don't think I can keep doing this. I've completely lost my way." Tears filled her eyes.

"Oh sweetheart, where's this coming from?" Michael sat forward in his recliner. "We thought it would take a few months to get going. You'll get there."

"No, it's more than that."

Alex took a deep breath and told her dad about her misguided trust in Olivia, the weird possessiveness over Harry, the theft of her play, her public humiliations, and being forced out of the flat. When she got back to London, she'd have a day or two at most to collect her things and get out.

"Unbelievable. And all because she thinks you and Harry?" He put his glasses back on and blinked several times.

"Basically, yeah. It's such a joke." Tears raced down her cheeks.

"Well, then we'd best get started, finding you a new flat." Michael grabbed his iPad from the windowsill. "Let's find some listings online—"

"Dad, you're not *getting it*..."

She pushed her bangs away from her forehead and tugged the cuffs of her black hoodie over her knuckles. "I can't do this anymore. Clearly, I'm not cut out for playwriting or London. I'm having more panic attacks. I've embarrassed myself."

Michael stopped scrolling on the iPad.

"Mom was right. I'll just keep struggling here with nothing to show for it. I'm kidding myself—coming here was a mistake. I need to go home. I need to go home and do something else. Office work, retail, anything but...*this*."

"But you don't have to go back to the States to do something else, love. You could stay in London, right? You've made some smashing new friends."

"Yeah, they're great. I wanted you to meet them. I didn't think I'd be here for Christmas, so I brought them with me for one last weekend before I say goodbye. I feel bad, though…I kinda brought them here under false pretences. Lucy thinks I'm asking you for help with rent money so I can move, but I've already made up my mind…to go back."

Alex wiped her nose with her cuff. "If I stay in London, I'll just be reminded daily of what I screwed up—every time I pass any of those beautiful theatres. *No thanks*. Writing is all that I've ever wanted to do…until now. If I'm not a writer, who am I?"

She brushed tears from her cheeks.

"I couldn't tell you all this over the phone. I had to see you—and Helen and Joan, too."

Michael pushed his eyeglasses up his nose. "I'm so sorry, love. I didn't know you'd had such a rough time."

He shifted from his recliner, cuddling his daughter. She sagged into his chest, her body giving in to wave upon wave of shoulder-quaking sobs. He stroked her hair and gently rocked back and forth as if his love could swaddle his baby girl in cotton wool, shielding her from further heartbreak and disappointment.

Alex felt like she was seven again…

"I think I started writing because my make-believe worlds were always happier than my real one."

Michael gave her a squeeze. "I should've done things differently. When the divorce happened, I should've fought harder to get custody of you, appealed the court's decision. Looking back, it's my biggest regret."

Alex found a tissue in her pocket, and wiped her streaming nose.

"I didn't do enough—I know that, and I know I can't make it up to you, all those missed moments—birthdays, Christmases…Well, I'm not making the same mistake again."

He patted Alex's shoulder and rose from the couch. He opened the drawer of the side table.

"I'm still paying the instalments on your university loan, but I can stretch a little further."

Alex scrunched up her eyebrows. "What are you doing?"

"I'm writing you that cheque to cover rent for the next six months. Leave Harry's flat when you get back home to London, but don't move into a dump or far out in the suburbs. I'd worry about you travelling on public transport late at night."

"But Dad, you're not listening. I need to leave, to go *home*… now."

"Alex, you *are* home. London's where you belong. Look, I know you're upset, you've been treated terribly, but you've come so far. Don't throw it away. Your life's here now."

"Did you slip some Bailey's or rum into your coffee this morning?"

Michael shook his head. "You're talented, sweetheart. I've always known it. You just need to believe in yourself. Once you get out of that flat, away from that horrible girl, I think you'll see things more clearly."

He finished writing and tore the cheque from the booklet.

"Please, Alex—promise me you'll give it another couple of months? If things haven't improved, if you still want to go back to Florida, I'll buy your plane ticket myself."

He placed the piece of paper beside her. She blinked several times to get a better look at it. His offer was so generous, but wasn't it just delaying the inevitable—at his expense?

"I can't promise you that. I wish I could. But I promise that I'll think about it…"

"What are you two talking about, then?" Joan strolled into

the room. "I was going to ask for a lift to the garage, but you seem to be in the middle of something." Her gaze shifted from Michael to Alex.

"More motorbike magazines, Mum?" said Michael.

"You've been crying..." Joan sank into the couch next to her granddaughter.

Michael eased back down on his recliner. "She's thinking of calling it a day, Mum, going back to Florida."

"Quit writing? Oh, Alex, no." Joan clasped her hand. "I'm so proud of you, my love. It's like you're following in my footsteps. I had to stop chasing my dream at your age, but you've got the chance to go further than I ever did. It's your *calling*. It's a chance to be yourself."

Alex wiped away lingering tears with her free hand. There was no point explaining her plan to leave to Joan. She was hell bent on Alex staying the course.

"If I could go back in time and talk to myself at age nineteen or twenty, I would've said '*Joan, you silly cow—life's too bloody short. Follow your dreams and don't let a man or bullies or anyone tell you to stop.*'"

She pulled Alex into a tight hug.

"Don't take the road I took. Don't have regrets. Don't become resentful. You can't give up, love. Get back to your writing." She pulled away and grinned at Alex. "Give me something new to brag about on Instagram. I've got 800 followers and they can only put up with so many photos of motorbikes and dodgy pottery."

Twenty-Two

"This place was made for you, Lex," said Freddie.

Lucy and Freddie linked arms with Alex and guided her towards Northern Soul Grilled Cheese.

"We found it a few hours ago, wandering around." Lucy looked at her phone. "Half two was our cut-off. If we didn't see you by then, screw it. We were going in without you."

"It's quite new. It definitely wasn't around when I went to uni here," said Freddie. "I would've known—I survived on food from the Church Street Market."

Alex dragged her feet. First her dad and Joan, and now Freddie and Lucy: everyone figured they knew what was best for her. "I'm not that hungry."

"Bloody hell. We waited for *this*?" Lucy scowled.

They passed a pretty strawberry blonde in a flowery dress and biker boots tearing her way through an overstuffed cheesy sandwich. Alex's eyes popped. "Good God, is that mac 'n' cheese in there?"

She hadn't eaten mac 'n' cheese since she left Florida. "Forget what I just said. I need *that*— now."

"Atta girl. I always knew you were a cheese-whore," said Freddie.

The trio joined the queue snaking around the small shop.

"How did the rent money talk go? Any joy?" asked Lucy.

"He wrote me a cheque. A big one."

"Thank fuck! You had me going there for a moment. You arrived in such a strop. I thought he said no." Lucy flattened Alex's inside-out hood. "You're quids in now."

"Operation Ditch The Bitch is go," said Freddie. "You'll be free, and Olivia can go back to storing her ugly designer clothes in that poxy box room."

Both friends looked at Alex, searching for a sliver of a smile. "Aren't you relieved?" asked Freddie, moving forward in line.

"Sorta, but I'm dreading it too." Alex's shoulders slumped. "Finding a new place, living with strangers? It's all such a gamble..." She tried to sound devoted to the cause for her excited friends.

"It can't be any worse than living with those so-called 'friends.' Don't worry, babe. We'll vet your potential flatmates." Lucy shifted closer to the counter. "You won't get stuck with losers. I was born to play judge and jury."

Alex hid behind her smile. Time to pretend, for everyone's sake.

☂ ☂ ☂ ☂ ☂

"I'm going to turn into a big lump of cheese. All these cheese sandwiches, cheese and onion pasties," said Alex. "Helen thinks I've lost weight. I've actually gained since May." She chewed a final bite of her mac 'n' cheese sandwich, her eyes rolling back in her head. "It's so damn good though."

"Chop, chop. Let's go exploring." Lucy brushed crumbs from her plaid shirt and hopped off her stool. Alex gathered their trays and trash, placing the pile at the end of the counter for the staff to collect.

"A day isn't enough to see all of Manchester, so I'll show you my highlights," said Freddie. "The old buildings are beautiful. The city's done a great job of modernizing without forgetting its past, you know? And the arts and culture is second only to London. Great clubs, music, bars, museums…"

"Football teams," said Alex. "Well, *one* specific footy team."

"Since we're already in the Northern Quarter, let's have a nose around here, then we can move on to the Cathedral, Albert Square, and if we have time, the Gay Village or Castlefield. Whatever you prefer," said Freddie.

"Castlefield has the canal-side bars, right?" asked Lucy.

"Yep. You'll love it." Freddie lifted the strap of his messenger bag over his head and onto his shoulder. "Alex, you should be proud of your birthplace. This city's creative, tolerant, and fun. Just like you, my little blonde friend!" He wrapped her in a hug and lifted her off the ground with a flourish.

Lucy groaned. "Freddie, you're so cheesy."

"Like me," said Alex, legs dangling. "I'm full of cheese."

Freddie laughed and lowered her back onto her feet. "This way, bitches."

He led the girls eastward along Church Street. Saturday afternoon shoppers searching for rare vinyl and secondhand clothes clogged the sidewalk, forcing Alex and Lucy to walk single file behind him until they reached Oldham Street.

"Okay, here we are. Afflecks! Four floors of shopping mayhem. My favourite secondhand leather jacket came from here.

Go forth and shop."

Lucy put her hands on her hips. "Not sure how much shopping's gonna happen. I only budgeted so much, and if we're hitting up Castlefield later, I'd rather buy food and booze than clothes."

Freddie's shoulders drooped. "Kick me where it hurts, why don't you?"

"I'll check it out. Looks cool," said Alex.

Lucy squeezed his arm. "Okay…but Freds…don't go nuts. You know what you're like."

They climbed the stairs to the first level where secondhand clothing, jewellery, tattoo, and piercing vendors elbowed for space with kitschy Japanese wares and a beauty salon.

Lingering outside the tattoo studio's entrance, Lucy rubbed her upper arm. "God, I thought the pain would never end. I almost bit right through my lip, didn't I, Freddie? I'd do it all again in a heartbeat, though. I love my tattoo."

"Yours is one of the best I've ever seen," said Alex. "I'd love another if I could decide on a design. I'd like a quote, from Shakespeare maybe… *'Oft expectation fails, and most oft where most it promises'.*"

The line from *All's Well That Ends Well* proved the great Bard was on to something. High expectations really were the root of Alex's heartbreak. Her chest grew tight.

Lucy snickered. "Well, that's fucking cheery. Why don't you get one that sums up your dedication to playwriting?"

"Or get a Union Jack, Big Ben—something that screams London," said Freddie.

An artist worked on an intricate flower design on a woman's shoulder. Alex's stomach lurched with queasiness. She couldn't do it. She couldn't keep the truth from her best friends.

"Look, I wasn't 100 percent honest with you guys." Her declaration pulled their attention away from the tattoo in progress. "I didn't ask Dad for money. I told him I wanted to go home...*home* as in back to Florida."

"You did *what*?" Lucy snapped. "I thought we agreed. You would ask for cash so you could move to another flat."

Freddie froze in a rare display of stunned silence.

"I never said I was going to ask. You assumed."

"No, you did. Why else are we here?"

"Lucy, I told you guys I wouldn't ask him for a handout. Remember? That day at the comic con?"

Lucy crossed her arms, frowning.

"I came here to tell him in person that I wanted to go home. He paid my university tuition. I couldn't tell him that over the phone or FaceTime. It was the decent thing to do, face-to-face."

"Wow. I can't believe I'm hearing *this*," said Lucy.

Freddie stepped in. "Hey, shhhh!"

The tattoo artist and her client glared at the trio. Freddie ushered his friends away from the shop's entrance. They shifted several stalls down and wound up in Pop Boutique, where they could be less conspicuous between the dense racks of secondhand clothes.

"Can we discuss this without involving all of Manchester, please?" asked Freddie.

"So you're still thinking about running back to Florida?" said Lucy. "Even though your dad wrote you a cheque...so he must think it's a bad idea, too, right?"

"I'd be lying if I said I wasn't."

"And everything that we've done to convince you to stay...was for nothing? Great. I could've used that seventy-two quid coach fare to replace my worn out boots or for groceries."

"Lucy, that's not nice," said Freddie.

"Well, she's being honest. I might as well be honest, too. Shame she wasn't honest about her intentions *before* we each forked out seventy-two quid."

Alex shoved a bunch of vintage dresses along a rack, avoiding eye contact. "I don't know why you're taking this so personally. You're acting like I'm doing this to hurt you. Whatever I decide, it has *nothing* to do with you, Lucy."

"And maybe that's the problem. I thought we were really good friends, best friends, but obviously I think more of our friendship than you do. Alex, for someone who goes on about people abandoning her, it seems like you really have no problem doing it to other people."

She stormed out of the boutique and down the hall.

"Let her go," said Freddie. "She's upset. Let her burn it off. She won't go far."

"I know she doesn't want me to go, but I have to do what's best for me. You get that, don't you, Freddie?"

"I do." He sighed. "But I don't want you to go, either."

He held a pinstriped jacket against his chest. "Lucy's been different since her grandmother died. She's more sensitive. She doesn't have anyone except me—and now you. She'd never admit it, but she's scared to be on her own. You two aren't that different.

"Yeah, I get it. Being alone's the worst."

"I know, but are you *really* alone? Devin and Taylor might be out of your life, but let's see..." He counted on his fingers. "...you still have your dad, Helen, Joan, your brother Robbie—they all love you. Who does Lucy have? She has no family left. So maybe you're not as bad off as you think."

Alex toyed with the sleeve of the pinstriped jacket. "I never thought of it that way. I always looked at both physical and emotional distance as abandonment."

"And it is abandonment, Lex. I'm not saying it's not, but you can still pick up the phone and call your dad or Skype with Robbie. Lucy can't call her dad. She has no siblings. God knows where her mum is; she hasn't seen her since she was three. She certainly can't rely on those hippie freaks living in her flat. You and I *are* her family. I think that's why she's taking your decision so personally."

He pulled a vintage red smoking jacket from the rack. "I'm not saying you should reconsider to make her happy. I just want you to know where she's coming from."

"I know. Sometimes it's hard to see beyond my own issues. I didn't mean to hurt her."

Freddie tried on the smoking jacket. He posed in the mirror and turned forty-five-degrees.

"That one looks good," said Alex.

"The sleeves are almost long enough. I can roll them up."

They stopped at the cashier's desk. "Lucy might kill me when she sees me walk out of here with this, but we can't please her all the time, can we?" He smiled at Alex and handed his credit card to a green-haired punk.

"But what about you? I know absolutely zip about your family. You never mention them."

"Not much to tell," said Freddie. "My family isn't the most 'gay friendly', put it that way. My twin's a good guy, but I don't see him that often. He lives in Kent."

"You have a twin? You mean there's two of you roaming the earth?"

"Yep, there's another me, although we aren't identical. In fact, Joe's chubby, blond and straight. Go figure."

🌂 🌂 🌂 🌂 🌂

Cigarette in hand, Lucy sat in a metal chair outside a coffee shop on Oldham Street.

"I figured you wouldn't get far." Freddie nudged Lucy playfully with his purple plastic bag.

"Since when do you smoke?" asked Alex.

"When I'm stressed. See, it turns out that online friendships aren't real friendships after all. There's so much you don't know about the other person."

"I guess I deserve that," said Alex.

Lucy looked away and blew smoke over her right shoulder.

"I should've been honest about my intentions for this trip. It wasn't fair to you or Freddie."

"You *think*?"

Freddie stepped in. "Hey, hey, c'mon. She's apologized."

"Did she?" said Lucy. "I didn't hear *I'm sorry*."

Saying 'I'm sorry' when it really mattered wasn't Alex's forte.

"Being pissy isn't helping anyone, Lucy. And it'll ruin the rest of our visit," said Freddie.

Alex gulped. "I'm…I'm sorry…and I'll find a way to pay you back the seventy-two pounds."

"I only said that to hurt you," said Lucy. "It's okay. I was having a great time up until thirty minutes ago. There's no need to pay me back."

"I hate when we fight," said Alex.

"Me too. Apology accepted." Lucy flicked the cigarette into the street.

"Okay, good," said Freddie. "Now make it official. Hug it out, bitches."

Alex leaned down towards Lucy who rolled her eyes at Freddie. They embraced briskly and let go. "But I'm still cross about the Florida thing," said Lucy.

"Dad wasn't happy about it, either. That's why he wrote the cheque—I didn't ask for it. He wants me to stick it out for a few months longer—he made me promise I'd give it more thought. He thinks that once I'm out of Harry's flat, things will improve—I'll be less stressed out, more settled."

"Yeah, that's what we've been saying," said Freddie.

"I guess, but it all depends on finding somewhere decent to live—and fast." Alex picked at her cuticles. "Otherwise, I'll be trading an umbrella for sunscreen."

Freddie showed off as much of Manchester as he could. They explored more of the Northern Quarter, including Forbidden Planet, roamed around the central retail district, and snapped photos in front of Manchester Cathedral. They skipped the Arndale Centre ("too many of the same shops we have back in London," reasoned Freddie), but made a point of finding the Royal Exchange Theatre, and Barton's Arcade, a stunning iron and glass-domed shopping arcade built in the 1870s.

Manchester Town Hall proved to be Alex's favourite. "It's so gothic and spooky, especially the clock tower. I love it."

"They do a lot of film and telly shoots here; that Daniel Radcliffe film *Victor Frankenstein*, one of the Downey Jr. *Sherlock* movies. But wait until you see this place in December," said Freddie. "The outdoor Christmas markets are legendary. You can shop and eat around the city centre and then pay the huge glittery Santa a visit at the Town Hall. He sits atop the entrance...it's magical."

"I had no idea Manchester was so cool," said Alex.

Lucy sighed. "Loving all the architecture and culture, but can we *finally* have a pint? I vote for the Gay Village."

"Really?" said Freddie, leading his friends along Princess Street. "What happened to your interest in Castlefield?"

"Nah, I want to visit your old stomping ground. My one and only visit here was just up and down to see Mark's play that time. Let's make up for it. As long as you're okay with it, Lex?"

"Lead on. I'm enjoying Freddie's trip down memory lane."

Lucy chimed in. "Maybe we'll run into your old ex."

"He wasn't *that* old," said Freddie. "He was only twelve years older than me."

"Cradle snatcher." Lucy smirked. "I know what you gave him, but what did he give you? A bunch of ancient Madchester records and a broken heart."

"And three years of unforgettable memories."

Alex grabbed his arm. "Aw, Freddie. Three years…that's amazing."

"My thoughts exactly." Freddie bounced on his heels and rounded the corner onto Portland Street. The girls upped their pace to catch him.

TWENTY-THREE

Alex pushed her chair back from the dining table and patted her mouth with a paper napkin.

"Helen, you've ruined meals for me. Roast potatoes and carrots, gravy, and Yorkshire pudding. I'll never eat this well again. I still think having dinner on Sunday afternoons is weird, though."

"It's tradition," said Freddie, savouring his last spud. "We used to have a roast every Sunday at one when I was a kid, and then we'd fall asleep in front of the telly."

"You sure you've eaten enough? You've got a long bus ride down south," said Helen.

Alex held her stomach. "I had two helpings of everything except the roast beef."

"I'm good, thanks. My plate was heaped three times," said Freddie. "Meat sweats, here I come."

"This guy can eat everyone under the table and never has to adjust his belt a single notch. So not fair," said Lucy.

Joan leaned in beside Freddie, who sat to her left. "I'm impressed, love. In my experience, most men who eat like you are football players or builders."

"Is *that* why I don't have a boyfriend? Do gays think I'm straight because I'm *not* watching my figure?"

"I've missed this. I love the gays, me!" Joan laughed conspiratorially with Freddie.

"Well, if you're all full, more pudding for me." Michael stood up, clearing an armful of plates.

"Hello? Have you forgotten your youngest daughter? I live for desser—pudding. That word still sounds weird. I haven't had an *actual* pudding in the American sense since I've been here. Yorkshire pudding doesn't count, which…let's face it, isn't *really* a pudding. It's not a dessert either. Weirdos."

Michael chuckled. "I guarantee you'll like tonight's pudding, love."

Alex and Lucy rose to help.

"Sit and chat with Joan, girls." Helen collected several platters and followed Michael into the kitchen.

Joan sighed. "It's been such a treat having you here. I don't know what you're all doing for Christmas, but I hope you'll celebrate with us. I may have spoken out of turn, but I'm sure Helen and Michael won't mind."

"I'm in," said Lucy with a bright smile. "Thanks for inviting me. Now you just have to twist Alex's arm. She's the fuckwit—" She covered her mouth with her hand. "Sorry, *I mean*…she's the one who needs convincing." She shot a look at Alex.

Joan leaned back. "Ha! Bloody Nora." She tossed her napkin down on the empty table. "Lucy, you're a girl after my own heart. Never apologize for cursing, love. If you can't hold your drink or swear like a sailor, I don't want to know you."

Freddie and Lucy laughed while Alex hid behind her hands.

"Now, I have a job for you two." Joan put her left hand on Freddie's knee and extended her right hand across the table to Lucy. "You need to help our kid stay on the *right* path." She nodded in Alex's direction. "I don't want to hear another mention of bloody Florida or leaving writing behind."

Alex half-frowned. "Joan…"

"You're a clever girl, and you come from strong Manchester stock," said Joan.

"She's right. Theatre's in your blood," said Lucy.

Alex bit her cheek just as Helen and Michael brought in a chocolate cake decorated with swirls of fudge icing, and a carton of vanilla ice cream.

"Sure your birthday was in July, but we couldn't let you head back home to London without cake and candles." Helen's eyes beckoned. "Make a wish."

Joan winked across the table at Alex.

The end credits rolled on Alex's third episode of *Jonathan Strange and Mr. Norell*. Three hours down, only two more to go until the bus arrived in London at five past nine. Her stomach snarled. She paused her iPad and lifted her laptop bag off the floor. Rustling around for her two packets of chocolate buttons lost inside, a folded piece of paper sliced her finger. She winced at the cut and pulled the prime suspect out of her bag—the folded cheque from her dad.

Studying the handwritten amount, Alex wasn't sure the cheque would stretch as far as her dad had hoped. At best, it would cover a deposit and *maybe* three months' rent. If she was searching in Manchester, she'd be okay—but London's rents were comparatively sky-high.

She traced his firmly crossed Ts and tilted consonants, each letter pressed further into the paper, each more determined than the previous one. His writing, his words—urging her to stick with it…

'*Once you get out of that flat, away from that horrible girl, I think you'll see things more clearly*'…

Maybe he was right. She had allowed Olivia's taunts and threats to grind her down, to poison her self-confidence. A bully. That's all she was. Olivia didn't hold the key to Alex's future.

A few months ago, quitting wasn't an option. Why should it be now? She owed it to her dad and Joan to try again. More than that, she owed it to herself.

Lucy and Freddie had tried all along to keep her on course—protective, supportive, always in her corner. Eyes closed beside her, Lucy's head bumped lightly against the window, her headphones emitting Sam Smith. Freddie's loud snores punctuated the air from two seats away, his long legs bobbing up and down in the aisle whenever a wheel hit a bump on the motorway. Alex's heart warmed at the sight of her two dear friends. Even if her dream career seemed out of reach, she had already won the lottery with these two.

A vibration buzzed Lucy's jacket pocket, interrupting her musical interlude. Her lids crept open. She yanked the headphone cord, spilling her phone onto her lap, the screen's glow illuminating her face.

"What?!" she screeched.

She thrust her phone in Alex's face.

"Look!"

'*Lucy. Good news—We rocked the Cornwall cheese festival. An A and R guy from Norway signed us to his label. Bad news—*

we're moving to Oslo in two weeks. Sorry to leave you in the lurch with the rent. Love and rainbows, Clem and Jasper'

Lucy beamed. "Cider with Rosie is leaving London!" She smothered Alex in a hug. "Hear that sound? That's your cell door opening. You're *free!*"

TWENTY-FOUR

Harry shrugged. "Who knew Scandinavians loved British folk music so much?"

Alex stifled the cheek-pinching grin that was threatening to overtake her face. A new sense of control electrified her. No more sitting back, allowing Olivia to derail her future—moving out, escaping her venom—just the start.

She wheeled her two overstuffed suitcases out of Harry's flat and into the hall where they joined her bulging backpack. Her laptop bag waited for her inside the lounge, basking in a mid-September sunbeam.

Harry scratched at his temple. "But living in a camper van in the middle of a Norwegian winter..."

Olivia, still wrapped in her silk dressing gown, hovered behind her boyfriend, a steaming coffee and the Saturday paper in her grasp. She glared at Alex over Harry's shoulder.

Alex bounced back into the flat and adjusted her *Batman* baseball cap with a snap of her wrist. "I know, right? They told Lucy living simply would feed their creative juices; make their music more grounded or earthy or...something. When the spring festival circuit starts, they'll be ready to roll. Literally."

She peeked back through the doorway, catching sight of Lucy reaching the top of the stairs. Lucy pulled the straps of Alex's crammed backpack onto her shoulders and winced as it kicked heavily against her back. She weaved like a drunk college kid, then regained her balance. She acknowledged Harry with a polite wave.

"Are you sure you don't want a tea or need a hand with your stuff?" asked Harry, waving back.

"Nah," Alex smiled at him knowing that Olivia couldn't miss it. "It was kind of you to let me push back my moving date a few weeks to coincide with Cider with Rosie leaving Lucy's."

Freddie stomped up the stairs and landed with a pout. He grasped a suitcase handle in each hand, and bumped and banged down the stairs towards the front door and the waiting taxi.

Olivia's face pinched tighter with each slam in the stair well.

"I'm just sorry I haven't been home much. Bespoke's been off the charts. I haven't had time to breathe," said Harry.

"Don't I know it," said Olivia, reminding everyone of her presence.

Harry sniggered and smiled at Alex. "Shame you couldn't stay longer, but I understand why you're going. A larger bedroom, your best friend? You'd be mad to pass that up."

"You've been wonderful hosts these past four months." She tossed her laptop bag onto her shoulder. Fibbing to Harry had become commonplace lately, though it still didn't sit well.

Tom stomped into the front room clad in only his boxer shorts. He bumped into his sister and hurled a scowl at her. "Why didn't you tell me she was leaving? Cheers, Olivia."

"I didn't hear you come home last night." She juggled the

newspaper that Tom dislodged from her arm.

"Who's going to feed my newfound Lucky Charms addiction, eh, Alex?" He wrapped himself around her shoulders, squeezing her close. "Maybe I'll see you at Broadway Market sometime. Or at the Royal Court. Give me a shout if you want a theatre buddy, yeah?"

Alex smirked at his boozy aroma. "Will do. Thanks, Tom."

"And if you want *me* to proofread your plays, Alex, just say the word." Olivia took a dainty sip from her cup and sat on the arm of the purple sofa.

Harry swiveled in place, nodding to his girlfriend. "That's my girl. I'm so glad you two got to know each other."

Alex sucked in a quick breath and widened her eyes before Harry turned back. "Yeah…"

"So, this is it, then." Harry ran a hand through his hair.

They both extended their arms at the same time. He lingered in their hug. "I'm always here if you need me, okay? Don't be a stranger."

Chin on Harry's shoulder, Alex met Olivia's stare, but didn't blink or look away. "I won't, I *promise*."

Olivia's eyes narrowed. Tom dropped down on the sofa, shaking its frame and unsettling his sister's perch.

"Before I forget…" Alex rifled through her hoodie pocket. A set of keys clinked in her hand. She handed them over with a big grin. "Thanks, Harry."

"Anytime. See ya." He stood in the doorway, watching her leave.

Tom hollered from the sofa as he crinkled the pages of Olivia's newspaper. "Bye, Miss America."

Olivia curled her lip. "Bye, Alex. Best of luck with your next play."

🌂 🌂 🌂 🌂 🌂

Lucy pushed the last of Alex's bags into her new bedroom. "I hope you didn't mind that we didn't come in to chat. I couldn't be held responsible for my tongue. It has a mind of its own."

"Fine by me," said Alex. "Olivia hung around like a bad smell. Heaven forbid I spend five minutes alone with Harry."

She dropped backward on the bare mattress and bounced several times. "A real bed. And a window and bookshelves…"

"It's definitely brighter and bigger than the bat cave at Harry's, and your female flatmate's much friendlier, too. Shame there's nothing here to match the titillation of Tom's midnight sexcapades." Lucy winked and skipped out of the room.

Freddie breezed in and flopped down beside Alex on the bed. "I'm famished. Time to pay your movers. A lovely bacon butty or sausage roll would be ace, *thanks.*"

"You dragged two suitcases down, then up some stairs. Hardly moving, Freddie."

"That's my cardio for the day. I'm knackered. I think I pulled a muscle, too."

"Lightweight," said Alex.

Lucy stamped up the stairs and into the room. "Here's a room-warming gift, courtesy of Cider with Rosie." Several pointy green arms stretched out in all directions from a huge clay pot.

Alex sat up. "Why would I want *that*? It looks like an octopus but with…spiky bits?"

"Or a bloody Triffid," said Freddie.

"What's that?" asked Alex.

Freddie smiled. "Google it."

Lucy shook her head. "It's an aloe vera plant. It wouldn't

fit in their camper van. Freds, you can have one, too."

He leaned on one elbow and adjusted his glasses to get a better look. "And let Moriarty fight with it? No, thanks. Take it to work. Your New Age sandwich bosses will probably chop it up into a salad or something."

"That's a crap gift," Alex pouted.

"I've got something much better than that horticultural horror show." Freddie stuck his hand into the back pocket of his jeans and yanked out his wallet. "Feast your eyes upon these gems." He held up four tickets, which Lucy tore from his hand. Alex followed their flight path with keen interest.

Lucy shifted the clay pot on to her hip, inspecting the tickets. She smirked at Freddie and handed them to Alex.

Her eyes popped. "Seriously? Tickets for Isabella's play?"

Freddie beamed. "Am I good or what? See, I'm much more than just a pretty face and a pert arse."

"Aw, thanks, Freddie. November 28 just can't come soon enough. It's all happening!" She flung her arms around his neck, knocking him backwards on the mattress.

"Actually, I can't take credit. Blame Mark. He picked them up."

"So all four of us can go!" Alex untangled her arms from his neck and shoulders. "I'll have to text him to say thanks."

"Mark's been working on getting tickets for a while. The run sold out, so I think he practically traded a kidney in exchange for them." Freddie ran his hand through his hair. "You were so low before the trip up north; we figured it might boost your spirits."

"It has!" Alex wasn't sure what thrilled her more—having tickets to Isabella's play, or the fact that it was Mark who got them for her.

🌂 🌂 🌂 🌂 🌂

"Did you know, it was a month ago today that I moved out of Harry's flat. I love it here, but my commute to work—*ugh!*" Alex mimed sticking her finger down her throat. She slung her laptop bag over her shoulder and walked down Henshaw Street.

"Welcome to London commuting hell." Lucy stifled a yawn. "I guess rolling out of bed on Martello Street and showing up behind the café counter in a few minutes looks *pretty good* right now."

Alex nibbled the edge of a barely toasted bagel. "I didn't think my new commute would be almost an hour long. It's double yours. Leaving our flat at seven thirty is killing me. It's just another incentive to find a new job."

They turned onto Balfour Street, barely dodging an older man and his hyperactive corgi storming out from the Victory Community Park. "I'm surprised you haven't bumped into Olivia in your old 'hood." Lucy hopped back onto the sidewalk.

"Greasy spoons aren't her style, darling," joked Alex, kicking her biker boots through a heap of crunchy brown leaves. "But yeah, it's just a matter of time."

"Have you spoken to Harry?"

"Once, last week. He asked about the flat, my writing. It still felt weird, not being honest about what went on with Olivia. I mentioned taking my laptop over to the National to write. He got excited by that, so that's all we talked about."

Lucy yanked at her black pencil skirt underneath her trench coat. "Sod it! This thing keeps twisting with every step."

"You look professional and pretty." Alex sighed at her jeans, and red and blue t-shirt underneath her open jacket. "I'd gladly trade places with you. I can't wear anything nice. It all

241

gets covered in grease spatters and coffee stains."

Lucy tugged at her waistband once more and gave up the battle. "Are you headed to the National after work?"

Alex looked ahead as they turned onto New Kent Road. A parade of five double-decker buses with steamed up windows chugged towards Elephant and Castle Tube station. "Yeah, but it's a pain. From London Fields station, it takes forty minutes to get there."

"Well, go somewhere else. You don't have to travel all that way."

"No, I like it there. I just wish it were closer. By the time I arrive and unpack my laptop, it's already two o'clock."

"You're just going there to see Mark." Lucy nudged her with her elbow. "Smitten kitten, *gagging* for a snog!"

Alex squinted. "I am *not*. I'm going there because it's a quiet, inspiring place to write."

"Think I was born yesterday? I've seen you stalk his Face-book page. So what did you drool over most? The shirtless vacation photos from Majorca? The shot of him giving his sister away at her wedding? No, I know! I bet you went all gooey over the picture of him riding his Vespa." Lucy sang out of tune. "*Memories…*"

Alex suddenly became very interested in chipping nail polish off her thumb.

"All his posts are tags from friends, funny that…well, if you do go, ditch that ponytail. Your hair looks much prettier down," said Lucy.

Alex squeezed her ponytail. "For your information, I'm making good progress on the play I started in June. The one about the women who built Waterloo Bridge."

The Tube station loomed straight ahead. Both girls pulled

Oyster cards from their bags.

"But you never talk about it. I think that means it's not grabbing your heart like your suffragette play did. You used to blab on about that one all the bloody time." Lucy looked at her friend. "There's no passion with this new idea, I can tell."

Alex waved her Oyster card above the ticket barrier's yellow disk and slipped through its gates, waiting on the other side. "I *am* passionate about it. It's still early days. But I'm also working on an outline for another idea in case the bridge story doesn't pan out. The new one involves time travel."

Lucy lifted her satchel through the barrier. "Ooh, *Doctor Who* influenced. Nice."

They stepped onto the escalator headed downwards towards the Northern line. Lucy sneered at the posters sailing by, advertising the latest Halloween slasher flick.

"If Olivia's theft taught me one thing, it's that I should have more than one idea in the works," said Alex. "It was naïve to put all my eggs in one basket. Live and learn. I won't make that mistake again."

🌂 🌂 🌂 🌂 🌂

Alex arrived at the National Theatre just shy of two o'clock. Normally, she would have four and a half hours before theatregoers started to overwhelm the halls, but today being Wednesday, a matinee had just begun in the Olivier Theatre. The place would be still until the play's interval in about an hour's time.

The cavernous building boasted many quiet nooks and corners spread out over several floors. Today, Alex picked a ground floor table just to the right of the theatre's bookshop. She released her hair from its high ponytail, her roots sighing with relief. A quick hair toss and make-up check in her compact's mirror...

"She lives."

Alex jumped, bobbling the compact. Mark stood in front of her, dressed in a blue t-shirt and black jeans, carrying a large box sagging with wine bottles. She followed the curve of his biceps, flexed hard under their weight. His brown eyes sparkled in the dim light. A car could have crashed through the lobby, and Alex wouldn't have noticed.

"It's been a while. I was beginning to think you were a figment of my imagination." He smiled warmly.

"Hello, stranger."

"Hey!" Alex waved enthusiastically and then felt silly for doing so at such close range. The lost compact on the floor could wait. "It's great to see you." She shot up to hug him, but he half-laughed and juggled the heavy box to get a better grip. Awkward.

Alex sat back down, her cheeks getting warmer. "I'm usually writing on the second floor by the windows, but workmen are repairing the heating in the ceiling there. How are you?"

Mark nodded. "I'm good, yeah. I wasn't scheduled to work today. A friend's at an audition so I'm covering for her."

Her? Jealousy pinched Alex's stomach.

"My turn's next week. I've got an audition for a TV series. Just a small part, but the director's a favourite of mine."

"That's amazing!" Alex angled forward. If her smile stretched any further, it would need a French postcode. "I can't wait to see you on TV!"

Mark tipped his head back and broke out into an eye-crinkling grin. "Thanks. We'll see."

"Text me, and let me know how it goes?"

Whoops. Too much? Alex dialed back her enthusiasm a notch. She felt like a popcorn kernel about to burst. What was it about Mark that made her so…giddy? She last felt like this three years ago when she fell for Devin.

"I will, but actually, I'm a bit of a Luddite with smartphones and social media. It took me an hour to figure out how to text you those photos."

"The wait was worth it, though," said Alex. "That shot of you balancing the Shard on your head? Classic."

"Ha, yeah, well, my favourite was the one of you pulling Big Ben up from its point."

"You're wasted as an actor. You should work for the London Tourism Board."

"If I don't win a BAFTA soon, I'm making that switch." He laughed. "Nah, who am I kidding? I'm a social media nightmare. I lasted on Twitter for a day. And why do people post photos of their meals?"

Alex snickered, but made a mental note to quit posting snaps of cake slices from Patisserie Valerie on Facebook and Instagram.

"I'm an old soul when it comes to techy stuff. I'd rather talk face to face, you know?"

"Yeah, nothing beats chatting face to face." Alex slipped under the spell of his smile. "It's more intimate."

"Exactly. See, you get me."

Alex blushed. "I do. And that's why I must thank you again for the play tickets…no texting emoji can match this face-splitting grin. And all the trouble you went to…"

"No trouble at all. I knew how badly you wanted to go," said Mark.

"I'll see you there, right?"

245

"You will. It's a date."

"Can't wait." A date! Alex lost the ability to blink...and speak. Damn that wine box...her body vibrated with the urge to touch him.

Mark raised his eyebrows at her laptop. "Wow, that's an oldie but a goodie. It's almost as old as mine. How's your writing coming?"

"It's getting there. I've been devoting every spare moment to it."

"I bet you've written some great stuff. I'd love to read it when you're ready to share..."

"Maybe you could act it out? Well...as long as you don't mind playing a woman."

"I'm nothing if not open-minded. I did a production of the *Rocky Horror Picture Show* once. My legs look smashing in fishnets and heels." He winked. "So, how's work?"

"Okay. Though, I'm looking for something better paid or theatre-related. There's not a lot out there."

He repositioned the box in his arms. "I heard someone talking the other day about upcoming postings for backstage tour guides. Sounds like a cool gig. It also involves working in admin and at the stage door."

Butterflies fluttered in Alex's belly. "Really? That would be perfect."

"Most of the jobs here require an online application, but I can put a good word in for you. It can't hurt, right? A few of the higher-ups drop by the bar on Fridays after six, and if the jobs haven't been posted yet, maybe you can get a jump on the queue."

Alex bounced in her seat, her hands flying to her mouth. "Oh, God. That would be awesome. Thanks! I'd love to work here. I know it inside out."

Mark laughed. "I heard. Freddie says you could teach the current guides a thing or two."

"I doubt that…"

"It would be a great fit. No promises, but leave it with me."

He nodded at a bartender who strode past. "That's my supervisor. I should get back before the interval. Maybe the next time I see you, we'll *both* be working here."

Mark sauntered off towards the Long Bar and looked back over his shoulder. Alex didn't peel her eyes away fast enough. He caught her gaze and unleashed a heart-stopping grin. She slid down in her chair and hid behind her hair.

TWENTY-FIVE

One month later

"Did you know that some of the National Theatre's props and costumes are available for hire?"

A chorus of "oohs" and "ahs" slipped from the lips of Alex's tour group of twelve theatre fans.

"With over 60,000 costumes in the theatre's collection—all crafted in-house—your fancy dress dreams can become reality. If you're looking for an enchanting Elizabethan gown or a knight in shining armor for a party or your Christmas celebrations next month, you've come to the right place. Why should the actors have all the fun?"

"Exactly," said one excitable American visitor.

"And with a return to our starting point, this ends our backstage tour of the National Theatre. We hope you've enjoyed your afternoon with us. Thanks for coming, and we hope you'll see one of our productions soon."

The group enthusiastically applauded Alex for a job well done.

"I'd love to rent something for my themed wedding," said a breathless bride-to-be as she handed Alex the fluorescent orange bib that all tour participants must wear. "Imagine dressing up in a gown worn on stage by Helen Mirren."

"We'll definitely look into it," said her doting mother.

Alex grinned as they headed towards the bookshop. Mark was right. This job was a perfect fit. Her enthusiasm and extensive knowledge of the National made her popular with visitors and her bosses. She had only been handling tours for two weeks when she was pulled aside by her supervisor and praised for her professionalism and breezy presentation. Her favourite perk—besides helping at the stage door and interacting with the actors—was the free ticket to every production at the National. In order to provide insider commentary, tour guides had to be up-to-date on every play performed. Watching Britain's best actors never felt like work.

It also didn't hurt that with this job, she saw Mark more often, too. She spent more time with him on her breaks and after her shifts than she did writing on her laptop on the second floor.

She grabbed her peacock-blue wool coat from the cloakroom and skipped to Kitchen, the National's café. Freddie munched on a half-destroyed piece of red velvet cake near the window, overlooking the South Bank terrace.

"Did you give away all the National Theatre's deepest darkest secrets?"

"Every single one of them." Alex sat down, adjusted her black pleated miniskirt, and let out a satisfied sigh. "You'll never guess what happened this morning. I touched Benedict's costume from *Frankenstein*. God, I love this job."

"I filed countless dusty copies of ancient BBC scripts. I almost sneezed myself inside out. Look! My eyes are still bloodshot. Envious?"

"Not a smidge, sorry. But tell me...how was Moriarty's appointment?" Alex looked at her phone. "It's only twenty past five. I didn't expect you here so soon."

Freddie handed her a fork. "He's fine. Turns out, his version of *The Reichenbach Fall* only resulted in a surface wound. Silly cat. I take a half day off, and it's a false alarm."

"Better to be safe than sorry, though." Alex pulled her coat over her shoulders to kill the November chill creeping through the window.

"True. I would've bawled if it was serious."

He shoved a large forkful into his mouth, mumbling through the cakey goodness. "But being stuck in the vet's waiting room did have its benefits. Guess what I spotted on Twitter? A huge con combining *Sherlock* and *Doctor Who* in January."

Alex gawped at him, dropping cake on the v-neck of her ruched purple blouse. "Seriously?"

"It looks pricey. Tickets go on sale next week, but I'm *soooo* going," said Freddie. "I'll deal with the financial punch to the face later. You're in, right?"

"I hope so." She swatted the cake crumbs from her boob. "The question is will my chequing account play along? I'm still waiting for my first payday."

"Borrow off Lucy. Get her to crack her rainy day fund. If there ever was an emergency, this is it. You were excited touching Cumberbatch's costume. How about touching HIM?"

"Cause of death: Benedict Cumberbatch." Alex licked icing from her fork. "But actually, I'm more excited to meet Andrew Scott. They can't leave out Moriarty, can they?"

Freddie's fork flashed as he stabbed the last bit of cake. "He got swarmed at Sherlocked. They'd be fools not to include him. Maybe this time I'll remember to show him a photo of *my* Moriarty." He glanced upwards. "Speaking of Irish actors…"

Mark strode over to their table. "There you are."

He nodded towards the foyer. "Lex, there's a guy asking for you at the bar. He went to the box office first and had no joy, so he came to us."

"Oooh, Lex! A mysterious admirer," said Freddie. "Hey, Keegs, does he have a telly in his belly and answer to Tinky-Wink—"

Alex kicked him under the table. "A guy?"

Mark looked blankly at Freddie and shrugged. "I've never seen him before. He's American, has a shaved head?"

Alex rose from the chair and draped her coat over her arm. "Must be from my last tour."

Mark laid his hand on the small of her back and guided her out of the café. Alex caught her breath. Mark's hand. *There*. The hairs on her neck silently stood to attention, craving so much more.

"By the way, I meant to warn you about next week. Isabella's play sounds totally off-kilter. We might have a 'rollercoaster situation', if you know what I mean. You'd better hold me tight—*just in case*." Mark's eyes wouldn't leave Alex's face. And his hand…now firmly planted on the curve of her waist.

"Not if I grab you first." Alex devoured Mark's gaze as his hand coaxed her closer. Her hip bumped his thigh, but neither pulled away. If only the American demanding her attention would vanish. She hated him already.

They approached the soft benches directly in front of the bookshop. A stocky guy dressed casually in beige cargo pants, a blue plaid shirt, and North Face windbreaker shot to his feet. A St. Louis Cardinals baseball cap dangled from the strap of a black backpack that rested on the seat.

The intoxicating smolder teasing Alex's body abruptly fizzled.

Devin.

Mark didn't clue in and reacted like nothing was wrong. "I'll see you later, okay?"

"Okay. Thanks." She swallowed, trying to wash away the lump in her throat. She didn't want Mark to leave her on her own...with him.

Devin swooped in for a hug. Alex stepped back sharply, her jaw snapped tight.

Mark's eyes narrowed. He slowed his pace towards the Long Bar and doubled back. "Lex, are you—?"

His supervisor intercepted his return, waving a list. "Mark, give me a hand with these cocktails for the Lyttleton reception..."

He half-listened to his boss, nodding while his eyes darted between Alex and Devin.

For Mark's benefit, Alex's face softened. She held her hand up and mouthed 'It's okay', releasing him to deal with his boss. When Mark didn't look back over his shoulder, she glared at her ex with a squint. "What are you doing here? How did you find me?"

He jammed his hands into his pockets, but his vivid blue eyes smiled easily. "Your friend Olivia. Your mom gave me your home number in June, but when I called last week, Olivia said you had moved. She mentioned something about you writing here, so I took my chances. I'm staying nearby at the Travelodge on Waterloo Road."

Alex crossed her arms and leaned away from him. "I almost didn't recognize you."

"The buzz cut?" He ran his hand over the brown stubble on his scalp. "Yeah, I shaved my head. If I'm travelling around Europe for a few months, it's one less thing to worry about. I was just in Italy." The skin on his sunburnt nose and cheeks pulled painfully tight each time the corners of his mouth leapt into a grin.

She stared coldly at the floor and noticed his footwear. White running shoes—so American tourist. "Are you here alone?"

Devin nodded. "Can we go somewhere and talk?"

"There's nothing more to say."

"I know you'd rather punch me in the face than have a civil conversation. And I deserve that. But…things were left unsaid. Give me five minutes of your time, and then I'll leave you be. Please?" His eyes pleaded.

She turned back towards Kitchen, catching Freddie on the approach. Alex's furrowed brow didn't go unnoticed. "Lex, everything okay?" He placed a hand on her shoulder and stepped protectively into the space beside Devin.

"Freddie, this is Devin. Devin…Freddie."

Devin extended his hand towards him. "Nice to meet you, man."

"Quite." Freddie stood firm, ignoring Devin's attempt at engagement. The American quickly pulled his hand away and stowed it in his jacket pocket.

"Devin wants to talk. Shouldn't be long. I'll meet you back here soon, okay?"

"I'm here if you need me." Freddie's eyes didn't budge from Devin. "Come to the Long Bar when you're done." He backed away, giving Alex a slight nod.

"Let's head outside," said Alex. "We can't chat here. I'm

done for the day, but my boss is still about."

She forced her arms into the sleeves of her coat and walked ahead of him, searching for a location that wasn't too comfortable; the less time spent talking to him, the better.

The theatre's glass doors slid open. The perfect venue stretched across the Thames in front of her. "Have you seen the view from Waterloo Bridge?"

Devin shook his head.

"Follow me."

They climbed the nearby cement steps in silence, Alex leading the way with Devin in her shadow. She stomped along the bridge's eastern sidewalk and stopped a third of the way across, the late afternoon's darkness dotted by office lights, illuminated attractions and the occasional helicopter slicing through the sky.

"You've come all this way. Say your piece." Alex fished a chewing gum packet out of her coat pocket. Her gaze swept across the eastern skyline, flitting from Somerset House and St. Paul's Cathedral to the Oxo Tower and the Shard.

"I see you're still wearing the necklace I gave you…"

Alex exhaled heavily and yanked her coat closed. She shoved a stick of gum in her mouth, her eyes still avoiding him.

"I made a huge mistake," said Devin.

A procession of four double-decker buses rumbled past, kicking up a blast of wind filled with crisp leaves across the pavement.

Alex brushed her wayward bangs out of her eyes, staring down at the muddy Thames, churning like chocolate milk in a blender. She snapped her gum and began to rip its packaging into shreds.

"I've felt sick about everything that happened. I'm not that person. I don't lie. I've felt like a fraud ever since," said Devin.

Alex tossed tiny pieces of gum wrapper one by one into the river. "Well, our relationship certainly was a fraud."

Devin shook his head. "Not in the beginning, it wasn't. Not for two years."

"And now you're with Taylor…so, all is right in the world." Alex chucked the last tatters of paper down to their watery grave.

"No, we broke up."

Alex snorted and raised her voice. "Fantastic. What do you want? Sympathy? I don't give a shit about either of you, okay? I'm only standing here to get some closure. You two tore my life to shreds. The two people I trusted more than anyone. What don't you get?"

Devin did a double take at the passing office workers glaring at them. He kept his volume low. "Alex, I get it. That's why I'm here. I treated you terribly. I'm so sorry."

"So you come here to apologize *now*? It must be nice to clear your conscience and move on. But I'm still dealing with being left and lied to. It's too little, too late."

"Maybe. But I owe you an honest explanation at least. I never gave you one."

Alex turned away and leaned on top of the white painted railing, gnashing her gum at a fast clip.

"…It wasn't planned. That's the truth. I know that sounds like a total cop-out, but I never set out to cheat on you. Taylor and I, we were both home in Louisville that summer. We hung out a lot. She was in a bad place. Remember how upset she was about her parents' divorce?"

Alex rolled her eyes skyward. "You're preaching to the converted."

"I tried to distract her—took her to movies, concerts. One

night we had too many tequila shots. She was really upset. One thing led to another. We kissed. I swore it wouldn't happen again, but it did."

"I don't need to hear all about your grand seduction. Just tell me. When did you *sleep* together?"

"Is the *when* that important?"

"Devin!"

"…That first night."

Alex threw her arms into the air, just missing a fast walking businessman on his smartphone. "You're disgusting. You couldn't get into her pants quick enough."

"I missed you. I guess I was…lonely." Devin scratched at the stubble on the back of his head. "This sounds terrible but…it felt exciting, risky…we both figured it would be a harmless hook-up that wouldn't survive beyond the summer. But it was hard to end once we came back to Emory."

"Yeah, and then you and I started up where we left off in the spring. I didn't leave your room for days, remember? No wonder Taylor was off with me that first week." Alex shook her head. "At least you didn't give me crabs or gonorrhea. I should count my blessings. God, I feel like a walking billboard for naivety."

"I always used a condom."

"Oh nice! That's you to a tee, Devin. Ever so thoughtful, even with a raging hard-on for my best friend."

"I still loved you—even in the middle of it all. I felt torn."

"But you didn't love me enough to keep it in your pants— or be honest about it afterwards."

Arms crossed, she leaned against the railing and bared her teeth. "You two danced around the truth for weeks. Taylor froze me out. All those cancellations, ignored texts. I felt guilty, like I had done something *to her*…and you, you were almost *too* attentive. Suddenly driving me to my part-time job. Surprising me in the library with cookies…and then—bam! One morning I'm cuddled up in your duvet while you shower, and a Snapchat message lights up your phone…"

Devin bowed his head.

"You know what's the worst part of all this…you were *everything* to me. You were the one who helped me deal with my panic attacks. By sophomore year, I didn't have them anymore, remember?"

He nodded, avoiding eye contact.

"You were always supportive, listened to my problems with my mom. Encouraged me to keep going in spite of her opposition."

"I tried to," he said softly.

"But when you fucked Taylor, all that foundation crumbled. The panic attacks started again and all that self-doubt I battled came flooding back. I felt abandoned all over again."

She jabbed a finger into her own chest, sniffing back tears. "I loved you more than anything. But that wasn't *enough*, was it? Mine wasn't the face you searched for on campus. It wasn't me you thought about before falling asleep…"

They both stared straight ahead down the Thames. Big Ben chimed six times in the distance behind them.

"Cast aside. Replaced. Forgotten." Alex wiped her eyes. "And now you *want* something, right? That's why you're *really* here. So, c'mon—what is it?"

He offered a weak smile, but pulled it back when Alex didn't look at him. "I know it's a big ask…I just wish you could forgive me. Or at least not be mad at me anymore. I think it would help you move on. It would help both of us."

A half-laugh rose in her throat. She pounded her fist against the railing. "Well, I can't. You lied. Pretended everything was normal. You broke my heart..."

She stopped short, her tight grimace breaking apart into a full-on laugh.

Devin flinched. "What's so funny?"

"Why didn't I realize this before *now*?"

"What?"

"God, I have to laugh. Otherwise..." She shook her head. "It's so *Gossip Girl*!"

"Sorry?" He shrugged. "You guys used to binge watch it on Netflix, yeah, I know..."

"I was Blair. Taylor was Serena. You were Nate. We were bloody *Gossip Girl*. The love triangle? Serena slept with Nate behind Blair's back at the Sheppard wedding."

"*Gossip Girl*, eh? That's funny," said Devin.

"Not for you, it's not. Sorry...I can't forgive you." Alex rubbed her nose and buttoned her jacket. "I'm sorry you came all this way for something I can't give. Wait—what the hell? Why am I saying sorry to *you*?"

"What happened between us is the biggest regret of my life. It's never too late to change your mind. I hope you'll be able to forgive me one day."

"You're going to be waiting a *long* time, Devin." Alex spat out her gum and hurled it into the Thames.

"Are you...seeing anyone?" His eyebrows pinched together. "That bartender guy back there, the one with his hand on your waist..."

Alex gripped the railing, her knuckles drained of colour. "What gives *you* the right..." She shouted at the rippling waves. "Is that it? Are we done?"

Devin nudged closer and leaned on the railing beside her, filling his lungs with cool air. "Alex, please...I know you better than anyone. I think you got on that plane to run away. To run away from the hurt I caused you. I'm just relieved to see you're making a fresh start after all that upset. At least something good's come out of all this."

Her head turned slightly towards his voice, but her gaze didn't budge from the river. The urgent lapping of the waves against a marooned barge fell into sync with her breathing.

"In college, it was clear to everyone that you had what it takes. I've since realized, I don't. You know Dad's always been on me to join his law firm. Well, after this gap year, I'm heading to law school. I need a fresh start, too."

Alex looked at him with narrowed eyes. "But you *love* acting?"

Devin winked. "Not to worry, babe. I'll save my theatrics for the courtroom."

A glimpse of the old Devin, bringing levity to a difficult situation. Alex cracked a half smile and then chastised herself for doing so. What's that saying? There's a fine line between love and hate...

"But you're not me. You're talented. I think coming here on your own is inspiring. I always knew you had it in you. *Always*. I know it might not mean much coming from me, but I hope you keep following your dream. Don't listen to your mom or anyone else who says you can't make it. You can. And you will."

A few cold drops fell from the evening sky, dotting the pavement.

Alex couldn't breathe. The pedestrians, the boats on the Thames, the buses whizzing by—it all faded away into the darkness, leaving only Devin's words suspended in her mind. She glanced up at his shirt; the first three buttons undone, revealing his slightly tanned neck and a fine sweep of chest hair. How often had she laid her head there? Safe, fulfilled—loved? Same old Devin...

He smiled warmly. *That smile.* Alex's heart skipped a beat. She trembled, but it wasn't because of the November rain.

"I guess I've said what I came to say. And I know you won't believe me, but I couldn't replace you, or forget you. Take care of yourself, Lexy."

Devin tossed his backpack over his shoulder and ambled down the bridge towards the steps to the South Bank.

TWENTY-SIX

Alex paused for a moment, unsure whether to chase after Devin or leave him be. A swarm of exuberant kilt-wearing schoolgirls unleashed from the National overwhelmed the sidewalk, so she could no longer spot him bobbing along the bridge.

She ducked her head into her coat's collar, trying to hide from the light drizzle, and jostled her way through the squealing herd. Her quivering legs made the trip down the cement stairs jerky and clumsy, like she was a newborn foal using its muscles for the first time. No sign of Devin in any direction. Alex wiped her nose with the back of her hand and hurried into the National's lobby.

"Finally." Freddie caught up to Alex in front of the bookshop. "I was going to send out a search party. How'd it go? You okay? You're shaking."

"I'm fine. Just cold and wet." Her flighty hands combed through her damp hair as her watery eyes stared past Freddie. "I need a drink."

"No worries. Mark's busy with his boss…Lucy's on her way from the office."

Alex's fingers grabbed at the waistline of her coat, desperate to pull it tighter.

Freddie's green eyes blinked rapidly. "Sure you're fine? You seem wobbly...want a brandy?"

"No. Jack and Coke."

Freddie pulled her under his arm, and they swerved as one through the growing pre-theatre crowd. "Sure thing, Little Miss Bossy. So...what did the frat boy have to say for himself?"

Alex sank down on a plastic white chair a few steps from the bar. "He's not a frat boy."

"Okay. Let me rephrase that...what did your shitty ex have to say for himself?"

"...He apologized."

Freddie sat down opposite her. "He must've said more than '*I'm sorry.*' You were gone nearly thirty minutes."

Mark rushed over with a hesitant grin. "Sorry. I couldn't get away...You okay, Lex? You look worlds away. Who *was* that guy?"

"I'm fine."

"She's not."

"I am."

"You're *not.*" Freddie waved Mark closer and lowered his voice. "The American bloke? Her ex. The one I told you about?"

Mark's eyes widened. "Oh, bollocks! Let me get you a drink."

Alex crossed her arms as Mark walked to the bar.

"You'll feel better if you tell me what happened." Freddie tousled his hair for a few seconds, then removed his glasses. "Does he want you back?" He rubbed his eyes so hard with his index finger that they watered.

"No! Maybe...I don't know."

"What are you going to do now?"

Alex tapped her foot against the leg of the chair, the heel of her shoe slipping off further and further with each strike. "Well, I'm not going to lock myself in my room with a pint of Ben & Jerry's, and Adele on a loop if that's what you're worried about. Where the hell's that drink?"

"So, you're *not* pining for him, then? Seeing an ex out of the blue can bring back all sorts of crazy feels—don't I know it," said Freddie. "Spotting mine in Manchester…Christ, I didn't last in that bar more than twenty seconds."

"It's complicated." Alex covered her mouth with her hand. "I'll always have a soft spot for him."

She caught Mark approaching with her drink and a pint for Freddie, and sat up straight.

"Jack and Coke? How'd you know?"

"Just a hunch." Mark smiled kindly. "It's on me."

"Thank you." Alex offered a slight grin.

"Nice. I'm here slogging away in the trenches, and Keegs gets the smile? Well, at least we're making progress." Freddie nodded at Mark as he reluctantly returned to the bar.

"I hate that Devin got the last word."

"Why, what did he say? Gimme details."

"He apologized. Several times. And told me his version of events with Taylor. My wild imagination can finally rest." Alex took a long gulp of her drink. She closed her eyes and shook her head as it prickled down her throat.

"Was it…incredibly dirty?"

"Freddie!"

"Sorry. Had to ask. So, do you feel any better about it?"

"No. It feels like I've been stabbed in the heart all over again. Seeing him was weird. It's stirred stuff up."

"Give yourself time. And booze...getting legless will defi-nitely help." Freddie picked up his pint. "So would a careless snog with a handsome devil, but maybe that's just me."

Lucy pulled up a chair beside Alex. "Hiya. Sorry I'm late. Jubilee line insanity." She dumped her satchel on the floor.

"You'll never guess who was on my train—Dominic West." She caught Freddie's frown. "Not that it *matters*...you okay, honey? I couldn't believe my eyes when I got Freddie's text. How did he ever find you?" She snatched the pint out of Fred-die's hand and took a long sip.

Alex sneered. "Olivia. Devin called Harry's flat.

"God, is there no end to her meddling? Conniving twat. So...what did he say?" Lucy swigged the pint again.

"He told me what happened. Apologized. He also said I'm 'inspiring', apparently. Shame my inspiration didn't motivate him to steer clear of Taylor's vagina."

Freddie snickered. Lucy spluttered on the pint.

"Too much?" Alex swallowed another large mouthful of her drink and winced. "Did you say hi to Dominic? I loved his danc-ing in *Pride*."

Lucy coughed, shaking her head. "You've got to stop beat-ing yourself up about what they did. Better you find out that he's a wanker with a wandering eye, and she's a deceitful prick tease. By all means, rage away. I would."

"No, no raging." Freddie crinkled his nose at Lucy, reclaim-ing his pint. "I think Lex should accept his apology and move on. Being angry, stewing over what happened? Don't. Grudges cause wrinkles—scientific fact. And ulcers. It's not pretty, any way you slice it."

"Seriously, Freddie?" Lucy's curls bounced against her shoulders with each shake of her head. "She shouldn't accept his apology. He's a pig and—"

Alex jumped in, holding up her drink. "All I want to do right now is get drunk. Become numb." She scrunched into her chair and swallowed the remaining liquid in her glass.

"Fair enough." Freddie shrugged. "I do think it says a lot how he came all that way to make peace with you. That's a pretty expensive apology. You'd only do that if you still loved the person…"

Alex buried her face in her hand.

Lucy scowled, smacking his arm. "Not helping!"

"*Just saying.*" Freddie winced.

Mark weaved through a cluster of theatregoers and placed a tray of drinks on the small table in front of his friends. "Get these down you. Final round before I cash out my shift." His eyes took in Alex, then shifted to Lucy. "What's on tap for this evening?"

"We should stop somewhere for a bite." Lucy glanced sideways at Alex, who tossed back her second drink, downing it in two gulps.

The blonde coughed and clasped her throat. "I don't need food, just another one of these."

Her three friends exchanged wide-eyed looks.

Lucy mumbled to the guys. "The booze isn't helping. She's a small thing. She can't keep this up."

Mark brushed Alex's shoulder. "I haven't eaten all day. Share a pizza with me? I won't take no for an answer."

"And then dancing, yeah?" Freddie winked at Lucy. "Good music, throwing some sweaty shapes on the dance floor…"

"I love the name of this place—Zippers. It's *soooo* funny!" Alex hiccupped between giggles and slurped another JD and Coke.

"Gay clubs have the best names. I'm glad you approve. And I'm happy you're dancing up a storm, not sobbing in the bogs." Freddie shouted over Donna Summer's *I Feel Love.*

Alex looped her arm around his neck, forcing him to hunch over. "The music's so good. It's just like the disco playlist Robbie made me a few summers ago."

The DJ mixed into *You Make Me Feel (Mighty Real)* by Sylvester, its beats taking control of Alex's hips. "Oh my God. I love this song! Robbie used to play it all the time." She shoved her empty glass into Freddie's hand and squeezed past an army of fit looking men, taking her place in the centre of the dance floor.

Freddie sat back down in their booth. "Do you think there's a chance her brother might be gay? I mean, his choice in tunes? Think about it."

Lucy rolled her eyes and yelled to Freddie. "She should've eaten more than one slice. She's out of control."

"Aw, bless. She needs this. Let her sweat it out. Look, they adore her," shouted Freddie.

Alex fluttered her skirt and grinded against two shirtless guys with glistening six-packs. Strobing lights lit up the trio in pulsating splashes of gold, blue, and red.

"I'll keep an eye on her." Mark laughed and knocked back a shot of sambuca. He slipped through the flailing arms and gyrating bodies on the dance floor.

"And I'll get more drinks in." Freddie bounced to his feet and around a group of guys in leather gear.

"Not for Lex...or me," Lucy shouted, guarding their booth.

Mark zigzagged his way to Alex, but found himself sandwiched between two well-groomed men wearing dark skinny jeans and black shirts unbuttoned to their waists.

"Alex," he hollered. "All right?"

"Mark!" She laughed with eyelids at half-mast and flung her arms around his neck.

"How 'bout we sit the next one out?" asked Mark, dabbing perspiration from his forehead. "I think you could use some fresh air."

The first notes of Robyn's *Hang with Me* flooded the dance floor. "Ooh, not yet. You've got to stick around for this one, Mark. Sing it with me!" Alex brushed against his chest, inhaling him in and swaying her hips provocatively to the beat.

Mark leaned in closer so she could hear him over the pounding sub-bass, his lips grazing her cheek. "Just this one, then. Let's see what you've got."

"I thought you'd never ask." Alex stopped mid-beat and pressed her lips against Mark's soft pout. He raised his hands in protest before dropping them slowly to rest firmly on her waist. Alex pushed her damp body into Mark's, her grip tightening behind his neck as she parted his lips with her tongue. If only she was wearing heels—his hair wouldn't stand a chance.

An over-enthusiastic dancer slammed into Mark's back, breaking their kiss.

Mark caught his breath. "You okay?"

Alex giggled and playfully slapped her hand over her mouth. Warmth crept across her cheeks, her whole body tingled. "I feel dizzzzzy."

"How many have you had?"

"Not enough," said Alex, biting her lip. "C'mon, Mark. *Play* with me." She grabbed hold of his t-shirt with both hands and started to peel it upwards from his low-rise jeans, exposing a trail of dark hair climbing towards his belly. "You like me, right?"

Mark swallowed. He nodded and clasped onto her hands, lowering their progress. "Yes, Lex. I like you. But I think you've probably had one too many."

"You taste like candy...licorice..." Alex slurred into his chest. "You're my *weakness*..."

He gently pulled her into his arms, guiding her off the dance floor while making sure she didn't stumble over dancing feet or discarded beer cans. "I think this is the booze talking, lady."

Her knees buckling, she waved a stern finger. "No. Freddie said getting Legolas would *help*."

Mark cracked up. "You mean getting *legless*..."

He picked her up and carried her the final steps towards the booth where Lucy and Freddie chatted. She clung on to Mark's shoulder like a rescued kitten, tucking her head into the nook of his neck. Once seated, the room flung itself into a stuttering spin. Alex wouldn't release her grip. Her short skirt lay rumpled, exposing her panties and sheer tights. Mark smoothed the skirt down with a single sweep of his hand.

"Ah, so funny...mmmm, kiss...*finally*..." mumbled Alex.

Lucy jumped up. "Is she all right?"

"Well, someone is," laughed Freddie. "Nice lipstick there, Keegs." He motioned to his friend to remove the burgundy smudge that overwhelmed his lips and part of his stubbly chin.

Mark flashed a cheeky grin and wiped his face with his free hand. Alex remained glued to his shoulder, rendering his right hand useless. "She's fine. Drunk, but fine."

"Mark, really...how *could* you?"

"C'mon, Lucy. I'd never take advantage." He pointed at his lips. "She pounced on me. I'm the perfect gentleman."

Freddie leaned across the table. "Don't tell me you didn't

enjoy that just a little bit."

Mark grabbed his pint and raised a roguish eyebrow at his friend.

Lucy collected Alex's bag and coat, and her own satchel and trench from the booth.

"That's enough excitement for tonight. Time to get this little one home to bed—alone."

"I mean it. I'm never drinking again. Even my hair hurts." Alex shoved her greasy bangs out of her bloodshot eyes. A chalky tablet fizzed in a glass of water on the table.

"Famous last words. Until your next ex shows up unannounced." Lucy yanked on a chair, causing it to squeal across the lounge's hardwood floor. Alex winced and snapped her eyes shut.

"I can't believe you made a move on Mark last night. Well done, you."

"God, how will I face him? He'll think I'm a slag."

"The girl with a single notch on her bedpost? I doubt it."

"Aw, Lucy. You didn't tell him that I've only slept with one guy, did you? Oh, *that's* attractive. I'm practically a nun..."

"I didn't. *I wouldn't.* But he might blame your shameless hit and run on the booze. If you really want in there, you should tell him how you feel—sharpish." Lucy bit into a piece of white toast slathered with marmalade. "Or miss your moment."

"If I wasn't drunk, I'd never have flown at him like that. God, I didn't grab his ass...or...did I?"

Lucy chuckled into her mug of tea.

Alex swiped her phone's screen. "I guess I could text him?

But he hasn't texted me. Is that a sign? I wonder what that means?"

"It means nothing. Mark's terrible with texts. Drives Freddie crazy. When was the last time you texted him and got a response?

"I always get a response." She stared at her phone as if telepathy would make him get in touch.

"You're the only one, then." Lucy shrugged. "Don't tell Freddie."

Alex began typing as Lucy crunched through a crust. "You haven't been sending him sexy Snapchats, have you?"

"Can you chew a little quieter?" Alex held her head. "You sound like a beaver chipping away at a log."

Lucy glared. "Did you just *text* him?"

"No. I was going to…but…I don't know what to say. What should I say? Lucy, help me—"

"Never mind that." Lucy yanked the phone out of her hand, setting it on the table. "Gimme details. The snog. How was it? Were tongues involved? Hands? Did he show any signs…you know, *pitching a trouser tent?*"

Alex blushed. "That kiss. I felt it everywhere. That I do remember. I wish we didn't get interrupted, to see where it could've led. Imagine, greeting the morning…with him, all naked and irresistible."

Her eyelashes fluttered closed, her eyes succumbing to visions of rumpled sheets and eager lips, his toned stomach and…

Alex's phone buzzed, shocking her back into the room. She snatched it quickly, checked the screen and then dropped the phone in her lap.

"I was all over him, wasn't I? He'll think I'm a tease."

"He *won't*." Lucy paused mid-chew. "He'll realize you're

keen. Nothing wrong with that. Personally, I think that kiss was *long* overdue."

Alex sampled the foamy water, now a murky orange colour. She stuck out her tongue and blinked. "Blech. That's disgusting! So, guess who just sent me a friend request?"

"Go on then. Is it one of those hunky gays you were grinding against?"

"No. Devin." A half-smile flitted across her face.

"Ugh, I would delete that sucker. Send him a clear message to piss off," said Lucy.

"Maybe later." Alex slid her phone into the pocket of her robe and inhaled deeply.

"What are you waiting for? Rip off that bandage. Let it hurt. Be furious. And then forget about him. He's such a shit, showing up like that."

"I can't just erase him from my life." Alex rose slowly to her feet, and gripped onto the back of her chair for balance.

"I thought you already had." Lucy shoved her crumb-filled plate away.

"I can't ignore what happened in the past," said Alex. "I thought I could...coming here, putting an ocean between us. Out of sight, out of mind, right?"

She pushed her hair out of her eyes. "But that distance disappears when you hear a song you both loved or get caught up in a random memory. And then the moment fades like an old photograph, and the distance settles in again. Seeing him *here,* though...stirred up so many buried feelings. It brought back all the happy times—and the bad ones."

"And that's why I'm so pissed at him. He's opened up all those old hurts. Doesn't he know to leave well enough alone? I don't get why you're not raging at him."

"Part of me is. I hate what he did to me. I hate that he showed up—and just when Mark and I got closer. It makes me feel…conflicted. And confused. But I'm handling it in my own way. Not everyone wants to start a world war like you do." She smiled at Lucy.

"If you let this arsehole get in the way of potential happiness with Mark, I will never speak to you again."

Alex rubbed her bloodshot eyes. "And I'm supposed to be the theatrical one."

TWENTY-SEVEN

Alex's first tour on Monday didn't start until noon, so she left her desk and went downstairs to check out the Long Bar. The supervisor and a delivery guy were shifting beer bottles. No Mark. She played with the scooped-neck of her knitted burgundy dress. Friday's kiss and the possibility of seeing him today kept her awake last night, teasing and tormenting her; the ache for him still constant, it warmed her like a fever that wouldn't break…

Where was he?

Back in the office, she pushed aside her spreadsheets and dedicated the rest of her morning to social media monitoring. She grabbed her charging phone. No texts. No photos. No joy. She hadn't received any texts all day Saturday or Sunday either. Now that Monday had arrived, shouldn't there be a funny message from Freddie about her slobbering over Mark or a cheeky hello from the snogging victim himself? Her screen stared back at her, blank.

Maybe Facebook offered some clues. Freddie last posted on Friday morning—before their night out—and Mark's page hadn't been updated for several months. Alex knew every photo, every comment by heart. What would it hurt to scroll through again? Go on, just a few minutes. His taste in pop culture made her swoon every time: *Eternal Sunshine of the Spotless Mind*, *Roman Holiday* (scooters!), *Before Sunrise*, Franz Ferdinand, Snow Patrol, The 1975—Tom Jones? That one always made her chuckle; she meant to ask him about that.

Alex sighed. She checked her email for the eighth time that hour. Nope, nothing except a promotion for geeky t-shirts at Red Bubble. She jumped between Instagram, WhatsApp, Snapchat, and Twitter, but her friends were all AWOL there, too. Why so quiet? Was a zombie apocalypse raging outside, or did her friends deem her too delicate to discuss Friday's wacko events? Maybe her behaviour horrified her entire social circle? *Oh God.* If no one wanted to talk about it, she must've made a massive fool of herself—again.

One tweet stole her attention…a *What's On Stage* post about five up-and-coming playwrights being showcased in an ambitious London-based workshop starting in December. She clicked quickly on the link.

Smiling confidently from the webpage in a beautifully staged black and white headshot…Olivia. Her bio listed her accomplishments, her BA in playwriting, *blah blah fucking blah…*

Alex's fingers scratched at her computer's touchpad, only slowing down when a certain word rolled into view— suffragettes. No need to read further.

"Cow."

Her phone pinged with a text from Harry:

'Hey Alex! Missing you 'round here. Hope all's well. Msg me when you can. H x'

She ignored it and opened a tour schedule spreadsheet.

☂ ☂ ☂ ☂ ☂

At quarter to two, Alex dropped off a tour in front of the National's bookshop and hurried across the lobby to Kitchen. The high-pitched growls multiplying in her stomach needed muzzling, pronto.

Her eyes flew around the room, pouring over each table and every customer holding trays in line. Still no sign of Mark.

She had arrived at the conclusion that apologizing was the right thing to do, even though she didn't want to apologize at all. The desire to kiss him had haunted her for weeks. Why should she be sorry? If only Mark would proclaim that their impromptu snog left him craving a repeat performance—then she could skirt 'sorry' altogether.

But what if he didn't enjoy it, if he was annoyed, or *worse* grossed out? She would deal with her embarrassment and go back to hiding her true feelings. She was getting rather good at it.

She grabbed a cute ladybug box that housed a kid-sized cheese sandwich on white, and a Pepsi, and joined the queue to pay.

"What's for lunch?" An Irish lilt floated over her shoulder.

His warm breath on her neck made her nerve endings sizzle. Found him! She scrunched her eyes and spun to face him, the pleated skirt of her dress whirling close behind.

"Wow. Fancy." He stepped back, taking in her outfit with approving eyes. "Are you just back from having cocktails at The Ivy?"

Alex smiled. "I didn't think you were working today."

"Yeah." Mark leaned in. "Scheduled every day this week, actually. But I'm hoping to get a call back this week. That TV series I was telling you about? I've read lines for the producer and director twice already. I think the third time might be the charm."

"Fingers crossed. Not that you need any luck. I'm sure you're perfect for it." She babbled and squeezed her cola can.

Mark grinned as the line shifted forward. He rested his hand on her back just long enough to nudge her ahead. "I wanted to check up on you yesterday, but my phone fell out of my pocket on the trip home Saturday night." He rolled up the cuffs of his black button-down. "Luckily I had the early shift yesterday, so I could spend the rest of the day getting a new one sorted."

Her gaze slipped between his eyes and his lips…searching for a sign…

"Next, please."

She placed her lunch on the counter with a fleeting nod to the cashier. Mark stepped up beside her, pulling out his wallet. "Let me get this. And could you add an Asian Vegetable broth, too, please?"

"You don't have to pay for mine."

"I want to."

Alex fiddled with her wallet's zipper. "Thanks."

Mark picked up the ladybug box. "That's not another cheese sarnie, is it? I'm going to start calling you Mouse."

She giggled and playfully smacked his arm. A silly grin crept across his face as he handed money to the clerk.

Alex chose the cozy banquette against the wall. Mark sat on the white chair across from her.

"It must have felt like a marching band pounding through your head on Saturday morning. You drank us all under the table."

"Yeah, it wasn't pretty." Alex popped open the ladybug

box. "I'm swearing off booze. My behaviour at the club…I'm surprised you're still speaking to me."

"Considering what you went through with your ex, I couldn't possibly pass judgment. A surprise like that is never easy." Mark smiled warmly but didn't make eye contact as he swirled his spoon in the steamy broth.

"But still. I should've known better. I was…inappropriate." She chewed a small bite. If the increasing burn in her cheeks was anything to go by, they must've been scarlet red. "I'm sorry, Mark."

"I'm not." He looked up with a smirk, and a twinkle in his eye.

Alex exhaled, her cheeks relaxing into a wide smile. *Mark enjoyed their kiss!* The desire to clear the table of plates and bowls with a single sweep of her forearm and leap across to meet his soft lips, short circuited her thoughts. Hungry café patrons carting trays stacked with cookies, coffees, and sandwiches, squeezed between tables and behind Mark's chair, creating an undulating wall between them and the restaurant. So tempting. If only they weren't at work…

Mark's eyes lingered, inviting her closer. He rested his hand on hers, its warmth passing through her body like an electric current. "Lex, you know I like you, and I was wondering—"

A tall, thin woman with light brown skin snaked behind Mark, swishing her shiny long black hair away from her face. In a single motion, she crouched down and dropped her slender fingers over his eyes. Mark flinched, his tender clasp of Alex's hand forsaken.

"Hey, Keegan. Guess who?"

His eyes masked, she twisted around and planted her plump lips on his mouth. When he squirmed, she released him, her fingers trespassing through his hair. With a satisfied smile, she swooped into the neighbouring chair.

Alex's eyes bugged out of her head. Who the hell was *this*?

Mark wiped her gooey red lipstick off his mouth with the back of his hand, his wide eyes betraying his embarrassment.

The woman rambled between breaths. "I'm so glad I found you! That part? The indie flick—it's mine! If you hadn't worked my shifts, I would've missed the auditions. Thanks, babe."

"Oh…" Mark didn't know where to look. "I didn't think I'd see you today. Weren't you off filming an advert?"

"Nah, the director's sick. It's been put off until next week."

Mark hesitated, then placed his hand—the one that was just holding Alex's hand—on the smoocher's back. "Alex Sinclair, meet Naomi Khan. Naomi, this is Alex."

"Hi, nice to meet you," said Naomi.

Alex's eyes darted from the brazen gatecrasher to Mark and back again. This girl was a total stunner, so exotic looking and friendly—so friendly that she placed her hand on Mark's upper thigh. Alex blinked several times to make sure her eyes weren't playing tricks. Nope. Actually, did Naomi's hand just slide further towards his crotch? Alex's stomach curdled. This chick wasn't subtle at all.

"Naomi just got back from a ten-month gig with the touring production of *Kinky Boots*," said Mark, shifting in his seat. "Alex's a playwright from Florida. You visited Florida, right?"

"We did. Performed in Miami. Extremely generous audiences. I loved it there," said Naomi.

Alex bit her cheek. *Great—so why didn't you stay there?*

Naomi faced Mark straight on. Her enviable breasts strained against her tight red top. Come to think of it, this girl would make the perfect Victoria's Secret Angel; striking, tall with long slim legs…a total nightmare.

"I can breathe easy now. I *had* to see you. Sometimes you're impossible to find, Mark…" Naomi beamed and abandoned his thigh to play with the hair above his temple.

Alex slumped back against the banquette and pushed her sandwich away.

"I'm chuffed it worked out." Mark glanced at Alex and moved slightly so Naomi's hand could no longer fondle his swept back locks.

The actress grasped her non-existent stomach. "I'm *starving*. I should've eaten before my shift." She helped herself to a spoonful of Mark's soup. "Mmm, love its crispy noodles. Alex, you should try this. I bet it tastes much better than—what is that? The cheese sandwich from the kiddie's menu?"

Alex wrapped her arms around her stomach and offered a tight-lipped smile.

"Lex has food allergies; she has to be careful," said Mark. "And the kids' menu's really good, actually. Don't knock it until you try it."

"You were always partial to a cheese butty." Naomi stood up, unfurling her skinny jean-clad legs. "I'm due upstairs in the Terrace Restaurant. I wish they'd stop stealing us Long Bar staff. I prefer working down here with you."

Mark stood up, giving Naomi a tentative parting hug.

She grabbed the Irishman, smooshing her chest into his, a sheet of paper couldn't squeeze between them. "Maybe I'll see you tomorrow on my break?" Naomi flipped a glance over Mark's shoulder. "Lovely to meet you, Alex. See you 'round."

Her perfect ass sashayed towards the lobby, collecting admiring looks in its wake.

Alex felt like she had been shoved off Tower Bridge. "Old

friend?"

"Kind of…" Mark rubbed an eyebrow. "We sorta *went out*."

Alex gulped. "Oh." Her suspicion realized.

"We hooked up a few times. She dropped me like a brick a year ago when she landed the touring *Kinky Boots* tour."

The blonde held her breath, trying to keep her heart from leaping out of her chest and dive-bombing the cold floor.

"I didn't hear from her until two months ago, just before she came home. She needed a gig, so I suggested she try here. It's a great place if you need time off for auditions."

"I bet…Do you help all the girls you know get jobs here?"

Mark's eyebrows scrunched. "*All* the girls…?"

Alex shook her head, unable to look at him. "I'm so dim. I didn't realize you had a girlfriend."

"I don't. Not now. Naomi's *just a friend*."

She'd heard those three words pass an actor's lips before.

"Really?" Alex scoffed. "She's *very* hands-on. Friends don't usually stroke each other's thighs."

Mark leaned forward, attempting to bridge the gulf growing between them. "Naomi, she's—" His arm caught the lip of the bowl, splashing hot soup into his lap. He jerked upwards. "Shit!" His hands scrambled across the table for napkins.

Alex snatched her wallet and scooted out of the banquette. "I've got tour prep to do."

"Lex! Wait."

Her eyes began to sting. She rushed through the café doors and out to the riverfront.

Alex signed off on her last tour, grabbed her coat, and slipped into the ground floor ladies' toilets. She hid in the farthest stall.

Mark had called three times since lunch. She listened to his messages:

'*Lex, where'd you go? I've been to your desk and searched every floor. Come see me at the bar, okay? Bye...*'

'*Hey, Alex. It's four thirty. I know your next tour doesn't start until five. Call me before you start?*'

'*Lex, my shift's finished. I'm sat right now in your writing spot. It's just gone six thirty-five. I'd really like to talk...*'

She frowned. The onslaught of messages could only mean one thing—guilt. He'd probably keep calling until she answered, or worse—he'd call Freddie and get him to find her; the fewer people in the mix, the better.

Watching Naomi in action, it was clear her designs—not to mention her hands—were all over him. How could she compete with Sex On Legs? Or trust him? How do guys say no to some one so obviously 'up for it'? Especially someone they'd slept with before.

She fanned her burning cheeks. It was foolish to think that Mark wouldn't be enjoying female company. Just because she wasn't into hook-ups or dating multiple people didn't mean that he wasn't. But sharing Mark with another woman? She couldn't do it. As much as she fancied him, she couldn't subject herself to the insecurity of another love triangle, the wounds from the Devin-Taylor entanglement raw again, thanks to his reappearance Friday. She'd cared deeply once, and it had nearly destroyed her. Perhaps it was too soon to get involved with anyone, anyway.

When the loo emptied, she abandoned her stall, blotting a damp paper towel over her forehead. She reapplied her smudged eye makeup.

Get it together, Alex.

She took a final deep breath before exiting the washroom. Maybe Naomi's epic timing earlier was a good thing. Since accepting the tour guide job, her writing had taken a backseat; all her free time here, devoted to Mark. Well, not any more. Time to wake up. Time to let him go. After all, unlike Devin, Mark was never hers to begin with.

She strode up one level of stairs, then another. On the landing leading to the second floor, she paused to catch her breath. Her heart beat loudly in her ears, blocking out the anticipatory buzz rising from tonight's theatregoers on the ground floor. A shadow stretched down the stairwell from above, blanketing her head, then her shoulders.

"Hello, stranger. I hoped I'd find you here." Mark grinned sheepishly as he hopped down the steps towards her.

His hair looked particularly hot tonight. Silky. Thick. Fluffy. What would it be like to grab fistfuls of it?

Alex swallowed and shook her head, erasing the image. Her hands trembled. She tucked them under crossed arms, hiding the evidence. "Sorry for leaving in such a rush earlier." Her eyes flitted to his chest. "I…forgot. My supervisor, she wanted to see me before my last tour."

Mark cleared his throat, his tone playing along. "Is everything okay *now*? Did you get it sorted?" His lips stretched into an impish smirk.

"I did, thanks." Alex glanced at his puppy dog eyes and then quickly diverted her gaze to the safety of the floor. She couldn't look at his eyes, lips, or that hair or else she'd stray. "Look, Mark, I didn't say everything that I wanted to say at lunch." She feared he could hear her heart pounding through her dress.

His face lit up. "Neither did I. Sorry for the interruption. I was going to a—"

Alex cut him off. "On Friday night, seeing Devin made me all nostalgic. You were there. I was drunk and…the kiss was a mistake; it didn't *mean* anything."

He shook his head, a concerned frown darkening his face. "…I don't think you really believe that."

"Putting you in an awkward situation like that wasn't fair to you. *Or* Naomi ...."

Mark stepped closer, his reassuring hands reaching for hers. "Lex, you've got this all wrong—"

"No, I *don't.*" Alex kept her arms crossed and backed up, the heel of her shoe scraping against the cement wall.

"I have a ton of writing to do, so I can't have another night like last Friday. I keep getting sidetracked…It's got to stop. Writing's my priority—"

Buoyant voices bent around the stairwell's corner, drowning out Alex's words. Three, four—six theatre patrons emerged into view, their light-hearted conversation drying up at the sight of Alex sloped against the wall and Mark, his lips only inches away from hers, resting his hand above her head.

The interlopers increased their pace, disappearing up the stairs.

Mark closed his eyes and sighed heavily.

She could breathe him in. So close. Close enough to kiss.

Alex's voice cracked. "Best to forget about the other night so we can both…move on." Her stomach churned like the Gulf of Mexico in a hurricane.

Mark swept his hair off his forehead. "Alex, I fully support your writing, you *know* that…don't do this. Let's go somewhere private to talk—"

Her eyes stung as his words fell to the floor, rejected. She raised her voice. "I *said* we need to move on. Can we drop it. *Please?*"

Mark rubbed his hands over his face. When they fell, he shifted backwards with a nod, but his dull eyes and slumped shoulders contradicted that assent. He scuffed the floor with his boot. "Sure. If that's what you really want."

"Please don't say anything to Freddie or Lucy. I'm embarrassed enough as it is."

Resting his hands on his hips, he tipped his head back, glancing at the ceiling. "Okay."

"Goodbye, Mark."

Head bowed, Alex squeezed past him. She rushed down the stairs as fast as her shaking legs could carry her.

On the journey home, Alex dried her tears, her mind and heart pulling in two different directions. Her thoughts lay tangled like a string of Christmas lights, while her heart felt hollowed out, a mere shell left behind. Turning onto Henshaw Street, the local kids were playing soccer on the road. She could relate to their deflated ball, kicked to the curb again and again. With a heavy sigh, she dodged around the erstwhile Ronaldos and Rooneys. There was no turning back—she'd get her head down, lock her heart away, and write through the pain. Full stop. She quickly closed the flat's red painted door on their joyful shouts.

"Hey, sunshine, good day at work?" Freddie cleared plates and cutlery from the table. The tomato-y aroma of spag bol saturated the flat.

"Don't you ever eat at home?" asked Alex.

"Ooh, a bit harsh. Someone's got the hump."

Lucy strode in from the kitchenette. "Was the Tube delayed at Lambeth North again? I'd be pissed, too…hey, did you talk to Mark?"

Freddie abandoned the table clearing and plopped down on a chair. "So, where's he taking you on your date? I want all the gory details."

"He's not."

"Why not?" asked Freddie. "I *know* he likes you. He was going to ask you out."

"I wouldn't know. It doesn't matter, anyway. I only have time right now for my first love…"

Lucy crossed her arms. "Bloody Devin? Fuck—I *knew* it!"

"Not Devin, Lucy. *Writing*. It's time to knuckle down. No diversions. No distractions and *definitely* no booze or boys."

"How boring," said Freddie.

She shook her head. "I've also got Dad's cheque to think about. He's put so much faith in me. I can't let him down. London's crazy expensive—and that money's not going to last forever—"

"But what did Mark actually say?" asked Lucy.

"Nothing much. He didn't have to."

"Well, if you blurted out that shit about 'distractions' and 'boys', you probably scared him right off," said Lucy. "You two could've been great together. I'm blaming you if it's awkward at the play next weekend."

"If I know Keegs, he won't give up easily. When he fancies someone, he's patient and persistent," said Freddie.

"Don't start writing your best man speech just yet, Freddie. Well, not for me and Mark, anyway." She mumbled under her breath. "Maybe for him and *Naomi*."

Lucy's ears pricked up. "Who's Naomi?"

"Naomi? Naomi *Khan*? She's back? That's weird. Mark hasn't mentioned it." Freddie shoved his glasses back up his nose. "Hmm. I thought she would've latched onto some rich bloke in the States, never to return."

"Somebody tell me. Who's Naomi?" asked Lucy.

"Remember that actress? Mark's co-star in that Simon Stephens' play, a year and a half back? The one at the Royal Exchange in Manchester?"

Lucy stared blankly at Freddie.

"Legs that don't stop, big boobs, beautiful light brown skin? Half French, half Indian?"

"Oh, God. *That* one. Yes, I do."

"That's Naomi," said Freddie.

"Well, *that* Naomi is back and has her claws into Mark," said Alex.

"I *doubt* that," said Freddie. "She moved on the moment she boarded that flight to New York last year. Sure, he was flattered. Who wouldn't be with all...*that*. It was hot for a spell, a right bonk-a-thon...I didn't see Mark around for weeks, but they quickly fizzled out. She's got bigger targets in her scope than Keegs. And it didn't take him long to figure that out, either."

"Didn't look like it this afternoon at the National. She practically unzipped his jeans right in front of me," said Alex.

"Fuck. I thought he was better than that. God, all men are pigs," said Lucy.

"*Ahem.* Not all of us, sweetie." Freddie picked up his phone. "Look, I'll text him. Find out what the hell's going on."

"No! Don't." Alex yanked her hair off her forehead. "I'm *serious*, Freddie. Don't. He's been a distraction. I didn't come here to find a boyfriend."

"But if you're really devoting 100 percent of your heart to writing, Lex, why are you blinking back tears? I think you doth protest too much, my darling."

Her bottom lip trembled. "It's been a long day. I'm tired. I'm starving. And I'm behind in my writing. Stop assuming I'm upset about *him*. I'm not." She pounded upstairs and slammed her door.

Lucy turned to Freddie. "And I'm Beyoncé."

Twenty-Eight

That night, Freddie and Lucy clashed over what to do. Freddie pleaded with Lucy— "just one text to Mark, go on!"—but Lucy stood firm. Two cups of tea and a packet of biscuits later, she'd won: Alex needed time and distance from Mark—not to mention Devin—to write and to heal her heart; she also needed their united support, more than ever. Alex had been panic attack-free since her move, and Lucy wanted to keep it that way.

Tuesday through Thursday, Alex couldn't keep tea or toast down. She didn't fight Lucy's suggestion of calling in sick and stayed bundled up in her bedroom, writing in between naps and sprints to the toilet. She blamed a dodgy chicken burger late Monday night for her digestive unraveling, but she didn't fool anyone.

Lucy occasionally knocked on her flatmate's bedroom door to check if she needed crackers or water, but got shooed away every time. When Alex fled to the toilet, she'd sneak in to leave behind a banana or a sports drink, worried that her friend was plunging further into dehydration and desperation. She knew Alex would kill her if she ever caught wind of her snooping, but

Lucy took a moment to scroll through the screen on the open laptop. Page upon page of writing met her intrusive eyes. Lucy smiled at her discovery. The taps in the bathroom squealed their alert, so she tiptoed out of the room and back downstairs.

Come Friday, Alex wobbled into work. Despite the dark circles and ghostly pallor, she donned her black pinstriped trousers, slim-fitting pink sweater, and flats, and acted the part of a happy, confident tour guide. Chatting with visitors boosted her spirits and by the end of her final tour at quarter to six, a slight smile warmed her cheeks.

Coat and phone in hand, she walked along the lip of the bookstore's entrance, keeping her distance from the Long Bar. A girlish howl filled her ears, coaxing her eyes where they didn't want to linger. There was Naomi, head thrown back, laughing and dusting something off Mark's chest. Fuck. Alex's delicate stomach deflated like a punctured Yorkshire pudding. Rubbing it in, a familiar chorus of Snow Patrol's *You Could Be Happy* taunted her from the bookstore's speakers. Great—one of Mark's favourites. She squeezed her eyes shut and turned away.

A buzz tickled her hand, halting her getaway.

'I see you! Got time for a brew? Harry x'

She scanned the foyer. There he was in a three-piece black suit, striding towards her from the main entrance. Any chance of escape, gone. His face lit up with a huge grin, and his eyes shone bright like a sunny afternoon.

"Hello." Harry pointed at the National Theatre security pass dangling from Alex's neck, and pulled her into a tight clinch. "Alexandra Sinclair, are you working in an actual *theatre*? I knew it would be just a matter of time."

"I'm a backstage tour guide. I'm moving on up."

"I'd say. Do you sleep here? I can't see you *ever* leaving

this place. It's your church."

Alex smiled.

"What's with the visit? This isn't your 'hood."

"We're seeing the play in the Lyttleton tonight. I had some time to kill, so I thought I'd wander around the South Bank. Actually, that's not true. I needed a wee, so I came in here."

Alex chuckled.

"Olivia won't be here for at least an hour, and Tom—God knows when he'll show up. Fancy a tea or a slice of cake or something? We need to catch up."

Her shoulders tensed. "Sure...I'm done for today." She threw one more look towards the Long Bar and herded Harry into Kitchen.

"So, what's new? How's the flat? You and Lucy aren't killing each other, I hope."

"Very funny. No, we're perfect housemates. We've worked out a pretty good system. I clean. She cooks. Everyone's happy. And then Freddie comes over and messes the place up and eats our food."

"And how's your writing going?" They circled around the centre table piled high with wooden slabs covered in cakes, cookies, and squares built from chocolate and marshmallow.

"Good. I've almost finished first drafts of two plays. I went all anti-social to really focus. I'm pleased with my progress, though. Two months ago, I only had a few scenes completed, but they're finally coming together."

"I'm not surprised. I blame our small room for all your writing problems. I don't know how anyone could be creative stuck in that cave. I'm still sorry about that—I should've taken Tom to task about it."

"Don't be," said Alex. "You gave me a place to crash.

That's all that matters." The old ease of chatting with Harry flooded over her. She missed it.

"Olivia's been writing up a storm, too. Remember her suffragette play? She's workshopping it with Isabella. They're raving about how good it is. Olivia mentioned a potential slot in some new writers' showcase at the Old Vic. I pressed her for more info, but you know Livvy…she plays her cards close to her chest. She's loving the program, though…I'm sorry that you couldn't be there, too."

Alex bit her tongue, thankful that Harry's attention was on the baked goods and not her face. "Sometimes it's not meant to be."

"Oh, your time will come. You're much too good to be ignored."

That's the old Harry she knew and loved—supportive, caring, like a big brother. Maybe she could ramp up the nerve to tell him about the suffragette play after all.

Harry chose a slice of banana bread. Alex plucked a container of strawberries from the cooler.

"What? No cake? No cookies? You feeling all right?" He playfully felt Alex's forehead.

"It's been a rough week. I'm trying to eat healthier. Baby steps."

"I'm impressed. Little Alex, you move out of my place and become all grown up."

"You sound like a parent."

"Got to get my practice in somehow."

"*What?*" Alex grabbed his arm. She swallowed and did a double take. She wanted to say '*Harry, did that bitch trap you?*' but instead whispered, "Olivia's pregnant?"

Harry laughed. "No! Well, not that I *know* of." He handed a twenty-pound note to the cashier to cover both of their snacks. "And a tea, please. Alex, want one?"

"Sure. Thanks. Three sugars."

He nodded at the cashier and placed their two teas on his tray. "But I do have news. Come sit."

They walked out of the café and past the bookshop, Harry choosing a small table hugged by two white scoop-back chairs, its vantage point offering a sweeping view of the National's lobby—and the Long Bar.

Alex's heart pounded in time to the fast circles she made with her spoon in the teacup.

"I've asked Olivia to marry me..." Harry beamed.

Alex halted her frenzied stirring, sending a hot jet of tea onto the table. Not the announcement she expected. Record booze sales at Bespoke, opening another club, even buying a larger flat...anything but a baby...or this.

"...and she accepted." Harry's eyes yearned for a reaction.

Alex dug deep, mining her theatre training to paint a convincing smile on her face. "Of course she did. Congratulations, Harry. You look thrilled." She blotted up the spill with a tissue.

"I was fit to burst." Harry leaned in. "The proposal came off even better than I imagined. I took her to Paris under the pretense of sourcing a new French wine supplier. I'd be in meetings all day, and she'd exercise her credit cards on Avenue Montaigne. She completely fell for it. Any chance for a designer shopping spree, right?"

Alex nodded. She'd never been on a designer shopping spree in her life.

"I booked the penthouse at the Hotel George V. It has this incredible 360-degree view of the skyline and a private terrace overlooking the Eiffel Tower."

"Are you sure you weren't a wedding planner in a previous life? Wow." Alex sipped her tea, unsure what more she could say.

He chuckled. "I arranged for fresh white lilies and roses, and candles to fill the space, and hired a string quartet. Perfect for the future Mrs. Manville. Olivia was speechless when she came back that evening." His eyes sparkled with joy and maybe a few tears.

"I thought the opening of Bespoke would be my proudest, most memorable moment this year, but this trumps it. She's made me the happiest guy on earth."

"Oh, *Harry...*"

His words kicked Alex repeatedly. In the glow of his euphoria, she couldn't be honest about Olivia. Not now. His princess bride had slammed that door shut. Why did she listen to Lucy in June? Now it was too late. She'd never knowingly hurt Harry, and on the heels of his gushy engagement story, that's exactly what she would do if she shared her secret.

"Of course, she wants the extravagant gown, historic church, all the wedding trimmings fit for royalty." He popped a piece of banana bread into his mouth. "And knowing her mother, it'll top all the society pages. I think they've already spoken to an editor at *Hello!*, can you believe it?" He chuckled.

Alex didn't just believe it; she expected it. She nodded with polite approval behind her cup.

"If Olivia gets here soon, you'll see her ring. I think everyone in London has seen it by now." He reached into his coat pocket. "Actually, let me text her and see how long she'll be..."

Alex nearly choked on a strawberry. "*No!* Please don't."

Harry blinked rapidly.

Her eyes watered. A few breaths helped her regain control.

"Please don't disturb her. She's probably still at work. I'm sure I'll see it soon."

"It's a beauty. You'll be proud of me." His hand retreated from his pocket, empty. "But enough about my love life. What's new with you? Put a spell on any English blokes yet?"

She inhaled deeply and peered over to the Long Bar where Naomi served a customer. Alex shook her head and stabbed another strawberry. "No, but Devin showed up unannounced."

"Seriously?" Harry blurted out amidst a mouthful of food. "The cheeky bastard."

"He's travelling around Europe and dropped in to apologize."

"I hope you told him where he can stick it."

Alex nodded between bites.

"Did you get, you know...*anxious*?"

"I was on the cusp, but I held it in. Just. I think I was more angry than freaked out. Afterwards, I completely lost my mind on Jack and Coke. Not my finest twenty-four hours."

"But justified, I'm sure. I'm proud of you, though, keeping it *mostly* together." He pulled her sideways into a hug.

She plunged into the embrace and glanced towards the Long Bar, this time locking eyes with Mark. Damn pink sweater—like a lighthouse on a dark night, it made her easy to spot. His pinched expression shifted to Harry, then back to Alex; it hurt like a knuckle-punch to a bruise.

"You could've called me afterwards." Harry released his grip. "We might not live under the same roof anymore, but I'm still here for you. I mean it."

"Same here." Alex bit into another strawberry, but instead of sweetness, it oozed sourness. Why did he have to show up and be so honest, kind, and supportive again? Their friendship had never been tainted by secrets and lies, but now it was—and she was the guilty party.

"And look who it is…" Harry looked past her and shot to his feet. Alex froze, her tummy capsizing from his wave of excitement.

Tom strolled into view, his typical disheveled yet chic self. "Hiya, mate…and Alex? My God, Miss America." Tom gave Harry a slap on the back.

Alex let out a staggered breath. No false fawning over engagement rings—yet.

"Gimme a hug, gorgeous. It's been too long." Tom yanked her from the chair, and planted a kiss on each cheek.

She squished into his navy wool coat. "Hey, Tom."

"I'm gagging for a drink. Want one?"

"Well, I…" She scrambled for an excuse.

"You can choose at the bar. C'mon." He threw a lanky arm around her shoulders.

She could see Naomi and Mark serving a cluster of customers. "Actually, Tom. I'd love to, but I'm working at the market research firm this evening. I should probably get a move on."

Alex hadn't worked there in over a month.

"Another time?" She shrugged her arms through her coat's sleeves.

He smiled, untying his black and navy checked scarf. "I'll hold you to it, darling."

"I still need that wee." Harry shimmied past Alex's empty chair. "Tom, grab me a pint. I'll meet you there."

He squeezed Alex. "I'm so glad I bumped into you. Let's not leave it so long, okay? And thanks for listening to all my soppy engagement talk. What am I like?"

Tucked into his hug, Alex frowned into her arm. "You're

the happiest man on earth." She pulled away with a smile and shuffled towards the exit.

Twenty-Nine

Alex and Lucy hustled along Upper Street towards the Almeida Theatre. Both wearing black dresses and tights underneath their winter coats, they bundled together for warmth in the nippy late November wind.

"I was worried earlier in the week when you were puking every five minutes," said Lucy. "The play's completely sold out, so you would've missed it if you were still poorly."

"I would've crawled here on my hands and knees." Alex pulled her wool coat tighter. The thought of talking to Mark for the first time in five days made her shiver more than the persistent gales. The more she thought about it, the more it became clear that avoiding him this past week was juvenile and cowardly.

Pushing through the Almeida's glass doors, Lucy spotted Freddie to her right, leaning over the box office counter.

"Made it with lots of time to spare." Lucy launched herself onto him. Alex smoothed her unruly hair.

"Hello, my darlings. Gorgeous as always. I'm glad you made it." He twirled to receive Lucy's hug. "Shame the same

297

can't be said for Keegs."

Lucy pouted, looking at Alex. "He's not coming?"

Freddie shook his head. "I just spoke to the box office manager. They'll take his ticket as a return and sell it. They've got a waiting list on the go since tonight's sold out."

Alex blinked rapidly, her mind a million miles away. She removed the tickets from her wallet, handing the fourth one to Freddie.

"I got his text just before you walked in. His boss called him into work. It's great he's making lots of cash, but their scheduling is seriously taking the piss and interfering with *our* social calendar. It's rubbish." Freddie tilted back towards the box office counter and surrendered the unused ticket.

"Mark must be pissed off," said Lucy.

Alex's eyebrows peaked. "Why?"

"Freddie said he *really* wanted to see this play. Wild horses couldn't have kept him away."

Alex swallowed and scanned the small rectangular-shaped lobby. Mark belonged to someone else, but that didn't excuse her behaviour this past week. Did her presence tonight make him feel so unwelcome that he couldn't bear to join them?

Maybe wild horses couldn't keep Mark away, but it seemed *she* could.

All two hours and fifteen minutes of Isabella Archer's play proved disturbing and unforgettable. It's dark, supernatural theme fitted perfectly with the season's dwindling daylight and London's chilly descent into the grip of winter.

Alex, Freddie, and Lucy stretched their legs in the minimalist white lobby, watching parched theatre fans pound back drinks at the Almeida's bar. The stage door, located just to the left of the box office, and down a few steps, flew open now and again to allow actors and production staff access to the lobby.

"Well, that was a bit weird," said Lucy in a hushed tone, leaning on the shuttered box office counter. "I know she's your idol, Alex, but she does come up with some nightmarish crap. I may have developed some new superstitions after watching that freak show, so be warned."

Alex shrugged. "I loved it. The thing she did in the script with the ghost and the farmer? I think it was a nod to Banquo's Ghost in *Macbeth*. It's unlike anything she's written before. It was so innovative. Must've been so challenging for the actors."

Lucy rolled her eyes.

"It was bonkers. But in a good way," said Freddie. "Mark's gonna be pissed when he hears about the complex performances. He loves those meaty roles. Maybe I'll lie and tell him it was rubbish."

Alex stared down at her shoes.

"That's what I'll tell him. No lies necessary," said Lucy.

Freddie jabbed her with his elbow. "Shut it, we've got *company*."

Isabella, cloaked in a knee-length black and white houndstooth coat, walked up the few steps from the stage door into the lobby. Most of the remaining theatregoers didn't recognize her, but Freddie, Lucy, and Alex snapped to attention.

The playwright strolled to the bar where she greeted a cluster of people, friends most likely, with hugs and kisses.

Alex looked for an escape route, her lungs begging for air. "Shit! You guys…" She hid behind Lucy.

"I know. I know. But you have to say hi," said Lucy, over a

shoulder.

"I can't. Can we go now?" Alex tightened her coat's belt.

Freddie fluffed up his hair. "I'll do it." He strode towards the bar, and pretended to mull over the cocktail menu, waiting for a break in Isabella's conversation before pouncing.

"Excuse me, Isabella?"

She turned, surprised that someone recognized her. "Yes?"

"Hi. My friends and I saw your play this evening. We *loved* it. Would you be so kind as to sign our programs?"

"Absolutely, what's your name?"

She took Freddie's pen and program and began signing. Alex was still impersonating a statue—albeit a quivering one—so Lucy tugged her along.

"Isabella, meet my friends Lucy and Alex. Alex is a playwright, too."

Alex's heart threatened to run away. Why did Freddie have to mention the P word? It was like painting a target on her forehead.

"Lovely to meet you both." Isabella stopped mid-signature on Lucy's program and gave Alex a double take. "Actually...you look familiar. Have we met before?"

Alex gulped. Time to 'fess up. "Uh, yes...briefly. In late spring?"

Isabella took Alex's program from her sweaty hands and began signing the cover. "Well, it's great to see you again and thanks for coming. I'm flattered you hung back to say hello. I'm not here for most performances, so it's a treat to meet theatre lovers afterwards."

Alex quietly exhaled. All that worry...for *what*? Isabella didn't remember her. Sure, her face seemed familiar, but that was it. All that nonsense from Olivia about bumping into Isabella at work and her remembering the horrific meltdown at the fundraiser? Total fiction. Her mind clicked into gear with question after question; it was like a starter pistol had gone off, and she was first out of the blocks.

"Isabella, I'm working on two plays at the moment. What advice would you offer to someone like me who's starting out and has zero connections?"

Lucy and Freddie exchanged glances.

"Well...don't shy away from writers' workshops. I'm currently holding one for five up-and-comers. New ideas and the people who create them fascinate me—plus it helps me keep my own inspiration topped up."

She paused to look directly into Alex's eyes, smiling warmly.

"I'll tell you what..." She began to write on the back page of Alex's program. "Here's my office email address. I can't offer you a place in the current sessions, but why don't you send me a sample of your latest work? I could have a quick look, give you a few brief pointers."

Alex's eyes couldn't open any wider. "That would be awesome."

"My pleasure. We have to support each other. God knows there are enough people out there trying to squash the arts." She handed the program back. "But most importantly, *keep writing*. The more you explore your stories, the better you'll tell them. And don't be afraid to be emotionally honest or raw. Audiences respond to what's real. Grab them by their hearts, and their heads will usually follow."

"I will...thanks. I'll send you something on Monday." Alex hugged her program.

Isabella nodded. "Thanks again for coming."

Outside, the collective wattage from the smiles of Freddie, Lucy, and Alex rivaled the brightness of the Christmas decorations strung along Upper Street.

"She's lovely," said Lucy. "I wasn't going to let you sneak away without saying hi. You do amaze me sometimes. We opened the door for you, and then—surprise—you walked right through it, chattering away."

She poked Alex in the ribs. "See, it's okay to accept help. If you were here on your own, you'd still be hiding in the corner. Admit it. You needed us."

Alex adopted a hard smile, hesitant to admit the truth. "Maybe."

"It's not a sign of weakness to accept or ask for help, you know?" Lucy pulled her into a side hug. "Silly Lex."

A rush of wind pushed them towards the road. Alex pulled both Freddie and Lucy closer. "Oh my God, you guys! Can you believe it? Me, Alex Sinclair…has Isabella's email address. How will I sleep tonight? I'm sending her an excerpt as soon as I can. There's no time to make it perfect, but it'll have to do. I can't mess up this chance."

"Aren't you the girl who said a few months ago that *'everything sucked'*?" Lucy tussled with her bag, her fingers digging deep inside for her Oyster card. She yanked at something stuck in its way, and a colourful postcard escaped skyward into the wind. It danced and taunted the trio above their heads for half a block.

Freddie jumped into the air, legs akimbo and arms stretching towards the stars. "Bugger. Almost had it."

Alex joined in, running down Upper Street, snatching at it with the hand that wasn't clutching her signed program.

"Just leave it! It's not important," yelled Lucy.

The wind took a breather, dropping the tattered postcard in an abandoned shop doorway clogged with curled brown leaves and discarded red Starbucks cups.

"Got it." Freddie wiped off the card, giving the photo a once over. "Ooh, someone's having a grand time on the French Riviera."

He flipped it over. His smile caved in.

"Alex. It's yours?"

Lucy bit her lip and sank into her wool scarf.

Alex peered at the image. Yep, the photo on the front was all sandy beaches and sturdy palm trees. Strange. Her forehead crinkled as she turned it over.

'Lexy. I'm taking a page out of your book (or should I say, play) and fearlessly travelling solo beyond my comfort zone. Keep showing us how it's done. I'll be leading the standing ovation. Much Love, Devin x'

Alex glared at Lucy. "Why didn't you want me to see this?"

"It's obvious, isn't it? Hello! *Lexy*? He's just one bloody pen stroke away from adding *Sexy*."

"But it's *my* mail. You have no right hiding it."

Freddie stood silent with his arms folded, his eyes volleying back and forth between his two friends.

The wind began to whistle again. "I'm baffled why would you even want it!" said Lucy.

Alex closed her eyes. "Not all of us move on as quickly as you do."

"And what good has it done, eh? Getting all sentimental? Reliving old heartbreak. Wounds never heal if you keep picking at them."

"I'm not lingering over old feelings. I'm finally making sense of them. If I don't, I'll never be able to move on. I've realized that what I'm missing is *the idea* of him, how things used to be before everything blew up," said Alex. "I know that person—that *time*—doesn't exist anymore. I need to let go. Devin asking for my forgiveness is a step in that direction, but I'm not there yet."

"Forgive? You're thinking of *forgiving* him? Why don't you forgive Olivia, too, while you're at it? Fuck, forgive everyone who ever stomped on you."

Freddie stepped closer. "Actually, forgiving's a good idea. Not only forgiving Devin, but also forgiving yourself, Alex. Give yourself a break. You've been blaming yourself for too long."

Both women ignored him.

"I thought I could run away from Devin and my problems…but it's not that simple. They end up following you, no matter how far you run. I can't change what's happened, I *know* that…I just hope I'll learn from it."

"I hope you do, too." Lucy backed down slightly. "Look, I'm sorry. I shouldn't have hidden the postcard. You know I only did it to protect you, right?"

"Yeah, I know, Mother Hen." Alex looped her arm through Lucy's and looked up at the red and white burger sign behind them. "C'mon, chips are on you."

THIRTY

Alex's eyes flew to the Long Bar as if on autopilot. Mark hadn't been at work for a week and a half. Even Freddie didn't know his whereabouts. His absence meant no more hiding behind tour participants or awkward sprints through the lobby. Life at work in early December clicked along at an easier, less emotional pace, but it was also dull and lonely. Alex hadn't spoken to him since that cringeworthy chat on the National stairs on November 23…seventeen days ago. Not that she kept track.

Weaving past arriving theatergoers, Alex ducked out of the National and inhaled the frosty evening air, the strings of lights stretching between tree branches along the South Bank, twinkling like strands of precious jewels. She patted her laptop bag, now her constant companion, writing before and after her shifts and through much of the night. Her obsession paid off. In the frantic week since chatting with Isabella at the Almeida, she had completed the first drafts for both her Waterloo Bridge and time travel plays.

It had been eleven days since Alex emailed Isabella an excerpt of the bridge play. Since hitting send, every ping from

Alex's inbox sent her madly clicking between programs. Her pulse would race and then stagger to a crawl once she clued in that the new arrival wasn't from the playwright. The cycle repeated again and again, but she remained hopeful. As a writer herself, surely Isabella remembered what it was like to be awaiting feedback.

The time travel piece had veered off in a more heartwarming direction. Isabella's simple advice seeped into Alex's core. She poured much of her own heart and soul into this work—a flood of prose had flowed through her fingertips and across her laptop screen without any coaxing into the early hours of each breaking day.

Alex craved some downtime. Lucy was meeting her in Soho at the Curzon cinema on Shaftsbury Avenue for the seven o'clock showing of *The Lobster*, Ben Whishaw's latest film. The Tube offered little breathing space. Early Christmas shoppers and their cumbersome bags of holiday cheer filled her carriage, jammed against cranky commuters, like cattle in a paddock. Alex fought the urge to 'moo' ironically. Thankfully, the crush didn't cause any delays between Waterloo and Leicester Square stations.

Dodging black cabs while crossing Gerrard Place, Alex spotted Lucy outside the Curzon, hopping from one foot to another, her gloveless hands tunnelling under her arms like two mice seeking shelter. "Hiya, Lex. God, I love my boss. He let us leave an hour early to get a jump on Christmas shopping. We've all been in the pub."

She spotted Alex's laptop bag. "Were you writing today? I thought the two plays were done."

"Just the first drafts, but I can't leave the bridge one alone. I keep finding things to tweak." Alex held the door open for her friend.

"I finished reading your time travel play." Lucy pulled out a folder containing a thick bundle of pages from her satchel. "It's even better than the suffragette one. I ugly-cried on the Tube this morning."

"Aw, I hoped for tears. I knew you'd love the grandmother…" Alex noticed blue smudges on the heel of Lucy's left hand. "Wait, what's that? Above your wrist…"

"Oh, just some marker. Got bored in a meeting and sketched the VP, as you do."

"Hmm. Most people *doodle* in meetings. They don't sketch. That's the artist in you screaming to escape."

Lucy rolled her eyes as she trotted down the steps to the cinema's lower level, still embracing Alex's play. "So, it's based on Joan, right?"

"Yep, she said something about going back in time, what she'd tell herself at age twenty if given the chance. It felt like a neat playwriting exercise. Basically, it's a love letter to her."

The girls stopped at the bar, Alex treating Lucy to her ticket, M&Ms, popcorn, and bottled water. It was the least she could do after being such a grumpy hermit since her argument with Mark.

"Joan will get a kick out of seeing her younger self choosing theatre over an early marriage and kids. I know she loves your dad to bits, but she must wonder 'what if' sometimes. The play's really uplifting. I felt empowered afterwards. Would it be okay if I read it again?"

Alex put away her change. "Sure, go for it. I'm not showing it to Joan yet. It's her Christmas present."

"It's *really* good, Lex." Lucy hugged the folder against her chest. "Please promise me, though, you won't hide it when it's done? Share it. Show it to Isabella, enter it into a competition—something?"

Alex shook her head. "Maybe one day, but right now my focus is on the bridge play. I'm dying to hear what Isabella thinks. I usually hate constructive criticism, but her advice could make a huge difference going forward."

Lucy gathered their snacks, glancing at the growing cinema crowd. "We better take our seats. The show's about to start."

The sunny, crisp afternoon on the second Saturday in December gave Alex the perfect excuse to bring Freddie and Lucy to Broadway Market in her old neighbourhood. Sharing the congested road with local hipsters, young couples toting bundled-up babies, and dogs hoovering discarded morsels off the ground, they were spoilt for choice. Stalls selling artisanal fudge and posh Scotch eggs rubbed shoulders with vendors peddling handmade scarves and antiques, while tables boasting handmade holiday decorations and spicy mulled wine did a brisk trade.

"Did we have to come all this way to find a Christmas tree? I bet we could've bought one near our flat." Lucy tightened her scarf. "We'll be really bloody popular on the Tube home."

Alex dropped fifty pence into the box belonging to four craggy old gentlemen singing carols near the northern end of the market, their warbling voices wrapping the street in festive cheer. "When I lived at Harry's I never brought you guys here, and look how freaking amazing it is. Shut up and eat your lunch. It's not every day I spring for food."

"This sandwich is to die for." Lucy chomped a fried egg, maple bacon, and cheddar creation stuffed into a steamed Bao bun. "Want to try?" She nudged her lunch towards Alex.

She scrunched up her nose. "Ew, as if."

Lucy laughed. "I knew you'd say that, Picky Pants. More for me."

"Not so fast." Freddie quickly chewed his pork dumplings. Lucy scowled, but handed over her sandwich.

Alex rolled down the lip of a green and white paper bag, revealing a pasty. "The lady in the Percy Ingle shop remembered me, wondered where the crazy cheese and onion girl went to. It's nice to be missed for a change."

She took a bite, and several pastry flakes fluttered down onto her wool coat.

"Hey, I finally heard from Keegs this morning," said Freddie.

Alex brushed her coat and poked her knitted hat away from her eyes.

"So, he remembered we exist, then?" asked Lucy.

"He's been filming a TV series in Aberdeen. He got the call on November 30, and was on a train three hours later. Showbiz madness."

"There goes my theory that Naomi had him handcuffed to her headboard. Kinky bitch." Lucy wiped a smear of gooey cheese from her chin. Alex shot her a dirty look. It flew away in the breeze, unnoticed.

Freddie pointed to a stall three-deep with customers. "Let's hit that Crosstown Donuts place, get a box, and overdose on sugar in the park."

Alex tugged the sleeve of his leather jacket. "No donuts will be consumed until we find the Christmas tree guy. I read that Whishy bought his tree here last year, so we'r—"

The *Sherlock* theme cut her off.

"Hello?…Yes, this is Alex…Hi!" Her eyes opened wide as she mouthed '*Isabella Archer*' to her friends.

"…You liked it?…" Alex stashed the half-eaten pasty in her coat pocket.

Both Freddie and Lucy stopped eating. When Alex didn't say anything for twenty-five seconds, they inched closer.

"…Really?…Stamford Street…Will do. Thanks, thanks so much…Bye."

Alex fist pumped the air. "Fuck, *yes!*"

"Ooh, rare F-bomb klaxon." Lucy grabbed Alex's arm. "What's so fucking amazing, then?"

"Guess who's been added to Isabella's workshop?" said Alex in a sing-songy voice as she bounced in her biker boots.

"How?" said Lucy.

"One of the playwrights dropped out because of a family illness. Isabella doesn't want to waste the spot. She liked my bridge excerpt, so I'm in! Next Friday night."

"Bloody hell, it's alllll happening. Come here, you!" Freddie pulled Alex and Lucy into an awkward embrace of arms, food, and plastic cutlery.

"It's at the Coin Street Neighbourhood Centre—that's close to the National—I can walk there after work. Fucking hell! I can't *believe* it. I've missed the first sessions, but I can catch up. I'm *so* doing this."

"Won't Olivia be there, too?" asked Lucy. "Aren't you worried about that?"

"What choice do I have? Of course I'll be annoyed seeing her there—with *my* suffragette play, but…it's hers now. I can't control that situation, so why try? I'll just burn out from frustration. It is what it is."

"I'm relieved to hear you finally say that. Enough is

enough." Lucy nibbled her sandwich.

"At least I have something Isabella likes that I can shove back in Olivia's face. I'm no charity case. I belong there. Enough time has passed, I hope she'll leave me be and just get on with it. Frankly, I'm too excited to care about all that right now."

"As you should be. Screw the donuts." Freddie tossed his empty food container in the trash. "Celebratory drinks—*now*!"

Thirty-One

"Why the fuck not me?" – Mindy Kaling

Six days later

Alex arrived at the workshop fifteen minutes early, fueled by nerves, excitement, and too much sugar. The meeting room in the Coin Street Centre was clean and bright with three long tables configured into a U formation. A smaller desk sat in the opening at the end, reserved for Isabella. Alex set up her laptop on the far table in front of the windows, taking the seat closest to Isabella's spot. Two male playwrights—one ginger, the other bald—followed Alex into the room and claimed their seats at the table across from her. A small Asian guy arrived five minutes later, choosing the lone spot in the bottom of the U; the only seat remaining, beside Alex to her left.

Just before seven, the sound of female laugher reverberated down the hallway and floated into the room. Isabella walked in first; wearing a white turtleneck sweater, black wide leg trousers, and a grey wool cape that draped below her hips. On her heels, chatting a mile a minute and auditioning for the role of Teacher's Pet, was Olivia in a cobalt blue jumpsuit and over-the-knee black boots, her long camel-coloured coat hanging on her shoulders for dear life. Alex thought the outfit would look ridiculous on anyone else, but the brunette managed to pull it off with style and aplomb. Alex swallowed slowly. She adjusted her red tartan pencil skirt, and the three-quarter length sleeves of her black v-neck sweater, then gripped her keyboard with both hands.

Olivia's gaze landed on Alex, her heels stuttering almost to a halt. Alex sat up straight and jutted out her chin. With any luck, the trapeze act swinging in her stomach would take notice and dismount.

Alex smiled widely like the Cheshire Cat. "Oh, sorry…did I take your place?" She spoke loud enough for Isabella to hear and hoped the irony wasn't lost on her rival.

"No need to move. There's room for everyone," said the award-winning playwright.

Olivia glared at Alex and set her Grande coffee cup on the table. Under the room's watchful gaze, she rested her coat on the chair, released her shiny laptop from its bag, and pushed her black leather Mulberry Piccadilly holdall to the side.

Isabella stood behind her desk, eyes absorbing the U. "Welcome back. Unfortunately, Gemma had to return to Scotland because of a family emergency, so we have a new recruit. Please welcome Alex Sinclair."

Three of the four writers grinned, nodded or looked pleased. Olivia frowned behind a sip of her coffee.

"As I mentioned three weeks ago, this workshop requires your utmost commitment. I'm not here to dish out compliments or hold your hands. I'm here to push you, to make you better writers. We're working on Olivia's play tonight. I trust that everyone's read it. If you haven't, you shouldn't be here..."

Alex's eyelids stretched open, catching Olivia's confident smile in their sights. Isabella the teacher was a different beast than Isabella the stage door idol. She didn't expect her to be such a hard-ass.

Isabella handed her a photocopy of the play. "Alex, my fault—I forgot to email your copy last weekend, so please work off these sheets and jump into the discussions where you can."

The play. It stared back at its rightful owner. Alex blinked several times, surprised to find tears threatening her eye makeup. It had been six months since she had held a copy. Six months! The fluorescent lights above her buzzed like hyperactive wasps in her ears.

The first fifteen minutes of the workshop consisted of Isabella commenting on why the suffragette play caught her interest.

"Stories of female equality and teamwork are needed more than ever. Women supporting each other, their drive to succeed and obtain what's fair and just—we can all relate to those struggles. Right, ladies?" Isabella glanced at Alex and Olivia. "That's why this play is so poignant. I wish this battle was ancient history, but it continues today. It's a war we're still waging."

Alex rifled through the pages, taking deep breaths. Word by word, the story was identical to her long-lost hard copy. Didn't Olivia tweak any of it? Even her character notes at the back looked the same. The only differences were that the font was Helvetica and the unblemished cover page had Olivia's byline in bold type.

"Okay, then. Let's discuss the protagonist of this true story. Emmeline Pankhurst, the woman who lead the suffragette movement. Olivia, some background, please..."

"Absolutely." Olivia's eyes darted towards Alex. "While our flat was being painted last year, I spent a week at Mummy's on Clarendon Road. I was walking down the street and discovered a round blue plaque at number fifty. It marked the address where Emmeline and her daughter Christabel lived."

Isabella jumped in. "Is that in Kensington? Must be beautiful."

Olivia grinned. "It's quite lovely, yes. The plaque piqued my curiosity. Who were these women? How did the suffrage movement change British society? I took the idea and ran with it that same day..."

A vein on Alex's temple twitched. She crossed her legs and tapped her foot against the table leg. Letting go was proving to be more difficult than she originally thought.

"The more I read, the more my admiration grew for these exceptional women. Since I'm all about 'girl power', I decided to make the idea my own and create a work that would spark conversations, educate, and entertain. As a Kensington girl myself, I wondered how Emmeline went from being a well-to-do socialite to a revolutionary figure that inspired—"

Alex slowly raised her hand.

Olivia pouted, and stopped mid-sentence.

"Is it okay to jump in?" asked Alex.

Isabella nodded. "Absolutely. We're not precious about decorum here."

Olivia clenched her jaw.

"Wasn't Pankhurst born in Manchester? Moss Side or somewhere like that?" Alex looked at Isabella. "She's a northerner like you, right?"

"A proud northerner. Something I can relate to," said Isabella. "Go on."

"Her northern roots are important because it was in Manchester that she met her husband Richard who was a key figure in the creation of Manchester's Women's Suffrage movement," said Alex. "His beliefs matched hers, and unlike most men of his day, he supported her attempts to improve society and get the vote for women."

Alex sat back in her chair, her nerves slipping away with each word spoken. "In fact, if she had been born in London, she wouldn't have met Richard, and her mark on history may have been quite different."

The hair on Alex's forearm spiked at the tense electricity vibrating from the seat to her left.

"Olivia...continue." Isabella waved her on.

Olivia resumed her presentation, but occasionally tripped over her words, mixing up Emmeline's associates and the dates of their most epic confrontations. Her wobbles hinted at forgetfulness, or worse, a shocking lack of knowledge. Alex's adrenaline was pumping, and she couldn't resist jumping in several times.

"...No, actually, Emmeline never did champion hunger strikes..."

"...I read that Emily Davison never intended to commit suicide..."

Alex politely corrected Olivia's errors, one after another.

Olivia glanced around the room, taking stock of her audience. She adjusted her notes and answered calmly. "Quite right. Thank you, Alex."

A smile crept up on Isabella's face. "You're well-versed on the British suffrage movement. Coming from an American, that's doubly impressive."

"I was born in Manchester. My dad's from Moss Side, so

the subject's close to home, I guess." Alex returned her smile.

The five workshop participants did a read through of the first act, making suggestions for staging and discussing the various character arcs. After an hour, Isabella paused the session for a fifteen-minute break. The room cleared leaving Alex alone with Olivia.

She scraped her chair towards Alex and snarled in her ear. "What the hell are *you* doing here?"

Alex continued to type. "I could ask the same of you. Shouldn't you be locked away in your coffin? Next session I'm wearing a garlic necklace." She chuckled. "Unlike you, Olivia, I have every right to be here. Not only did Isabella like my suffragette idea that you're passing off as your own, but she's also keen on another play I've written. I'm here because I'm a good writer. Period. I didn't have to steal someone else's work to get a spot."

"You just couldn't help yourself, could you—correcting my mistakes?" Olivia's eyes checked the doorway and flew back at Alex. "You're going to tell Isabella the play's yours, aren't you?"

Alex shook her head. "You can have the suffragettes. I'd never hurt Harry. He means a lot to me, and he's been a good friend. It would hurt him, telling Isabella that you're a thieving, lying cow."

She patted the side of her laptop screen. "I'll just keep my suffragette play locked up in here as a reminder of how far I've come. Besides, I've got plenty of other ideas where that one came from. I've been writing like a whirlwind since moving away from you."

"Your devotion to Harry is cute." Olivia waved her sparkly rock; the diamond's size would make the Crown Jewels blush.

"See this? He proposed. I'm now wearing your entire family's net worth—and then some—on my left hand. I've won. I've got the play and the guy."

Alex halted her typing, making eye contact with Olivia for the first time. "Look, for some reason he's besotted with you. I still don't get it, but whatever. Let's just move on, okay?"

The whites of Olivia's eyes shone. "I don't trust you, Sinclair. In fact, I can't bloody stand you. I've *never* wanted you as a friend—and I certainly don't want you as a colleague, either. I just want you *gone*. Out of both our lives for good...so, how much?"

Alex scrunched up her face. "How much what?"

Olivia tossed her hair, reached into her Mulberry bag and pulled out a chequebook. "How much to send your Yankee arse back to Florida? Or New York...I don't care where, as long as Harry and I don't have to see you again. Name your price. Fifty thousand pounds? A hundred thousand?"

Alex's jaw dropped. "Paying me off?" She laughed. "Oh, Olivia. Your money doesn't interest me. I'm probably the only person in London you can't buy. Nice try. This Yankee's staying put."

Olivia's hands shook. She shoved the chequebook into her handbag, her pretty face now contorted with barely contained rage.

Alex stood up calmly and headed to the water cooler. The other writers would be back any minute.

The brunette bolted to her feet, teeth clenched and nostrils flaring like a cornered mare. She snatched up her coffee, raising it to her lips, then hesitated. A wicked smile spread across her cheeks. She popped the lid and poured every ounce of the hot, milky liquid into the keyboard of Alex's laptop.

Alex heard the splash and turned sharply away from the water cooler. A torrent of excess coffee dripped along the edge of the table, pooling on her chair, the floor, and staining her laptop bag.

"Shit! What have you *done*?"

Olivia cocked her head and sneered. "Whoopsie." She tossed the empty red cup down to the floor.

Alex leapt towards her computer, elbowing Olivia out of the way. She jabbed at the keys, summoning documents, but the screen turned a sickly grey hue.

"You did this on *purpose*!" She grabbed the soaked device and shook it upside down, but the liquid had already done Olivia's dirty work.

Two of the three playwrights ran back into the room, followed by Isabella. "What's going on? I could hear you in the ladies' toilets."

Alex's voice croaked. "She dumped her coffee all over my laptop. It's ruined!"

Olivia covered her mouth with her hands. "Oh God, it was an *accident*. I'm so sorry. My heels are slippy. I lost my balance." She peered over Alex's shoulder. "Is it working? Is it? Oh God, *how* did this happen?"

Isabella swept over. "Try a restart. Maybe the shock of the liquid put it to sleep temporarily? Don't panic yet."

Tears streamed down Alex's cheeks and quivering chin. She couldn't pull up any documents on her screen. No email. No Internet. Nothing. It wouldn't reboot, either. Her shoulders sagged. "It's destroyed. Everything's...gone."

"Oh, no..." Olivia turned away from the panic and slyly smirked behind her hair.

The ginger-haired writer scrolled through his phone.

"There's a computer shop two minutes down the road, beside Waterloo Station that's open until half nine. If you rush, they might help you before closing."

"Thanks." Alex grabbed her belongings and dashed out of the room, praying her laptop could be saved.

Alex stood watery-eyed in front of the computer genius hoping for a Christmas miracle.

"I'm sorry, love. This thing was dead on arrival." The expert shook his head. "There's nothing to salvage from this dinosaur." He handed back the sticky laptop. "Bring us your backups, and we'll get you a new laptop up and running."

Alex rubbed her bloodshot eyes, her hand flecked in smudged mascara. "Thanks for trying." She bowed her head, exiting into the rain. A new laptop? Not on her wage. And worse, she stupidly hadn't backed up her files for at least…what, three weeks now? The entire second act of the bridge play was gone. The hard copy Lucy returned of her time travel play was the first draft from early December; weeks' worth of writing, wiped out.

She needed someone to lean on. She called Lucy. No answer. The Pret Christmas party was this evening, and Freddie was her date. She tried her dad—a busy signal. She tried again…still busy. With Mark gone astray and Harry off-limits, she felt more alone than she had in months.

THIRTY-TWO

Alex turned up her collar against the bitter wind gusting between the National and the BFI building. She wasn't scheduled to work this Saturday morning, but after last night's run-in with Olivia, she needed a peaceful place to think about her future. Lucy snored loudly in a post-party coma at the flat, and Freddie's phone skipped straight to voicemail, so she still hadn't shared last night's disaster. Even her dad, Helen, and Joan were out of reach this morning with either busy signals or voicemail on each attempt. She longed to speak to someone, anyone.

She passed strangers in groups of two or more, sharing laughs along the South Bank's riverside terrace. How could they carry on without a care in the world when her life was in tatters? They appeared buoyant. Happy. How dare they.

She grabbed a hot chocolate from Kitchen and a copy of *Time Out* magazine, and trudged up the stairs inside the National, seeking solace in the familiar. Her second floor spot with its striped cushions and soaring windows, welcomed her into its bosom. Without her beloved laptop for company, she draped her coat over her black jeans, and sighed. Her hands flipped through the magazine, her eyes barely absorbing the text and colourful photos on its pages. She gulped her drink and stared straight ahead.

In the shadows, a figure passed by on the far side of the floor near the stalls entrance to the Olivier Theatre.

"Mark?" Alex hollered and caught her breath.

He stopped and peered her way, like a deer trapped in car headlights.

Her heart did a somersault. She waved him over, desperate for a friendly face, or even a not-so-friendly face. She regretted how they'd parted a few weeks ago. She slapped on a smile and adopted a breezy tone.

"Hello, stranger. I heard you were filming in Scotland. The TV role?"

A tight-lipped nod greeted her as he stashed his hands in his front pockets. "Yeah."

"Mark, congratulations. That's massive."

He shrugged, his eyes briefly meeting hers. "Not really. It's just a small part."

"It's still a huge deal."

"Thanks." He pivoted his body towards the stairwell. "I should get back. I was looking for tumblers at the Olivier's bar, but they're not there, so…"

Alex knew that the tiny bar on this level was closed for re-furbishment.

"I've missed you." Alex blurted out. "I mean our chats… I've missed our chats."

"Me too." Mark nodded towards the floor, his hands still in his pockets. "But I thought you wanted space, so…"

Panic rose in Alex's throat. She couldn't let him slip away. "I've been a totally selfish brat. Blaming everyone but myself for letting my writing fall by the wayside..."

She yanked the cuffs of her black cardigan over her palms.

"...not listening, thinking only about myself and what I want..."

"We're all guilty of that sometimes," said Mark.

"But I heard only what I wanted to hear. I didn't let you explain—and that's not fair. Friends don't do that to one another."

He looked up and pulled on the edge of his grey v-neck sweater. "So...we're *friends* again...are we?"

"Yeah, I'd like to be, if you'll have me."

Friends...friends would have to do. A few weeks ago, they were on the cusp of so much more. The knot in her stomach loosened just enough to allow a deep breath to escape from her chest. "I'm...I'm so sorry, Mark."

His shoulders relaxed, and he sat down beside her. "I'm sorry, too." He smiled softly. "I hated how things were left. You were so upset...I've thought about it a lot. I should've handled things differently...told you about Naomi coming back to London, working here..."

He stuck a finger into a small rip in the knee of his jeans. "That night on the stairs, it took every ounce of my self-control not to run after you. But the last thing you needed was pressure from another bloke. I'm sorry I hurt you, Alex. It was never my intention."

Mark opened his arms, and Alex welcomed his hug. She closed her eyes, inhaling slowly. He smelt heavenly, reminding her of when she first saw him. How stupid to risk losing...this. Her eyes grew misty.

"One piece of advice, though—please don't assume that you have to tackle problems on your own. Life can be a bastard.

Don't push people away, especially when you need them the most…" Mark showed no signs of letting go. "It's like you're afraid of being left. I think maybe you pull the plug before it happens to you."

"I know. I've been an idiot." Alex blinked, trying to rein in the tears while he couldn't see her face. "I never ask for help. Be gentle with me, okay? It's a new thing, relying on other people."

"Not *other people*—your friends, okay?" said Mark. "And you can count on me. I'm not going anywhere."

He squeezed her and pulled away with that cheeky grin.

Alex took a deep breath. Time to test Mark on his word. "Even if you know my secret—that I have panic attacks?"

Mark held her hand. "Even if you have panic attacks—at least you keep things interesting!" He smiled. "I mean it. I won't disappear on you."

Alex sighed. That was easier than she had expected. Mark wasn't put off, at all. Could he be any more perfect? A heavy tear escaped down her face, a reminder of her current reality. No wonder they were back in the Friend Zone—why would he want to kiss her when she was such a mess? She probably looked like a doll left out in the pouring rain—a mess of melted mascara, puffy eyes, and splotchy skin. She dropped her gaze to the floor, and in the absence of a tissue, hid her nose behind her free hand.

"Hey, now what's the matter? You couldn't have missed me that much."

Alex wanted to laugh because she had missed him terribly, but his kind words unleashed a procession of silent tears. "I've been trying to hold it in…"

"Is it your dad? Your gran?"

She shook her head. "No, thank God. It's Olivia—again. She dumped a massive coffee all over my laptop last night. Fried the hard drive. The computer guys couldn't save it. What good is a writer without a laptop? I'm basically screwed."

"Shit! They couldn't save *anything*?"

"Nothing. My current projects, all gone. And before you ask about back-ups, I always do back-ups. I just haven't for a few weeks…"

"Oh, Lex!"

"I know, I know. Losing my computer's bad enough. I've had it forever, and I can't afford a new one, but it's my plays that…" The tears streamed fast and furious down her cheeks. She raised her hands to hide her ugly crying face; Mark didn't need to see that.

"C'mere." He gathered her back into his arms. "We'll fix this." He held her close in silence, thinking. Alex sank in and held on.

"I'd spot you a few quid, but I'm totally skint right now. My flight home for Christmas cleaned me out. You can borrow my laptop, though. It's not fancy, but it'll do the job."

Alex tilted back, wiping her nose. "I can't take your laptop."

"Yes. You can and you will…and what are you doing this afternoon?"

"Feeling sorry for myself. Why?"

"There's a private function in The Deck restaurant. The one on the roof? They want to pinch some of us, but we're already short-staffed. You could go in my place. All you have to do is carry a tray of appetizers. Easy money, right? The quick cash can go towards your laptop fund. And if you're free in the evenings this week, you could work their other private parties as well. Christmas is crazy busy around here."

She blotted her eyes.

"I wish I could help with what you've lost writing-wise, but that's out of my league. I'm sure it's all still up there in that smart brain of yours, though..."

"You'd do all this for me? Why?"

He smiled. "Do you really have to ask?"

Alex bit her lip.

"I could get used to playing the hero." He glanced at his phone. "Shit. My boss will have my balls if I'm not back downstairs. So, the private party starts at two. You've got two hours." He stood up and extended his hand. "Come. There's a brew downstairs with your name on it. My treat."

Mark was right; circulating trays of appetizers was a no-brainer. The party of investment bankers from the City was more interested in Naomi and the continuous flow of booze than Alex's prawn bundles. She took a breather in a nook at the far end of the venue, checking her phone. Both her dad and Joan had left messages. A power cut and depleted phone batteries, the reasons for their disappearances earlier. She sent two texts back, saying she would call after work.

Naomi ducked into the hideaway. Alex looked up from her phone, swearing under her breath. The beauty had been chatty each time they bumped into each other, but the blonde wasn't buying it. The images of her fondling Mark were still plastered all over her brain. She felt relieved that she had mended fences with Mark earlier, but could do without this afternoon's reminder of what Naomi had that she didn't.

"If that slime pinches my arse one more time, I'm going to *lamp* him." Naomi pointed to a lanky fifty-something banker with a greasy comb-over.

"That I'd like to see." Alex frowned.

"Not in the holiday spirit?" asked Naomi.

"You could say that."

"I've been there. Say no more." Naomi nudged her with a bony elbow. "But this year, I think Father Christmas is *finally* bringing me Mr. Right. It's been a bit stop-start, but I think we're finally on the right track." Her face shone brighter than her empty silver tray.

Alex dreaded the name that would spring from Naomi's pillowy lips.

"We went out for drinks after work and ended up at mine. Neither of us got much sleep that night." A loud laugh escaped from her throat. "Start as you mean to go on, Naomi."

She knew it, her suspicions now proven right. It *was* back on—Mark and Naomi's bonk-a-thon. It wasn't any of her business, but a part of her wanted more details, even if they hurt. At least she'd have closure. "You're lucky. Mark's lovely." As soon as the words left her mouth, Alex wished she had a recall button. Whatever Naomi spilled next would only make her feel bad. Too late now.

"Mark?" Naomi's pencil-thin eyebrows pinched. "No, he's just a friend. Well, that's not *totally* true. We had a little fling last year, so we have history, but it's ancient. I slip into my old flirty ways with him sometimes, but no, he's not my type."

The blonde's mouth gaped open.

"*You* should go for him." Naomi's elbow jabbed her again. "You look cute together."

Alex did a double take. Naomi nodded. "I'm serious. He talks about you *all* the time. If you're interested, you should definitely let him know. Mind you, he works too much. And he's got that awful scooter…"

"He talks about me?"

"He was raving about your play the other day—something about a bridge? I feel like I know you, he goes on so much…" She scrunched up her perfect nose. "Actually, I might owe you an apology…that day in Kitchen? I'm such a terrible flirt; it's my default setting. I didn't realize you guys were having a moment when I interrupted…I'm sorry."

Alex nodded, speechless.

Naomi leaned in. "I know he's really into you, but listen. Fate can be a lazy bitch. Don't wait around for her. Make it happen with Mark. That's why I've devised a battle plan to hook my new fella. Don't leave anything to chance, sweetie. Ever!"

She winked and strutted off towards the chef to refill her tray.

Alex briefly closed her eyes, a slow grin winding through her freckles. All the resentment and jealousy she had been feeling towards Naomi slowly fell away with each elated breath.

In the three days running up to Christmas Eve, the National hummed with back-to-back holiday parties. Alex worked every catering shift available on top of her regular job. Throbbing feet, skipped meals, and zero face time with friends plagued the hectic week, but each pound earned brought her closer to a new year's purchase of a good secondhand laptop.

Before staff scattered at noon on December 24, Alex met Mark for a quick goodbye in Kitchen. His flight to Dublin was leaving from Gatwick in three hours, and he was headed to the airport straight from work.

He handed over a burgundy laptop bag that had seen better days. "I wish I could give you a proper Christmas present, but this will have to do. I'm in no rush to get it back. Keep it for as long as you need."

Alex hugged the bag against her geometric-print blue and black sweater dress. "This is the best present anyone could give me. Thank you."

He grinned mischievously. "Okay, I lied. I do have something for you."

"Cheater." Alex swatted at him.

"It's just a little something. Close your eyes."

Mark only had five minutes to spare, so she didn't put up a fight. All the rustling and crinkling raised her eyebrows.

"Now open."

Four large packages of Twizzlers rested on the table—strawberry, and black licorice twists.

Alex squealed and snatched a package to her chest. "I've been having sugar shakes. How'd you find them?"

Mark beamed. "A friend brought them back from the States. I've had them for two months, waiting for the best time to give them to you. Thank goodness for lengthy expiration dates."

"Would that friend be Naomi?"

He nodded, his grin fading. "Yeah, Naomi..." He cleared his throat. "She really is just a friend. Nothing more."

Alex bowed her head. "I know." Her eyes glowed, and a slight giggle escaped from her lips.

A smile meandered across Mark's face as he lifted his backpack to his shoulder. He exhaled slowly, hesitant to look away.

"Wait. I have something for you, too." Alex slid a Christmas card across the table. "Lucy used to call me the 'Card Lady' because I never missed an occasion to mail a handwritten card. I'd hit all of them—birthdays, Easter, Christmas. Although that nickname's probably dust now. I couldn't afford to send any this year."

Mark tucked the red envelope into his jacket pocket. "Do you mind if I save it until Christmas morning? It will give me something to look forward to."

"If that's the highlight of your Christmas morning, times are tough," said Alex.

He chuckled, raising an eyebrow. "Good things come in small packages, right, Mouse?"

She blushed.

He pulled his duffel bag closer to his seat and slipped his other arm through the backpack strap.

An empty, sinking feeling overwhelmed Alex. If her heart pounded any harder, the British Geological Survey might issue an earthquake warning. She stared at his lips and curled her fingers around the edge of her chair.

"Mark, before you go, I..." She leaned in, her lips parting slightly. "...I just want to wish you a Merry Christmas." She tossed her arms around his shoulders. He met her hug with a warm squeeze. She closed her eyes, deflated. Not the holiday greeting she planned to deliver. Bottled it.

Pulling away, she looked up at him. "Thanks for everything. I'll see you on the other side?"

"Definitely. Enjoy Manchester and make sure Freddie behaves." Mark picked up his duffel bag and set off. At Kitchen's entrance, he looked back over his shoulder. Alex waved with a sigh.

He turned around again, this time kissing his palm and waving the captured smooch her way.

Thirty-Three

"Happy Christmas, kids. Having you here's the best gift." Joan beamed at Alex, Lucy, and Freddie as she sipped a can of lager. "Anyone else fancy some cheer?"

Freddie shot up from the floor, a pair of fuzzy reindeer antlers jiggling atop his head; the comical accessory contradicted his dressy white shirt, red smoking jacket, and black trousers. "Drinking at 11 a.m.? I like your style, Joan."

He whipped into the kitchen where Helen and Michael toiled away, the mouth-watering aroma of turkey cooking in the oven hinting at the delicious meal to come.

"My first Christmas with you, age twenty-two. Crazy." Alex hugged her gran tightly. "I need this after the year I've had." A toasty fire glowed in the lounge's fireplace while the Carpenters' Christmas album warbled from the stereo.

"That's the best part of the holidays. A clean slate's just around the corner." Lucy stooped down, marveling at the blanket of presents under the tree.

"No, the best part's the grub." Freddie returned to his fireside spot on the floor with an open beer in his hand. "Turkey, roast spuds, pigs in blankets, Yorkshire pudding—I haven't had a traditional Christmas meal in…forever."

"Don't you go home, love?" Joan took pride of place on the cushy sofa. She was bundled in a blue and white Fair Isle sweater, an early Christmas gift from Helen.

Freddie shook his head and shifted closer to the sparkly tree, the tint of his face fluctuating with each blink of the candy coloured lights. "Nah, Lucy and I typically hang out over Christmas. My parents misplaced their welcome mat years ago."

"Me and Freddie have been celebrating Christmas Jamaican-style the last few years—roast chicken, rice and peas, a bottle of Sorrel—raising a glass in honour of my gran. And we always splurge on Christmas crackers. Freddie's fetching in a paper crown," said Lucy, sitting down beside Joan.

"That sounds wonderful, love. It's important to keep up family traditions," said Joan.

Michael weaved his way around his guests, carrying a tin of Quality Street chocolates and a large tub of Celebrations. Alex and Freddie swarmed his delivery before it could land on the coffee table. Freddie loaded his hands full of mini Maltesers, Twix, and Galaxy chocolate bars.

"Ooh, calling dibs on the Bounty bars." Alex playfully shoved Freddie with her woolly white elbow. The sweater made her look like a fluffy Christmas snowflake.

Freddie laughed. "Bounty? Are you joking?"

Alex shook her head, munching on the small bar. She folded her legs under her blue tartan miniskirt and sat beside him on the floor.

"It's the least popular one." Lucy dug a green triangle out of the Quality Street. "The sad little Bounties always get left behind."

"Once an outsider, always an outsider. Nice one, Lex." Freddie gave her a peck on the temple.

"Alex, did you hear from your mum?" Michael upped the fire's flames with a remote control.

"She sent a card saying she was off to Antigua with her greasy boyfriend; some resort where Oprah goes, apparently. Robbie and Kathryn were invited, too, like I care."

"Now, Alex, come on…" Michael raised an eyebrow, his mouth a wry smile. Despite his dislike for his ex, he still expected his youngest to show her mother respect.

Helen trotted into the room, wearing a tacky snowman Christmas sweater that matched Michael's. "Let's open the presents before we eat. Everything should be ready by one."

"Perfect. Then we can watch the Queen's Speech at three," said Joan.

"Really? The Queen addresses the nation today?" asked Alex. "Weird. Can't see the President doing that."

Helen pulled gifts from under the tree and placed them into eager hands.

Joan's face lit up. "And we'll look through the photo albums you brought too, Alex. We got your annual school photos, but that was about it. Your mum was quite stingy."

"Still is…well, with *me* she is. I haven't looked through those albums for ages. So embarrassing. Bad haircuts. Horrible clothes, and the acne…"

"They're going to be hilarious. Lex wouldn't let me take a peek. God knows, I've tried," said Lucy, adjusting the hem of her grey sweater dress as she joined her friends on the floor.

For the next fifteen minutes, wrapping paper and bows overwhelmed the lounge, and laughter overtook the Carpenters' holiday harmonies.

"Lex, you outdid yourself." Freddie gazed at two *Doctor Who* Titan figures. "How on earth did you remember? And where did you find them? The green-windowed TARDIS and the blue-shirted eleventh Doctor are rare variants. They're impossible to get."

"All hail eBay," she smiled. "Why go blind boxed, when you pick and choose?"

"They must've cost a mint. Thank you so much. I'm speechless…"

Alex shook her head, tearing the final piece of paper from Lucy's present. "Anything for you, Freddie."

"Speechless, Freds?" asked Lucy. "Enjoy this moment, everyone—God knows it won't last long!"

"Wow. Lucy's creative talents strike again! Love it. Thank you." Alex flipped through a one-of-a-kind book filled with photos and Lucy's drawings. "Here's the first photo we took together at the Fox and Hounds near Sloane Square. Oh, and look Joan, here's all of us at the Castle pub. Check out Mark's face."

"Are we talking about Mark…*again*?" Lucy scrunched up her nose and elbowed her best friend. "See, this year wasn't all bad."

Alex smiled at his photo. "Yeah, I'm an idiot. I'm glad we're speaking again."

"Hopefully that's not *all* you'll be doing!" Lucy smirked.

Alex playfully smacked her friend. "Lucy! Open your present."

She ripped open the candy-cane striped paper, revealing the back of a CD case; it featured imagery of tall fir trees against a starry sky, no track listings. Confused, she flipped it over—a male and a female smiled up at her, both dressed in gaudy Nordic clothing and carrying lutes. The title declared CIDER WITH

ROSIE *Odin's Magical Spear*.

"Straight from their website." Alex beamed expectantly at Lucy. "I was worried it wouldn't get here in time. It's number three on the Norwegian folk charts—*seriously!*"

"Ahh, nice one, cheers, Lex. That's brilliant." Lucy adopted a *trying-my-best-not-to-hurt-your-feelings* smile and held the gift up for everyone to admire.

A few seconds in, Freddie broke the room's polite silence, doubling over with laughter. "Oh God, YOUR FACE, Lucy!"

Alex and her family joined in the wave of giggles, all in on the joke.

"I'm *sorry*, babe! Did you really think I'd give you such a crap gift?" Alex handed her a bendy rectangle covered in reindeer paper.

Lucy's mouth fell open in relief. "I was gonna say—you don't even *know* me."

She removed the wrap in one go, smiling widely. A *Watchmen* graphic novel greeted her. "Now that's better. I've always wanted to read this one, and I forgot to buy it at the con. Cheers, Lex!"

"Look inside…" said Alex.

Her friend cocked her head to the side and opened the cover. A pamphlet from the University of the Arts London slipped onto her lap.

"What…the…?" Lucy clutched the pamphlet.

"Your gran was so proud when you got accepted into their animation program, and I know it broke your heart to drop out. Lucy, you're really talented, so I signed you up for three nights of cartooning fundamentals, to dip your toe back in."

Lucy's eyes glowed with tears, her hand clapped over her heart. "I can't believe you did this for me. No one's ever done something like…" She leapt into a hug with Alex.

"You and Freddie mean the world to me. I wouldn't have lasted here five minutes without you. It's my way of thanking you guys—for everything. I've never had friends who meant so much to me—I love you both…" Happy tears welled up in Alex's eyes.

Freddie squeezed his way into the hug. "Who says family's only connected by blood, eh?"

"I don't think it's a coincidence that my panic attacks have faded. You two, you're my safety net." Alex smiled into Freddie's shoulder.

Michael put his arm around Helen. "I don't worry so much about Alex, knowing she has these two around."

"Ah, it's not a proper Christmas without a bawl. Even the Carpenters are getting to me." Joan waved her hands by her face. "I blame the drink. Can't get too sauced before the turkey."

She finished her lager and sailed her fingers along the smooth, cool silk of the scarf from Alex. "It's beautiful, love. I just wish you wouldn't spend your hard-earned money on me."

"If I can't spend it on you guys, who would I spend it on?" Alex wiped away a lingering tear. "The extra cater-waiter hours helped. I only dipped into my laptop fund a little bit. It was more important to give special presents to everyone—this year of all years."

"As much as I love the scarf, the play's the best gift you could've given me. Oh, Alex, I can't wait to read it after dinner. *Me*, back on stage, who'd have thought?" Joan beamed, flipping through the pages. "You're so busy with your job and writing for the workshop. How you ever found time to write about silly old me, well, I'm gobsmacked, love."

"My plan was to give you the finished piece, but Olivia's

coffee had other ideas." She frowned. "At least the first draft is better than nothing."

"If that's what your first drafts look like, you're even more talented than I thought." Joan waved her son over. "Michael, can you give my gift to Alex?"

He handed his daughter the last present lying under the tree, its box wrapped in Christmassy Paddington Bears and crowned with a red foil bow. "Let me guess. A coffee table book about *Sherlock*? *Doctor Who*? You're easy to buy for," he said.

Alex chewed another Bounty. "You mean *predictable*, Dad."

She tilted the box to her ear and shook it. "Is this one of your pottery masterpieces, Joan?"

Her grandmother zipped her lips. "I'll never tell, but it's fragile so..."

Alex picked apart the tape, preserving a section of paper Paddingtons for safekeeping.

A white box with a familiar logo stole her breath. "Oh...my God..." Her mouth gaped open as the last shred of wrapping gave way, a tremble travelling to the tips of her fingers.

Lucy set down her pamphlet and leaned into Alex. "Now *that's* a gift. Take a bow, Joan."

Alex's vision blurred. "Joan!" She handed the box to Lucy and bounced to her feet.

"Wow, it weighs next to nothing," said Lucy. "Freddie, lift it."

Alex dove into Joan's arms. "It's incredible, but these laptops cost a fortune..."

"I've missed out on years of treating you. Just say I'm making up for lost time."

"I don't know how to thank you."

Joan's eyes shone. "You want to thank me? *Keep writing.* Make me even more proud, love."

"But how did you know what to get?" Alex leaned out of the hug. "Did the instructor at your seniors' computer class help you out?"

"The instructor? Love, I *am* the instructor!" She shook joyously with a throaty laugh that drowned out the Carpenters. "Those coffin dodgers do my head in, though. They're so slow on the uptake sometimes."

Freddie and Lucy burst into laughter.

"I booked an appointment at the Covent Garden Apple store for when you get home," said Joan. "They'll transfer everything you've saved on your external drives. And do me a favour, Alex, back up *daily* to the Cloud from now on."

"I won't make that mistake again." Alex opened the box's lid just as a phone buzzed and scooted across the coffee table.

"Alex, yours." Lucy handed the smartphone to her friend. "One guess." She nudged Freddie's leg with her foot.

Alex sat back on her heels as she read the text:

'Someone's naughty! Tickets to Les Liaisons Dangereuses at the Donmar tucked into my card? You weren't supposed to do that. Love it! Thank you. Happy Christmas to you and your family. Wish I was there keeping you warm under the mistletoe. I'll make it up to you on New Year's Eve, I promise. Missing you, Mouse. Mark xo'

The message arrived with a photo of Mark wearing a crooked red paper hat from a Christmas cracker, captioned *'Honey, you should see me in a crown.'* He might be out of the loop on all things *Doctor Who*, but he got her BBC *Sherlock* fascination…and if his text was anything to go by, how much she fancied him.

She re-read the text twice and swallowed, easing the lump in her throat. "It's Mark. He's wishing all of us a Happy Christmas and says he'll see us at New Year's."

"Aw, bless," said Joan. "I think I'd like this Irish fellow. Send him our love." She grabbed the two photo albums that stuck out of Alex's red National Theatre tote.

"Ooh! I knew I forgot something…" Helen set off towards the dining room.

"Anything else you'd care to share, Lex?" said Freddie. "Kisses, hugs, declarations of true love?"

The blonde stopped texting. Her furrowed brow instructed Freddie—not in front of her family.

He crossed his arms. "Spoil sport."

"Leave the girl to her crush." Joan waved Freddie and Lucy over. "Come see these photos. Our Alex, such a cutie in her pigtails and striped t-shirts."

Helen returned, carrying flowers in a simple vase, tied with a wide silver ribbon. "Sorry, my sweet. I forgot to give you these earlier."

Alex did a double take and dropped her phone in her lap. A snug bundle of snapdragons—as red as a London post box—rose above the glass, their unique blooms bouncing up and down like the jaws of chatty teenagers.

"They arrived yesterday along with a note from Mark, asking us to give them to you today."

Alex swooned. "They're gorgeous! But how did he know? I never told him…"

Lucy high-fived Freddie. "Yes!"

"You guys!" A wide smile spread across her flushed cheeks. She pressed one of the soft velvety flowers with her finger, its jaw snapping the tip.

"Seems like a nice lad," said Michael, patting his daughter on the shoulder.

"And he supports United, Dad! He's a Red."

Michael grinned from ear to ear.

Alex kept one arm wrapped around the vase while she resumed texting with her free hand.

"Joan, Lex still rocks striped t-shirts. Can't keep her out of them," said Freddie, taking ownership of the second album.

Alex hit send on her text to Mark:

'Snapdragons! So beautiful! Thank you. They'd be rather fetching with your majestic red crown—if only you were here. Please wish your mum and family a Merry Christmas. I'll be waiting impatiently on New Year's. I'm easy to corrupt, remember? Lex xo'

Freddie howled. "Ooh, and there's the obligatory nudie photo in the bath…"

Alex snapped out of her reverie. "Oh, good God. I wish I left these books in the back of my closet—better yet, back in Florida." She set her phone and flowers on the table. "Let me see…"

She shuffled on her knees towards the tree and playfully yanked the album from Freddie's hands. A bundle of stapled papers flew out of the album and across the lounge. It landed underneath the coffee table like a disheveled butterfly.

"What's this? The Secret Diary of Alexandra aged ten-and-a-half?" Lucy fetched the splayed pages and twirled the sheets around so the cover page faced up. Her eyes bugged out of her head as if she had just seen a ghost. "Holy shit. Lex?"

Alex continued flipping through the album with Freddie. She figured that Lucy's find was another cringeworthy slice of her Floridian past. A bunch of old notes passed to her best friend in grade six? A childhood story typed one letter at a time on her mom's old typewriter?

Lucy swallowed, her eyes still wide. "It's your *play*...the original suffragette play. Look." She stuck the pages underneath her friend's nose.

Alex dropped the photo album into Freddie's hands and grabbed the stapled document. Her eyes poured over the title page. She spotted her name, her play's title, and smudged March 2015 date stamps from Emory University, as well as comments and her grade—an A—left in red pen by her professor.

Her hands shook as she turned the pages over one by one, the words all too familiar. Bringing up the rear, her complete play notes, listing sources used in her research and a brief synopsis on why this subject matter was important. The hardcopy hadn't been snatched after all.

Freddie hovered over Alex's shoulder, staring at the pages. "I thought Olivia took it. How is this even possible?"

"Maybe she read it and made a photocopy?" said Lucy. "You said the version she had in Isabella's workshop was identical, right?"

Dazed, Alex could barely speak. "Yeah...every word. Even the notes..."

Michael leaned in, getting a better look. "Bloody hell."

"She replaced the title page, it had her name and everything, but yeah...she must've copied it and put the original back. But *when?* I came home the night she read it and it was in my room. The front page was folded back, but apart from that, everything was just as I'd left it..."

"All she'd have to do is scan it on her printer using OCR, and she'd have a text file. I can't believe someone would stoop so low as to steal like that," said Joan.

"I still don't get how it ended up in your photo album," said Freddie.

"Didn't you say Harry has a cleaning lady?" asked Lucy.

Alex nodded.

"Maybe she moved it. How many times did you knock over those book stacks? I bet the cleaning lady crashed into them hoovering your room. Stuck the play in the largest book she saw?"

"Oh, Lucy. Stop it. I'm getting aroused. You sound just like Benedict, deducing like Sherlock." Freddie fanned his face.

"Freddie!" yelled Lucy. Joan laughed.

Alex scratched her brow and stood up. "I guess it's possible. She had a heck of a time in there. I always knew when she'd knocked over the books because I'd find them piled up different-ly when I came home. And Olivia never claimed to have the original hardcopy, so..." She sank down beside Joan.

"But she still took the play and said it was hers," said Joan. "I would stick it to her. Tell that writer lady what that girl's done." She pointed at the papers in Alex's hands. "You have all the proof you need right there. It's even got your teacher's marks all over it."

"Never mind New Year's. Here's the real fireworks." Lucy unwrapped a Quality Street orange cream. "Do it. Show Isabella. Can you imagine Olivia's face? Man, I want to *be* there."

"You've changed your tune," said Alex. "After she stole it, you persuaded me not to get into a battle with her, she's so well-connected..."

"Things are different now. Olivia destroyed your laptop, all your work. Now you've got Isabella's ear *and* the hard evidence to take the bitch down."

"Lucy's right," said Michael. "Olivia can't argue against

solid proof like that. Blow the bloody doors off. I would."

"But how would I even bring it up to Isabella, though? And what about *Harry?* What will he think?"

"Who cares!" said Freddie. "If anything, you'll be doing him a favour, exposing his fiancée's true colours."

Michael adjusted his glasses. "He's engaged to her now? Christ…"

"You don't have to make your mind up now, love, but think about it," said Joan. "You have options now. Ten minutes ago, you didn't. There's nothing better than a surprise gift at Christmas, is there?"

THIRTY-FOUR

Freddie and Lucy fell asleep on the butt-numbing Sunday afternoon journey down to London. With the heat pumping on the bus and the lolling motion along the motorway, they were goners within twenty minutes of their Manchester departure. But not Alex. The unexpected surprises of the past two and a half days were the gift that kept on giving. Her mind wouldn't rest. She still couldn't believe Joan's generosity or the miracle wedged into her childhood photo album. The unexpected text and flowers from Mark were the icing on the Christmas cake. Her lifelong hatred of surprises ebbed away with each passing mile.

She wouldn't forget this Christmas break for a long time—lounging around in PJs, eating her weight in chocolate, and playing tipsy charades—it all served to temporarily push the anguish of the workshop to the far reaches of her mind, if only for a while.

The two or three times she had felt on the verge of a funk, Freddie and Joan cheered her up with their gut-busting double act. Thinking back, Alex chuckled out loud and clutched her ribs, still sore from the hilarity that ensued Christmas night. With her dad and Helen safely ensconced at the neighbourhood pub, Freddie cracked open *Cards Against Humanity*, daring Joan to join in—a challenge she wholeheartedly accepted.

The semi-detached house shook with politically incorrect laughter for hours. Alex wheezed like a bagpipe gasping for air, and Lucy had to run upstairs to the bathroom, frightful that she was about to pee her pants. At one point, the neighbours banged on the common wall, demanding that the Sinclair household shut up or they'd call the cops—the crowning moment to an epic night.

But now her biggest challenge lay ahead—Wednesday, January 6—the date of the next workshop. Still a week and a half away, but there it loomed, not budging from her path, snarling like a rabid dog. Her breath grew short.

What to do?

She pulled the hardcopy of her suffragette play from her tote bag. Two years of determination, passion, and plenty of tears lay within its pages. The frustration. How she'd pull her hair out when characters wouldn't cooperate or the story arc unraveled on a whim.

Would it be so wrong to stick to The Plan—to let the play and its tangle of emotions and memories go for good? To remain at a distance and let the story live on in Olivia's hands? Alex tried to analyze her own motives honestly…self-preservation was a biggie. She had never met anyone as intimidating as Olivia. And then there was saving Harry from the upset of exposing his girlfriend. The path of least resistance—avoiding conflict, running away…before Alex arrived in London that had always been her M.O., so why change now?

Besides, she'd resigned herself months ago to the idea that she'd watch the play's progress in silence from the sidelines, only a select few knowing that she gave life to those characters.

But that was *before* Christmas—before she had options and damning proof, back when her dusty photo album kept its secret at the bottom of her overstuffed closet on Henshaw Street.

Alex recalled her dad's words:

"Blow the bloody doors off."

She flipped through the crinkled pages of the first act and then the second. Strong confident women spoke her words under the bus's dim night-light. Forget the superheroes that she loved and often imitated in cosplay; these characters—some invented, most pulled from the pages of history—were the real wonder women.

Something clicked.

All three of her most recent plays—the suffragettes, Waterloo Bridge, and Joan's time travel adventure—were populated with trailblazers, outsiders, and rebels…women who fought the good fight and shook the foundations of society. They lived with fervor and courage, overcame seemingly insurmountable odds, and ultimately succeeded. How ironic that she hadn't taken a page out of one of her own plays…

Until now.

Alex looked at the page open on her lap and blinked several times, fighting sleep. As she closed her eyes, the characters seemed to whisper, 'Don't let us down.'

To Alex, December 31 had a hugely exaggerated reputation. In her life, only two New Years were in any way 'happy'—the two she spent with Devin. Their first was at a house party off-campus, only memorable because it was the first NYE far from home with a boyfriend, while the second unfolded at a four-star hotel in downtown Atlanta. Devin didn't spare any expense, booking VIP tickets to an exclusive bash seventy-three floors above the city. That night, after dancing for hours and downing enough champagne to make Alex hiccup, giggle and sneeze simultaneously, Devin gave her a small black velvet box at midnight. Inside she found her beloved silver A necklace resting on a bed of purple satin. Following their prolonged midnight kiss and another twirl around the ballroom, they continued their revelry between the sheets in their hotel room. Despite the heartbreak that followed just ten months later, Alex still wasn't sure another New Year's Eve could match it.

But this afternoon, she felt hopeful...out with the old, in with the new. With Freddie throwing his annual year-end celebration in his flat, and Mark promising to make their reunion special, this New Year's Eve took on new significance. And to Alex's delight, for the first time ever, her attendance was requested at more than one venue; Harry had also invited her to Bespoke's private party, but she begged off, blaming co-hosting duties at Freddie's as the reason why she sadly couldn't make an appearance.

The National gave Alex a half-day off, so she surrendered fully to the NYE cause—to look and feel confident, gorgeous, and sexy. Nails polished, hair pin-straight, legs and bikini line waxed, smoky-eye makeup applied—she wasn't sitting back, letting the new year fold in around her. Nope. She would kick it into gear with her amazing friends and a passionate kiss with Mark. She had one wish for tonight—to pick up where they left off at Zippers, but without her drunkenness and Devin's shadow looming over them.

She arrived at three thirty that afternoon to help Freddie set up. Lucy would follow after work, and Mark was due after that—his flight from Dublin landing at six thirty. Co-workers from the BBC and Pret, friends from Freddie's clubbing exploits, and a few mutual stage door buddies of Lucy's were also expected to join the festivities around nine o'clock.

With Prince's Greatest Hits blaring at full volume, Alex danced around Freddie's flat, dusting his shelves and swaying her ass, all the while breathless in anticipation, her mind stuck on nothing but Mark's return and that longed for midnight kiss. It created the most welcome distraction, something exciting to dwell on, shifting the January 6 workshop out of mind.

The previous seven months had been tough, but optimism wiggled its finger, urging her to enter January with a bounce in her stride and a fresh mindset. As a first step, Alex accepted Devin's Facebook friend request. There was no longer any love there, or anything to yearn for where he was concerned. She was ready to close that chapter of her life—for good. What better time than a new year to move on, forgive, and remember the lessons learned along the way? She felt lighter, more confident, cutting away all the anger and sadness that had been twisted like barbed wire around her heart. And Freddie was right—she needed to give herself a break, too.

She eyed the navy sheath dress she'd worn to the Bespoke dinner hanging from Freddie's bedroom door. Though pretty, it was meant to be the understudy, not the lead. The day before the December 18 workshop, she had purchased a shimmery black and silver dress from Topshop, but after the destruction of her laptop, spending hard-earned cash on clothing was unjustifiable. The dazzling party frock was swiftly returned for a full refund. At least her faithful navy number had won Mark's approval once before.

Around half past four, Lucy bundled through Freddie's door, carrying a garment bag and an old shopping tote from Marks and Spencer, a bottle of something tucked under her arm

"Hey, auld acquaintances? You didn't forget me, did you?"

"Ask me that question tomorrow morning. Memory loss is a sign of a good time." Freddie popped out of the bathroom, a damp sponge in his rubber-gloved hands. "Let me ditch this cleaning crap, and I'll help you with that."

"I'll take the bottle. I've got the drinks trolley organized, and I don't want it messed up." Alex rolled a blue IKEA cart from behind the breakfast bar of Freddie's kitchen. "We should get one of these things, Lucy. It's so cute. We could fill it with baking supplies."

"Right. I may have to rethink my New Year's resolution to bake with you. Can you imagine the arguments? And honestly, I bet more of the icing will end up in your gob than on the cupcakes." Lucy disappeared with her bags down the hall to Freddie's bedroom. She returned a minute later with a de-gloved Freddie by her side.

"Alex. Come sit. Freddie and I have something to show you."

The blonde stopped fiddling with the metal cart and bit her cheek. "That sounds ominous."

She plunked herself down on the sofa, cuddling a squirmy Moriarty.

Lucy eyed the cat. "Freds, can you stick that soul sucker in the loo or something?"

Upon the feline's banishment in Freddie's bedroom, Lucy sat down.

Freddie set a box wrapped in green and silver paper on the coffee table. "We forgot one of your Christmas presents. It's all

Lucy's fault."

"It's not *my* fault. Well, okay, it was…sorta…I left it at the office by mistake. Anyway, it's here now. Open it. It's from both of us."

Alex went to gnaw a freshly painted fingernail, but thought better of it. She gazed at all the pretty. "It's beautiful. I saw this wrapping at Paperchase."

"I know. I was there, remember? Open it," said Lucy.

She tore the paper easily, thanks to Lucy's economical use of tape. A Topshop box greeted her. "What?" She flipped open the lid and gasped. The glittery dress—the same one she had re-turned—lay amidst red tissue paper.

"You guys!" Happy tears sprung to her eyes. "You didn't!"

Freddie beamed. "We bloody well did! Isn't it *glorious*?"

"You shouldn't have to pay for Olivia's bitchery with your New Year's Eve dress," said Lucy. "You haven't bought anything special since May. This dress just screams cocktails and confetti."

"When I heard you returned it, I ran out on my lunch hour and stuck it on my card. We tucked it away at Lucy's office so you wouldn't find it during one of your crazy housecleaning sprees."

Alex held it up against her ratty Gryffindor tee. "But you guys can't afford this. The other dress would've been fine for tonight."

"Fine, sure, but not spectacular," said Lucy. "What good are the holidays if you can't share a little love and sparkle with your best friend?"

☂ ☂ ☂ ☂ ☂

Alex steered clear of booze, determined to keep a clear head. She wanted to remember every detail tonight. The black dress skimmed her body like it was tailor-made, fine lines of delicate silver beading twirled like glittery tinsel to its mid-thigh hem. The thin straps and deep v-neck showed off a sprinkling of freckles on her shoulders as well as her small tattoo. Alex loved how the dress put the spotlight on her boobs—built-in cutlets magically boosted her chest to a B-cup. Eat your heart out, Caprice! For once, Alex felt like a woman, not a kid playing dress-up.

The flat vibrated with high-spirited pleasure-seekers and a never-ending soundtrack of Madonna, Michael Jackson, Kylie Minogue, and seventies disco. Lucy's co-workers mixed easily with Freddie's clubbing buddies while the BBC gang roared with laughter playing *Cards Against Humanity* with the London fandom posse. Even the chippy owner ventured up from the shop downstairs to partake in a toast to Freddie and his noisy bunch of merry-makers.

Freddie's and Lucy's co-workers and friends were chatty and funny, but there was one problem—no Mark. Alex had received a text from him around five saying he'd be there, but as of ten o'clock, the Irishman remained a no-show. His flight was due hours ago, and a pit stop at his East Acton flat shouldn't have made him this late. His absence was further concerning because his flight wasn't appearing on her tracking app. She tried calling him, but her attempts bounced straight to voicemail.

Lucy noticed Alex's sneaky glances at her phone. Enough was enough.

"You're not going to make him arrive any faster by checking your phone every five minutes." Lucy snatched a mushroom pizza bite off a tray and popped it into her mouth. She straightened the slit of her merlot-hued halter-neck dress while she chewed.

Alex slumped against the kitchen counter, kicking off one of her heels. "I just figured he'd be here by now."

"Stop leaning. You'll get creased." Lucy sipped her white wine, her eyes pouring over her friend's dress. "It's stunning, Lex. You've got boobs!"

On Lucy's orders, Alex shifted, but jutted out a hip in protest. "He's having second thoughts, isn't he? I blew my chance. Otherwise he'd be here." She nudged a tray of sausage rolls along the counter.

"Mark likes you! He'll *be* here. Stop stressing. You'll laugh about this at midnight. He won't be able to keep his hands off you. I hope you've got some condoms in your bag, lady."

Alex bit down on a slight smile. "I do, actually. Freddie made sure of that."

"You slapper!" Lucy winked. "Stop worrying. Think about the fun you'll be having later."

Freddie bounded over, dolled up in a secondhand black tuxedo, a crisp white shirt, and a dapper bowtie. "Whatcha talking about, chickies?"

"Were you spying on us, Mr. Bond?" Lucy set down her empty wine glass. "We're discussing Alex's not-so-secret plans for Mark tonight."

"Poor guy's gonna be begging for mercy. I bet that's why he's late. He's *girding his loins*."

Alex smacked him playfully in the stomach.

He grabbed both friends by the hand. "C'mon, enough counter-surfing. The accountant from Pret's setting up his portable karaoke. We must have a go."

"Fredd-ie! Fredd-ie! Fredd-ie!"

The chant overtook the flat as the half-cut guests beckoned their host to be the first to take the mic.

"Me? Oh, go on then. Let's have a little *Into the Groove*, shall we? My Madonna anthem. Hit it."

"This should be good," said Lucy, donning a pointy New Year's hat.

Several other guests followed with renditions of songs by Oasis, Ed Sheeran, and Rihanna. The accountant from Pret did a spot-on impression of Drake—dad dancing and all—much to the crowd's howls of amusement. Lucy took her turn, waving her arms to the heavens in a peppy version of *You've Got the Love* by Florence and the Machine. While at the mic, she caught Alex's optimistic facade crumbling with each passing verse, her dull eyes staring at her phone.

Lucy hauled her friend towards the microphone.

"Alex is *dying* for a turn."

"No, Lucy—*c'mon*, don't make me do this..."

"Oh, you're doing this. Anything to spare another moment of watching you moon over your phone."

Alex scowled at her friend and whispered to the accountant from Pret. She grasped the microphone tightly. The music to *When Will I See You Again* by the Three Degrees filled the room. She didn't need the screen prompt. She knew all the lyrics by heart.

Lucy elbowed a sweaty Freddie. "How apt."

🌂 🌂 🌂 🌂 🌂

By five minutes to midnight, most of the partiers had clambered up to the rooftop deck of Freddie's building, waiting to catch the fireworks launching at midnight from a distant pier near the

London Eye. Squished and jostled, Alex sulked at her phone. The thin straps of her dress slipped down every time her body shuddered under the late night chill.

Lucy nudged the straps back up. "Why didn't you wear your coat?"

"I thought Mar—*someone* would be here to keep me warm," she said, wiping her nose.

"He still has a few minutes."

"Face it, Lucy. He's not going to rush in at midnight and kiss me. That only happens in romantic comedies. I'm not Bridget Jones."

Freddie pushed his way through to his friends, a glittery party tiara nestled in his hair. "Sorry. Just had to make sure that Moriarty was safely stowed in his carrier. Fireworks give him the willies."

He couldn't ignore the glum expression on Alex's face. "Don't pout, darling. I know it's not the same, but I'll kiss you at midnight." He shrugged off his tuxedo jacket and covered her quivering shoulders.

Alex's phone pinged, lifting her scowl and sending her pulse on a tear. Her eyes flew downwards to the Facebook messenger app notification.

'*Happy New Year, Lexy. I hope this year's everything you want it to be. Much love, Devin xo*'

Her heart sank. "Not you. Not…*YOU!*"

She tore at her neck, snapping her necklace. The A charm fell away from the busted chain and catapulted across the deck like a wayward silver bullet. Her eyes cursed its existence as it vanished into the fickle shadows of swaying bodies, glowing cigarette ends, and glinting beer bottles. Good riddance.

Lucy nudged Freddie behind Alex's back. They simultaneously looped their arms around her shoulders.

The rooftop revelers began their rowdy countdown to midnight.

"Ten, nine, eight, seven…"

Alex tossed a look over her shoulder to the door leading downstairs to Freddie's flat.

"Four, three, two, one…HAPPY NEW YEAR!"

Ear-popping bangs, rumbles, and high-pitched whistles erupted in the distance, echoing through London and overtaking the squawking party horns on the rooftop. Electric bursts of red, blue, and white illuminated the inky sky, eliciting "oohs" and "wows" from the easy-to-please audience.

Alex's view grew blurry. At this moment, she hated everyone and everything.

Happy couples and pissed strangers grasped each other for snogs and polite pecks. Freddie seized both Lucy and Alex and laid boozy wet kisses on their cheeks. "Happy New Year, you two. I couldn't start a new year with two better accomplices. I love you, my fangirlies!"

A quartet of BBC buddies began to slur their way through *Auld Lang Syne.* The accountant from Pret accompanied the singers on a green and orange party horn that seemed to sneeze tissue streamers with each raspy puff of air.

Lucy chuckled at their shenanigans, then thought better of it. Alex's eyes didn't leave the wooden planks on the floor. Lucy tightened her hold around her friend's slumped shoulders.

They stood silently as the partiers whooped and cheered each explosion in the sky. The breathtaking display wowed London for close to fifteen minutes.

Alex trembled despite the warmth of Freddie's jacket and retreated downstairs to his flat.

Once out of Alex's earshot, Lucy had a go at Freddie. "Mark better have a good explanation. I really thought he'd be here. My heart's breaking for her. Such a bastard—"

Freddie nodded. "Couldn't agree more. But the angrier we get, the worse Alex will feel. She needs to forget this mess. I feel so bad for geeing her up." He let a bunch of his friends exit down the stairs first. "Grab her a drink, keep her occupied. And let's save the review of Keeg's behaviour until tomorrow afternoon, okay? God, the fact that I'm being rational proves I'm not nearly pissed enough. Let's remedy that."

Upon entering his flat, he snatched a bottle of vodka from the cart and threw himself into a twirl with the disheveled Pret accountant and a curvy BBC receptionist, all three singing Kylie's *Can't Get You Out of My Head* at the top of their lungs.

Alex weaved through the flailing arms and wobbly drinkers, tossing empty beer cans into a large trash bag.

Lucy clutched at the bag. "Lex, stop. The party's still in full swing. Come dance."

"I'm not in the mood. I'd go home, but I can't afford a cab on my own. I need to keep myself busy. It's all I can do not to cry, so, *please*...let me do this. If I dance, I'll want a drink. Dancing and drinking didn't end so well last time."

"I'm sure Freddie appreciates you keeping everything tidy, but if you're still doing this at 1 a.m., I'm forcing you to dance. Cleaning's no way to welcome in a new year." She sighed and leapt into the dancing fray, joining a twerking Freddie.

Alex did three laps of the crowded flat, clearing abandoned cans, bottles, and overflowing ashtrays. She refilled bowls of crisps and heated up four more trays of mini sausage rolls and pizza bites. She glanced at her phone—12:58 a.m.—and began another sweep of the room for stray cans.

Something tugged at the trash bag trailing behind her.

"Lucy, look, I'm gonna get going…"

A familiar sexy scent—spicy cardamom, juniper berries, and leather. The delicate hairs on the back of her neck stirred. "Hello, stranger." Mark whispered in her ear.

Her heart fluttered, as effervescent as a champagne bottle about to pop its cork.

She spun around. His leather jacket rose and fell with each laboured breath, his black hair disorderly and teasing above his determined brown eyes. His forehead glistened with perspiration, giving him an otherworldly glow.

The bag slipped from Alex's grasp, her eyes afraid to blink in case he vanished. The throbbing sub-bass of Kylie's *On a Night Like This* faded into the background, her ears hearing only his sensual Irish lilt. A room crowded with forty people and only one person existed stood inches away, stealing her heart.

One hand gently held her waist, the other caressed her cheek. Mark tilted his head towards Freddie's muted TV, broadcasting New Year's countdowns around the world. "I knew I'd make it in time…see, it's now midnight…in *Greenland*."

He leaned down and kissed her tenderly. Alex threw her arms around his shoulders, months of longing and tension melting into the desperate embrace. She pulled away to smile and lose herself in his brown eyes. "*Greenland*? You better show me how they keep warm, then." Mark laughed and swept her into a deeper, more passionate kiss.

Seeking some liquid refreshment, Freddie broke free of the disco inferno and spied his friends in a tight clinch. Alex's hands were lost in Mark's hair while his were claiming ownership of her ass.

"*Oh, mmmyyyy!*" Freddie slurred his best George Takei impression, a cheek-pinching grin spreading across his flushed face. He hugged Lucy, who let out a high-pitched squeal. Tipsy and teary, she began to hiccup with glee.

Thirty-Five

The evening Alex both dreaded and welcomed had arrived. Tonight—January 6—the first workshop since Olivia poured her bitter revenge all over Alex's future.

She spirited away to the second floor of the National, her cold hands fiddling with the hem of her grey knee-length skirt and the nape of her neck, but her A necklace—her crutch—no longer hung in its faithful spot. Lost among discarded beer bottles and glittery cardboard hats somewhere on Freddie's roof, the gift—along with the boyfriend who gave it to her—belonged firmly in her past.

She checked her phone. Only an hour stood between her and the big reveal. Only an hour left to rehearse what she wanted—no, *needed*—to say.

It didn't help her nerves that the window behind her howled in distress. Heavy rain-soaked gusts bombarded the glass, prompting Alex to smother her white blouse with the coziness of her fuchsia cardigan. She inhaled deeply, hoping the incoming breath would hush the jitters that needled her chest and harassed her mind. Just fifty-five minutes now until her performance...*actors to the stage, please. Take your positions...*

"I wanted to wish you luck."

Mark sat down and leaned in, delivering a trail of kisses along her neck while his fingertips stroked her arm. Alex's whole body loosened with his touch. She closed her eyes and ran her hand through his tousled hair, begging him not to stop. His lips met hers urgently, coaxing her to abandon the laptop beside her.

A P.A. announcement regarding a platform discussion in the Lyttleton Theatre disrupted their smoldering reunion.

"Wish *me* luck? More like you're trying to *get* lucky, not that I'm complaining. It actually made me relax a little." She stroked his stubbly chin and smiled. Since New Year's, time together had been limited. Mark was juggling his shifts along with a lead role in a BBC radio drama while Alex had been setting up her new computer and re-constructing the lost second act of her Waterloo Bridge play.

Their belated New Year's kiss nearly didn't happen. Fog had played havoc with flights departing from Dublin. After several delays, the airline finally cancelled Mark's flight, offering him the option of flying out of Cork on Ireland's southwest coast instead. They paid for his train trip and somehow got him on the last flight arriving at London's Stansted airport at 11 p.m. He tried to call Alex and Freddie, but all the phoning around to arrange last-minute tickets had killed his battery.

When Mark slipped into the noisy party at 12:57 a.m., he stood silent for a minute just watching her wandering through the crowd, detached. She had no clue he was there, her gorgeous dress hugging every curve, inviting him to take hold and never let go. Their initial kiss stretched into a breathless twenty-minute snog until Freddie threatened to douse them both with a bucket of ice water.

Lucy offered to stay over at Freddie's, allowing Alex and Mark the luxury of spending their first night together alone at the flat. The stubble burn on her face and elsewhere may have started to fade, but the dizzying memories of his lips exploring every inch made her want to surrender all over again. Once the workshop wrapped tonight, they could tumble back into bed and get reacquainted.

Mark held her hand. "You'll be fine. I wish I could watch you kick some Kensington arse."

Alex chuckled.

"Go ahead and laugh, but I totally believe in you. Look what you've achieved in the past few months: you moved abroad, found a new flat, got a job you love, and wrote two new plays."

She wrinkled her nose.

"Scoff all you want, but you're the bravest person I know. Standing up to a bully is never easy. Just a few months ago you'd be having a panic attack at the very thought of it, right? But now look at you, you're *this close* to taking back what's rightfully yours."

He brushed Alex's bangs out of her eyes. "You walk in there with your head held high, okay? Grab Isabella alone during the break. Send me a text when you're done. I'll meet you."

"I wish I could see myself the way you see me," said Alex.

He squeezed her hand. "I had a snoop through your Pinterest boards ..."

"Oh God..." Alex curled forward. "You must've hated that. Did you break out in hives?"

Mark scrolled through his phone. "Okay, here's one. You pinned this quote from Yvonne Pierre—'*Use what you've been through as fuel. Believe in yourself and be unstoppable'*. See? That must've resonated with you if it's in your collection."

"Or was I just feeling sorry for myself one evening? I probably pinned a bunch of cupcake recipes and Whishaw photos at the same time."

"Alex, don't sell yourself short. Most people in your shoes would've been long gone by now, running for the hills. You're my hero, no bullshit."

She grimaced.

"You are! You're so much stronger than you realize. You just have to recognize it, and believe in yourself. You can do this."

Alex smiled and leaned her forehead against Mark's. "Great minds...*you can do this*—that's what I always tell myself, too."

His fingers caressed her cheek. "There you go, then. Maybe the best inspirational quote is actually your own."

Alex rounded the corner on to Stamford Street and spotted the glowing tail lights of a dark green sports car, hugging the curb in front of the community centre. Her stomach plummeted like an elevator snapped free of its cables.

Harry—dropping off a flawlessly presented Olivia, not fifty feet away. Her purple and red tapestry Erdem coat fluttered over a long tapered black skirt and Louboutin heels, a hastily opened golf umbrella shielding her from Mother Nature's wrath. Even the downpour couldn't dampen her aesthetic perfection.

Alex paused beneath her bobbing brolly, hoping its fight against the elements wouldn't register on their radar. A gaggle of teenagers piling out of a Nando's restaurant on the main floor of the Coin Street Centre provided perfect cover from the future Mrs. Manville. Once Olivia swept indoors, Harry revved his engine and sped off, propelling a swell of dirty sludge towards the chairs stacked up outside the eatery.

That tiny glimpse rattled Alex's resolve. Two minutes ago, she was determined to unload to Isabella. Now she wasn't so sure. Why did Harry have to appear today of all days? She'd spent her post-Christmas week erasing any concern of hurting him. Easy to do at a distance—it was much harder with him smiling in his Jaguar only a few feet away, giving Olivia a peck goodbye. Now he was *real* again, a friend who didn't deserve to get hurt in the post-Apocalyptic fallout.

She hurried out of the deluge and into the building. Pausing to gather herself, the elevator jerked open, revealing her three male colleagues. They held the doors, beckoning her to join them on the ascent to the third floor.

"Happy New Year, Alex," said the ginger one. "Could they save your laptop?"

She fussed with her windblown hair. "Afraid not. The computer guy said he was a genius, not a miracle worker."

The male trio chuckled sympathetically as the doors opened on their floor. Alex walked behind, taking deep breaths to stifle the acrobatics in her gut. She passed the door to the ladies' toilets and considered stalling in there with just her anxiety for companionship, but Mark's words—*her* words—nudged her legs forward: "*You can do this.*"

It wasn't a surprise to discover Olivia sat closest to Isabella. She was welcome to that chair; bad karma had seeped into every fibre. Alex sat down next to Olivia, the only chair still available.

Olivia leaned sideways, as if whispering to an old friend. "Oh, did I take your place?"

"You know you did." Alex didn't even blink.

Olivia responded with a snort.

"Happy New Year, everyone," said Isabella, unpacking a stack of folders from her satchel. "Now that the holidays are over, let's jump into the process with both feet. We'll be joined tonight by actresses doing a staged reading of Olivia's suffragette play. They won't be off-book, but seeing Olivia's words come to life will spotlight any problems. And just a reminder, as per Olivia's instructions, even the male characters will be portrayed by women."

Olivia shot to her feet. "Actually, during the holidays, I gave the text a makeover. I've got revised copies for everyone."

"You know your work better than anyone," said Isabella. "If it needs tweaking, I'm all for it."

Olivia handed scripts to each person. "I've highlighted the changes so you can see what's been improved and modernized. It's more *accessible* now."

Alex flipped past the cover page, her eyes zeroing in on several yellow highlighted blobs. Her eyes widened further and further with each line skimmed. Improvements? That's what Olivia was calling this bastardization of her story? Vandalism, more like. Jarring new dialogue on the pages interrupted her beloved characters' conversations, and historical facts were changed. She skipped frantically ahead in the script. Names were modernized for no reason at all—Emily Davison became a trendy 'Emi' and Sophia Duleep Singh, the Indian princess who fought alongside her white British counterparts, was renamed 'Sophie'.

Giving the characters a sugarcoated Hollywood overhaul tore their authenticity to shreds. She turned more pages, shaking her head at the ridiculous updates, oblivious to the troop of actresses assembling in the middle of the U of desks.

Olivia's haughty tone snapped her back into the room.

"Sorry to interrupt, Isabella. I'm having a difficult time picturing Emi." Olivia crossed her arms. "Can we swap out actresses? No offence, darling, but you're a bit too...*plus sized*. Emi's the heroine of this story and would be slimmer, you know?"

Alex's jaw dropped. Two of the men shared a did-I-just-hear-that look, while the third stifled a snicker. The so-called plus sized actress, no bigger than an American size ten and hardly chubby, turned scarlet, her shoulders slumping under the weight of the room's scrutinizing gaze.

Isabella swallowed hard. "Olivia, we don't have time to shuffle roles and the suffragettes weren't striving to be beauty queens, you know that. If your play moves forward into actual performance—and that's a *big* if—you can make your casting preferences known then. Ladies, please continue, top of page eight ..."

The brunette frowned and fanned herself with the script.

The actresses read on. Alex watched as Olivia pinched her lips together whenever the size ten actress spoke. She noticed how Isabella leaned forward, studying every word, every nuance of the read-through. More than once, she was certain that she'd seen Isabella frown at some of Olivia's attempts to modernize dialogue, or alter characters, scribbling red notes on the margins of her manuscript.

Alex returned her attention to the actresses reading the now clunky lines. At the end of the first act, they reached a poignant scene—she could remember sweating over every line of the original, playing the roles out in her head a hundred times. Olivia's reimagining of the scene unfolded. 'Sophie' was married to a new character called 'Kale'.

Alex winced. Naming characters from the early 1900s after today's *trendy veg*? She glanced down at the page. 'Kale' wasn't the worst of it. She gasped in horror at the new notes accompanying the scene—Olivia had even changed 'Sophie's' ethnicity. She was no longer an Indian princess. She was now a white socialite from Chelsea.

Are you fucking kidding?

She bit her tongue and tapped her foot impatiently on the floor, watching the hands of the clock on the wall crawl towards the scheduled break, still twenty minutes away. Her temples began to throb under the strain of her now constant scowl.

Olivia's romcom-worthy love scene veered towards diabetes inducing. It concluded with Sophie the suffragette standing by her man and promising to scale down her efforts in order to keep him sweet.

Alex's chest rose and fell in quick bursts. Changing names and races of real-life people was offensive and inexcusable, and now she was changing the suffragettes' courage and beliefs, too?!

Olivia had poisoned Alex's self-confidence, bullied her out of London Fields, damaged her friendship with Harry—but there was no way in hell Alex would let her degrade these women and their story in such an obnoxious manner.

She couldn't bear to hear another word...

"Enough!"

Every head in the room swiveled towards Alex.

Thirty-Six

The actresses froze, their wide eyes flitting between Alex and Isabella, waiting. The male playwrights shifted in their chairs, unsure where to look. A flush of redness flooded Isabella's pale cheeks while her breathing picked up pace.

Olivia looked like she was chewing on a wasp, all bulging eyes and skewed jaw. "Alex, are you still cross with me about your laptop? You *know* it was an accident...if you're trying to make me feel worse, well, you're doing a brilliant job—"

Alex threw her hands in the air. "I can't stomach any more of this farce. Emi? Kale? Sophia is *white* now? —What the *fuck*?" She leaned over the table, shaking off Olivia's shadow to address Isabella. "Sorry to interrupt, but I *really* need to speak to you—in private."

Isabella squinted back, her soft tone masking her displeasure. "Alex, it's out of order for a student to call a halt to a workshop, and I won't tolerate bad language." Her stare took an upward detour to the clock. "We're close to break, so let's take fifteen to regroup, everyone. Alex, come here, please."

The award-winning playwright clenched her jaw, watching

the room empty. Everyone scuttled out except for Alex and Olivia, the unsettling silence broken only by the closing metal door.

Olivia launched upwards atop her Louboutins, her nearly six-foot frame towering over both women, her eyes wild and wide.

"Are you going to stand for this, Isabella? What right does she have to heckle my work like some football hooligan seeing theatre for the first time? It's inappropriate."

Isabella nodded. "She's right, Alex. I can't allow such disrespectful interruptions during sessions. I have to say, I'm disappointed in you—it's inappropriate and unprofessional. If you have another outburst like this one, I'll be asking you to leave. Consider this a warning."

Alex rose to stand, her heart hammering against her chest.

"Inappropriate and unprofessional?" She pulled papers out of her bag and walked around Olivia to Isabella's chair. "Well, so is stealing another writer's work."

Alex handed her original manuscript with its bent pages, university date stamps, and scrawled professor remarks in red ink to Isabella. She could practically feel Olivia's stare singe the back of her neck. She briefly looked sideways. Yep. Her nemesis quaked, ready to erupt like a volcano.

"What's this?" Isabella's face tightened.

Olivia jostled Alex out of the way. "Don't fall for it. She has no reputation, so she's trying to smear mine."

Isabella's eyes raced over the title page and through the corresponding sheets, stopping several times to digest the text before flicking to the final pages and the attached notes. Her puzzled eyebrows leaned heavily onto her eyelids.

"Alex…this play's yours?"

She nodded, holding her breath. "I wrote it in college in Atlanta. Until a few months ago, Olivia and I were flatmates. She read my play as a courtesy and then presented it as her own at the young playwrights fundraiser, the event at Bridgewater House. Where I first met you."

"Oh for God's sake, *she's lying*!" said Olivia.

Isabella ignored the fretting brunette. "I knew you looked familiar at the Almeida. Why are you just telling me this now?"

"She completely blindsided me that night. She pitched my idea to you! I was reeling, had a full blown panic attack. When I got home, I looked for this hardcopy, but it was missing. Without proof, why would you believe me? You don't know me. I'm a nobody."

Alex swept her hand towards Olivia. "Look who I'm up against. She's rich, powerful, well connected...as she's reminded me repeatedly. Everyone *adores* Olivia and her fundraising for the arts—"

"You should've tried me." Isabella interrupted.

Alex shook her head. "It's easy to recreate someone else's work on a computer. If I'd shown you my saved version, you wouldn't have believed me. I needed the original hardcopy to prove that I wrote it. I found it over Christmas."

Olivia crossed her arms. "Okay, I know why she's doing this to me. The truth is, I *do* remember Alex and I talking casually about a suffragette idea last year. That doesn't mean I 'stole her play'—I just sat down at my laptop and actually *did* something with it. And now she's obviously getting her revenge. You can't copyright an idea, Alex! Isabella, don't fall for this ridiculous university manuscript rubbish. Some people will stop at nothing to discredit people with talent like you and me—"

"Stop!" Isabella slammed her hand on the table. Her water glass skipped two inches.

She sat back and continued to speed-read page after page, exploring the contents. The air in the room crackled with electricity, Alex and Olivia both fearful of breaking the silence...

"Olivia, the original draft you submitted—it's practically identical to this hardcopy. The directions about casting. The dialogue. Characters. Even the notes at the back."

"Of course they're identical. I wrote it!" Olivia shouted. "She must've gotten into my computer somehow, copied the Word files, I don't know—come on, Isabella. You *know* me..."

Isabella pointed to the hardcopy. "Okay, let's say this is a copy of your original work, yes? Then what about words like *'color'* and *'behavior'*? They stuck out during my first read through—why would a British writer use American spellings? On first reading, I dismissed it as spell check failure..."

She locked eyes with Olivia. "Plagiarized work? How could you *be* so stupid..."

Olivia searched for a response, but remained silent, her eyes narrowing.

Alex stepped closer to Isabella, taking a deep breath. "I'm sorry for disrupting the session, but I couldn't allow this charade to go on any further, regardless of the consequences. Better to be honest than secretive and scared. Even if I'm banned from this workshop, at least my conscience is clear now."

The door nudged ajar, the three male playwrights checking if the workshop was about to restart.

Olivia leaned so close to Alex that she could feel the brunette's hot breath on her face. "Oh, cry me a river, you stupid little slut. Don't give me this 'butter wouldn't melt' act. You're the thief. You're the liar."

The women's raised voices sent the door flying shut with a metallic bang, the break extended indefinitely.

Olivia jabbed a manicured finger at Alex. "Stop playing dumb. I'm sick of it. Tallahassee Thanksgiving 2014? Ring any bells? I saw the photos...your cozy sleepover with my Harry."

Alex's eyes bulged like the secrets of the universe had been revealed.

"Shall I refresh your memory? Harry's plastered all over that album—laughing as he carved your turkey; smiling with a forkful of pumpkin pie..."

"Oh, for fuck's sake!" Alex crossed her arms. "Photos? *That's* why you stole my play?"

"...kissing whipped cream off your nose! Playing stupid American football and—I bet you remember *this* one—you straddling Harry in a pile of leaves. It's photographic proof, the two of you, caught in a blatant lie. And none of the photos with Harry were tagged. Trying to hide the evidence, were you?" Olivia flailed her arms, her engagement ring sending out glinty flares with each unhinged flap.

Alex frowned. "Tag them? What? It wasn't important. A missing tag isn't proof of, of...anything."

Olivia dropped her hands to her hips. "Photos never lie. You and Harry should've at least had the sense to get your stories straight—"

"Okay, you want the true story? Yes, I'm *guilty* of abandoning Harry on a holiday long weekend. I'm *guilty* of calling him at the last minute with an invite to his first American Thanksgiving. I'm *guilty* of goofing around, snapping silly photos—the turkey, the whipped cream on my nose...but straddling him? That was an ill-timed football tackle. Totally harmless and PG—we were surrounded by kids! I've told you a million times. *Nothing happened*! I know what it feels like to be cheated on. I'd never do th—no. You know what, I'm *over* trying to explain something that never took place! Your insecurity is your problem. I'm done with you."

"Well, I've not even started with you. You're accusing me of plagiarism—fine! Don't you know who my father is? We'll sue you for defamation, libel—*whatever*. You'll be tied up fighting the lawsuit for *years*. If you want your family to be financially ruined, keep this up. I don't need to listen to your fairy tales."

Olivia straightened her skirt. "And Isabella, I respect you—you know that—but if you choose to believe her over me, well, that's your funeral."

The door to the meeting room squeaked open again.

"Guys, five more minutes!" shouted Isabella. Alex figured that some of the actresses were dying to have a front row seat to this performance.

A familiar face appeared around the door's edge.

Harry.

Both Alex and Olivia gasped as one.

Pale and crestfallen, his hands clenched Olivia's Swarovski bedazzled iPhone, presumably left behind in his car.

"Is this true?"

Olivia unleashed the waterworks. "Darling, they're accusing me of all sorts. I've done nothing wrong..."

He strode into the room towards his princess, his beige cashmere Burberry coat billowing behind him like a superhero's cape. "Answer me. Is this *true*?"

Alex stood frozen, her breathing halted.

Harry's fiancée clambered to his side, all pleading arms, sniveling tears, and streaky mascara. He flinched backwards, his lip curled.

"Harry, look—she sold her play to me...for rent money.

She's always broke, you know!"

Alex rubbed a raised eyebrow. She didn't feel anger anymore, just…pity.

Every time Harry stepped back, Olivia edged closer. "She wrote the original draft, but I've improved it so much since then, so it's mine really…"

Isabella exhaled and stood up. "Olivia, stop."

"And you still won't tell me the truth. *Me* of all people." Harry's hands were shaking. "I heard everything. The stealing. The cheating allegations—I would never…" His voice broke as he covered his mouth with his hand. "Apparently I had more faith in you than you *ever* had in me…I've heard enough."

"Harry, please…"

He stormed out of the room. A cluster of eavesdropping actresses and the other playwrights swung their heads back and forth between Harry's exiting blur and the three women. Olivia scrambled to collect her belongings, dashing towards the doorway.

"Olivia, your actions cannot be tolerated. Until I can investigate further, and make a phone call to the professor at Emory, your involvement in this workshop is suspended," said Isabella. "I also don't take kindly to threats. I suggest you refrain from any actions, legal or otherwise, until you hear from me."

"I was only trying to protect what's mine," Olivia shouted, amidst tears as she clicked down the hall.

"Yeah, so was I," said Alex.

THIRTY-SEVEN

One week later

Perched on a wooden bench beside the front window of Freestate Coffee on Southampton Row, Alex took a quick sip from her soothing cup of hot chocolate, waiting for her guest's arrival. She arrived before the lunch rush to grab this perfect spot, knowing she could lose herself in the passing double-decker buses and impatient black cabs. Eight months on from her arrival last May, she was still smitten.

A friendly face waved from the doorway, prompting Alex to stand up.

"Thanks for meeting me." Harry hugged her quickly. He eased out of his Burberry coat, but Alex noticed something was up. Normally well-groomed and fashionable, Harry looked like he had grabbed whatever clothes were lying on the floor of Tom's room. His grey point collar shirt was wrinkled and buttoned up incorrectly, and a rare five o'clock shadow crept above his lip and along his cheeks and chin. His usually sparkly blue eyes were sombre and sleepy, sinking into purple circles. He didn't smell clean and sweet like Harry, either. If Alex didn't know him better, she would've assumed he'd been on a bender.

"I love this place." Alex smoothed her black sweater and skirt as she sat down. "I don't get to stop in too often, but it came to mind when you suggested somewhere off the radar." She couldn't avoid the obvious. "Harry, you look shattered."

"I've had better weeks." His smile didn't quite reach his eyes. "Let me grab a tea, and we'll catch up."

A few minutes later, he returned with his Earl Grey, a plate crowded with two large chocolate brownies, and a pair of shiny forks.

"Someone's trying to butter me up." Alex laughed.

"It's nice to be in the company of a woman who eats without counting calories."

"Why bother? I'm terrible at math." Alex dug into her brownie, scooping a bite too large for the fork. "I'm glad you texted. I thought I might never hear from you again. You wouldn't be in this mess if I had stayed in the States." She savoured the chocolate's brief sweetness and swallowed.

Harry looked down at the table. "You should've told me about the play earlier, but I understand why you didn't. Olivia has a talent for making people do exactly what she wants. Once upon a time, that was one of the things that made me fall for her, the way she knew her own mind, her self-confidence."

"How's it at home? I bet she'd freak if she knew you were meeting me."

"That's why I wanted to meet somewhere she doesn't frequent. Another confrontation is the last thing I need. Home's been good, actually. Best thing I did was chuck her out of my flat."

"You threw her out? Tom, too?"

"Yep. We had a huge row at home after the workshop. I told her that she had to be gone by morning. Tom was great. He just shrugged in his typical style and offered to move on, but Olivia begged. That wasn't pretty."

"Ouch," said Alex.

"It's done; we're officially...over." He exhaled heavily, swirling a spoon in his tea. "Her stealing and bullying—it was horrible, completely inexcusable. What she put you through, Alex, I'm horrified you were put in a position where you felt you couldn't tell me. And if you thought you couldn't trust *me*, then who have I become? Olivia didn't exactly bring out the best in me. I see that now."

His eyes wandered towards the window, staring into nothing. "The fact that she doubted my fidelity and commitment to her was the last straw. I can't be in a relationship with someone so easily poisoned by jealousy. Shame it took me four years to figure that out."

With a frown, he plunged his fork into his brownie, chipping away a miniscule bite.

"Mmm. Now I know why you like this place. Delicious." He didn't return for another taste, but his hand clutched the empty fork.

"I'm ashamed of how I got sucked in. I never saw how manipulative she could be. She was charming, popular, a beautiful girl with *everything* going for her. And best of all, she was crazy about me. Obviously, a little *too* crazy as it turns out. I thought I knew her, but—"

"Harry, cut yourself some slack. She was obviously on her best behaviour whenever you were around."

"Probably. I've been thinking about it a lot...what turned her into such a scheming, possessive mess. Before we began dating, I was never without female company—and I mean, *never*. I lost my virginity at thirteen."

"Harry!"

He rolled his eyes and looked sheepish. "I know, eh? I was quite experienced by the time we got together, and she didn't have the best role models for a healthy relationship—her dad had an affair with her nanny when she was a kid." He stabbed at the brownie with his fork with no intention of taking another bite. "God, I've been so blind."

His chin shot up, his eyes capturing Alex's gaze. "I'm not making excuses for her. Whatever happened, it still didn't give her the right to bully or steal from you. Or accuse you of sleeping with me."

Alex smiled softly. "She made me feel guilty even when I wasn't."

"You too?" He half-laughed, shaking his head. "I never cheated on her. That's the kicker. Any hook-ups, secret snogs, it was all in her imagination. I never looked at another girl. I thought she was The One, that we'd spend the rest of our lives together..."

He blinked, but not fast enough for Alex to miss a tear or two moistening his eyes.

"I'm ashamed and so sorry. About everything, looking back. The terrible box room, the fundraiser embarrassment..."

He dropped the fork and pushed his hair back, kneading his forehead as if each squeeze might dissolve the upsetting memories. "And I had your friend fired, too. What the hell was I thinking? I did it for Olivia. She was in meltdown mode and seeing her so distraught tore my heart out—she played me like a fiddle. I'm usually a pretty fair guy, but I didn't even give him a chance to plead his case. I had no clue that you knew him...until Tom mentioned it last week. The bloke must hate me."

"I think it bothered him for about a day, and then he moved on. Mark's not one to dwell on stuff like that. He's pretty positive," said Alex. "A good guy."

"He sounds it."

Harry did a double take. "My God, Alex. I could use that glow to light my way through London Fields at midnight. Is there something you care to share?"

"Maybe."

"I think wee Alex has got herself an English fella."

"He's Irish."

"Oh, that's right. Well, he's a *lucky* Irishman. I'm happy for you."

"Thanks." She smiled through her next bite of brownie. "What are you going to do now? All those wedding plans to cancel…"

He sighed. "Ahh, it's only money. Better to lose a couple thousand quid than have a lifetime of marital misery. I haven't been off the dating track or without a girlfriend since I was twelve. Time to fly solo for a while. I'm looking forward to it, actually." His tentative smile tried to convince Alex—and himself.

"And I'm also hoping *we* can still hang out, despite my stupidity and terrible track record in fiancées?"

"Absolutely." Alex smiled warmly, covering his hand with her own. "Maybe it's time we tricked a few people on this side of the pond with our brother-sister act. You game?"

Thirty-Eight

Alex, Lucy, Freddie, and Mark pressed through the crowds to join the long queue for a photo with Sherlock himself, Benedict Cumberbatch. The actor and his co-stars, plus the cast and creatives from *Doctor Who,* were in the midst of a weekend-long comic con in late January at the ExCel in London's Docklands.

"I was worried your old uni professor may have fucking died or something. Two and a half weeks to respond to Isabella?" Lucy scratched the shoulder of her red pleather jacket, her Martha Jones cosplay in full effect. "Thank God he finally came through yesterday and backed you up."

"He'd never forget me; I was such an annoying perfectionist," said Alex. "I bet he was happy to see me graduate."

"So, now that the suffragettes are yours again, does that mean you have two plays getting the Isabella treatment?" Freddie admired his recently autographed Martin Freeman photo.

Alex nodded. "Yep, Isabella said it's not the norm for a student to have two entries, but then nothing about the Olivia situation was ever normal."

"Wow." Freddie raised his eyebrows. "Such an overachiever. Do your workshop mates have a hate-on for you? Making them all look lazy..."

"Hardly." Alex smacked him on the butt. "Actually, I think they're relieved. She spends so much time taking me to task— they get away scot-free. Honestly, though, I'd take her tough love over compliments any day. Wait, did I just say that? I never thought those words would come from *my* mouth. Anyway, her criticism is improving my writing, big time."

Mark pulled Alex into the chest of his cozy navy sweater, giving her a lingering peck on the top of her head. "It sounds crazy, but your battles with Olivia kinda prepared you for everything Isabella's throwing at you—you're not getting bowled over by it, right? That's a victory in itself."

"Should I send Ms. Chadwick-Smythe a thank you card?" Alex straightened her red tartan kilt, careful not to bend the signed photo with Steven Moffat in her hand. Her white blouse, black cardigan, tights, and ankle boots completed her Clara Oswald Christmas 2013 cosplay outfit. "It feels good speaking up, standing my ground. I'm definitely not fretting as much as I used to or feeling the need to control every little thing. Not sure if it's connected, but I'll take it."

"And no more panic attacks. I'd say it's connected." Lucy stepped forward with the queue.

"I think it has more to do with you guys." Alex smiled warmly. "I've finally found my London family, and I hate to break it to you, but I'm not going *anywhere*. I'm home at last. You're stuck with me."

Freddie adjusted his black tie, channeling Jim Moriarty in his choice of outfit. "America's loss is Britain's gain."

"And ours." Mark gathered his girlfriend into a kiss.

Lucy elbowed him in the ribs. "God, Keegs. Save some for

later."

A loud roar erupted from the curtained-off area where a special effects panel was taking place. The applause and whoops from the hidden audience continued for a few minutes, blending in with the *Sherlock* theme.

"Moffat was lovely—discussing writing with me." Alex smiled at her signed photo. "I just hope the organizers sort out the conflicts. Capaldi's photo op is at the same time as Andrew Scott. I can't have th—"

"Alex? Is that your phone?" asked Lucy. "I thought the theme was coming from the panel, but your bag won't shut up."

"No one I know would call at a time like this. Don't they realize that Cumberbatch lurks behind that wall?" Alex frowned, spotting 'caller unknown' on the phone's screen, and answered.

"Hello? …Yes, speaking…"

Freddie, Mark, and Lucy carried on behind her, laughing at Freddie's photo with Rupert Graves. The *Sherlock* actor, grinning wildly, was giving him a precarious piggyback.

"I'm fine, thanks…" Alex covered her other ear with her free hand. She glared at her noisy gang, motioning for them to hush.

"Who is it, then?" asked Freddie, not really expecting Alex to answer.

She remained riveted to the mysterious voice, her eyebrows reaching their upper limits with no further space to roam. The absence of blinking and breathing drew Mark's concern. He stared at his girlfriend, hoping to catch the gist of her conversation, but Alex turned her back, desperate for quiet and privacy amid the noisy line of fans.

"I bet it's Isabella." Lucy tugged on the con lanyard around her neck. "That woman's a robot. She has no social life. It would be just like her to hassle Lex over the weekend."

Alex turned around, facing her friends. "When?...Sure, I can, yes...and thanks again for the call...Yes, you, too. Bye."

The line surged forward, but Alex didn't budge, tears brimming in her dazed eyes. She bobbled her phone trying to stuff it into her bag. "Oh my God. Oh my God..."

"What's wrong?" Mark moved closer, offering a gentle one-armed embrace. Alex grasped at his hand resting on her shoulder. She squeezed her eyes shut, her chest chasing breaths lost during the phone conversation.

"You're freaking me out. Who was it?" asked Lucy.

Alex covered her mouth with her hand. "The literary manager at The Royal Court Theatre."

"Seriously?" Lucy's voice squeaked.

Freddie yanked his glasses from his face. "No way!"

Alex nodded, a wide smile lifting her cheeks and sending her tears on a happy slide down her face. "My time travel play. They read it, *somehow,* and want to put it into production this summer."

"In *production*? Not workshopping or adding you to a playwriting program? Actually performed on stage with actors ...in front of a paying audience?" asked Freddie.

She wiped away her tears. "Yes, in the Jerwood Theatre."

Mark hugged her tightly. "Holy shit! I *love* their upstairs space. So intimate—only ninety seats. The actors are so close to the audie—"

"Not *upstairs*." Alex peered up at him through her bangs. "The Jerwood Theatre, *downstairs.*"

Her cheeky grin grew brighter by the second.

"Bloody hell! That's the main auditorium. *Four* times the size..." Mark trailed off, speechless.

"I thought it was a joke at first, but they knew the play. They want me to come in next week to discuss possible edits, meet the director. I didn't know what to say. I didn't want to let on that I didn't even *submit* it—"

"Hang on—so how did they read it?" asked Freddie.

An uncharacteristically shy hand rose from their huddle. "I did it. I sent it in."

Alex pulled away from Mark's hug, her jaw slack. "What?!"

"I worried that you'd just show it to Joan and that would be the end of it—but it was so good, Lex—"

Freddie's eyes bulged. "Lucy, you crafty little minx!"

"Look, I know I should've told you," said Lucy. "But I fell in love with it. Not just the grandmother stuff—all of it: love, regret, second chances, chasing your dream...I couldn't stop thinking about it, so when you let me hang on to it, I might have made a few copies and mailed them off..."

She laughed, rubbing the ink stains on her left hand. "What can I say? I'm pushy! And besides, you named it *Thirteen*, for fuck's sake! I had to get it out of the house, try to override its bad mojo."

Alex yanked Lucy into a tight hug. "You superstitious freak! I promise I'll never make fun of your weird phobias ever again. But, I'm shocked they liked it *as is*. I planned at least two more rounds of edits. I guess we'll discuss that next week."

"Remember I told you months ago that your perfectionist tendencies might be holding you back? Yeah...*that*," said Lucy. "Not everything has to be 110 percent shiny and polished, you know."

"I'm starting to realize that..." Alex chuckled, her damp face leaving Lucy's shoulder. "I've spent so much time the last few years trying to be perfect…and independent. And in the end, a rough draft and my friends made the difference."

She blotted her eyes. "Thank you—for having so much faith in me. I can't believe you did this, Lucy."

"I didn't *do* anything. It was all you." Lucy grinned. "It's your writing they fell in love with. I just gave it a friendly shove out the door."

THIRTY-NINE

Thursday, July 21, 2016—7 p.m. PRESS NIGHT

THIRTEEN
By Alexandra Sinclair
14 July – 3 Sept

Jerwood Theatre Downstairs
Tickets: from twelve pounds

Playwright Alexandra Sinclair makes her London debut in the Royal Court's Jerwood Theatre Downstairs.

After a week of previews, the buzz surrounding Alex's play hit a fever pitch just in time for its press night, every leather seat filled by ticket holders, invited guests or theatre critics—all eager to see what the young American playwright had to offer. Alex's worries proved to be unjustified. Two standing ovations and rumours of a four-out-of-five-star review had the theatre company popping champagne corks and sighing with relief at the after-show bash in the downstairs bar.

"That looks perfect. *Smile!*"

A photographer was wrapping up a quick photo call with Alex and her cast in front of the red wall overlooking the Royal Court's main bar. Two acclaimed actresses in their mid-sixties shared the spotlight with a handsome twenty-something actor, a blonde starlet just out of RADA, and Naomi.

"The photos and review will be featured on our *What's on Stage* website by morning," said the affable shutterbug. "Looks like you've got plenty of admirers this evening. Enjoy it, love."

"I'm still trying to catch my breath. Thanks so much." Alex smiled, running her hand over the cowl neckline of her purple lace pencil dress, anxious to be reunited with her loved ones. This moment had to be shared. Her actors shuffled back down the few stairs to the dimly lit bar, but Naomi stayed by Alex's side, giving her a peck on the cheek.

"I'm so proud to be in your first play, babe." Naomi playfully dabbed at the lipstick smudge left behind on Alex's face. "I never dreamed that we'd work together. Now look at us. Forever connected because of your art."

"Art? Is that what we're calling it now?" A clean-shaven Tom in a lilac-coloured tie, white shirt, and slightly wrinkled white linen suit strode up to the two women, smiling widely. He wrapped his arms around both of their waists, but only one was the recipient of a steamy kiss.

"Is this what happens now? No bouquets at curtain call, just big juicy snogs?" Alex laughed and threaded free of Tom's grasp. "I'll leave you to it. Have fun, guys."

Her elegant black lace-up heels tapped down the steps, letting the happy couple go at it from a safe distance. A wave of hot, humid air greeted her at the bottom, the July heat and crush of bodies—four deep at the bar—conspiring to suffuse everyone with a natural celebratory glow. Alex zigzagged towards the spot where Michael, Helen, and Joan stood wide-eyed and laughing with drinks in hand.

"Alex, love, aren't you glad you didn't quit?" Michael's smile practically stretched to Manchester and back. "When the car dropped us off at the front door, I couldn't help myself. I cried like a baby."

"We all did," laughed Helen.

"Seeing *Alexandra Sinclair* in neon lights above the theatre's entrance…are you trying to give your poor old Dad a heart attack?"

"Never mind you. What about me?" Joan took a quick sip from her pint of ale. "It's not every day you have a play performed about your life." She kissed Alex on the cheek. "I'm so proud of you, love, we all are. I take it you saw your mother's Facebook post? I always knew she was a braggart, but chasing up her local paper for an interview?"

Alex nodded. "Yeah, the *Tallahassee Democrat*. Anything to boost interest in her real estate business, I guess. Did you see the photo they used of the two of us? She really had to dig to find that one."

Joan rubbed her granddaughter's back. "She's the one missing out, love." She peered towards a man standing a few feet away. "See that reporter over there? He wants a word with me, 'the real Joan'. Wait until I post photos from tonight on Instagram. My followers won't know what hit 'em!" She toddled over to the scribe, pint in hand, to bask in her second chance at fame.

"Did you get the bouquet of snapdragons from Robbie?" asked Michael.

"They're gorgeous! I put them in a vase in the dressing

room. I'll collect them when we leave tonight. I wish he could've been here. He said he'd try for closing night if the hospital gives him time off. Glad I never became a doctor. I like staying out late too much."

"Lex!" Lucy and Freddie bobbed through the crowd, careful not to spill their drinks. "Did you see who's *here*, talking to Isabella? Only Amanda Abbington." Lucy nearly tripped over her own feet in excitement. "Here's your chance to right a wrong. Go have a word."

"She's here with Molly, too—I *mean*, Louise Brealey. She's lovely." Freddie craned his neck back towards the corner nook. "I know you met Loo at the con back in January, but you can play your *I'm a Celebrity* card now. And then you can introduce me and Lucy."

"Are you *using* me, Freds?" Alex laughed.

"Well, knowing the playwright certainly has its benefits. Sobbing through your play, the cute guy next to me handed me a tissue—and his mobile number. *Thirteen* might become my lucky number."

Alex hugged him. "Anything for you Freddie, anything." Her eyes settled on the stairs. "And we'll meet Loo and Amanda in a sec. There's someone I have to see first."

She pulled away from her friends and family, approaching a single figure walking down the stairs.

"I'm so glad you made it," said Alex.

Harry hugged his friend. "My God, Alex. A standing ovation—*twice*. Your name lit up outside the theatre. You've come so far."

"Isn't it crazy?"

"And look at this crowd." Harry surveyed the room. "They're all here because of your writing. That's got to feel good, especially with everything you've faced."

Alex blushed. "Well, 'that which does not kill us makes us stronger', right?"

"So true. I hope you don't mind, but when I sell my flat, I'm mentioning in the listing that a Royal Court playwright used to live there. I think that will instantly give it an increased cool factor. The Hackney hipsters will be biting my hand off."

"Just don't divulge that I lived in the closet. I've got a rep to think about." Alex winked.

"I'd never," said Harry with a smirk. "Hey, did you hear? Olivia's moved abroad. She's trying her luck in New York City. London can breathe easy."

"Tom told me." Alex leaned in. "Can you believe it? He's been dating Naomi exclusively for nearly *eight* months. She tells me all the Olivia gossip, so I'm up-to-date whether I want to be or not. I think Tom's breathing easier, too. He seems happier, and he's been going on auditions! Blame lust...or *love*?"

Harry grinned. "A lot can change in a year."

"Correction. A year and...two months," said Alex.

"I thought you were terrible at maths?"

"I still am. Why do you think I'm in the arts?"

"Well, it looks like you're not the only rising star in attendance." Harry pointed to three blushing young women squeezing past, clutching autographed theatre flyers.

"Come." Alex gripped his elbow. "Say hi to Mark."

Hugs, air kisses, and words of congratulation greeted Alex through the busy bar. As they reached the end of the counter, Mark was saying "thanks for stopping by" to four more fans of his new TV series, the BBC's latest hit.

"*There* you are. Hello, stranger." Mark gave Alex a lingering kiss on the lips. "I saw Naomi and Tom getting busy on the landing. I didn't want you feeling left out."

She beamed at her boyfriend. "I don't. Not with you."

"Oh, get a room!" Harry laughed. "Who am I kidding? You two don't need any encouragement. Great to see you, Mark." He slapped the actor on the back, and the two men shook hands warmly. "So, do you always bring your own fan club with you?"

"Feels like it lately." Mark widened his eyes. "The morning after the first episode aired, I started getting recognized. It's been fun—so far. No creepy autograph requests in the men's loos or people following me—nothing like that, thank God." He laughed. "Never underestimate the power of a role in a BBC drama."

"I almost never watch TV and even I'm hooked, so that's saying something," said Harry. "When's the second series being filmed?"

"We've already started. I had to beg for two days off so I could be here for Alex." He squeezed her waist and drew her closer. "This time tomorrow, I'll be back in Aberdeen. Work's been mental. Since May, we've been apart more than we've been together."

Alex agreed with a small nod.

"Nice to be in demand, though." Harry smiled. "I hate to be the first one to leave, but I must whip back to Bespoke before last call. I'll say a quick hello to Michael and Helen, and be off." He gave his friend a hug. "Congrats, Lex. You did it!"

"Thanks, Harry." She smiled and adjusted his bent lapel.

"Mark, look after our girl. She's a keeper."

"Will do, Harry. Cheers."

Alex nuzzled into Mark's neck and gently pulled on his black tie. Her left hand continued its journey down his purple shirt, resting just above his belt. "So, tell me, Mr. Keegan, how does it feel to be back here, where we first set eyes on each other?"

He dropped his left shoulder and pivoted, wrapping both arms tightly around her waist. Face to face, their bodies leaned together, not even a whisper could float between them. "Actually, I'm kicking myself I didn't snog you right there on the spot. Baggy *Captain America* t-shirt and all."

Alex winced. "Ergh, don't remind me. I'm lucky you gave me a second look."

"Well, it wasn't just about looks, Mouse." His finger lingered softly over her mouth. "Although there's a lot to be said for those pouty lips of yours...and how great your arse looks in yoga pants." He playfully grabbed a handful and winked. "But at the pub, when you spoke in your cute American accent about writing—TOTAL turn on! I said I only liked you for your accent, remember? I told you that on our first date..."

"Our first date? On the Vespa? You consider that our first date?"

"Why wouldn't I? I asked if you fancied a little London adventure—you accepted. I think the best dates feature new experiences, easy conversation, and the girl you fancy rotten holding onto you for dear life. As beginnings go, *yeah*—I'd say it was pretty epic!"

"I thought you were lovely, but as for getting it together, we were hopeless."

"I know." He pressed his lips against her forehead. "Blame the workaholic in both of us...and certain...extenuating circumstances..."

"To think, I almost ruined our chances. Stupid baggage, getting in the way. Things could've turned out so differently. I'm glad you never gave up on me."

"The course of true love never did run smooth, and all that. But cheer up, Mouse—we made it...and so did your play! Just look at tonight—London is yours. I'm not surprised, not at all. It may have taken you a while to realize it, but you can do anything you put your beautiful mind to."

He kissed her on the nose. "And if a little corrupting takes place along the way, well, so be it."

"You're a bad influence, Mark Keegan."

"So I've been told. But you do realize, don't you? You're everything to me, Alex Sinclair. I won't risk losing you again."

A twinkle of mischief lit up his eyes. "You and me, we've only just begun our adventures together. Vespa Rules from now on: hop on, hold tight, and remember to enjoy the ride."

Alex laughed and kissed Mark tenderly. She slipped her arm tightly around his waist, leading him towards her family and friends. A discreet new tattoo, a *Doctor Who* quote in Cocktail Script, peeked out from the inside of her forearm—

'We're all stories in the end. Just make it a good one.'

WANT TO KNOW WHAT HAPPENS TO
ALEX, MARK & FRIENDS NEXT?

Read the sequel *London, Can You Wait?* today!

Acknowledgements

It can be a grammatical nightmare when you're a Canadian writer creating a story about an American gal living in Great Britain, so I hope my Canadian spellings were easy to follow!

Music plays a huge role in my life and in my writing process, so it was natural for me to include specific songs through the novel. Consider their mentions 'Easter Eggs' (using the old DVD term) of a sort. If you have a listen to these tunes, you might unlock further insight into the characters' motivations and thoughts in those particular scenes.

A huge thank you and tons of love goes to my husband, Darren Lee and my sister, Heather Middleton, who read endless drafts, offered clever suggestions, and never made me feel guilty about running away time and time again to London—"It's for *research!*"

Cheers to Judy Faulds and Dee Asprey for answering my questions about what it was like for a Canadian and an American moving to London and Manchester respectively. Your early insight was so helpful. Next time I'm in the UK, the hot chocolate, and grilled cheeses are on me.

A very special thanks to Emily Cline, Renate Lameraner, and Gabrielle Domingues who went above and beyond the call of duty—advice mavens, readers, editors, and beloved friends.

To my favourite gals, my partners in fangirl crimes, who share my passions for theatre and pop culture, and friendships beyond borders: Vicki Angel, Charlie Roberts, Paula Wiseman and Cristina Baptista—I love you, girls— "It's all happening!"

They say you should never meet your idols, but in my case, it gave me the much-needed kick in the pants to start this book. To Stephen Beresford, whose enthusiasm, humour, and thoughtful answers to my questions about writing for stage, screen and TV were just what I needed to commence this journey—thank you! And if you haven't seen Stephen's award-winning film *Pride*, please do. It is everything!

Love and hugs to my family and friends—my ultimate cheerleaders who always believed: Dad, Zoey, Bill & Tobey, Val, Tony & Jason, Sally & Bruce Gibbs, Esther Layland, Sheila MacDougall and Maria Mackay.

Warm thanks to my writer friends: Carolyn Leslie, David Burga and Tracy Abrey—your encouragement and advice was much appreciated.

In a story that features pop culture idols, I'd be amiss not to celebrate some of mine. Many are already mentioned in this book, but I'd like to thank Andrew Scott, Ben Whishaw, Louise Brealey, Matt Smith, John Barrowman, Bertie Carvel, Saint Etienne (Bob, Pete, and Sarah), Simon Stephens, and Steven Moffat for their inspiration and talent—and for being kind and generous with their fans. I'm so proud to call myself one.

To my two favourite cities, London and Manchester—I owe you so much.

And to everyone who bought, read and hopefully enjoyed my first novel, thank you! Xoxo

Enjoyed this novel? Please consider leaving a review on Goodreads.com or the retailer's website!

Stay in touch!
Follow Jacquelyn on:

Twitter: @JaxMiddleton
Instagram: JaxMiddleton_Author
Facebook: JacquelynMiddletonAuthor
Web: www.JacquelynMiddleton.com